BREAKING THROUGH

BOOK 2 OF THE SEAL TEAM HEARTBREAKERS SERIES

TERESA J. REASOR

Breaking Through
Copyright © 2012 by Teresa J. Reasor
Cover Art by Tracy Stewart
Edited by Faith Freewoman

Contact Information: teresareasor@msn.com

Teresa J. Reasor
PO Box 124
Corbin, KY 40702

Publishing History: First Edition 2012
ISBN 10: 0985006935
ISBN 13: 978-0-9850069-3-8
Print Edition

Dedication

To all the men and women of the armed forces who help to preserve our freedom. God Bless you.

And to the Lethal Ladies. You are the bomb!

And to my children, Sarah, Daniel, and Jennifer. I love you.

Table of Contents

PROLOGUE

B rett "Cutter" Weaver drew a deep breath and reached for patience. *Jesus.* Why couldn't Derrick let it go? He'd been harping on it for the last ten minutes. Stewing about it for the last two hours.

"Damn stupid you getting between me and the kid, Cutter." Derrick Armstrong's voice grated over the loud whomp-whomp of the helo's propellers. "He hated us. You heard him. We were protecting his ass, and he fucking hated us for it."

Brett swiveled in his seat, pushed his face close to Derrick's, and stared him in the eye. "If I hadn't stepped in, your ass would be in the brig right now. *Move. The. Fuck. On.*"

Derrick's features hardened his expression sulky. "We'll be facing him down the barrel of an AK-47 in less than a year. He's probably working for al-Qaeda already."

Leaning back, Brett pinched the bridge of his nose. *Probably so.*

Maybe he shouldn't have kept Derrick from ripping the kid's head off. But he was a *kid.*

After the way Derrick had grabbed him, the boy had to have bruises. He had to be some important Iraqi citizen's son, too. Otherwise they wouldn't have been called out on protection detail just before this mission.

The fifteen-year-old had hunkered sullen in the back seat for the last ten minutes of the ride, his eyes filled with hate and hurt.

The helo hit a patch of turbulence and bounced. Brett braced his feet and his adrenaline jumped. He shook it off.

Across the compartment from him, Greenback grabbed the edge of the metal seat to keep from being pitched head first onto the floor. "I want my fucking airfare back."

"You didn't have to pay for this ride. Uncle Sam did," Bowie shot back, his west Texas drawl thick as Greenback's New Jersey accent.

Brett blocked out the team's good-natured banter. "You need to talk to Hawk about what happened or we'll be up to our necks in shit. The kid's bound to talk."

"It's his word against ours, Cutter."

Brett's stomach plummeted, and it had nothing to do with the rise and fall of the chopper. *Was that what it had come to? His word against theirs?*

"I want you to put in for some counseling, Strong Man."

Derrick snorted. "That little bastard spent twenty minutes pissing on us and our country, and I'm the one who needs counseling? That's bullshit."

"Did you get another letter from Marjorie?"

Derrick's expression went flat. "What does that have to do with anything?"

"Every time you get a letter from home you get fucked up. If her letters make you—"

"Leave it alone, Cutter."

Fuck. This was way out of his league. Though he'd had training, he was no psychologist. Derrick's rage was out of control. He was close to slam-dunking his career right into the nearest latrine.

Brett had to talk to Hawk about this.

Otherwise, he'd see his own career trashed by association.

Brett's attention shifted across the helo to his other teammates. Hawk was looking over a schematic. Flash studied him and Derrick, a frown hardening his features.

And what the hell was going on with Flash? He'd been stewing about something, too. Secretive. He'd had a hush-hush meeting a week ago and been different ever since. He'd even quit gambling. Something was up.

When Brett had approached him about this sudden shift, he'd gotten the same three words kicked in his face, *Leave it alone.*

Brett rolled his neck trying to relieve the tension in his shoulders. He had to take a step back and get his head into this mission.

He ran both hands over his close-cropped hair. *We've been down range too long. God, I want to go home.*

The landing controller's voice came over the bitch box. "Ten minutes out."

"COM systems on," Lieutenant Hawk Yazzie ordered.

Brett breathed in the rubbery-smelling air, a blend of machine oil and ammo, and pulled on his gloves. He gripped Derrick's shoulder. "Forget about the shit that happened this morning and get your head in the game. Everything else needs to stay on board this chopper." He adjusted his throat mike.

Derrick's expression grew sullen but he nodded. "As long as you have my six we're good, Cutter."

The sound of the CH47 Chinook's propellers reverberated through the compartment as it hovered over the drop site. The rear hatch lowered. A crewmember tossed out the rappel rope, while another manned the machine gun mounted at the bay door.

Hawk signaled and took position. The team rose as one. Hawk was first on the rope and down. Greenback, Bowie, Doc, and Flash slipped into the darkness behind him. Brett grabbed the rope and rappelled down, his gloves absorbing the heat and keeping his hands protected. Seconds behind him, Derrick's feet hit the ground.

"Down and clear," Brett said into his COM.

The downdraft from the helo's props pounded them as it bugged out to the east. Brett ran west twenty yards looking for cover and dove behind a knoll of sand. In a country ninety-five percent desert and the other five percent sand with vegetation, you took whatever crappy cover you could find.

As the dust devils settled, a taut waiting silence hung thick around them. Five minutes passed, ten, as they waited to see if the drop had been spotted.

"Fall in," Hawk's voice whispered in his ear through the COM.

They gathered in a designated area only a few hundred feet from their drop sight.

"Cutter, take point," Hawk said. "When we're within distance, we'll leap-frog in and out. Greenback, you have our back door. You know the drill."

The mile-long trek to their target area would be cakewalk until they reached the outskirts of town—as long as they didn't run into any hostile patrols.

Silence, broken only by the occasional rustle of clothing, dogged them all the way in. Brett fought to keep his mind on what lay ahead, but Derrick's volatile actions and attitude weighed heavily in his thoughts. They'd been swim buddies all the way through BUD/S training. Derrick had changed since then. But so had he.

Brett signaled a stop as he scanned the burned out shells of bombed buildings spanning the immediate horizon. How could the innocent civilians trapped between them and the Taliban or al-Qaeda keep from hating both sides? With their homes and businesses destroyed and their families displaced, it was no wonder some looked at every man in uniform with hate-filled eyes.

And now some bomb-making terrorist fuckers had taken up residence.

Brett went over the mission one last time in his head. Having all five men inside the structure was a risk, but it would take one man, or even two, too long to wire the structure and get out, leaving discovery a strong possibility. At least with five men they'd have a chance at shooting their way clear if everything went to hell.

Flash, positioned atop one of the abandoned buildings, could cover them outside with his M-12 sniper rifle, and though Greenback was covering their back door, he'd take up a defensive position and keep the fuckers in crossfire.

Knowing he had backup inside the building and out made it easier for Brett to focus.

Using hand signals, Hawk conveyed his orders. They donned their NVGs. Light reflected easily off the sand, but within the unlit streets visibility would peter out. Brett led off, and they leap-frogged to the buildings, hugging the shadows and signaling to each other. They'd practiced the maneuver until it was second nature.

Darkness lay like a threat over the streets as they worked their way north following the GPS coordinates secured by Intel. Six blocks into the district, the building came into view. Not a house, but a business of some kind.

Greenback peeled off to the end of the block to guard their back door. Their escape route.

Surrounded by the abandoned husks of empty buildings, the light bleeding from beneath heavy fabric on the second floor window screamed occupancy. Hawk signaled for them to fan out and take position.

Placing every foot with care, Brett worked his way to the east corner of a building diagonal from his target area. He focused for a time on the rooftop sentries, then scanned the east side of the building. A window in the middle of the first floor was positioned where none of the sentries could observe it. If he could get it open, he could just waltz right in and set his charges.

A figure slithered up to the opening. *Jesus, Hawk was a smooth operator.* In less than a minute he had cut the glass, disengaged the lock, and slid the window open. Then he shimmied into the room and disappeared. A prearranged click on the COM signaled he was on target.

One of the sentries on the roof turned and ambled toward the other side of the building. Brett eased from his position. The unexpected crunch of concrete beneath a boot heel zapped his nerve endings. He froze. Controlling his breathing with a practiced effort, he shadowed back into the alley and against the wall.

The tango walked past him, his rifle cradled in the bend of his arm. The pungent scent of his sweat blended with the oil used to clean his weapon.

The man suddenly tensed. Who did he see?

Brett eased his KA-BAR from its sheath. When the tango raised his rifle, Brett covered the man's mouth with his gloved hand and plunged the knife into his back at an upward angle, piercing his heart. The terrorist's grunt of pain was cut off. He dropped as though his legs had been kicked from beneath him. His body sagged. His rifle slid toward the ground. Brett jerked his hand upward, holding the body's weight by the jaw and snagged the rifle sling with his other hand. The firearm pendulumed just above the ground. *Holy fuck, that was close.*

Brett dragged the body into the alley and rolled it flush against the building, concealing the rifle behind it. He then wiped the KA-BAR clean with the tango's shirt and replaced it in its sheath.

How long before the man would be missed? *Not long enough. Got to get moving.*

Two clicks sounded in his ear. Derrick had made it inside. So the guy had been aiming at him. Strong Man needed to practice his stealth skills.

Watching for any movement on the roof, Brett eased from the alley and worked his way from shadow to shadow toward the building. He paused behind a small patch of scrub that offered only the minimum of cover, then broke into a full-out run and zigzagged across the last twelve feet, every inch of his body tensed for the strike of a bullet. Reaching the building, he flattened himself against the side of the structure. No cry of alarm followed. No one opened fire. He drew a deep breath and shook off the adrenaline humming through his body.

He secured his rifle sling over his shoulder, gripped the bottom of the window, braced a foot on the rough concrete, and boosted himself up and into the opening. His pack dragged at the edge of the frame, making a soft sound like a zipper being worked. He froze, listening for any enemy response. Nothing. He wiggled gently, disengaging the pack, and climbed through.

Although the lower floors remained pitch-black, his NVGs illuminated everything in green. Two tables separated by crates sat against one wall with rifle parts lined up carefully across them. The faint odor of machine oil hung close.

He paused to click his COM system four times and moved on. He approached the door, leaned forward, and pressed an ear to the panel. Silence breathed back at him from the hall on the other side. Another series of clicks signaled Bowie's entrance into the building.

Brett eased open the door a slit and peered out. All clear. Sliding silently through the opening he turned left, hugging the wall as he crept down the hall. The last room on the left was his target. He pressed his ear to the door. Emptiness pinged back at him. And no light shone from beneath.

Twisting the knob, he eased into the room and shut the door. Long rows of wooden boxes lined the interior. One lay open and next to it, a pile of packing material. Brett approached it. AK-47's, lying in neat stacks and cushioned by straw, filled the crate.

Bingo.

He set aside his rifle and shook free of his pack. Drawing a deep breath, he worked the straps free and opened the flap. He pulled out his supplies and laid them on the floor in neat order. Moving quickly, he positioned plastic explosives against the interior weight-bearing walls. When set off, they would collapse the building inward and bury anyone inside. Just in case, he decided to create a circuit of charges with DET cord around the boxed weapons. He had just finished the last circuit when the door swung open.

Every nerve in Brett's body jumped to high alert. He grabbed his Sig Sauer sidearm and jerked it free.

Recognition momentarily drained the strength from his arms and he lowered his weapon. *Shit.* He'd almost blown away one of his guys. What the fuck was going on? Hawk's and Bowie's charges were already set, Doc's, too. He'd heard the clicks. *What the fuck was Derrick doing here?*

Derrick pressed a finger to his lips and rested his ear against the door listening. He gave the all clear and signaled for him to hurry.

Brett nodded, thrust his pistol into its holster, and turned back to the task of arming the charge. *Derrick shouldn't be here.* This change in plan put them both at risk.

Just get this done and get the fuck out of here.

He checked his watch, then set and switched on the timer. Sensing quick movement to his right, he jerked to the left. A metal gunstock slammed into the side of his head with the force of a baseball bat, tearing the NVGs from his face. Blackness crashed over him.

CHAPTER 1

Three months later

"I t isn't aphasia."

From his seat across the desk, Brett looked up. Dr. Stewart's expression offered no clues as to how he should feel about his announcement. The doc's normal hangdog expression remained the same.

"That's what I was told after I woke up from the coma, sir." Brett said when the doc continued to wait for a response.

"Any time there's an injury to the brain, and there's a problem with speech, there's a list of things it can be. Aphasia is only one of them."

Brett nodded. "What does this new diagnosis mean?"

"Well, Ensign, it means you're not going to receive a medical discharge from the Navy. Yet."

Medical discharge. *Medical discharge!* The blood drained from Brett's head. Nausea hit him like he'd been kicked in the nuts. "What do you mean *yet?* Nobody said anything about a discharge. I'm getting better. I'm working my way back."

"That's why we don't believe you're experiencing aphasia. If you were, you wouldn't be progressing, you'd be learning to cope."

A surge of adrenaline kicked Brett's heart into overdrive. "Then what the hell is it?"

"Your speech pathologist, Miss Myers, thinks the blank spots in your memory are stress-induced rather than physical." Captain Stewart rose to his feet, moved around the desk to lean against its edge, and crossed his ankles. "When you were in elementary school or middle school, did you ever pull a blank during a test?"

"Sure. Everybody's done that at one time or another. But the information eventually came back to me."

"But with aphasia, it wouldn't, Ensign Weaver. You'd learn coping mechanisms to help you come up with a substitute, for the word you couldn't remember, but you wouldn't ever recover that word in that instance. You might substitute another one totally unrelated to what you were trying to say. To make explaining simple—if you were trying to think of the word dog you might call it … ice cream, though you knew up here," he tapped his temple, "exactly what a dog was. The correct word just wouldn't route itself to your speech center."

The tight feeling banding Brett's chest began to ease. "I don't do that. I can't think of the word at all and have to concentrate on it, circle it, until the original, or a substitute that makes sense, occurs to me."

"And we all do that. You just happen to do it more frequently than the rest of us. Because of all the behaviors you exhibit inconsistent with aphasia, your wide-ranged articulation in particular, we've changed our diagnosis. We believe you're suffering from PTSD."

Bullshit! Brett shook his head. "I'm not stressed now. I'm home, I'm with my family." *I'm awake for the first time in a month.* "And I'm still doing this shit." He heard the anger and frustration in his own voice and drew another breath. "Sorry, sir."

Doctor Stewart's long face became serious. "How angry are you about being denied the opportunity to train and deploy with your team, Ensign?"

Brett eyed the doctor. Was this a test? A trick? If he admitted to his anger, would it affect his final prognosis? Could they kick him off the team for this shit?

Stewart shook his head and took the seat next to him, putting them on a more even keel. "You can't ignore the physical and mental trauma you endured in Iraq. It isn't going to go away."

Everyone always pussyfooted around what Derrick had done. Having one of your best friends try to kill you—*twice*—was a little more than just a trauma. It moved way beyond trauma right into ... *Shit!* Maybe if he thought of a word that would encompass the experience, he'd be cured.

Brett turned in his seat to face him. "Look, I'm not trying to ignore what happened. I'm dealing with it. And not being able to train, to do what I'm meant to do, is just going to make this thing I have worse. I need something physical to set my sights on. A goal I can work toward, not some '*maybe.' I need to get back to my team."*

"That's exactly what we want to happen, Ensign. But it's going to take a lot of work, and a little cooperation on your part."

Any time these fuckers started mentioning cooperation, they wanted either a quart of blood, or to inflict pain, or both.

Brett studied the doctor through narrowed eyes. He scrubbed a hand over his close-cropped hair.

Okay, think. Stewart wouldn't be saying this if he didn't have a shot at returning to his unit. From the look of things, if he didn't cooperate, he had zero chances. *Fuck.*

"Put me back on light duty at least. I'm going crazy sitting around."

Stewart's eyes glinted. "It's only been twelve weeks since your surgery, Ensign Weaver."

"Yeah, I know."

Stewart rose to his feet and moved to sit behind his desk. "No calisthenics and no strenuous exercise."

Brett suppressed the grin that threatened to break through. "Agreed."

Stewart continued to eye him, a hint of suspicion in his gaze.

"I'll have a letter for you by the end of office hours today."

"Thank you, sir. Now, what do I need to do?"

Zoe Weaver stared at the plastic stick from the home pregnancy test. Her shoulders were so knotted with tension the muscles ached.

They weren't ready for this.

After a rocky patch, she and Hawk had just gotten things ironed out enough to enjoy each other. She couldn't be pregnant.

Her brother Brett had just come out of his coma. Her sister Sharon was recovering from an emergency C-section and hysterectomy. Derrick Armstrong's trial was coming up in a month or two, but she could handle that. But this—She swallowed against her rising panic.

She loved Hawk. No doubts—no holding back—she was committed.

He said he loved her. Showed her on a daily basis. But she refused to pressure him into marriage with a pregnancy. The words had to come without that hanging over his head. They had to come from his heart. When he was ready.

A plus sign appeared in the window on the stick. Her breath caught and her hand crept upward to cover her mouth. Was it a shout of joy she was suppressing, or a groan of despair? Trapped between the two, she couldn't decide.

A quick tap on the door startled her.

"Zoe, you all right in there?" Hawk's voice laced with concern brought tears to her eyes. She brushed them away.

"I'll be right out." She stuffed the plastic stick back in the box and crumpled the instructions into a tight ball. She had to think about what she was going to do. She couldn't just spring it on him.

He was so observant. He'd know something was wrong if she didn't pull herself together. Taking several deep breaths, she reached for calm. She tossed the crumpled paper into the trash and covered it with a piece of tissue. She shoved the home pregnancy test to the back of the bathroom cabinet behind rolls of toilet paper and bottles of antiseptic.

She washed her hands, dried them, and, drawing one last calming breath, opened the door.

Hawk looked up from the end of the bed. "You okay?"

"Yeah. I just lost track of time. I didn't mean to hog the bathroom."

"We have two." He shrugged then continued to tie his shoes. "I've been called in to base to take an instructor's place at the pool. His kid is having emergency surgery. They think it's appendicitis."

"Okay." The calf muscle of her damaged left leg tightened as she limped forward and sat next to him on the bed. She brushed back the black hair at his temple with her fingertips. Would the baby have Hawk's wonderful high cheekbones and dark hair? Would it have his Native American heritage stamped as strongly on its features? Her voice sounded husky when she said, "I hope he'll be okay."

"I'm sure he'll be fine." He looped his arm around her and drew her in against his side. His gray eyes looked intent as they studied her face. "What time's your interview?"

Lord, after the shock of the pregnancy test, she'd completely forgotten about her hospital interview. Her gaze darted toward the clock. "Not for a couple of hours yet."

"It's a relief your application for your license went through so quickly. Right?"

"It had to be some kind of record. I didn't think any kind of bureaucracy worked that fast. You didn't have anything to do with it, did you?"

"No." He shook his head. "Maybe they just realized California needs a really great physical therapist. And I think Dr. Connelly might have called and spoken to someone."

Zoe's brows rose. "How do you know that?"

"Because I asked him to." He brushed a stray curl back from her cheek. "I wanted you here with me. And now that Brett is back on his feet, I knew you wouldn't be happy unless you were doing what you're supposed to do."

The words '*I wanted you here with me*' captured her attention. The rest just seemed to blend into the background. She turned his face toward her and kissed him.

Hawk took advantage and eased her down onto the bed. His hand worked beneath her t-shirt to cup her breast. And when his fingers toyed with her nipple, a titillating heat arrowed down her torso.

"You're not pissed because I interfered?" he asked as his lips left hers to nibble her earlobe.

She shivered. "No, of course not. I want to be here with you, too." Her hand slid over the front of his desert camouflage uniform pants and found evidence of what he wanted. She'd never get enough of this, or of him.

But how was she going to tell him about the baby? He'd just decided he could handle a commitment to her, though he could be deployed any moment. If he went wheels up, how would he feel leaving her behind—pregnant?

It would drive him crazy. He'd worry about her. He'd be distracted, and he might not be as careful as he needed to be. No way was she telling him. Not yet.

"If you have time," she whispered in his ear. "I could use a little added incentive to do well on my interview."

Hawk laughed. He raised his head to look down at her. "I might need a little encouragement to do well at the pool, too. I wouldn't want sexual frustration to distract me."

"We wouldn't want that," she agreed and lifted her head to kiss his throat.

He rushed to untie his boots and they hit the floor with a thump.

Another laugh bubbled up from inside her. "I think that may be the sexiest sound I've ever heard, Lieutenant Yazzie."

Hawk's smile promised more. "I think we can do better." He pushed her t-shirt up and lowered his mouth to her breast.

CHAPTER 2

Two Weeks Later

Yasin al-Yussuf narrowed his eyes against the painful glare of the late afternoon sun. A wave of anxiety cramped his stomach. Sweat ran down the middle of his back, dampening his cotton shirt, already wilted from the heat. As he passed an old man squatting in the dirt outside the low-level apartment complex, he averted his face. It would not do for anyone to recognize him here.

The building, three stories high, had circular pits of recent small arms fire scarring the west corner. Small patches of grass clung to the narrow strip of sandy soil between the structure and the cracked sidewalk.

So this is what he had come to. This is what the Americans had forced him to become. The very thing he had fought against for so long.

He turned the corner. A slow-moving car swung onto the street. He bent his head and focused on the sidewalk, then threw up a hand to conceal the side of his face as it passed.

A large chunk of concrete, blown from the top edge of the building, propped open the front door. He ducked inside and paused to allow his eyes to adjust.

A narrow flight of stairs disappeared upward, while a lower level hallway shot back into a dimly lit passageway. The smell of cooking fish had nausea gripping his stomach and twisting it.

He could leave this place. He had not gone beyond the point of no return. No one knew he was here.

But what of his son? Where was Sanjay? The two American men who had driven him home had to have played a part in his disappearance. They had surely killed him and buried his body somewhere in the desert. But why? He was only a child.

While the American military continued to drag their feet and offer him platitudes and empty sympathy, he and his wife had clung to their hope and to each other.

Four long months had passed since he had seen his son. Four months filled with an unrelenting fear and grief that he could no longer bear.

He had watched Levla change from a vibrant, joyful woman to a shadow. She disappeared into her grief more and more each day. Though she never spoke the words, he knew she blamed him for trusting strangers to deliver their only child home. He blamed himself. He had allowed his work to devour his life, and now his son was gone.

Anger and grief twisted together, clawing at his insides, burrowing into his brain. The men who were supposed to keep him safe and see him home safely had to pay. They must have killed him. He gripped the railing, and with steps heavy with determination, he trudged up the stairs.

At the top, he turned left down a hallway lit by ineffective intermittent lights and a dingy window at the end. Halfway down the passage he paused before a door with the numbers he sought.

Once again nausea struck him, and he drew deep breaths until the feeling passed. He had waited long enough. The Americans didn't care about one lone Iraqi child. And his own people had been unable to find anyone who had seen his son since the moment the two Navy SEALs had taken him. *They were responsible. And they had to die.*

He knocked on the door.

After too short a time, the hollow panel swung inward, and a man stared out at him, his dark eyes flat and hard, his skin dusky from the sun.

Suddenly desert dry, Yasin's tongue lay useless in his mouth.

"What do you want?" the man demanded.

Yasin swallowed. "I wish to speak to you."

"About?"

"The two Americans who killed my son."

The man studied him, his features sharpening with recognition.

A shudder shook Yasin. He knew him. He had come too far. There was no going back. "They were two Navy SEALs. The same ones who killed your brother in the explosion."

The man's eyes widened, then shifted and became predatory. He swung the door wide. "Come in."

Captain Russell Connelly paused just outside the luggage claim area and scanned the crowd. People stood queued up around the conveyor snagging their suitcases. The crowd parted to spit out two lucky men with their bags, then folded back in on itself. Neither man was Evan.

He checked his watch. Thirteen hundred hours. He had to report to the hospital at sixteen hundred for a meeting with the surgical staff, and he hoped to get Evan settled and share a meal with him before the meeting.

The dull florescent light caught the copper highlights in the auburn hair of the woman tugging a huge suitcase behind her. Something about the way she walked seemed familiar. As she moved closer, a smile of recognition curved her lips.

"Captain Connelly, how are you?"

"I'm good, Mrs. Weaver."

She smiled again. "Clara. Surely you can call me Clara now."

Why hadn't he noticed this beautiful, vibrant woman two months ago?

Because she'd been the mother of his patient, and he'd been keeping his professional distance.

But also because she'd been under tremendous stress.

Her son had lain in a coma. Her older daughter had had an emergency C-section, a baby girl, if he remembered correctly. And the same team member rumored to have injured Brett and caused his coma had nearly killed her youngest daughter.

Jesus.

"How are your children doing?" he asked, then mentally slapped his forehead. He braced himself for the inevitable outpouring.

"Brett is doing well, thanks to you."

Heat crept up the back of his neck at the look of gratitude she shot him. He shook his head. "He's doing well because he's a resilient young man. The medication I gave him may, or may not, have had a bearing on his regaining consciousness.

"You never gave up on him. You kept trying, and that's what counts."

"Your daughter Zoe would have kicked my butt all over the hospital if I'd ever hinted at quitting."

Clara laughed. "She's a force to be reckoned with. She's a real steel magnolia—soft, southern and feminine, but with a core of steel."

"Like her mother."

Soft color touched her cheeks and she shifted the strap of her purse over her shoulder. Her blouse parted, showing the lacy camisole-style t-shirt hugging her breasts and offered him a glimpse of cleavage. "Thanks for the compliment, but I think all my children got more of that from their father."

"And you're here just for a visit?"

"I haven't made up my mind yet. After everything that happened in June, I decided to take early retirement and explore my options."

How old was she? She looked too young to retire.

And why was he speculating about her age?

Because for the first time in a very long while he was noticing a woman. *Really noticing her.*

"Dad."

Evan's voice just behind him caught his attention. He tore his gaze away from Clara Weaver to face his son.

Time stopped. His heart plunged. *My God. What the hell happened?* He barely bit back the exclamation. *What's wrong?*

Evan looked pale, and his face was thin. Dark shadows formed crescents beneath his eyes and accentuated the sharp thrust of his cheekbones. His clothes hung on him as though the cloth found it painful to touch his bony frame.

Six months. It had only been six months since they'd seen each other. *How had this happened?*

A soft hand gripped his, and he glanced down at Clara Weaver.

Her shoulder brushed his as she leaned forward and offered her other hand to Evan, filling the awkward silence, giving him time to recover.

"Hello, I'm Clara Weaver. My son was one of your father's patients a couple of months ago."

"Evan. I'm Evan." His smile appeared strained as he accepted her hand. His brown eyes looked overlarge in a face that seemed to have shrunk.

"I'm glad to meet you, Evan." Clara's gaze swung upward to Russell's face, searching, concerned. "It was good seeing you, Dr. Connelly."

His mind, sluggish with shock, began to function again. "Russell," his voice sounded rusty. "Please call me Russell."

"Russell, then. I'll be staying at Brett's apartment. Perhaps you and your son can come to dinner one night." Releasing his hand, she rifled through her purse, then withdrew a pencil and a scrap of paper. She jotted something down and pressed it into his hand.

A knot the size of softball lodged in his throat. "Thanks, Clara."

"I hope to see you both soon. Evan." She nodded to them and, gripping her suitcase handle, sauntered out of the baggage claim area and down the terminal.

Russell opened the paper to read the cell phone number and the note, *If you need anything at all.* He tucked it into his pocket. "Let me take your bag, Evan."

"I've got it."

Russell matched his pace to Evan's as they strolled up the terminal to the exit. He made a point of pausing at the artwork displayed along the way, giving Evan time to rest.

His mind raced with possibilities as he studied the way Evan moved, the color of his skin, looking for clues. Though they were the same height, Evan had always been less muscular. But now he'd lost at least thirty pounds, maybe more.

They caught a shuttle to the parking lot. Dread slowed his pace as they walked the short distance to the car. He hit the button on his key ring to unlock the doors and raise the trunk lid. Evan stuffed in the bulky case. Russell slid behind the wheel and waited for him to get in and buckle his seat belt.

He rested his hands on the wheel, but didn't start the car. Emotion tightened like a steel band around his chest and choked off his air. "What is it?" His voice sounded hoarse.

Evan's brown eyes grew glassy and his throat worked as he swallowed. "I have AIDS, Dad."

Clara gripped the steering wheel as she pulled out into the stream of traffic traveling east away from the airport.

My God, what a horrible way to find out your child is ill. The blatant shock on Dr. Connelly's face had torn through the surprising pull of attraction she'd felt toward him and spurred her to offer him support in the only way a stranger could, through physical contact.

How long had it been since he'd seen his son? It was obvious he hadn't seen him recently.

In the military, separations came so often and lasted anywhere from a few months to more than a year. But that was usually during deployment or training. Dr. Connelly was stationed here, had been for some time, or that had been the impression she'd gotten while Brett was ill.

Why hadn't he seen his son? An estrangement? Could it be that Evan hadn't wanted his father to know he was ill? But why?

She had no right to speculate. But the look on Russell's face—Russell. The name suited him. The streaks of gray hair at his temples stood out against the sun-kissed tone of his skin. He must do some kind of outside activity.

His hand had gripped hers more out of an automatic response than an acceptance of the comfort she was offering.

He'd been so stunned.

She'd paused long enough to observe them out of concern—and curiosity.

He and his son hadn't embraced, even after she'd left them. Pain had lain between them like shards of glass. How awful for them both. Was the distance a normal dynamic? Had it been shock that had held them apart, or was their relationship as strained as it seemed?

But after the shock, when Russell had begun to recover, she'd seen the look in his eyes and recognized it. The same look had stared back at her from the mirror for a long endless month until Sharon had recovered from her emergency surgery, and Brett had awakened from his coma.

Fear. Fear for your child, and helplessness, because there wasn't a damn thing you could do to stand between them and the pain they were experiencing.

It had been etched into her husband Joseph's features every time he'd seen Zoe in pain after the accident that had nearly cost her a leg. Not being able to shoulder their daughter's pain had eaten at him. And her.

Evan had the hollow-eyed look of a cancer patient. The measured way he'd moved, as though he was conserving his strength between each step, spoke volumes. Whatever it was, it was bad.

Why wouldn't he have turned to his father, a doctor, from the very beginning?

The question burrowed into her thoughts.

They owed Russell Connelly so much. Was there some way she could help? Would he even welcome the offer? He had her number. She'd just have to wait and see.

CHAPTER 3

"**A**re you going to tell Mom what Dr. Stewart said? Zoe asked.

"Are you going to tell her you're sleeping with Hawk?" Brett shot back as he loaded the dishwasher. *Jeez.* How the hell did the place get in this kind of shape with only him here? He scanned the living room for any dishes he might have missed.

"That's probably something I don't have to say. She already knows—has known for some time."

Brett's head whipped around. "Damn, Zoe. That isn't the kind of thing you talk about with your mom."

"I'm living with him, Brett. We share a house and a bed." Her dark blue eyes gleamed wickedly. "Do you really think she doesn't know her children have sex lives?"

"If she ever asks, I'm still a virgin," he said.

Zoe laughed. "Too late. She knows you and Jennifer Taylor swapped cherries in the back seat of her car on prom night. If you're going to have sex in the family vehicle, at least get rid of *all* the condom wrappers."

Brett squeezed his eyes shut. "Man. It sucks when you can't hide anything from the women in your life."

Her expression grew serious. "You already keep so many secrets. It helps us feel connected when you share the emotional parts of your life with us."

"Not this, Zoe. I don't want Mom to look at me as though I'm defective." *Like Captain Jackson does.*

The bland expression never wavered. But had he seen a small flinch of pain in her blue eyes?

Ah, shit!

"Mom would never think that about you," she said.

Damn. She would take the high road instead of bashing him. And now he felt like an asshole. "Zo—"

"It's all right. You don't have to tiptoe around me, or my leg, Brett. You of all people should know that." She bent to pick up a dishtowel from the floor and limped into the small laundry room. "I'm still on my feet. I'm still mostly in one piece. A bit dented here and there, but I'm good."

Damn his big mouth. He leaned against the doorframe as she loaded the sheets he'd stripped from the bed into the washing machine and started it. There was no one on the planet he loved more than Zoe. She'd stood by him, done physical therapy on him, read to him, talked and fussed and begged him to wake up the whole time he'd been in the coma. She'd never given up. Damned if he'd repay her with thoughtless comments like that. He tried to formulate an apology.

"Did he give you any timetable as to when you can start full training again?" she asked.

Brett shook his head. "He's finally given his consent for some running and calisthenics."

"Which you've been doing for a month now." Zoe broke in.

Brett narrowed his eyes. *How did she know?*

"We both know you have. I do pick up your clothes every time I come here."

Shit. He'd always been more squared away than this. He was going to have to get his act together. Get his discipline back. "Until he releases me to train I'm still stuck on desk duty and paperwork."

"It beats sitting here looking at the walls and driving yourself crazy."

Captain Jackson was sure to come up with some unique torture. Guaranteed. He'd test him and zero in on his speech problem. *Damn him.* Jackson had focused on the term "brain injury" in his doctor's report, and, as far as that prick was concerned, it meant he was unfit for duty. *Forever.*

Zoe's arms slid around his waist, and she rested her head against his chest. "It's going to be all right, Brett."

He could always depend on her belief in him. It never wavered. He rubbed her slender back and rested his chin on the top of her head. "Damn straight," he said, giving her hazelnut-streaked ponytail a gentle tug.

He had to get into the right mind-set to prove to Jackson he was still in the game. Being a SEAL was all he'd ever wanted. He wasn't going to allow Derrick and Captain SOB to steal it from him.

"When are you going to put Hawk out of his misery and marry him?"

Zoe pulled away and leaned back against the kitchen counter. She averted her eyes, and a frown crossed her features. "I'd marry him tomorrow if he wanted it. He still doesn't think he's atoned enough for breaking things off with me a few months ago. And he wants me to be sure I can handle being separated for such long periods of time when he's deployed and training."

"I can set him straight," Brett said "You're like a bad penny, a burr, gum on the bottom of a shoe. There's no getting rid of you."

"Thanks," Zoe's tone was dry. "I really want him to think of me in those terms."

Brett grinned. "I'll try and pretty it up for him then. "V-V" *What was the fucking word?*

Zoe's expression remained passive, patient.

He grinned when it came to him. "Vel-Velcro maybe."

The phone rang. He strode to it and snapped it up. Captain Jackson's secretary spoke on the other end of the line. He listened intently.

"Who was it?" Zoe asked as soon as he hung up.

"I'm to report to Captain Jackson ASAP. He has an assignment for me."

"Good! After my interview, I'll stick around and get Mom settled." She punched him in the arm. "You're getting out from behind the desk. This is what you wanted, what you've been waiting for, isn't it?"

"Yeah." But what kind of assignment was it? Jackson was going to put the screws to him. He knew it.

Brett strode down the hall. With every step, he seesawed between excitement and anxiety. Reaching his destination, he paused outside the office door. Maybe they were going to allow him to return to full duty. Naw—Doc Stewart would have let him know. He was doing speech therapy one day a week, his psych therapy twice a month, and taking a language class. *Goddamn.* What else did they want him to do to prove his fitness for duty? How much longer was he going to have to wait?

Brett took a deep breath to offset the quick flash of anger tightening the muscles of his face. He tapped at the Captain's door with a little more force than was necessary.

"Enter." Jackson's muffled tone carried through the barrier.

Brett opened the door, reached the desk in two strides, then snapped to attention. Jackson continued to look over some paperwork on a clipboard while Brett maintained his posture.

"At ease, Ensign. How do you feel about public speaking?"

Dread hit the pit of Brett's stomach with the punch of a grenade launcher. *Ah, shit.* He spread his feet, folded his hands behind him, and focused his attention out the window just beyond Jackson's shoulder. "I think it should be left to priests and politicians, sir."

Jackson studied him, his expression impassive. "Our public information officer has developed a staph infection and has been hospitalized. He was scheduled to deliver a speech about SEAL team training to the San Diego Women's Political

League. You have been chosen to take his place this afternoon."

Shit! "I'm not much of a public speaker, sir."

Jackson eyed him. "It's important for us to keep our best foot forward in the public eye, Ensign. Especially now."

"Yes, sir."

"I'll be attending as well, but the bulk of the information will be coming from you."

"Yes, sir." Another damned test. That's what it was. "Permission to ask a question, sir."

Jackson's eyes narrowed. "Permission granted."

"How many ladies will be attending, sir?"

"About two hundred."

Two hundred women he could humiliate himself in front of by forgetting the word he wanted, or not being able to come up with a substitute. Great, just freaking great. "Where is this meeting to be held?"

"In the Crown Room at Hotel del Coronado. You have two hours to prepare, Ensign. You're dismissed."

Brett focused on Jackson's face. The son-of-a-bitch had probably waited until the last minute to call him in. "Yes, sir." He saluted, swiveled on his heel, and left Jackson's office. He strode down the hallway to the elevator. The doors opened and he stepped in. Blessedly alone, he painted the air blue with a stream of swear words that would have had his schoolteacher mother slapping him upside the head. *Why the hell didn't he ever forget any of them?*

Teresa "Tessa" Kelly shifted from one foot to the other as she stood at the back of the sprawling, richly paneled Crown room. The meal had been well prepared and delicious, but she had barely touched it. A girl had to watch her figure. She looked forward with more enthusiasm to the entertainment part of the session. At least she'd have something to write about after it concluded.

This lifestyles page assignment was a never-ending afternoon-tea hell. If she had to swallow one more canapé, or rub elbows with one more SEAL team groupie, she would scream. Being in a war zone dodging bullets and bombs would be preferable to this. Her pale redhead complexion had already turned pink though she had layered on sun block before leaving her apartment. She should have forgone the poolside drinks.

Captain Jackson rose to speak to the group. He looked tall and imposing in his whites, his prematurely gray hair gleaming beneath the lights as he climbed the steps to the small podium. She was sure what he had to say to the ladies would be some of the same things all the Naval speakers said about the war on terrorism in Iraq and Afghanistan. And as important as the subject was to her assignment, Tess's attention wandered back to the young officer sitting at the table with Barbara Hanover, their hostess. Ensign Brett Weaver.

Tess clicked on the small mini-recorder she carried so as not to miss any part of Jackson's speech. But her thoughts turned to the younger officer who had accompanied him. What was Brett Weaver doing here? Was he going to take part in some way?

The brief news article that had followed his injury, followed by the meltdown of one of his team members and the disappearance of another, had piqued her interest. If she could just get an exclusive interview with him, she might be able to convince her editor to move her from the lifestyles page to the political beat. Luckily, this assignment did have political overtones, otherwise Captain Jackson would not have attended. That's what was giving her an itchy feeling between her shoulder blades. Why was he doing a PR stint when he could have sent any junior officer to handle the San Diego Women's Political League? If only she could ferret out exactly what she was missing.

Brett Weaver turned his head to speak to the woman next to him. The strong line of his jaw appeared masculine and clean. His brows, darker than his hair, followed a strong brow ridge. His sun-bleached hair was cropped close to his head. Would he be going wheels up soon, as the teams called shipping out?

As though sensing her interest, Weaver looked over Barbara Hanover's shoulder directly at her. In the past, she had thought blond men washed out. There was nothing watercolor-soft about this man. He looked fit and focused. Even across the room, his eyes pinned her with a steady, bold look that triggered a quiver in her stomach.

Captain Jackson's comments wound down too quickly, and, surprised, Tess's attention shifted to him. "I'm sure you'd rather speak to a younger member of the teams. Ensign Weaver will be happy to answer any questions you may have."

Tess's brows rose. She hadn't known he was going to speak. Her heartbeat started to drum, and she hurried forward to find a closer seat.

Brett climbed the two steps to the platform. God, he'd rather be three feet deep in a foxhole with bullets whizzing overhead than standing up here in front of two hundred women. His heart was running like an engine stuck in high gear. Sweat ran down his back, making his shirt cling to his spine. He shifted, trying to relieve the discomfort. Fuck! Just how many more hoops was he going to have to jump through before they judged him fit?

His attention fastened on the face of the redhead he had noticed eyeing him earlier. Her long, steady stride ate up the distance as she walked up the aisle between the white linen cover tables. Her steps flipped up the hem of her yellow sundress, baring shapely thighs. Color flared across her cheekbones to match the soft, sun-kissed pink of her nose. With a brush of her hand, she shoved her skirt down and slid into her seat.

Distracted from his nervousness, Brett's lips quirked up. Legs that long and beautiful needed to be insured, or at least declared a national treasure. If he could get a closer look at them after this was over, it might even be worth the discomfort he was feeling.

He waited for the woman to get settled then said, "Good afternoon, ladies." *God, his Kentucky accent sounded so much thicker over the PA system.*

"I understand you have some questions you'd like answered about the SEALs and our training. I've been a SEAL for three years, and I can tell you from experience the training is rigorous and sometimes dangerous. But there are other facets to it as well. While I wait for my next deployment, I'm taking a foreign language class so I'll be able to communicate in the area I may be deployed to. So, contrary to popular belief, it isn't just about fighting a war, or quelling violence and aggression, or taking down terrorists. It's about saving as many lives as we can, and having the skills we need to do that successfully. Now what else would you like to know?"

Fifty hands went up all at once, among them the redhead's. Brett called on a woman closer to the front of the group whose hand wavered tentatively. "Will you tell us about your experience during BUD/S training?"

For a moment, Brett thought of Derrick and the ordeal they had faced together as teammates and swim buddies. The loss of his friendship, his comradeship, still hurt.

He jerked his attention back to the question. "It was tough. The instructors pushed us to the limit, but we pushed ourselves as well. If we hadn't, we wouldn't have made it through. It taught us to work as a team, and it conditioned us mentally to withstand a great deal of pressure."

"Mental pressure. I thought it was just physical punishment," the redhead said.

Bret paused a moment. "When you're swimming in the ocean in the dark, you link together to make sure you don't lose anyone. You're cold and wet, and the sand is sticking to and scraping the skin off of places you wished it wasn't—" He smiled as a smattering of laughter broke out. "You know you aren't alone, because you have a brotherhood of men around you experiencing the same hardship, the same discomforts. You come out of the ocean, and you layer yourselves together to conserve body heat because you're a unit, and you take care of each other. Because your strength lies in keeping all the members of your unit strong and ready to act. It's as much a mental preparation as it is physical."

He focused on the redhead's heart-shaped face. Her eyes were dark, instead of the green he was expecting.

"Have you been cleared for active duty yet?" she asked.

Surprised and a little wary of the interest in his personal life, Brett hesitated before answering. "For partial duty. I'm doing some training with another unit, preparing for when I'm cleared to return to my own."

He pointed to a heavyset woman dressed in a brightly flowered sundress.

"How are you feeling after your injury?" she asked.

"I'm fine. I returned to training about a month after my discharge from the hospital." Against doctor's orders. "I'm back to full strength now. Thanks for asking."

"How many languages do you speak?" asked a pretty blond at the third table to the left. She flashed him a saucy smile.

"I'm learning some Farsi right now. Kurdish, Spanish, French, Arabic, and some Gaelic."

"Gaelic! Why Gaelic?" she asked.

"Well ...." He dragged out the syllable a smile tugging at his lips. "I was on leave in Ireland, and I met this girl ... "

Laughter broke out and some of the his tension eased. It was going okay. He hadn't forgotten a single word or needed to pause to get one to come.

A dozen questions later, the redhead raised her hand again.

"How do you deal with the danger of what you do?"

He caught a glimpse of the recorder she held. Press. Was she press or just a groupie? Wariness brought an instant tension to his back and shoulders. For a moment, his mind went blank. *Focus! Focus, circle the word.* Ter- ter- Tr- Tray "Training." He took a breath. "And more training, and more training. The more you repeat a skill, the more confidence you build, the more able you are to deal with things when they don't go according to plan." God, he could be a poster boy for the National PTSD Association with that one.

"I've earned my wings, so I can pilot a plane if I need to. I've been trained in hand-to-hand combat, underwater demolition, and high-altitude parachuting. I can pilot any kind of watercraft and fix an engine with duct tape, bailing wire, and Band-Aids. You don't only have to be physically fit, you have to keep yourself mentally sharp, and you have to be able to think on your feet and be flexible in intense situations."

"And you really want to go back to that?" An older woman at the front table asked.

"Yeah." Brett remained silent a moment. "This is going to sound corny as hell, but ... This is my country. I want to keep it safe. I'll do whatever I have to do to secure it. If that means standing between the citizens of the U.S. and whatever threat is out there—" He shrugged. "That's what I'll do, and I'll continue to do it until I can't any more."

Silence followed and embarrassed heat hit his face. "Thanks for having me, ladies."

Amid eager applause, Brett settled back at the table and felt a hand touch his sleeve. He turned his attention to the woman beside him. In her late twenties, her skin was smooth, her lips lush, and her pale blue eyes more than a little avid as they settled on his face. But the ring on her finger screamed married, even if her attitude didn't. And he definitely wasn't interested in getting mixed up with a married woman.

"Thank you so much, Ensign Weaver," said Barbara Hanover, the President of the San Diego Women's Political League. The smile she offered him held a hint of flirtation and her voice sounded just breathy enough to suggest more. "You were everything the ladies expected a SEAL to be, and more."

A wry smile twisted Brett's lips. "I'm glad I haven't disappointed any of them."

"I know this isn't your normal job. Captain Jackson said Master Chief O'Connor has been hospitalized and you stepped in at the last minute."

"Yes, ma'am."

"God, please don't call me that. It makes me sound so old. I can't be more than three or four years older than you."

"It has nothing to do with age, ma'am. My mother believes in old school manners, and she'd skin me for addressing you, or any other married female, with less than complete respect."

"How quaint," Barbara's tone remained sweet, but held a brittle undercurrent. "Please excuse me, I have to go and make my concluding remarks." She ran a smoothing hand over her perfectly coifed honey-colored hair.

He rose in a polite gesture, and rested a hand on the top of her chair when she shoved it back.

She shot him a wry smile over her shoulder and paused to lay a hand on his arm as she brushed by him. "What would you be calling me if I weren't married, Ensign?"

He studied her expression, trying to judge her mood. When her gaze remained fixed on his, he grinned. "Honey, babe, darlin', or any combination thereof. Ma'am."

Though regret flickered across her features, she laughed. She took her place behind the podium and flashed him another smile.

He nearly sighed aloud with relief as he regained his seat. This public information gig was like a thirty-yard run through mortar fire. God, he felt as though he'd just run the O course. The next time he saw Master Chief O'Hara, he was going to slap his back and offer to buy him a beer. He caught Jackson's attention resting on him and frowned.

The Captain leaned across the space between them to speak for his ears only. "You've done such a fine job today,

Weaver, I may file orders for you to take O'Connor's place until he can return to duty."

Fuck! Brett barely bit back the exclamation. "I think that would be a waste of training time, sir."

One dark brow rose. Jackson eyed him with a flat assessing look. "You just told these ladies there's more to being a SEAL than war games. Just think of it as a different type of training."

Brett drew a deep breath. Had he just been ambushed? "Public relations isn't my thing, sir."

Jackson nodded toward the podium. "Could have fooled me."

Brett clenched his teeth against the urge to argue. For a moment he thought his head might explode from the rush of angry heat.

Were they trying to give him shit details to get him to resign? Was something else going on? Something he wasn't aware of.

He probed Jackson's expression through narrowed eyes, but the man had already returned his attention to Barbara Hanover's closing remarks.

This wasn't the place or time to ask, but goddamn it, he was going to as soon as they returned to base.

CHAPTER 4

Twenty minutes after Captain Jackson's escape, Brett broke free of the women surrounding him and strode down the hall to the nearest exit. Stepping out into the afternoon sun, he drew a deep breath of the salt-tinged air and narrowed his eyes against the glare. Sun worshippers, slick with oil, reclined on striped lounges arranged in synchronized order around the pool. High-pitched squeals came from the shallow end where four children played with a beach ball.

The damn place was like a maze. He shoved his sunglasses on and descended the closest concrete steps leading down to the beach. The white sail of a small watercraft stood out against the deep blue of the open ocean glittering to the north. He watched the small scrap of white as it worked its way closer. Tension drained from his shoulders.

"Ensign Weaver."

Damn. He'd almost escaped. He turned to face the woman. Sunlight emphasized the copper highlights in her chestnut hair. The sun-blushed tint of her cheeks and nose gave her pale, smooth skin a touch of color. As she sauntered toward him, the slender length of her legs snagged his attention again. A vision of those long legs wrapped around his waist while he thrust into her flashed through his mind. His body responded with instant eagerness.

"My name is Tess Kelly, Ensign Weaver. I'm a reporter from the San Diego Tribune."

Shit. So he'd been right. Brett remained silent as she stopped before him.

"I'd like to interview you for the paper."

Brett scanned the area around him. Did she have a photographer stashed somewhere? That's all he'd need, his picture plastered across a newspaper. He'd lose his anonymity and be useless to the team. "Sorry, we don't do interviews."

Her brown eyes narrowed and her lips tightened. He read determination instead of anger in her expression.

"You just did an interview in there for the ladies," she said.

Brett shrugged. "Then you should have everything you need."

"People are very curious about what happened a few months ago. They'll want to know how you're doing. How your sister is doing."

He raised a brow. He could take care of himself, but Zoe was still ... emotional. Something was going on with her. "I already answered that question in there." He nodded his head toward the hotel. He then changed his stance, aligning his six-foot frame so he invaded her personal space. He caught a whiff of her floral perfume, the heat intensifying the scent. Her apple shampoo blended with that and some other fragrance, maybe a lotion she used on her skin. *Her smooth, creamy skin.* Awareness zipped through his system. The back of his neck grew hot and his heartbeat fired into overdrive. Sweat trickled between his shoulder blades. *Jesus.*

Despite the high-alert status of his cock, he dragged his attention back to the current problem and gave her his best hard-edged stare. "As for my sister, she values her privacy as much as I do. And she doesn't need any shit from you. So don't even think about harassing her."

Tess held her ground, but beads of perspiration moistened her hairline, and her gaze shifted away.

"Is this how all you guys control the women in your life, threats and fists?"

Brett suppressed the urge to flinch. Derrick's actions had given the whole team a black eye. It had brought spousal abuse in the Navy into the public forum and set off a firestorm of questions and suppositions. Hell, by now it had probably sparked a study or two.

He drew a deep breath and kept his voice even. "I have three women in my life. My mother and my sisters. I've never raised my hand to any of them. And I'd make anyone who did w—" *Think!—What's the word? Will- wit- wis-h*

Her reddish-brown eyes, the color of milk chocolate, homed in on his face, a speculative gleam in their depths.

Every muscle in his body tightened. "—wish they hadn't." He finished the sentence and heard the panic in his own voice.

God, he'd never run away from anything in his life, but he had to fight not to run now. He stepped away from her, and swiveling on his foot, walked away.

"Why did Derek Armstrong attack you?" she asked.

Though she was speaking about the more public spousal abuse case between Derrick and his girlfriend Marjorie, Brett's thoughts went to Iraq. Why—why—why? He'd asked that same question a hundred times since discovering Derrick had been the one who tried to bash his skull in.

He left me to die. After everything we'd been through.

What had he done to set Derrick off?

He paused on the steps to the pool and looked over his shoulder at her. "I'm not at liberty to talk about the case, ma'am. The Navy is conducting an investigation."

"Which will keep everything hush-hush, of course." Her tone held a note of accusation.

"I don't know what they'll do." *I just want to get back to my team.*

Making it to the top of the steps, he paused to glance back, and his gaze swept her legs one more time. Damn shame she was a journalist.

Movement to his right snapped his attention in that direction. "Ensign Weaver, sir?" Two young Warrant Officers came to attention and saluted.

Returning the gesture, Brett gave a nod. "What can I do for you?"

"Captain Jackson needs you back at the base now, sir."

Had something happened to Hawk? His gut clenched. What was going on?

Aware of Tess climbing the stairs behind them, Brett nodded. "I'll come right now." He dug his car keys from his pocket.

"I'll need you to ride with me, sir."

Brett paused to study the young sailor's face. He tossed the keys to his partner. "It's a cherry red mustang parked in front of the motel." He narrowed his eyes. "Take good care of it."

"Aye, sir."

"Is there a problem, gentlemen?" Tess asked as she reached them.

"No problem," Brett answered. "I have to report to base ASAP. Let's go, Warrant Officer."

"Aye, sir."

"Miss Kelly," Brett nodded toward her.

"Ensign Weaver." She slid a business card into his pocket. "Just in case you change your mind."

The air inside the pool facility hung sticky and moist. Dressed in black swim trunks and a t-shirt, Hawk followed along the edge of the water, keeping pace with the eight men swimming below him. Though the duty was dull and repetitive, in this second phase training it was necessary for the men to grow as comfortable in the water as they were on land. The only way for them to do that was to spend hours swimming, scuba diving, and practicing water skills and tactics.

As the swimmers reached the side of the pool, each surfaced and went into a head back position to clear their airways and rest.

"How are you feeling, Mr. Lucas?" he asked one of the men who seemed winded.

"I'm fine, sir."

Hawk nodded.

Ensign Zac O'Connor, known as "Doc," sauntered up to stand at his elbow, a video camera pointed at the men in the pool.

"What's up, Doc?" Hawk asked.

Doc shot him a look over the extended viewer of the video camera. "HQ wanted some footage of the men training for a video. So they sent me out. How's Zoe?"

"Good. She's going for her interview at the hospital today."

"Sounds good. It'd be a great fit. Hope she lands the job."

"Thanks."

Doc pushed the off button on the video camera and lowered it. His expression changed from its usual easygoing half-smile to serious. "Have you heard any news about the investigation into Flash's disappearance?"

Hawk's facial muscles tensed. "No. I've had more communication with a sponge on the ocean floor than with Naval Criminal Investigative Service," he said, with sarcastic emphasis on the word investigative. "And I've called NCIS several times in the past few weeks." Frustration ratcheted his heartbeat up a notch. "The official word is they can't talk about an open and ongoing investigation."

Doc swore beneath his breath. "Flash had his problems with the gambling, but Jesus!" Doc rubbed a palm over his short auburn hair, then dropped his arm. "He should be here waiting for orders to go wheels up just like the rest of us, not—" Doc made a cutting gesture. "You think he's dead?"

Hawk remained silent a moment. He'd gone over and over the last days he'd hung out with Flash. He'd been secretive, agitated. They had no definitive proof identifying him as the man who had smuggled the ancient Iraqi seals into the country in Brett's gear. Even if Flash had been responsible for the smuggling, the artifacts wouldn't have brought enough on the black market to bankroll him for the rest of his life. If he was alive, he'd have to surface sooner or later.

He looked up to find Doc still waiting for his answer. "Against all odds, Brett came out of a coma. I'm not ready to write Flash off just yet either. Even if he was in over his head with gambling debts, and he took this route to cover them, there's no real proof he did it. I can't see him ditching the only family he has, his team. Not unless he had no control over what went down."

"So you think maybe someone kidnapped him, or he's on the run from someone?"

"He has skills. We disappear into a jungle for days at a time. We can survive in the desert with one canteen of water, a compass, and a KA-BAR. Why wouldn't he be able to survive under the radar?"

The other instructor, Petty Officer Second Class Frank ordered, "Prepare for subsurface."

The men straightened from their laid back positions in the pool.

"Go subsurface." Frank's voice bounced off the walls in an echo.

The men took a deep breath, pushed off the pool wall, and swam underwater the length of the pool. Doc and Hawk fell in alongside the swimmers until they surfaced and went heads back to rest again.

"But what about the blood in the car?" Doc asked.

"Not enough for him to be dead. Wounded yes, but not deceased. I saw that myself."

"So, you think he's alive?"

"Until someone shows me his dead body, that's what I'll believe. He's a SEAL."

The tension in Doc's face relaxed. "You're right. If they didn't find a body, he's in the wind." He grimaced. "He had to be the one who smuggled the artifacts in, though. Right?"

"My gut says he did it," Hawk said, though he flinched at the admission.

The feelings that acknowledgement provoked lay between them for several long moments. The whole team was still reeling from Flash's disappearance and Derrick's arrest. Every time he thought about the domino sequence of events that had led up to both, a painful ache settled in the pit of his stomach. These were guys he'd trusted with his life. How could they have both betrayed their team, and themselves?

"The only proof we had was that he helped pack Cutter's gear, and that's circumstantial," Hawk said. "Anyone could have slipped the stones into Cutter's bag between the time it was packed and the time we caught the transport home. But his disappearance points a finger. And the signs of a struggle inside his car point to more."

Doc nodded and looked away. "You know that saying about how we never leave a fallen man behind? It feels as though we have. We should have pursued the investigation ourselves."

"And we'd have all ended up in the brig for interfering in a federal investigation."

"Better that than this damn limbo," Doc muttered bitterly. He glanced at his watch then across the pool. "It feels like we've lost an arm." He glanced at Hawk. "Know what I mean?"

"Yeah, I know."

"Prepare for subsurface." Petty Officer Frank's voice carried across the pool once again. "Go subsurface."

Grateful for the interruption, Hawk shifted his attention back to the men in the pool.

Doc slapped him on the shoulder. "I'll see you later." He sauntered toward the exit.

"Sure." Hawk paced down the edge of the pool away from him.

"Hey, Hawk." Doc's called, his voice echoing across the distance between them.

He paused and glanced over his shoulder.

"My place, seventeen hundred, tomorrow night." Doc continued talking while he walked backwards. "Steaks on the grill. Bring Zoe and some beer. I'll call the rest of the guys and have them bring their girls."

Maybe that's what they needed, a good steak and some hang time with the other team members and their families. It couldn't hurt. "Zoe's mom is coming in."

"Bring her. She can be my date. She's hot."

The image of his future mother-in-law, Clara, as a cougar dating Doc flashed through his head. Hawk laughed. "She'd eat you for breakfast."

"I'd hope," Doc shot back, his grin wide. The door slammed behind him.

Hawk laughed, and the smile lingered for several seconds. Until his thoughts shifted back to Flash.

He'd give NCIS time to do their thing, and if they hadn't come up with some answers in a couple more weeks, he'd have a meeting with the rest of the guys, and they'd do their own investigation. As Doc had said, they never left a man behind.

CHAPTER 5

Brett's gaze traveled from Captain Jackson's face to the two NCIS agents. Damn, he'd thought the investigation into Derrick's meltdown was finished. What else was there for them to ask about? So why had they sent the military police to pick him up? An edgy tingle started just between his shoulder blades, as though a sniper had him in his sights. What the fuck was going on?

"Do you have any objection to my staying, Ensign Weaver?" Captain Jackson asked.

"No, sir."

"Why don't you have a seat?" One of the agents, the one who had introduced himself as Agent Wright, motioned with a hand the size of a dinner plate to a hard-backed metal chair. The man was at least six foot six, and probably two hundred and fifty plus pounds, with café au lait skin, dark brown eyes, and hair cropped close to his head.

Though the urge to remain standing was strong, Brett took the seat.

"You were sent to Iraq in two thousand ten and served seven months there, correct, Ensign Weaver?" Agent Wright asked.

"Yes, sir."

"On April twenty-eighth, 2011, you were assigned to a protection detail for a fifteen-year-old boy by the name of Sanjay al-Yussuf."

The day of the mission. Shit.

"Can you corroborate that for us, Ensign?"

"No, sir, I can't."

Agent Wright's brows rose and he glanced at his partner.

Agent Scott, five foot nine and about one hundred forty-five pounds, with shaggy light brown hair, was physically less intimidating than Wright. But his green eyes were sharp as he leaned forward in his chair. "Why not?"

"I was injured during a mission later that day. I was in a coma for a month afterward. My memory of anything that happened that week has been completely wiped out. The last thing I remember is training the week before for the mission on April twenty-eighth."

Both agents leaned back in their chairs and continued to stare at him. "Do you have medical proof of this, Ensign?" Agent Wright asked.

"Contact Captain Russell Connelly at Balboa Naval Hospital. He was my doc until I was discharged. Dr. Ronald Stewart is my doc now."

"You'll sign a release?"

Brett shrugged. "After you tell me what happened to the boy."

Wright's eyes narrowed. "Why would you think something happened to him?"

"You wouldn't be here asking questions otherwise. We traveled in caravans throughout the city. We'd have had cover front and back. Why don't you just ask the other guys on the detail?"

"Because they're dead," Wright said, his voice flat.

No! Each Humvee would have had a crew of four. Eight guys dead. "*Jesus.*"

"You and Ensign Armstrong are the only survivors of that detail, Weaver. And he ain't talking," Scott said. "You got any idea why he'd refuse to tell us what happened that day?"

"No, sir." Had something happened during the transport?

"He tried to kill you twice. And you don't know why?" Scott asked.

Alarm bells clanged in his head. They were acting as though they had proof Derrick had tried to kill him. If he wasn't talking—

"I can't testify as to how I was injured during the mission later that day, Agent Scott. I don't remember even leaving base. As to the incident at Lieutenant Yazzie's house, I was standing between Derrick and his girlfriend and my sister while he threatened them with a loaded gun. He didn't much care for the interference." Bitterness edged his voice.

"If he'd done something to the boy, and he was afraid you'd talk—"

Prickles of shock raced down Brett's throat into his torso, and then rage flashed deep into his gut. His face flushed hot. He met Wright's stare head on. "No way, sir. *No fucking way.*"

"Weaver—" Captain Jackson's tone held a warning.

Ignoring Jackson, Brett remained focused on Wright's face. "He's a kid. *An unarmed civilian.* We wouldn't have laid a hand on him." He drew a deep breath, forcing calm, forcing his anger back. "Had there been any sort of altercation, the eight guys covering us would have reported it."

"They never had the opportunity, Ensign." Scott's voice held a note of quiet finality.

So they'd been killed that same day. *Fuck. Eight guys. Jesus.* Brett drew another calming breath, trying to slow the harsh beating of his heart, and tamp down the sick feeling in the pit of his stomach. He turned his attention to Scott. "We don't kill innocent civilians. Our mission there is to preserve the safety of innocent civilians and of our men. Al-Qaeda and the Taliban don't agree with that. Our being there is reason enough for them to try to kill us. Plus they're always on the lookout for new recruits, and they don't give a damn whether the guys they pick up are interested or not. I'd be looking at the possibility the kid was kidnapped by one of the teams they have cruising the neighborhoods."

"That possibility is being looked at, Ensign," Wright said.

Brett relaxed a minute degree. "Good. I hope they find him."

The agents rose. Brett did as well.

"You'll be hearing from us, Weaver," Scott said.

Was that a threat? Neither agent offered his hand. After a brief nod to Jackson, they filed out of the office, leaving a void behind them.

Jackson resumed his seat. Brett remained standing and faced him, waiting to be dismissed.

The silence hung between them heavy with tension. Brett searched the man's expression and looked away. *No backup here.*

"For what it's worth, Weaver, I don't believe you had a damn thing to do with that kid's disappearance," Jackson said.

Surprise held Brett immobile. "Sir."

"What I believe, and what you can prove are two different things. Someone high up sent those two assholes here. Someone who wants answers and wants them quick. If I were you, I'd work on trying to remember all I could about that protection detail."

Simple for Jackson to suggest. It would be easier to pull memories out of a black hole than his brain. Brett remained silent.

"Dismissed, Ensign."

"Aye, sir." Brett pivoted on his heel and marched from Jackson's office. In the military, you were guilty until proven innocent. How could he fight that with a memory full of holes the size of mortar shells?

Russell lifted the cartons of Chinese food out of the bag and put them on the small kitchen table, releasing the aroma of ginger and peppers. His apartment was utilitarian but clean. He'd given Evan the master bedroom and bath in consideration of his condition. There were so many things going on with his son, and he hadn't been aware of any of them. Why hadn't Evan called?

"Are you having any intestinal distress?" he asked as Evan came into the kitchen from the hall. "I thought Chinese, since it's pretty much steamed vegetables and rice, would be—"

"I'm good, Dad," Evan said, cutting him off. "This looks fine." He pulled out a chair and sat down.

Russell got clean plates and silverware from the dishwasher and set them on the table. "How's your mother?" he asked as he got ice tea from the refrigerator and filled two glasses.

"She's fine." Using chopsticks, Evan placed an eggroll on his plate. "She and Carl took a second honeymoon in England a couple of months ago. She came back with pictures and souvenirs from every castle there."

Evan grasped the container of fried rice, tipped some on his plate, then reached for the General Tso's chicken.

"I'm glad she's found someone who likes to travel." Russell set the glasses down on the table and took a seat. He filled his plate.

"You mean travel together, don't you," Evan's tone was an accusation.

Russell concentrated on his chicken and broccoli. "I couldn't very well take you and your mother to a war zone, Evan."

Gloria had ruthlessly implanted her feelings of bitterness, rejection, and disappointment from their ten-year marriage into their son. His deployment schedules had disrupted his visitation with Evan, and she had manipulated her custody status as a way to control and punish Russell for what she perceived as his marital shortcomings. She'd used Evan like a weapon until he'd moved out of the house to go to college. And by then the damage to his relationship with his son had seemed beyond his ability to repair. Why had she felt the need to drive a wedge between them?

Seeing the same bitterness in his son's green eyes that he'd had aimed at him from Gloria's over the years triggered a rage toward her he'd suppressed for most of their relationship. Evan was no longer a child. And if his condition was as dire as he suspected, it was time for him to make an effort to reach him.

"Why are you here, Evan?"

"You've been gone a while."

No. He wasn't getting away with that. "We saw each other six months ago, when I first got back. I've called numerous times and gotten your voice mail. You've never returned my calls."

Evan stirred the food on his plate. "I was busy with several cases at first, then in the hospital for a time."

"Did your mother know?"

Evan remained silent a moment, avoiding his gaze. "Yeah."

"You could have asked her to call me. There might have been something I could have done for you."

"I have doctors, I don't need another," Evan said, his tone sharp.

"I wasn't speaking as a doctor, but as your father."

"It's a little late for that."

Pain lanced through Russell, shoving him to his feet. He carried his plate to the sink, the food barely touched. Gloria had enjoyed thirty years of uninterrupted participation in their son's life. He'd had to be satisfied with the scraps she and Evan would allow him. How pathetic was that? He couldn't shake the need to hurry and make up for lost time.

"I've never spoken with anything but respect for your mother to you. I've never told you how I felt about the divorce. Or my feelings about having another man raise my son."

He turned to face Evan. He looked frail, ill. If the disease was raging through his system he'd only grow weaker. Their time might be too short to peel the bandage off slowly. He'd waited twenty years for Evan to allow him into his life.

"I don't suppose you remember any of it. You were only eight. Your mother waited until I was in a war zone to file for the divorce and sole custody." *She was dating Carl before I deployed. Something I didn't know until I got back nearly a year later.* "She and Carl were married a week after the divorce became final. I was still in Iraq."

"The court system didn't care about my military status or the legitimate reasons behind my absences. They awarded her sole custody, but gave me visitation rights. When I returned home, I filed for more frequent visitation, and she played the military card. My household wasn't a stable environment. I was an absentee father. There were guns in the house, and she was worried about supervision. And then she tried to get me to sign over my parental rights so Carl could adopt you." *When I refused, she launched her campaign to undermine my rights any way she could and to keep me from seeing you.* He looked into Evan's pale features. "And she had the best legal advice money could buy, her own husband."

"But you never relinquished your rights."

"No. I'd have never done it. You're my *son.*" His voice cracked on the last word. He glanced at his watch to cover the loss of control. "I have a meeting at the hospital. I won't be long. I'll be off for the next few days. We'll have plenty of time to talk."

Evan drew the ice tea glass closer and cradled it between his hands. "Why didn't you tell me about this before?"

"Your mother has always been important to you, Evan. I didn't want you caught between us, then or later. By the time you started college—" *I'd lost you.* "A pattern had been set, and ... you didn't seem interested in changing it."

"Is there any proof?"

Russell flinched, then ground his teeth. Was it the lawyer in him coming through? Or was he truly his mother's son in every way?

Russell strode from the kitchen, turned left down the hall to the master bedroom, and went to the closet. From a shelf above the clothes bar, he dragged a cardboard box down and laid it on the dresser. He removed the lid and withdrew a thick file bound together by brittle rubber bands. The faded pages represented more pain than anything else he'd ever experienced. The dissolution of his family, and the loss of his child. Tears shoved a knot the size of a soft ball into his throat.

It was indisputable proof that every word he'd spoken was true.

Was Evan strong enough to handle it?

Evan shuffled through the door.

Too late to back down now. Russell stepped forward and extended the file. "Here's your proof."

CHAPTER 6

Where was Brett? He was supposed to be back hours ago. Typical man. None of them had any sense of time.

Zoe eyed her mother as she poured a cup of coffee in Brett's small kitchen. The aroma of the casserole she'd prepared permeated the room. Instead of enticing her, the smell made her nauseous. Was this the beginning of morning sickness?

"So, is there any news you want to share with me?" Clara asked as they sat down at a kitchen table barely big enough for four.

Had she sensed something? Or was it the marriage thing again? "I think my interview went very well this morning. They said I should hear back by the end of the week."

"Good. How are things with Hawk?"

"He's wonderful. He hasn't gotten his orders yet, but the team is training again. They never truly stop. He thinks they'll be going to Afghanistan next. He's filling in for one of the instructors today whose little boy is sick."

"He's a gem, Zoe."

"Yeah, he is." She met her mother's gaze. "I love him so much, Mom."

Clara smiled. "I'd have never guessed. What's up with your brother?"

"He's started getting in shape again. He's running and swimming. And he's taking a language class, one of the Afghan dialects."

"But?"

"I think he's having trouble with someone at work."

Her mother's features settled into a frown. "Do you know who it might be?"

"He doesn't say much about what happens on post. None of them do." Zoe drew a deep breath. "I guess that's a good thing. I'd worry more if I knew everything they did." An instant memory flashed through her mind of Hawk, his cheek swollen and his eyes enflamed, after being hit in the face by a Simunitions round. It could have been so much worse.

Though her stomach roiled, she cleared her throat and continued. "If I had to hazard a guess, it would be his commanding officer. He's been dragging his feet about assigning Brett to duty."

"But you just said a minute ago that he gave him an assignment."

"A public speaking engagement in front of two hundred women."

"Oh—" the word came out in a whoosh of air. Her expression grew fierce. "*That asshole!*"

Zoe laughed. "That was my take on the whole thing, too. I texted Brett right after my interview. He said everything went fine." Her eyes strayed to the clock. "That was two hours ago."

"He'll be here in a minute. And what about Hawk? Will he be joining us for a meal?"

"Yes, he will. But he may be a little late."

"I'm anxious to see him." Clara grew quiet a moment. "I saw Dr. Connelly at the airport."

Instant interest had Zoe's brows rising. "Oh, how was he?"

"He looked fine. A little tired. He was picking up his son." She cupped the tea in her hands as though warming them.

Zoe took a sip from her cup. "I didn't know he had a son. I knew he was divorced. All the nurses would primp a little before he came on the floor. Even the younger ones. He's older, but still a hunk."

When Clara's cheeks grew pink, Zoe studied her.

He's very ill. The son, not Dr. Connelly. He looked so frail, so thin." Clara reached out to lay a hand over Zoe's. "I mentioned we'd have them for supper one evening. Would it be all right with Hawk if we invited them to his house instead of here?"

"You know it will, Mom. And you know you can come stay with us whenever you like. We have extra bedrooms."

"I want to spend some time with Brett first. I haven't really been able to since he got out of the hospital. I hope he doesn't feel as though I didn't want to be here for him." A worried frown creased Clara's brow.

"Of course he doesn't, Mom. He knows Sharon needed you more urgently than he did. And Hawk and I were here for him. All you could have done was sit by his bedside, like I did, and wait for him to wake up."

"Has Derrick Armstrong confessed why he tried to kill Brett?"

"Derrick's denying he ever tried to hurt him."

"But he admitted it in front of you, Brett, and Marjorie."

"He's backpedaling on it now." And the statement he'd murmured while holding a gun to Brett's head had been too ambiguous to prove. *Damn him.* "I haven't seen Marjorie since he attacked her. I think she's gone back to live closer to her parents."

"But she'll return for the trial?"

"I don't know, Mom. I'm sure she'll have to testify. She's the one Derrick was after that day. I think he'd have killed her. He's unbalanced."

"Every time I think of Derrick leaving Brett in that building unconscious, and of Hawk going in and rescuing him—" She reached for Zoe's hand. "Had Hawk been any less the man than he is ... " Obviously close to tears, she shook her head.

Zoe gave Clara's hand a squeeze. "But Hawk is who he is, and Brett's fine now. If he can survive getting up in front of two hundred women and talking about what he does, he's good. He's been training on his own. And just waiting to be released to return to full duty."

"If he isn't able to do that …" Clara began.

Being a SEAL was all he'd ever wanted. He'd move on. But he'd never truly bounce back. Zoe shoved the thoughts away. "As Hawk says, he's done hard before, and it wouldn't mean as much if it came easy. His speech glitch is getting better all the time. He's going to be just fine."

At the sound of the apartment door opening, she caught back a sigh. She didn't wish for Brett to be on the hot seat with their mother, but seeing him would set Clara's mind at ease. Clara rose and Zoe followed. Dressed in his summer whites, Brett wore the uniform as though he'd been born to it. The grim set to his features kicked Zoe's heart into an anxious gallop. Something had happened.

His eyes homed in on Clara, and a genuine smile flashed across his face. "Mom." He pulled her in close and gave her a fierce hug.

Clara buried her face in his chest and gave him a squeeze.

He kissed the top of her head. "I'm glad you're here, Mom."

Zoe frowned. What was it she heard in his voice? Stress and what else?

"You've done something to your hair," he said, with a frown.

"Just a few highlights, nothing drastic." Clara pulled back to look up at him and touch his cheek. "You look good. Strong."

"My hair's growing back." Brett grinned and rubbed his hand over his hair so it bristled up.

"I can see that." Her brows rose. "Your new assignment?"

"I filled in for a public information officer today. I'm buying him a beer as soon as he's out of the hospital."

"That bad huh?"

"I'd rather have my nose hairs pulled out one at a time."

Zoe laughed. "Makes my eyes water just thinking about it. You said it went all right."

"Yeah, it did. But it's not something I'd want to do all the time."

"Out of two hundred women, did you meet anyone interesting?" Clara asked.

A slow grin worked across his lips. "Yeah. Got her number, too." He patted his pocket. Let me get out of this monkey suit and we'll eat. Something smells good, and I'm hungry." He sauntered into the bedroom and closed the door.

Zoe frowned at his quick escape. Something was definitely wrong.

Brett closed the bedroom door. He closed his eyes and for several moments breathed in and out slowly to relax the tension.

As much as he'd looked forward to seeing her, his mother couldn't have picked a worse time to visit. Shit was going to hit the fan. He could feel it. And he was going to be trapped in the middle of it.

He removed the card Tess Kelly had tucked inside his shirt pocket and studied it. If he could get one member of the press on his side .... But how was he supposed to do that and not divulge any military secrets? As far as the mission went, he was safe. He couldn't remember shit about it, so that wouldn't be a problem.

But the investigation into the Iraqi kid would be something Tess Kelly would want to sink her teeth into.

Agents Wright and Scott had blinders on. As far as they were concerned, they'd found their men.

But they weren't taking into consideration that he wasn't Derrick Armstrong. He might not remember anything about what had happened that day, but he knew what he was capable of. And killing a defenseless kid wasn't one of those things. *No fucking way.*

But how was he supposed to prove it? Why wouldn't Derrick tell them about the protection detail?

Because if something happened during the transport, it could be Derrick's motive for trying to kill him.

Shit. If only he could *remember.*

He set aside the card on the dresser and changed into jeans and a pullover knit shirt. His eyes strayed to the card again. His thoughts went to Tess Kelly. Heart-shaped face. Chestnut red hair just a little deeper hue than his mother's. Her eyes weren't just brown but a warm—*Jesus, what am I doing?* He blew out a breath.

If he didn't have this damn speech thing, he'd have already called her.

If she weren't a damn reporter, he'd have already called her.

If he had any balls, he'd have already called her.

He'd just be upfront about the speech thing. It was no big deal. She wouldn't think anything of it. Or would she?

A knock sounded and his head went up. In one stride, he was at the door and jerked it open.

Zoe stood on the other side, a frown on her face. "You okay?"

"Yeah, I'm fine."

"Hawk's here, and we're ready to eat."

"Good." He'd fill Hawk in after dinner. See if anything was screwy about the way he and Derrick had acted before the mission.

She reached up and smoothed his hair down. "You didn't lose her number, did you?"

He smiled. "No."

"I think you need to give her a call. You haven't been out since you left for Iraq. Ten months is a long time between dates."

How long had it been for her before she met Hawk?

"I allowed my leg to keep me from enjoying so many things. If it wasn't for Hawk, I'd still be in that same stunted place I was back in college." Her dark blue gaze fastened on his face, her expression earnest. "Don't blow this little glitch you have out of proportion, Brett. In the grand scheme of things, it doesn't even register."

She was always trying to build him up. Always had his back. He drew her close and gave her a hug. "Thanks, Zo."

He looped an arm around her shoulders as they strolled into the kitchen together.

"Doc has invited us all to dinner tomorrow night, seventeen hundred. All we have to bring is the beer and the girls," Hawk announced as he took his place at the table. "He's invited you as his date, Clara. I told him what a cougar you are, but he said he'd take his chances."

Clara's eyes grew round, then she laughed. Zoe joined her.

"You boys are something else," Clara said with a shake of her head. She turned to Brett as he pulled a chair out and sat down. "Why don't you call the woman you met at the speaking engagement today? I bet she'd love to go."

A reporter at a SEAL barbeque. The guys would love that. "I was hoping to start out with something a little less—" He searched for the word.

"It isn't like being thrown in a shark tank. We survived it. She will too," Zoe said while spooning casserole onto her plate.

"Yeah, but you and Mom are already used to the guys. She's not."

"What's to get used to? It's a barbecue," Clara said.

Shit. He'd have to tell them. "I wasn't thinking of her getting used to us. It's the other way around. She's a reporter for a local newspaper."

He glanced at Hawk to check his reaction and caught a frown.

"It's not like you guys go around talking about SEAL tactics or secret missions when you're with your families, Brett," Clara said.

"As long as she comes with the understanding that this is a family barbecue and not an interview opportunity, it should be fine," Zoe said.

His sister was too damn trusting. She hadn't seen that avid hunger in Tess Kelly's eyes. The woman was eager for any kind of scoop. Maybe he could use that to his advantage. But he wouldn't allow her to use his family or friends.

"I think I'm going to shoot for something a little less rowdy for a first date. I haven't gotten to hang with the guys much, so I'm going to go solo this time. Maybe I'll bring her next time."

The tension at the table relaxed and the conversation turned to Zoe's interview and news from back in Lexington, Kentucky.

When Zoe and Clara rose to clear the table, Brett used a hand signal to get Hawk's attention.

"Balcony in two," he mouthed.

Hawk nodded. "Sure."

Brett wandered through the living room, opened the sliding glass door, and, leaving it open behind him, went out onto the balcony. In the west, smattering wisps of cumulus clouds drifted across a dark purple sky. Brett braced his elbows atop the railing and looked down into the street below. Clean sidewalks, streetlights, and evening traffic, a welcome sight after the dusty streets in Iraq. He breathed in the fresh breeze that whipped across the platform, and he detected a hint of the ocean. He'd never gotten used to the smell of raw sewage fouling the streets in the towns they'd cleared of terrorists.

Hawk wandered out to stand beside him, a beer in each hand. "It looked as though you could use this." He offered one of the bottles.

"Thanks." Brett accepted the moisture-glazed container and rolled it between his hands. "I had a visit from a couple of NCIS agents today at the base. In fact, they sent a detail to drive me back to Jackson's office for questioning."

Hawk's expression sharpened, his gray eyes intent. "Why?"

"Do you remember Derrick and me going on a protection detail before our mission?"

"Yeah. Headquarters needed a couple of SEALs to impress some Iraqi liaison. You guys drew the short straw and had to deliver his kid home. You were only gone a couple of hours."

Brett straightened and set the beer on the plastic table. "I need you to remember everything you can about when we left, how long we were gone, and what time we got back. If you saw us when we returned. Anything about that detail."

"It would all be in the report." Hawk's black brows clashed. "Ah shit! You were injured and weren't able to file a report."

"Would Derrick have done one?"

"He may have after the mission. He should have. We couldn't take a dump without filing one. What's going on, Cutter?"

"The kid we escorted home disappeared after we dropped him off. NCIS is circling me and Derrick. They're looking for an excuse to hold us responsible. I think someone high up is trying to find a scapegoat instead of the truth, and because of Derrick's current status, they've found an easy answer."

"You'd have had cover front and back, Cutter. You wouldn't have traveled alone."

"They're dead. All of them."

"Jesus—" Shock streaked across Hawk's features, then his expression blanked.

"My ass is hanging out there with this, Hawk. I can't remember shit about that week." Brett shoved both hands through his hair. "They think we did something to the kid."

"No way." Hawk shook his head. "Derrick maybe, if he'd been alone. Toward the end of the tour he was strung out. But you were still rock solid. You wouldn't have stood by while he hurt the kid, and you wouldn't have laid a hand on him yourself. I'd stake my career on it."

Brett drew a deep breath. Having Hawk back him up beat some of the edges off his worry. "Thanks for saying that." But Hawk's beliefs weren't tangible evidence. He drew a deep breath. "Will you pull up Derrick's report and see what he filed?"

"Yeah, I can do that." Hawk took a swig of his beer. "When we were investigating who was responsible for your injury, Greenback said you tried to counsel Derrick and Flash just before the mission. He said Derrick was upset about something. You may want to talk to him. See if he remembers anything."

"Roger that." Finally, something proactive he could do.

"There'll be radio transmissions logged. When you dropped the kid, you'd have radioed to let base know he'd been delivered. There'll be a record somewhere."

"I hope so. Otherwise—"

"Don't go there. We're going to sort it out." Hawk slapped him on the back.

Despite Hawk's reassurance, Jackson's words still taunted him. All of this was tied to Derrick Armstrong's anger management problems. In Iraq. Here at home. Brett's gut clenched. And it was going to cost him everything if he couldn't fucking remember.

CHAPTER 7

Tess Kelly ground her teeth against the angry words and scowled at her editor, Elgin Taylor, from across his cluttered desk. How many times did they have to have this argument?

The thin walls did nothing to block the telephone ringing somewhere down the hall. The smell of burnt coffee intruded from the kitchenette just off the main office. Though his office looked out onto what had once been the bullpen of the paper, very few people stirred there. Reporters today could work from anywhere and submit the story with one click of their mouse.

"Your lifestyles article was good, Tess. Why can't you be satisfied with a brush now and then with politicians, military personnel and their wives? Why do you want to be in the thick of things?"

Because that's where all the good stories are. Because my father wouldn't be standing on the sidelines.

Shifting her weight, she drew in a deep breath and folded her arms against her waist. "I've been doing the stories you assign me for more than a year, Mr. Taylor. When you hired me, you promised you'd give me the opportunity to stretch my wings as a reporter. The events I usually cover are not what I would call an opportunity."

"You're offering our readers something they want to read, whether you're interested in it or not. We have to pander to our readership in order to survive. Do you know how many traditional papers are going down? We're all having to go to this ePub bullshit to keep the doors open."

"The ePub model is allowing you to reach a wider audience while saving resources and money, sir. More people can subscribe and read our paper without the cost of printing or distribution. It's the same paper, just a different delivery format."

"Maybe I should transfer you to the marketing department since you understand it so well," he said, his tone sour.

God forbid. "What will bring in a wider readership, sir, are hard-hitting stories that play on current interests. We're sitting in an area rich with story opportunities. Going at them from a sharper angle will garner wider attention. I don't have to tell you that."

Taylor sat up, resting his elbows on his desk. His thick gray hair, more salt than pepper, gleamed beneath the florescent lights. "Sharper angles, huh? Any time you start talking sharper angles, I have to call the legal department and vet something to make sure we don't get sued."

"I'll always have three dependable sources before I write the story, Mr. Taylor."

He waved a hand in a dismissive gesture. "I know." Then he scrubbed his face irritably. "The problem is that, for every story we find, there are five people jumping on it, and it's blasted across the television news, blogs, and cell phones before we can even get it into print. It isn't the quality of your work, Tess." His gaze raked her face. "You'd be better off trying to join some local news program and getting your face on camera. You're pretty, young, and sharp. You'd probably make it to the top in nothing flat."

"I don't want my face on television. I'm a writer, not a public speaker." She drew a deep breath. "Most stories are written in a hit, then move on, format. The human element is totally missed. I want to delve more deeply into issues, not just skim the surface. Most of the stories we cover are about people. Why can't we concentrate on bringing the human-interest angle to the forefront instead of the issues? Once your readers identify with the people involved, they'll want to read more."

His brows rose, speculation in his gaze. "What do you have in mind?"

Tess's cell phone rang. She jerked it from her pocket and glanced at the ID. The number seemed vaguely familiar. She pressed the on button. "Hello."

"This is Brett Weaver."

An instant rush of adrenaline surged through her system. Heat rose to her face, and her heart raced. "Yes. What can I do for you?"

"Will you join me for lunch at the Sheerwater today?"

Aware of Taylor listening to her end of the conversation, she hesitated. "Is there some specific reason you're asking me to lunch?"

"Besides the fact that you're beautiful, and have gorgeous legs?" His husky male tone shot sex appeal across the line.

She bit her lip to hide the instant response that triggered a flush to her skin and dampness between her legs. *How could he do that with just his voice?*

"There will be a story in it for you."

Was he just playing her? Or was he serious? SEALs had a reputation for being players. But he was asking to meet in a public place. A very beautiful public place. *A hotel.*

An image of the two of them in one of the rooms exploring— *Oh, shit. She couldn't go there.*

What kind of story could he possibly have for her? Nothing with too much political substance. He'd not risk his career to offer her any military secrets. But if she didn't go, she'd never know what he wanted.

His patient silence on the other end of the line broke through her anxious speculations. "What time?" she asked.

"How's eleven?"

"Eleven will be fine."

"I'll see you then."

Tess hit the off button, and her attention shifted to Taylor. "That was," she started to say Brett Weaver but changed it to, "a source. Possibly a lead on a story."

"Was he asking you out on a date?"

A sudden shot of anger made her voice tremble. "I don't date my sources, Mr. Taylor. You know we women are liberated enough that we don't have to resort to using our bodies to—"

He raised a hand. "I was out of line." Taylor said, cutting her off.

Tess took several deep breaths to calm herself. Had every man in this business remained stuck in the chauvinistic seventies like her father? "He says he has a story for me."

"About?"

"An inside look at the SEALs. In particular, Brett Weaver."

"The guy who did the speaking engagement yesterday."

"Yes. People are interested in him because his buddy allegedly tried to kill Weaver and his sister along with some girl he was dating. This guy may be willing to tell me about that."

"If you can get info and corroborate it I may be tempted to allow you to do the series you're angling for. You were angling for a series?"

She hadn't been, but a series would be great. Female readers would eat up one about SEALs. Perhaps he wanted to discuss why he'd been escorted back to base yesterday. He'd played it down, but there had been more than one tense moment in his encounter with the two military policemen.

Excitement jogged through her system and her heart caught the rhythm. Maybe he'd actually open up, and she'd find out what was going on.

And pigs could fly, too.

Clara spooned meringue atop the banana pudding. Everyone liked banana pudding, didn't they? He wouldn't think she was being pushy by delivering something home-cooked to his door. Would he?

She couldn't shake the image of Russell Connelly standing with his son, his very ill son, at the airport. Every time the thought came to mind, it gave her heart a squeeze. They'd both looked so ... alone.

Strong arms came around her waist from behind and she jerked, startled.

"Sorry, I didn't mean to scare you," Brett said as he gave her a squeeze. "That's a lot of banana pudding, Mom. Think the team will be up to eating all that?" He kissed the top of her head.

"I think your team could eat sauerkraut and wieners cooked in an old Marine Boondocker. They all have cast iron stomachs."

Brett laughed. "Yeah, they pretty much do." He released her and leaned against the kitchen cabinet next to the stove.

"I'm fixing a pan for Dr. Connelly and his son."

"Oh. I haven't seen him since I was discharged and turned over to Dr. Stewart."

"I ran into him at the airport." She set aside the mixing bowl and spoon, opened the oven door, and slid the two glass casserole dishes into the oven.

After setting the timer, she focused on Brett. His skin was tanned, his hair, always blond, tipped with lighter tones from being in the sun. Dressed in a t-shirt and running shorts, he looked fit and strong. But there were shadows beneath his eyes as though he hadn't slept. Was there more going on than just a difficult relationship with a commanding officer?

"You know I can sleep on the couch. You didn't have to give up your bed for me," she said.

"I'm fine on the sofa bed, Mom. I can sleep anywhere. Why are you making banana pudding for Dr. Connelly?" he asked, speculation in his gaze.

"His son is ill. You know how I used to make you banana pudding when you were sick?"

"Yeah. 'It goes down smooth and replenishes your potassium.' How old is his son?"

"I'd say close to your age. Maybe a little older." She touched his smooth-shaven cheek. "Dr. Connelly was so good to you when you were his patient. I just want to do some small something in return."

"How are you going to get it to him?"

"Hawk got his address for me. I thought I'd take the dish over while you're out running." She glanced at his running shoes. "That is what you're getting ready to do?"

"Yeah. Just a few miles."

"Uh-huh." A few miles to him meant five or six. She didn't know how he did it. Or maybe she did. She studied his features, so much like his father's. A wave of longing struck her. What would things have been like if Joe—She wouldn't let herself go there. It had been too many years.

"Your father would be so proud of you, Brett."

His eyes, a lighter shade of blue than Zoe's, focused on her face. "He'd be pissed off I joined the Navy instead of the Marines."

She laughed. "Maybe just a little. But he'd have been proud of your accomplishments, too."

"I know." He was silent a moment. "Remember that wooden pistol he gave me that shot rubber bands?"

She folded her arms against her waist and said, sternly, "I remember you shooting your sisters in the behind with it."

He grinned mischievously. "I practiced for hours on the cardboard targets he made for me. Shooting a moving target was more fun."

"I don't think your sisters had quite the same perspective."

"Dad threatened to turn it into kindling and burn it if I didn't quit. He said he'd given it to me to teach me gun safety, not to torment my sisters."

"And he took you out on the target range and let you shoot that twenty-two he'd won at a match."

"Yeah. Beautiful pistol. Got me hooked on real guns."

"It's still at the house if you'd like to have it."

His eyes lit up. "Sure. I carry Dad's, you know."

"Yes, I know." She took in the control in his expression. "Whatever it takes to keep you safe, Brett."

He nodded. "There's a line we don't cross, Mom."

Something in his voice drew her eyes to his face.

His features had grown empty with control. His fists clenched and unclenched, tightening and releasing, and his biceps swelled with the action. "Even though we're soldiers, and we follow orders, we still have a moral code we follow. If it's morally wrong, we don't ... follow through."

Had all he'd endured driven him to a crisis of belief in himself? Or what he'd chosen as his calling? The idea thrust her heartbeat high into her throat. She shoved away from the counter to stand in front of him. "What you do in war, you do to save lives. That's why your father went to war, and that's why you did. I know that the actions you've taken in battle were done to preserve morality, not to pervert it. I know you know the difference in right and wrong, because I raised you. I've seen you train and strive to be the most professional, honorable soldier and human being you can."

The tension in his body relaxed somewhat and his expression lightened. "Thanks, Mom."

Her throat was too dry to swallow. "You aren't doubting that, are you?"

"No." He shook his head. "Someone said something yesterday that's been going through my head. And I was thinking more of you than me."

"Me?" Her mouth parted in surprise, she sucked in a breath. "You don't ever have to doubt my belief in you. You're a good man, Brett. A good human being. And a good soldier. Don't ever let anyone tell you you're not." A thought had anger climbing into her chest and she gritted her teeth. "Especially Captain—*Asshole.*"

Surprise crossed his face. He threw his head back and laughed.

"Zoe told me about the assignment yesterday, and I was just—"

"It was a test, Mom. I'm used to having harder things thrown at me. I admit I was sweating bullets a time or two, but for the most part it was okay. And the ladies were very receptive."

"Meaning that several hit on you."

He chuckled again. "Yeah. But I'm beyond the SEAL groupie thing now."

"This coming from the man who had a number tucked in his shirt pocket when he got home last night."

"Yeah, but she's different. Definitely not a groupie."

Clara raised her eyebrows, instantly interested. What kind of girl was she? "Hum." The timer went off and she picked up oven mitts from the counter.

Brett pushed away from the cabinet. "I'm going running. Be back about one. I have an appointment on Coronado afterwards."

She recognized his need to escape before she asked any more questions. Was she being a busybody? A pest? She'd have to be careful about that. Her children were leading their own lives and no longer needed her counsel. "Take your time, Brett. You don't have to entertain me. I'm good."

The door closed behind him. She removed both casserole dishes from the oven and set them atop the stove to cool.

She'd have to call before she delivered the dish. Why was she so nervous about calling Russell Connelly? Her stomach grew hollow with nerves. She pressed a hand against her midriff.

Because she was thinking of him now as Russell, and not Captain or Doctor Connelly. She'd felt that moment of connection. Felt the brush of his gaze over her face, her breasts, and recognized the male interest in his expression.

After so many years as a widow, she'd thought that sweet feeling of response had been lost to her.

She'd tried dating a little when the kids had gotten older and were out of the house, living their own lives. Loneliness had driven her to it. But it hadn't felt right.

She hadn't been as receptive to the men's sexual overtures as they'd expected, either. They'd desired a quick, easy conquest instead of having to woo her. As though being a widow made a woman desperate for casual sex, or at least more open to it.

She'd been looking for more. She'd been looking for what she'd had with Joe. But she'd never found even a hint of that special something with the four men she'd gone out with.

Then on her fiftieth birthday—She cringed at the memory. Charlie Cooper was a nice guy. But she'd felt self-conscious and uncomfortable afterwards. Guilty, too. Though he'd called and tried to ask her out several times, she'd never seen him again.

Her gaze rose to her reflection in the microwave door above the stove. She touched the fine lines around her eyes and mouth. What was it Russell Connelly saw when he looked at her?

She turned away from her reflection. Fifty-five was worse than fifty. Five years worse. Pathetically worse. If Russell were interested, how would she feel if he wanted more? The panicked beating of her heart was her only answer.

CHAPTER 8

Clara stood before Russell Connelly's apartment. She balanced the casserole dish of banana pudding, still warm from the oven, and tapped on the door. It swung open almost before her hand had dropped.

"Hello." Russell smiled. Dressed in knee-length khaki shorts and a t-shirt that hugged his broad shoulders and chest, he looked masculine and fit. "Come in. Evan's still asleep but should be up any moment." His large hand rested at the small of her back as he guided her through a small but neat living room. "I don't sit in here much, I guess you can tell. I prefer the kitchen." He gestured to the right.

The kitchen was clearly the heart of the apartment. Sunlight streamed through a sliding glass door at the end of the room, brightening the interior, and the pale yellow walls reflected the natural light. A laptop and several files lay on the table.

"May I take that?" Russell asked, nodding toward the dish she held.

"Certainly. If you like it hot I can pop it back into the oven."

He set it on the stove. "I have to confess, I've never had homemade banana pudding, just the boxed stuff. I'm not much of a cook. But like most men, I'm a master at the grill."

Did her smile look as nervous as she felt? Had she ever been this tightly wound with a man before?

She drew a deep breath. "I'm just the opposite. I'm more at home in front of the stove. If I light the grill without starting a brush fire, I think I've done something special."

He chuckled and leaned forward to pull the aluminum foil from the dish. "This smells wonderful. Evan needs the calories and the potassium." He smiled again. "I probably don't, but I'll have my share."

"My children swear by it, like grandma used to swear by chicken soup. It might help Evan's meds go down easier, too," she said.

"Would you like to sit out on the balcony with me until he's awake?" he asked. "I have iced tea."

Was he asking her just to be polite or did he truly want her company? She glanced at her watch, though she didn't have any place else to be. "If you're not busy. Brett's gone for a run and has a lunch appointment, so I'm on my own for a while."

"I'm just wading through some paperwork. You'll be the perfect excuse to ignore it." He got glasses out of the cabinet, filled them with ice, and poured the tea.

Clara accepted hers and wandered to the sliding glass door. She unlatched it, pushed it open and stepped out onto the small balcony, a twelve by twelve space at most. The metal railing beckoned, and she leaned on it, looking over the vista of multi-level buildings, all steel and concrete.

Russell set his ice tea glass on a small table and closed the door. "Not much of a view," he said, joining her.

"I've lived in the same subdivision house for twenty years. There's not much of a view there either, but I have small things. An herb garden, some flowers, and some bird feeders."

Glancing at him, she found him studying the balcony and turned to scan it herself. The grill was pushed against the wall at one corner. A small table with four chairs took up the bulk of the remaining space on that side. Two lounge chairs with a small square table between filled most of the additional space. Everything was aligned with military precision. And everything was white or gray.

Clara smiled at his rueful expression. "You're not home much. What would you do with pots of flowers when you're not here to water them?"

"Thank you for giving me an out, but to be honest, it never occurred to me to add those things. I spend most of my time at the hospital. But I do manage to run three days a week."

Thus the tan and the muscular calves displayed by his khaki shorts.

"Maybe a cactus."

He laughed. "How long will you be here visiting?"

"I don't know, yet. I've taught for so long. I've lived for my own children, then other people's. Now it may take me a while to find my way."

"You could start a whole new career."

"Maybe so."

"A flower shop."

She smiled and shook her head.

"Your husband was military."

"Yes. A Marine. He was killed by friendly fire during Desert Storm."

His expression blanked, then settled into a frown. "Jesus. I'm sorry."

Always the same reaction. Shock, regret, and then sympathy. A life cut short. But not wasted. Joe had given her children, and so much more. "It's been a long time."

"You never remarried."

She shook her head. "Evan's mother?"

"We've been divorced since Desert Storm. She remarried and lives in Los Angeles." He leaned down to rest his arms on the railing. "I've had several deployments since then. This last one will probably be my last. I'm getting a little old for battlefield medicine."

"Not if you still have a passion for it."

"Thanks. But I feel as though I'm doing more good here now. They're trying to nudge me toward a more administrative position at the hospital. Head of my department, but I'm not sure that's what I want."

He glanced at the sliding glass doors. "I've taken some leave while Evan's here. Maybe It will give me time to decide."

"So it seems we're both at crossroads," Clara said, taking a sip of her iced tea.

"Not always the most comfortable place to be."

"No. Retiring has been the riskiest thing I've ever done. But after everything that happened last April, I—wanted to be free to enjoy my family, certainly. But I wanted to see what more I could do besides teach."

"What do you think you want to do?" he asked. He took a drink of his tea, his throat working. He was bigger than Joe, over six feet. His hands were square and large.

His eyes weren't green or gray, but hazel. With his face so close to hers and his gaze focused on her so intently, Clara became self-conscious and looked away. She concentrated on her ice tea glass, uncertain of what she'd read in his gaze. "When the kids were little, I used to have a passion for photography. I even won a contest once. It was a picture of Zoe." She fell silent a moment. "I've saved a little cash. I thought I'd invest in a really good camera and see where it takes me."

"That sounds like a plan," he said.

She glanced in his direction to find a smile curving his lips. "It may be a pipe dream, but I'll have fun with it," she said and shrugged.

The sliding glass door opened behind them and they turned to see Evan standing in the doorway. "Hey," Evan nodded to Clara. "May I speak to you, Dad?"

Russell set aside his ice tea and entered the apartment.

"What's she doing here? Is she one of your women?" Evan asked, his voice carrying before the door closed.

Clara's face burned and her stomach dropped. Evan didn't want her here. Though the knowledge hurt, she understood he was ill and might not feel up to having a stranger visit. Trapped on the balcony, Clara turned away to avoid witnessing their discussion through the glass door. Humiliation whipped through her, curdling her stomach.

One of his women? Was Russell Connelly a player?

Tears burnt her eyes, and she blinked to clear their sting. She took a sip of the tea and then another, seeking calm, though her chest felt tight. Russell and Evan's voices carried through the glass as she approached the door. She flinched and tried to block out the words. She tapped to warn them she was coming in.

Their heads whipped around as she slid it open. "I have to leave." She stepped into the kitchen. The tension between the two men hummed in the air. "We're attending a barbecue tonight, and I need to prepare some things." She plastered a smile on her face as she nodded to Evan and avoided looking at Russell altogether. She set her glass in the sink and collected her purse from the counter. "I'll see myself out."

"Clara—let me see you to the door," Russell said, following her.

"It's all right."

"No, it's not," The frustration and anger in his voice made his tone adamant.

She forced herself to look at Russell. "He's ill. He needs your undivided attention right now. I've intruded and it was never my intention—" *Or was it?* "I hope he gets well soon. Truly I do." She fumbled for the door, but Russell's hand was there on the knob blocking her escape.

"I'm sorry, Clara."

She nodded. "I have to go."

His hand rested against the small of her back, the pressure light, his touch comforting. Warmth tumbled through her. Her heart clenched.

Her gaze rose to his face. The look of pain and confusion she read in his expression triggered an ache of loss beneath her breastbone. "It's all right."

Russell opened the door. She escaped out into the hall. Though the urge to rush was strong, she forced her steps to remain slow and measured, aware he watched her walk all the way to the elevator. She pushed the button. *Come on, come on.* Drawing several deep breaths, she closed her eyes against the fountain of tears pushing against her lids, and practically leapt aboard the elevator when the doors opened.

Brett scissor kicked, straightening his body and digging deep with the next stroke. His shoulder and leg muscles burned as he reached the end of the two-mile swim. The familiar approach to the beach in front of the Hotel del Coronado loomed in the immediate distance. He turned inland, and the gradual rise of the bottom finally allowed him to stand in the chest-high water. Hearing the rumble of a boat motor approaching close behind him, he turned and floated on its wake as it pulled beside him.

"Your best time yet, Cutter. Two miles in seventy minutes. That's impressive," Greenback said from the small skiff's driver's seat, his New Jersey accent exaggerated by excitement.

"Thanks." Brett breathed in several gulps of air. "It won't mean a damn if I can't convince the Doc and Jackson I'm good to go."

"He'll come around, man. Give it some time. It's only been two months."

"Time passes more slowly when you're sitting on your ass waiting to get back into training."

Greenback's expression settled into sympathetic lines. "You are training."

"Yeah, I guess. I appreciate you spotting me, Greenback."

"No problem. I'll give some thought to what we talked about earlier. If I remember any more, I'll call you."

"Thanks. Got a hot date waiting for me. Gotta go." Brett said. He offered his wet hand. Greenback clasped it in his own briefly.

Greenback turned the boat into the surf and shot away. The skiff took on more speed as he traveled east toward base.

Brett swam closer to shore, and when he reached shallow water, removed his flippers. He walked up the beach toward the hotel. The sand clung to his wet feet and then crumbled away. Memories of being cold and wet and coated in grit flashed through his mind. Every time he walked this beach, the events of Hell week came back to him. He'd gone through more than two years of training since, and a deployment to Iraq, but that week was what stood out when he walked this stretch of sand. It had been the beginning of his SEAL career.

Five minutes later he reached the car. He tossed his flippers and his dive knife with its rubber sheath into the trunk, exchanging it for his towel-wrapped clothes and shoes. Making a quick stop at one of the public restrooms that serviced the beach, he showered, dried off, and changed into street clothes.

He paused by one of the mirrors over the sink to run his fingers through his short-cropped hair and shove it into place. His fingertips followed the shallow scar ridge left along his temple, a reminder of the blow that had left him in a coma. There were other smaller, less distinct, scars where they'd drilled into his skull to relieve the hematoma. But this one seemed to stay tender, though the dark red had lightened to pink.

A hard knot of pain and anger gathered in his chest. He drew a deep breath.

Derrick had cost him his position on the team. And now he was doing it again by not talking to the NCIS agents.

Brett rolled the swim trunks up in the towel more securely. It was his own mind betraying him now. If stress was causing his language problem, then why not the holes in his memory? He had to break through it somehow to get back to where he wanted to be. He *would* break through it.

He glanced at his dive watch. Almost time to meet Tess. He tucked the damp bundle beneath his arm, shoved his sunglasses on, and strolled from the restroom, up the network of sidewalks to the street.

He went over the information his internet search this morning had garnered. Finding out she was Ian Kelly's daughter had been the clincher. The man had connections. He could put pressure on sources that might open things up and force headquarters to get their collective heads out of their collective asses and find the kid.

Brett breathed in the moderate California air and smelled the rich scent of hibiscus blooming along the walk. The whole thing could come down on him like an anchor. Or it might not. Jesus. Flash was the gambler, not him. And look where it had gotten him. Brett's gut clenched. Well, if he got a bad feeling about this whole meeting, he could always walk away.

The Hotel del Coronado sprawled before him, and his pace quickened. Would she be waiting for him, or would she keep him cooling his heels? Nerves knotted his stomach. He'd had a good day so far. Just pulled a blank a time or two while talking to Greenback. The stress of the conversation had probably been the reason.

He rolled his shoulders and neck to relieve tension. A four-mile run and two-mile swim had depleted his reserves. He needed to replenish them, and his stomach growled as he worked his way around the hotel to the restaurant.

He'd called ahead and made reservations. The place was a little expensive, but the food was incredible. Had he chosen it to impress her, or because it was close to where he'd end his swim? Probably a little of both.

He spotted Tess sitting at a table beneath one of the square umbrellas. He studied her profile as she looked toward the water. Though she appeared lost in thought, he read tension in her posture. She gripped a glass of water and raised it to her lips. The peach blouse and cream linen pants she wore emphasized the graceful length of her limbs. Her hair was pulled back and bundled at the nape of her neck with a large tortoiseshell clip.

The hostess appeared at his elbow. "May I help you, sir?"

"I see the woman I'm meeting." He nodded in Tess's direction.

"Please join her. I'll send a server over immediately."

"Thanks." He approached Tess from behind and to the right so the sun wouldn't be in her eyes when they met.

When he crossed within her view, she glanced up. Her sunglasses blocked his ability to read her expression, but the bulky frames and opaque lenses didn't detract from the perfect proportion of her cheeks and jaw. The tug of attraction he'd felt the day before returned with a vengeance.

"If only you were sixty, two hundred pounds and homely ... I might be immune," he said.

Tessa's lips parted in an oh of surprise.

Good enough to kiss.

He was still waiting for her retort when he pulled out the chair on her right and sat down. He set the soggy bundle he carried on the sidewalk next to his seat.

As promised, a server arrived to take their drink order and give them menus. Tess ordered unsweetened tea, Brett orange juice. He needed instant energy to ensure he was at the top of his game with her.

"I read some of the articles you've written in the last six months," he said as he studied the menu.

Her auburn brows rose just above the sunglass frames.

Though she attempted to appear relaxed, her hands gripped the menu, bending it. She was either nervous, barely able to contain her curiosity, or both.

"You don't strike me as someone who would be interested in San Diego social life, Ensign Weaver."

"I'm not. I wanted to get a feel for how you approach things." He set aside the menu. "Call me Brett."

Soft color touched her cheeks. She focused her attention on arranging her silverware.

So she wasn't as immune to him as she tried to appear.

"You mentioned you had a story in mind," she said her gaze averted.

"I've run four miles and completed a two mile swim this morning. I'd prefer to eat before we talk."

Her brows climbed higher. "Have you been released for full duty now?"

"No."

"Should you be training so hard?"

He smiled. "If you don't train, you get out of shape. If you get out of shape, you put your team and yourself at risk. You're a liability if you're not at peak performance. If I wait until I'm released to train—"

"You'd be a liability," she finished.

"Exactly."

The waitress arrived with their drinks. Brett set aside the menu and downed half his juice while Tess ordered an asparagus and wild mushroom pizzetta with boursin cheese. He ordered a white cheddar burger and fries.

"Why the SEALs?" she asked breaking the silence that fell once the woman had left.

"My dad was a Marine. Semper Fi all the way. He thrived on challenges. I took after him." He studied the curve of her chin. "You know about following in your dad's footsteps?"

"Yes." She looked away toward the beach and the distant gleam of the water.

"Ian Kelly is a legend in journalism," he prodded.

"Some people say that."

Brett leaned forward and rested his elbows on the table. "What do you say?"

"I'm not here to share confidences, Ensign Weaver. I'm here for the story."

Were they estranged? It wouldn't help his cause if they were. "You may need his help with this story."

Her head jerked around. "Why do you say that?"

"He has connections, and you're going to need connections to get at the heart of this."

Tess's lips compressed. "So it has an international component?"

"Yeah." Brett removed his sunglasses and tucked them into his shirt pocket. Would she have the guts to come out from behind her dark lenses so he could read her reactions more easily?

"Are you at liberty to speak about the particulars?"

"It wasn't top secret. And no one has ordered me not to."

Tess jerked her sunglasses from her face and set them aside. "All right. Tell me what this is about."

He studied the intensity in her sherry-brown eyes. He might have smiled had the situation been less serious. He hoped fervently he was doing the right thing in opening this can of worms.

"I think I'm being investigated for murder."

CHAPTER 9

A fter watching Clara enter the elevator, Russell closed the apartment door. "Jesus Christ. What the hell just happened here, Evan?"

"She probably buys into that old adage that the way to a man's heart is through his stomach."

His snide tone sounded so much like Gloria's, Russell fought the urge to punch something. "She brought the pudding for you. She thought it might help your medications go down easier."

Evan's eyes widened. "You told her?"

"No. But she isn't blind." He shook his head. "How could you be cruel to someone who was showing you an act of kindness?"

"It didn't look as though she were here to see me." Conflicting emotions raced across Evan's face, anger, frustration, and something more until his features took on a sulky look. "I didn't want her here."

"You made that clear enough, and she's gone." Clara wouldn't be back. Regret lay like a weight inside his chest. He raked both hands through his hair.

They had been making a connection. She had been uncertain, shy. And he had been more attracted than he'd been in … ever.

And his son had purposely hurt her.

"You called her one of my women. You know nothing about my life. You've never wanted to. What kind of bullshit did your mother serve up to you to make you think I was running around acting like a wartime lothario? If that's the tripe she's fed you, she's a fucking liar."

Evan flinched and looked away.

Russell had taken enough of Gloria's vicious punishment to last a lifetime. It had made him gun-shy in his other relationships, what few there had been. No more, damn her. "Was I supposed to pine for her for the rest of my days while she moved on with her life?"

Evan tugged at the belt of his robe. "Yeah, I guess you were."

The sudden acquiescence to his accusations brought Russell up short.

Evan shuffled to the overstuffed sofa and sat down. "I read the legal file last night. She was involved with Carl before your first deployment to Iraq. She remarried the day after the divorce was final. Yet she harped on your being unfaithful."

"Never." He sat down in a chair across from Evan. "I'm not perfect. I was a neglectful husband. I had med school, my internship, and residency. Then you were born. The Navy paid for my education and training. I owed them." He leaned forward and rested his elbows on his knees. "I can understand your mother's reasons for looking elsewhere for what she needed. I can understand her seeking a divorce. But I was never unfaithful."

"What about Valerie?" Evan asked. "I remember her."

"I'm surprised. You only saw her once. I met her eighteen months after the divorce. You were almost ten by then."

"What happened to her?"

Old pain jabbed him with the sharpness of a scalpel and twisted. "She died in a car accident." After nearly a year of dating, they'd been talking about marriage versus living together. Just a few days later she was gone.

"I was in my mid-thirties when Valerie died." His voice sounded rusty. He cleared his throat. "I've dated my share of women since, but none—" He shrugged. "Now, I'm racing toward the end of my fifties, and I'm alone. That wasn't what I planned for myself."

"No, I don't guess so," Evan looked away again. "This isn't exactly what I planned for myself either." He gestured to his scrawny frame. "It seems we've both been unlucky in love."

Though he'd worked hard to accept who his son was, there were times Evan's openness about his lifestyle made him uncomfortable. "How is Simon?"

"Still healthy. I'm trying hard not to hate his guts."

"How about I hate him enough for both of us," Russell said.

Evan laughed. "That's the closest thing you've ever come to saying something that even remotely sounded gay."

"So glad I'm finally picking up some of the nuances," Russell said, his tone dry.

Evan's smile was brief. He swallowed. "I'm sorry I pulled the pissy gay guy thing."

"I'm not the one you owe an apology to." It would do no good for him to harp on it. Evan was an intelligent man. He knew what he needed to do. But his disappointment in his son's behavior lay between them as unavoidable as the pall of sickness.

Tess studied Brett's expression as they left the restaurant and strolled down to the beach. His features remained closed, unreadable. It was frustrating as hell.

Brett paused at one of the coupled lounge units owned by the hotel and raised the umbrella. He motioned for her to take a seat.

"Where did you grow up?" he asked.

"For a while, all over the country. But when I was ten, my parents divorced and my mom and I settled in New York." She sat down, swung her legs up on the lounge, and relaxed against the back of her chair. "Who's interviewing who, Brett?"

"I'm about to place my Naval career in your hands. I want to know something about you."

Her pulse leapt and her eyes focused on his face.

He folded his tall, muscular frame onto the lounge and stared out across the ocean. Though he appeared relaxed, a muscle pulsed in his jaw. "Is your mother still living?"

"Yes, she's an interior designer in New York. She remarried when I was twelve. He's a very nice, very rich banker. His name is Milton Chase."

"My mom's visiting me and my sister. She arrived yesterday." He glanced at his watch and frowned. "When my dad was killed in Desert Storm, she held the family together. She's a tough lady. My sisters are, too. I can always count on them to have my back." His gaze swung to her face. "Who has yours?"

Tess remained silent a moment. Her mother and stepfather would certainly stand up for her, but would her father?

No. The story always came first. Before birthdays, Christmas, or any medical catastrophe. Some day he'd die in a distant country, searching for something neither she nor her mother had ever been able to give him.

"If you need someone who'll dig for the truth and damn the consequences, you can trust my father to follow through. But you can't depend on him to care too deeply for anyone. Not even those of us who have a genetic tie to him."

"I'm sorry."

She deflected the feelings his sincerity triggered with a shrug. "I'm used to it." *Liar.* She swung her legs off the lounge and, leaning forward, rested her hand on his arm. "Why don't we just cut right to the heart of it?"

The muscles in his forearm grew taut beneath her touch. The warmth of his skin seeped into her fingers. His pale blue gaze, lighter gray-blue around the pupil and darker around the rim of the iris, delved into hers. And when his lips parted, her gaze dropped to them. The structure of his jaw was undoubtedly masculine, his lips not too thick or thin. What would they feel like— *Whoa*—Hadn't he just said he was being investigated for murder? She had no business even sitting close to him, let alone touching him.

She withdrew her hand and clasped her fingers together in her lap. She cleared her throat, though it did nothing to cut the regret settling like a knot at its base. "Whatever you tell me today will have to stay off the record until I have other sources willing to verify it. How difficult is that going to be?"

"Damn near im—" He paused and color crept into his cheeks. "Damn difficult."

"You started to say impossible."

"Yeah. There may be people in Iraq with information about what happened."

"You don't know?"

Brett shook his head. "I don't remember what happened that night or the week before."

"What are they saying you did?"

"Derrick and I had a protection detail. We delivered a kid home in the heart of a certain city. His father was an Iraqi big wig. Some kind of liaison with the military. The kid disappeared after we dropped him off. NCIS is trying to say we're responsible for his disappearance. They're sniffing around like we hurt the kid. Derrick's history would give them an out, an easy way to placate the Iraqi and the State Department. The guys covering us were killed that same day. All eight."

Shock ricocheted through Tess. She pressed her fingertips against her lips. "So, you're basically saying you can't even prove you dropped the boy off."

"Yeah. That's what I'm saying."

"What about Armstrong?"

"He won't talk to NCIS. Which makes us both look guilty as hell, since he's the only one with a memory."

"He's just playing it smart." She pointed at him. "You shouldn't say anything without legal representation, either."

"I don't think that will make a difference. My CO thinks someone's pushing for a quick resolution."

"Why not just find out what happened to the kid?"

"One kid in a sea of missing and displaced people? Communications are spotty, intel is too. It's like looking for a newborn star in the next universe." He looked out over the bay. "NCIS must have hit a wall or something and now they're looking around for some passable theories. It's been more than two months. The Iraqi government must be putting diplomatic pressure on someone."

"The Navy has hundreds of thousands of dollars invested in your training, Brett. They'd be throwing all that away."

"To prevent an international incident. To give an important contact in Iraq closure, and ensure continued cooperation. They give murderers in this country free passes all the time in exchange for their testimony. If you don't think they'd burn me and Derrick both at the stake, you're mistaken." He sat up, and his knees brushed hers, then settled on either side of her legs. "In the SEALs you plan for the worst so you're prepared if it happens. If you have a choice between rations and a full magazine, you take the bullets. I've not sat on my thumbs waiting to train, and I'm not sitting by while they tank my career and my reputation for an easy fix to a diplomatic problem."

He leaned forward. His hands cupped her linen-covered legs at knee level, his thumbs rubbing back and forth across the top, setting off nerves she hadn't even known existed. And though he seemed unaware of what he was doing, Tess felt every stroke through the fabric as though it hit bare skin. Her breath caught in her chest and swallowing grew impossible.

His gaze held hers, intent with outrage. "I have a clean reputation in the SEAL community. More than a few commendations. I've got proof if you need it. I may have a Swiss cheese memory as to the events of that day, but I know myself. I sure as shit didn't touch that kid. And if Derrick—I'd have stopped him."

Tess moistened her lips and covered his hands with her own before the urge to slide closer overwhelmed her. "Brett." Fire blazed across her cheeks at the husky sound of her voice.

He released her and held his palms up in surrender. "Sorry." His grin held rueful chagrin and more charm than she could ignore. "I wasn't purposely putting a move on you. Not that I wouldn't want to, when all this shit is over."

She shook her head, more to clear her hormone-fogged brain than in denial of his statement. "What is it you expect from me?"

"You said you wanted an interview. I'm prepared to give you whatever information you need, without any of the secret stuff of course. In exchange, I want you to contact your father and put him on the scent of this new story possibility."

"You realize that could blow up in your face? He won't pull any punches."

"Whatever happened to that kid, I had no part in it. That's the only thing he's going to learn about me. So, I'm good."

He seemed so certain. Confident. But if he had no memory … She didn't want him to be guilty of anything. But what if he was?

"What do you think happened?" she asked.

"I think the al-Qaeda or the Taliban scooped him up as soon as we left. They might have thought he could tell them something useful. Or they might have sent him to one of their induction camps to train him. Or both. Whatever happened, I don't hold out much hope that they'll ever find him. But if your father can keep the pressure on, some clue might shake loose." He glanced at his watch. "My mom's probably waiting for me."

He rose and stepped clear of the lounge.

"When do you want to meet for the interview?" she asked. She accepted his hand to get up, and told herself it was just to be polite.

A slow smile built into a devilish grin as his palm came to rest on the small of her back while he urged her up the trail back toward the hotel. "How would you like to attend a barbeque? Doc, our medic, is throwing on some steaks tonight. The only thing is, it's a family thing, and you can't interview anyone. And you'll have to come as my date; otherwise the guys will be circling you like sharks."

It would give her some insight into their home life and his. "Sounds dangerous. But I think I can handle it."

Brett chuckled. "I don't doubt it."

CHAPTER 10

Clara spread her purchases out on the bed. Camera body, twenty-four hundred dollars, check. Zoom Wide Angle-Telephoto 24-70 mm lens, twelve hundred, check. 70-300 mm lens, three hundred, check. Speed light, four hundred and fifty, check. Spare battery, charger, and remote shutter release, one hundred-sixty, check. Two sixteen-gigabyte SD cards, eighty dollars, check. Sling bag for her equipment, one hundred-seventy-five, check. She'd spent nearly five thousand dollars, and the store had thrown in lens cleaner, some cloths, and a few extra lens caps. Thank you very much.

She lowered herself to the bed, breathed in the new plastic smell emanating from all the wrappings, and stared at the camera. *Five thousand dollars.* The hard knot of guilt that was lodged just beneath her breastbone twisted tighter. She had never bought expensive items for herself. When the kids were growing up, every dime went for keeping a roof over their heads and food on the table. Now she was alone, and she was still struggling with the mentality that she had to earn any small extra thing *she* wanted.

She should have waited until the emotional sting she'd suffered earlier had settled. Instead, she'd gone off half-cocked and spent damn near every dollar in her savings account.

What was I thinking?

That she needed something more. Had that been what the visit to Russell Connelly's apartment was about? She flinched at the thought.

She had to look inside for what she needed, not to other people. She knew that. Understood that. But sometimes the loneliness was as smothering as the grief she'd felt after Joe died. She no longer had her children to fill her days and nights. She no longer had a job to bury herself in. Propping her elbows on her knees, she rested her head in her hands.

"Where do I go from here?

The instruction booklet for the camera lay in the box at her feet. She dragged it free from the refuse and flipped it open.

This was as good a place as any to start.

The thing he hated most about being in charge was paperwork. He understood the purpose for it, but it still sucked.

When the phone next to Hawk rang he almost welcomed the break. But the whole time he was discussing the logistics problem for the upcoming training op, his mind was still on the missing paperwork from Brett's protection detail in Iraq.

Hawk rubbed a hand over his face as his gaze traveled around the nondescript office he used when on post. A desk and chair, standard issue, two chairs for visitors, some filing cabinets. A phone. He could run his team from the field as well as he did from this office.

He'd been going over reports for hours trying to find one Derrick Armstrong might have written around April twenty-eighth. He couldn't find a damn thing. So Armstrong hadn't filed a report. Which didn't help him or Brett one damn bit.

But there had to be logs of their communications with HQ during that time. In the sea of paperwork every mission and maneuver propagated, the chances of him finding it logged into the system were slim to none. Hell, it might be six months before the paperwork cropped up. It would take a federal court order and NCIS's demands to get it done quickly. *Fuck.*

At a knock on his office door, he glanced up with a frown. "Come in."

He rose as the door opened and two men entered his office. No uniforms, military bearings, and all business. NCIS. The larger of the two closed the door behind them.

After the introductions, Scott, the shorter member of the team said, "We're here to speak to you about two of your men, Lieutenant."

Hawk motioned to the two seats in front of his desk. "Have a seat."

Five minutes into the conversation, Edwards said, "We know you have an ongoing relationship with Weaver's sister."

"Yes."

"You can't afford to allow that relationship to encourage you to cover for him."

Rage surged through Hawk, and his gaze focused on the man. "I don't have to cover for Ensign Weaver. I'm sure you're going to interview the other members of the team, if you haven't already. They'll agree Brett is as rock solid as I've just told you."

"But Armstrong is a different story."

"Ensign Armstrong started counseling right after we shipped home."

"For anger management issues."

"Yes. Attributed to PTSD."

"What would have stopped him from directing those issues toward Sanjay al-Yussuf?"

"First of all, Ensign Armstrong's issues seemed to center around jealousy directed toward his girlfriend, Marjorie. But he isn't just the man who's sitting in the brig facing charges stemming from that. Derrick often went into the villages and passed out candy and rations to the children. We all did, but he was more dedicated. He once carried an injured child five miles in from the field for medical treatment. He took issue with the al-Qaeda using children as suicide bombers. He spoke to me and the other members of the team often about it. If those feelings hadn't kept him in check, Brett Weaver would have."

"Yet he tried to kill Brett Weaver during your last mission in Iraq."

"He hasn't been charged with that. And there's been no evidence discovered that anyone on our team is responsible for Brett's injuries."

"But Brett Weaver believes he did," Agent Wright spoke for the first time.

If Brett said that to these two, I'll eat my dress uniform bonnet. "Since Ensign Weaver was unconscious when I discovered him, I doubt he made such a statement."

Wright's eyes narrowed.

"Your CO has recommended you for a commendation for saving Weaver's life in Iraq," Scot said.

What the— Jackson had said promotions and commendations were frozen until the investigation into what had happened to Brett was finished. Hawk shrugged. What was Jackson up to? "We don't do the job for medals or commendations."

"You must have some idea who attacked Weaver during the mission," Wright said.

"Yeah. One of the eight or nine terrorists inside the building with us." Hawk answered, his sarcasm thick.

"You don't believe that any more than we do," Scott said.

Hawk raised a brow. "Are you going to try to convict one of my men using speculation just so you can tie up loose ends?"

Wright's expression grew flat. "We don't work that way, Lieutenant."

"I'm glad to hear it."

"Has there been any progress on the investigation into Second Lieutenant Carney's disappearance?" Hawk asked, partly to needle them, but also to find out what they were doing about Flash's Houdini three months before.

"We're not attached to that investigation, Lieutenant," Agent Scott said, his expression deadpan. "We wouldn't be at liberty to discuss the case if we were."

"Meaning you still have no leads?"

"It seems your entire team fell apart as soon as they returned home, Lieutenant," Wright said.

Hawk controlled the urge to rise to the man's bait. "My team had just come off a tough seven-month tour of duty. I suggest you stop judging them and start looking at things using more than the parameters you've been directed to follow." *And get your head out of your ass, dickhead.*

Ignoring Wright's look of outrage, he continued. "If you're at liberty to pass on some information to the as—agents who are in charge of that particular investigation, there has been some talk about Flash—Lieutenant Carney, receiving visitors just before returning home. Perhaps you should look into who those visitors might have been, and whether they're tied to his disappearance."

Wright's features grew tense. "What sort of visitors?"

"Visitors dressed as military, but who wore no rank or insignia. I thought they might have been attached to your agency."

Wright and Scott looked at each other.

"And you're just now mentioning this?" Scott said.

"I've called your office every week since Carney went missing. None of your agents was interested in speaking to me."

Scott's jaw clenched, and a muscle began pulsing there. "We'll see the information is passed on."

Hawk nodded.

"Someone will follow up with you about it."

"I'll be holding my breath, Agent Scott."

Knowing a dismissal when they heard it, the agents rose.

As soon as the door closed behind them, Hawk allowed himself one brief smile of satisfaction before he went back to his computer search.

This shit was getting out of hand. It was time the team became involved.

Music, its rhythm pounding in a steady beat, traveled from behind the four-plex, while the distant sound of the surf attempted to wash it out to sea. The timbre of rumbling conversation and warm laughter added to the clamor. Zoe swallowed against the nausea plaguing her. The smell of the hard-boiled eggs she'd used to garnish the huge bowl of potato salad drifted up into her nose. Her stomach rolled, and she looked toward the scattered bushes in the side yard in case she lost control. *Morning sickness at mid-evening. Great.* She wiped a sleeve over her forehead to get rid of the beads of cold sweat, then used it to cover her nose.

Hawk balanced the bowl of potato salad on one hand, and used the other to guide her to the back of the complex. The building looked like a large cube with big windows and an entrance to each apartment on the four corners.

"Won't Doc's neighbors be disturbed by the noise?" she asked, desperate for any distraction.

"All four apartments are occupied by SEALs, and they've all been invited," Hawk said.

The single guys trained hard and partied harder. Zoe hadn't seen that in Hawk, but she and her family had invaded his house while Brett was in the hospital, and when they'd had their breakup, she'd only left for a brief time. He'd pushed her away, fearful of how she would react if something happened to him. Being separated for those two weeks had been torture, and he had caved. It was harder being apart than living together with the ifs.

But it went deeper than that. Guilt over being 'down range' while his mother was dying of breast cancer had made him hyper-vigilant about his responsibilities to the people in his life. That hadn't changed. He worried about her leg. About her ability to stay independent when she grew older. She couldn't have him worrying about her while he was training or out of the country. He had to stay focused to stay safe.

So she'd stay on her feet the best way she could, and she'd keep quiet about anything that could cause him any added distraction. That was the plan.

He'd be leaving in seven days for a three-week training operation. Desert training to freshen their skills for another deployment. He hadn't said, couldn't say, but she guessed Afghanistan this time.

Dear God, how she dreaded it. Not because of the baby, or because she'd be alone, though those thoughts entered into her worries. But because she wouldn't know how he was from one moment to the next. The not knowing would drive her crazy.

The back yard opened into a large concrete patio surrounding a rectangular pool. A grassy divide lay between the beach and the house. A volleyball game was in progress, the net set up in the sand.

"Yo, Hawk," Greenback yelled, from his position on the back line. "We need you, man."

Hawk raised the bowl he carried.

"I can take that," Zoe said, reaching for the container. She needed him distracted until either her stomach settled or nature took its course.

"Thanks, babe." He brushed her cheek with a kiss and jogged across the yard to join the players.

Zoe limped to the long, dish-laden buffet table and maneuvered the bowl into place between containers of coleslaw and a vegetable casserole. She twisted away from the table with a shudder. The sight of food made her nausea worse.

Doc, his dark auburn hair damp around his face, manned the large double-layered grill, long-handled tongs in one hand and a beer in the other. His black t-shirt sported the image of a large bull seal and the logo SEALs Do It On The Beach. "Hey, Zoe. Want a beer?" he called out as she wandered toward the cluster of wives and girlfriends sitting near the pool.

"How about a soft drink?"

He pointed at one of the coolers. "Help yourself."

Trish Marks waved from her seat. The high-pitched squeals of the children splashing in the pool traveled to her, making her jittery. The hodge-podge of lawn furniture beckoned. Maybe if she sat down she'd feel better. She chose a soft drink from the cooler and crossed the patio. Just as she reached Trish, the wind shifted, shoving the scent of grilling meat at her. Zoe clamped her hand over her mouth as the urge to gag rose. Bathroom—Lord, she needed a bathroom. *Now!*

Trish frowned in concern, and scrambled out of her chair. She half pushed, half guided Zoe toward a door.

The gray rug beneath her feet was the only thing Zoe saw as she fought to hold back the wave of bile. The sight of the white porcelain commode was a relief. Falling to her knees, she heaved and heaved until there was nothing left in her stomach.

Trish held a cold, wet cloth against her forehead when the urge eased and shoved the handle down, flushing away the evidence. "I'll go get Hawk."

Zoe grasped her wrist. "No, it's passing—I think."

"I can drive you home so you can lie down," Trish offered.

Zoe shook her head. The movement stirred the nausea again, and she stopped. She braced an arm across the commode seat and rested her forehead on it. "I'm not contagious," her voice sounded hollow as it bounced around the toilet bowl.

Silence filled the small space. Zoe tilted her head back to look up into Trish's freckled face. The woman's blue gaze held hers, a silent question lying heavy between them, until Trish drew a deep breath and voiced it. "Are you pregnant?"

CHAPTER 11

"Yes. I'm pregnant." Just saying the word somehow made it more real. "I haven't told Hawk yet. They have that training thing coming up next week, and you know how he is."

"Oh, Zoe." Trish's smile held joy and understanding. She bent to give her a hug.

"Look, I know you don't hold anything back from Langley, but please don't say anything to him." Zoe forced a smile to her lips, though the urge to weep rose strong. "They may be good at keeping national secrets, but I don't think family stuff counts. And as close as he and Hawk are—"

Trish laughed. "Hawk will be so thrilled."

Zoe bit her lip. Would he? They had talked marriage, but hadn't settled on anything. "I hope so. This wasn't exactly planned."

Trish shrugged. "Sometimes it happens that way."

"You're the only one who knows. I haven't even told Mom or Brett. I've been building up my nerve to tackle Hawk first. He worries about me, and I don't want him to be distracted while he's training."

Trish knelt and brushed the damp curls away from Zoe's face. "He's tough. He can handle this. He'll need time to process it and accept it before ... "

Before their next training run. Before their next deployment. Before they risk their lives again.

Zoe's vision blurred, and though her queasiness hadn't quite dissipated, she forced herself to her feet instead of giving into it, or the tears. "I'm good now. Any suggestions for how to deal with morning sickness, or in my case anytime sickness?"

"Crackers, crackers, and more crackers. And potato chips. The salt seems to do something for it. And lemonade."

"Okay." She gave a nod. "There has to be crackers or potato chips out there somewhere. Do you think Doc would be insulted if I looked in his medicine cabinet for toothpaste?"

Trish laughed. "I don't think he'd mind at all."

Zoe opened the medicine cabinet in search of toothpaste, and, finding a tube, squirted some onto her finger to brush her teeth. The taste of mint seemed to sooth her upset stomach. Turning on the water, she rinsed her mouth and spat, then shut the tap off. "Let's go find something salty."

Brett's hand rested against Tess's waist as he guided her along the sidewalk that meandered around the apartment complex. His mother walked ahead, the strap of her camera bag thrown over her shoulder. The bag wallowed against her hip as she moved, too heavy to bounce. The two women seemed to have hit it off. No surprise, his mom got along with just about everyone. But something was off with her. She'd been quiet. Kind of distracted. And she'd gone out and spent a shitload of money on camera equipment. What was up with that?

The elusive scent Tess wore teased him once again. It wasn't floral, but something citrus. The delicate curve of her cheek, the soft, pouty shape of her lips, and those warm, sherry-colored eyes just ... did it for him. The curve of her waist fit his hand as though made for him. Her long legs, bared by shorts, stretched pale and smooth. He'd start at the small knob of bone at her ankle and work his way all the way—*Hold on. Can't go there.* But, Jesus, he wanted to.

After all this shit ended, he'd be after her like a bird dog scenting quail. He had trouble suppressing a grin. Like

Romeo after Juliet. It would probably shock the shit out of her to know a military guy could be romantic. He'd show her. Would she go for a guy who did do the hearts and flowers thing?

"Cutter." Bowie's shout reached him almost before he'd made it around the corner of the apartment building. Bowie paused long enough to hug Clara before moving on to extend his hand. Brett clasped it and bumped shoulders with him.

"You're missed, man," Bowie said, pounding him on the back hard enough to hurt.

"Thanks. I haven't missed your sorry ass at all," Brett said.

Bowie laughed and turned his attention to Tess. Brett had seen that wolfish grin and flash of dimples before. He sent a narrow-eyed look of warning at his teammate and received a smirk in return.

"Tess, this is Ensign Dan Rivera."

"Everyone calls me Bowie," Rivera said, offering his hand.

"Is that a call sign?" Tess asked as she accepted his grip and shook briefly.

"Yes."

"So you're nicknamed after a knife?"

"Sort of. Mostly after Jim Bowie who fought at the Alamo. I'm from Texas."

"I recognized the accent."

A small crease of concentration appeared between Tess's brows. She was already in observation mode as she looked up at Brett. "And your call sign is Cutter?"

"Yeah." Every part of his training could make him a murderer in her eyes, but avoiding her question would only make her suspicious. "I'm good with sharp weapons, particularly knives."

"Oh." Her lips pursed on the word. "You'll have to demonstrate for me sometime."

His brows rose. "If you like."

Would that be part of the story she wanted to write? It would be a distinctive detail that could identify him. He'd have to talk to her about keeping his part in all this anonymous. Jesus, this whole thing was like tiptoeing through a minefield. One wrong move or word and he'd be eating his discharge papers.

His gaze scanned the players involved in the volleyball game. Hawk, Langley Marks, Oliver Shaker, and Doc's neighbor Seaman Jeff Sizemore comprised one team. The other was made up of Bowie, Doc's neighbor, Seaman Carl Tanner, and the two new guys in the team, Seamen Jack Logan and Kelsey Tyler. Brett threw up a hand in recognition as Jack Logan called to him. Logan and Tyler had filled Flash and Derrick's places. His own spot was still open, but that could change at any time.

The thought scared him more than the threat of being arrested. This was what he was supposed to be. Sure, he had a backup plan, but if he had a record or a dishonorable hanging over him, what the fuck kind of life could he be looking at?

He caught Hawk's frown as he noticed Tess standing beside him. It was already too late. He'd invited her right into the heart of the team. He just hoped to hell he could show her they were all just people, living their lives. Raising their families. But they were professionals, too. Not killers.

"Come meet the ladies," he suggested.

"Sure."

Clara, having gone ahead of them, stepped back from giving Zoe a hug.

"Tess this is my sister, Zoe."

"Nice to meet you." Tess offered Zoe a nod and a smile.

"You, too."

Brett went around the circle of eight ladies introducing the other men's girlfriends and wives.

"I got word from the hospital this morning," Zoe said. "I got the job."

"I knew you would," Brett said. He tugged her close and gave her a hug.

Zoe leaned into his side. "I start next Monday."

"I'm sure Hawk's pleased."

"Yes. He was talking about how much it would cost to start my own clinic if the hospital job didn't come through."

"You're not a doctor?" Tess asked.

Zoe laughed. "No. But there are times I feel as though I've had enough experience and education to be. I'm a physical therapist. I'll be working with patients with debilitating injuries or amputations."

"That sounds challenging," Tess commented.

"It will be, but I'm up for it. It's been a long two days waiting for the news. It was a tough interview, too."

"I'm sure. Obviously you did well."

"Why don't the two of you sit down," Clara said. "I'll get us some drinks."

"I'll get them, Mom." Brett waved her to a seat. "Orders, ladies?"

With a mental tally of everything they wanted, he wandered off to the cooler and paused at Doc's side to slap him on the back. "What's happening?"

"Almost through here. We'll be eating any minute now." Doc's green gaze appeared more serious than his words. "NCIS was on post asking questions about you and Derrick today."

Brett's stomach dropped. "Shit. I was expecting it, but still."

"These guys really have a hard-on for you both."

"I know."

"What are you going to do about it, Cutter?"

"Since they're not willing to look beyond the send of their noses, I have a plan."

"Such as?"

"You know that phrase we hear sometimes, 'plausible deniability?'"

"Yeah."

"Well, this applies. The less you know, the less they can ask you when the dust settles."

Doc's expression grew grave. "They can't charge you with anything if there's no evidence, Cutter."

"They're going with the idea that the lack of evidence points to us having done away with the kid, Doc. I've done a lot of things in the line of duty, but cold blooded murder isn't one of them."

Doc presented a fist and they knocked knuckles.

"Who's the legs?" Doc asked, tipping his beer in the women's direction.

Brett grinned. "Tess Kelly. She's a reporter for the San Diego Tribune."

Doc stepped back and eyed him, his amazement clear. "Is she part of your plan?"

"A very small part. She's here as my date with the understanding that this is a family barbecue and off limits to the press."

"And you trust her?" Doc said as his brows rose.

"No, not entirely. But then she probably has bigger balls than you or I do."

"Why's that?"

"Would you go out with someone suspected of murder?"

Doc's features hardened. "You haven't been charged. You're not going to be charged."

If only he could be sure. "You know that itch you get between your shoulder blades when you know someone has a bead on you?"

"Yeah, I know it well. It's saved my life more than once."

"I've had that itch ever since NCIS showed up in Jackson's office." He slapped Doc on the back. "Got to get drinks for the ladies." He opened the cooler and dug in to retrieve a couple of beers and several soft drinks. "Thanks for having my back, Doc."

"Always, Bro."

But the thought he'd just voiced to Doc set a niggling worry crawling through his gut. How far would Tess go for a story?

Tess stretched her legs out and crossed her ankles. She couldn't say that the SEALs and their families weren't capable of feeding an army, or a navy as the case might be. She'd definitely eaten far more than she needed. They didn't lack for social graces, either. The conversation had run the gamut from movies they'd seen to the best techniques for surfing. Something Logan and Tyler, the newest members of the SEAL team, seemed enthused about.

The two 'new guys' left after eating to catch a few waves before sundown.

Clara moved around the crowd taking candid shots of the men and their dates and the children. The kids hammed it up for her.

"Is your mom a photographer?"

"No, a retired school teacher. She showed up at the apartment with all that camera equipment this afternoon." He shook his head, clearly baffled.

"If she's just retired, maybe she's looking to remake herself. Madonna's done it."

Brett flashed her a smile. "If she starts wearing skin tight leotards with cones over her breasts, I'm calling an ambulance."

Tess laughed. "She may be good at this. Up until now she's probably lived her job to provide for her family. Most single parents do."

"I guess you're right. She shouldered all the responsibility after Dad died. And with Zoe's condition, that wasn't easy. After that, she helped us all with college. Then my sister with her kids. She's like the Pied Piper with children."

Clara said something to Doc. Then she and the children went into his apartment.

"Told you. They'll follow her anywhere."

What would he do if something happened to end his career?

"What are you going to do when you retire from the teams?"

"Most of the guys go into some sort of security work because of the training. I have an engineering master's from University of Kentucky. I'll dust that off and go back to school and see what happens."

An engineer. He could have made a fortune working for private corporations. "With an engineering degree, you could have worked anywhere. Why the SEALs?"

"I wanted to serve my country. Most of the officers have college degrees of some sort. Even most of the non-commissioned have college hours. We're not just guys toting guns. There's more to the training than that."

She leaned back to digest everything he'd said while idly watching Zoe and Hawk's progress around the patio as they swayed to the music. With the back of her leg completely exposed, the extent of Zoe's injuries was open for anyone to see. Nearly half the calf muscle was gone. Scars from skin grafts patch-worked up both legs to disappear beneath her shorts. Tess flinched away from the sight.

"If she catches you looking at her with any kind of pity, she'll verbally kick your ass," Brett said from beside her. He shifted in his seat to stretch his long legs out.

"I wasn't staring out of morbid curiosity. It's just—" She swallowed to clear the knot from her throat. "She's beautiful, and it hurts to see that marred in such a brutal way."

"Yeah. It does." He focused on the soft drink he'd been nursing nearly half an hour. "A drunk driver came through our subdivision. It was summer and there were kids out all over our street riding their bikes. He managed to miss all of them, until he passed out at the wheel and hit Zoe. She was all tangled up with the bike." He flinched and closed his eyes as though the memory was still too fresh to think about "She was in the hospital for months. It took nearly a year for her to learn to walk again."

"And the guy who hit her?"

"He was an habitual drunk driver. He got ten years, but he died of liver cancer before he served five."

"At least he can't hurt anyone else."

He nodded. "There is that. She's good now. There have been some rough patches for her. Girls being petty bitches in high school. Guys being assholes in college. She and Hawk are good together."

Her gaze wandered to the couple. Hawk rested his chin against Zoe's hair and she nestled against him. He spoke close against her ear and she tilted her head back to look up at him. The smile she offered him was so open, so intimate, Tess looked away.

"It's pretty clear they're crazy about each other," Brett said.

"Yeah, I can see that."

"If she'd hooked up with any other guy on the team, I'd have had to step in. But Hawk's solid."

He was also intimidating as hell, even from a distance. He'd been cordial enough at dinner, but watchful. And he hadn't wasted any time in steering Zoe away from her. What was he afraid of? Zoe wouldn't know any SEAL secrets. But she had been a witness to, and a victim of, Derrick Armstrong's meltdown.

The last vestige of sunlight dipped beneath the waves, and the evening air began to cool. Doc switched on the pool lights, and the exterior lights came on with them.

Her attention shifted to Doc's neighbors. Carl Turner and Jeff Sizemore lounged around the pool with their girlfriends, talking with Ensign Shaker and his wife Selena. Their nine-month-old was passed around and rocked by the women while they visited.

For a moment she dwelt on the connection these people had to one another. They were like an extended family, and a support system for each other.

Despite his earlier flirtatious smiles, Bowie and his date, Angela Melzonni, seemed deep in like as they sat close together on the edge of the pool holding hands. Doc slouched in a lawn chair talking with them.

"You seemed to know Angela well." She tried to ignore the stab of jealousy she had no right to feel, and to sound impartial as she asked, "An old girlfriend?"

"She was one of my nurses in the hospital."

"Oh." The resentment she'd fed to help hold her attraction at bay dissolved. *Shit.*

Chief Petty Officer Langley Marks and his wife Trish glided by in perfect rhythm. Brett set aside the soft drink, rose, and extended a hand. "Come dance with me."

Thus far she'd managed to keep a distance between them with a running barrage of questions. He'd answered every one. But it seemed that was at an end.

She was supposed to be his date but … No, it would be okay. She was in control, as always. Besides, she wasn't interested in getting involved with a man who would be as absent from her life as her father had been. She needed someone who would be there every day when she got home from work. Someone she could depend on when emergencies arose. Someone dependable in every way a dependable man was supposed to be.

The moment she placed her hand in his, her breathing grew unsteady. He tugged her to her feet and into his arms with an ease that had her breath catching altogether. At five foot five and a hundred and twenty pounds, she'd thought herself sturdy, but held against Brett's six-foot frame with his broad shoulders and chest stretched before her, she felt delicate.

His hand splayed against her back, but he didn't pull her in too close. He guided her just near enough for their bodies to brush as he led her into a slow, swaying rhythm, part seduction, part torture.

She couldn't have sex with him. He was a source.

He was in trouble, but every time she looked into his baby blues, she just couldn't believe him capable of cold-blooded murder.

And the more she got to know him, the more she was drawn to him.

But could she trust her instincts?

She gnawed her lower lip.

"Relax, I don't bite," he said, resting his cheek against her hair.

"It isn't that. I'm more at ease in the professional realm than I am the personal one." *Oh, shit. Did I just admit that?*

Dancing with this man was personal. She was sharing her space with him. But it didn't feel like an invasion for him to hold her. It felt—amazing. She wanted to lean into him. He smelled like laundry soap and grill smoke, blended with the light fragrance of cologne and the underlying scent of *him.*

The pressure of his hand guided her closer, and she had no choice but to relax when every muscle turned to liquid. A rush of need set afire every nerve. Her hand slid from his shoulder to rest against his chest, the muscle there evident beneath her touch. "This isn't a good idea." Her voice came out just above a whisper.

"We're just dancing. What's not good about it?" His husky voice wreaked havoc on the aching heat growing between her thighs.

What could she say when every inch of her was alive to every move he made? Had they been alone, she'd have been tempted to hook a knee around his hip and press against the growing bulge that brushed against her belly.

Oliver Shaker spoke before either of them was aware of his approach. "Call me if you need anything, Cutter." The baby lay nestled against his shoulder asleep, her little form so relaxed her limbs looked boneless.

"Thanks, Greenback," Brett said.

"Good night," Selena offered, her soft voice almost carried away by the stiffening breeze.

Though Brett continued to hold Tess for several moments, the interruption had broken the spell. She pulled away and slumped back into her chair, feeling like a teenager caught necking in the back seat of a car.

This was the first time she'd gotten so twisted up over a man that she actually wanted to throw caution to the wind. Brett Weaver was dangerous.

CHAPTER 12

Yasin al-Yussuf scanned the dusty streets. Every business they passed needed repairs, their facades pockmarked by shrapnel, bullets, or age. Every home lay behind short garden walls. What little privacy the walls provided, they didn't block the sight of peeling window facings, broken glass, and dilapidated roofs. His driver, Aban, sped through the poor neighborhood with little regard for the people walking along the roads. The rule stated, the faster the vehicle moved, the harder it was to overtake. The man took the directive very seriously. The second rule was they never took the same route to Yasin's home. Aban could be trusted to follow that one above all others.

But the vehicle's speed didn't prevent Yasin from seeing the people's struggle to overcome what war and terrorism had done to their neighborhoods, their lives. He had struggled to help his country rebuild. And what had he received in return? Betrayal from the very people he was working for. They viewed him as a traitor for dealing with the Americans, yet they wanted the money the Americans paid for services, and the opportunity to make more. It was not freedom they wanted, but money, and power for themselves and for their families.

He ran a weary hand over his face. He had wanted to create a more stable homeland for his family. He'd wanted to fight al-Qaeda and rid his country of those who thrived on social unrest and tried to suppress their freedoms. It had been for his people he had worked so hard, but more for his son.

And now Sanjay was gone. He studied the dismal landscape outside. It was growing harder to believe that what he did was worthwhile.

His cell phone rang. He pushed the accept button and identified himself.

"The bird has flown." The caller disconnected.

He did not recognize the gravelly voice speaking Kurdish on the other end of the phone, but he understood the message. He struggled to suppress the anguished cry that rose from deep in his chest. With this act, he had become one with the terrorists. Tabarek had made it through airport security and had boarded a flight for the United States. Now he had only to make it through Homeland Security when he landed in Los Angeles.

When the SEALs who had transported his son home those many months ago were dead, he would know justice. But he would never know peace. Sanjay was dead. And he had become a murderer.

Tess paced the floor of her apartment with the phone pressed to her ear. Through the living room into the kitchen, around the limited floor space of the bedroom, and back again.

"Why do you think I'll be interested in this story?" Ian, her father asked. The connection faded in and out as though he were on the move.

"Because it has all the elements you love in a story. This has a wounded hero, falsely accused. A fifteen-year old boy who has disappeared. A government agency more interested in settling for the easiest answer than searching for truth. And it's happening in Iraq where your contacts are strongest. And best of all, no one is going to scoop you on this, because no one else knows about it."

"And you're giving the story to me because?"

Was that suspicion she heard in his voice? Had he been burned recently and covered a story he couldn't sell? She hadn't seen his byline coming across the wire services as often. But sometimes it took time to cultivate leads and figure out the spin.

"I can't do the story myself. Being a woman in a Middle Eastern country trying to do a story like this would be impossible. I don't have the international contacts you do. And as much as I'd like to say I was brave enough," *crazy enough*, "to cover the story, despite bullets flying and bombs going off around me, I know I'm not cut out for that kind of journalism."

When his silence stretched long enough to be uncomfortable, she said, "Why don't you fly in and meet Ensign Weaver? If you still aren't interested, I'll see who else might be."

"Are you sleeping with this guy?"

Now an accusation. What was going on with him? "No, I'm not sleeping with him. He's a SEAL. He's gone nine months a year on training ops and deployed six months at a time. I'm not interested in an absentee lover." She flinched. Was that not what her mother had said to him? For a moment, strident voices raised in argument battled in her head. They echoed inside the apartment. She closed her eyes and struggled to block the memories out.

"You're sounding more and more like your mother every time I speak to you, Teresa. I hoped you could be your own adult rather than follow in her footsteps."

He always called her Teresa when he was about to make a point. And he'd made a valid one. What had happened between her parents those many moons ago was over. Had he not walked away from her as well, she might not still be feeling the sting of the divorce long after her parents had put the mess behind them.

He drew a deep breath. "Why don't you tell me why you're so interested in this?"

"I believe there's someone high up pulling the strings to either make this international situation go away fast or milk it for all it's worth. Whoever this Iraqi liaison is, he must be very important to the military, or someone else."

"Because?"

"I don't know yet. But there's something more going on behind the scenes."

"I'll never get the thing across an editor's desk, Tess. And they won't want your SEAL's identity released. When their names are known it puts them and their families at risk. And makes them a target for every terrorist cell they've ever attacked."

"You won't have to release his name if you angle the story from the Iraqi point of view. Families have lost children to al-Qaeda and the Taliban. They indoctrinate those kids into their terrorist networks. And no one is looking for them."

"Your Special Ops friend believes this kid was kidnapped by al-Qaeda?"

"Yes, he does. They're using children in despicable ways. You know that better than I do. They're turning them into terrorists whether they want to be or not. This is a human rights story."

Ian remained silent for a moment. When he spoke, there was resignation in his tone. Was he finally running down? Was the lifestyle he'd led all these years finally getting to him? "I'll want to talk to this SEAL myself."

The very thing she'd asked for had come to fruition, but now dread hit her. If Ian came to San Diego, Brett would meet her father. Ian could be charming and resourceful, but he was single minded and relentless, and he'd bury Brett Weaver if he thought there was a story in it. She held the phone between her shoulder and her ear and rubbed her temples where a dull ache throbbed.

"Do you want me to have him call you, or do you want to meet him face to face?"

"Face to face, darlin'. I want to meet the man. I'll fly out on Wednesday. I'll call you with the details."

"All right."

Tess hung up the phone, but continued to stare at it for several moments. She hoped Brett Weaver knew what he was getting into.

The thirty-eight foot deep sea fishing boat wallowed as a set of waves rolled beneath her. The sea was tinged battleship gray on the horizon, the early morning light dulled by a hint of a storm out to sea. Russell eyed Evan for signs of seasickness.

Evan zipped his jacket, turned his face into the sharp pacific breeze, and smiled. "Relax, Dad. I'm fine. I have been on a boat before."

"I brought some Dramamine just in case," Russell said, keeping his tone casual.

"Your friend, Clark, seems pleased you're on board," Evan said.

"He and I met about ten years ago when I chartered a larger vessel for a group of Naval medical staff. We had the idea that we would fish along the southern coast for a couple of days. Half were sick before we made it out of port and we had to turn around and drop them off."

Evan laughed. "That didn't include you."

"No. I usually reserve the right to puke my guts up during storms. As long as it doesn't get any rougher than this, I'm good. We've been going out one or two days a year ever since. Monica is his private fishing vessel. He doesn't charter it out."

They left the bay and the large inboard motor vibrated beneath their feet as the boat took on speed. Evan gripped the chrome bar that ran along the top of the starboard side of the vessel. Russell stepped in close in case he lost his balance.

"If it gets too windy for you we can go below until we get to a place where the yellowtails are running," he yelled close to Evan's ear.

Evan gave him a thumbs up signal and sat down on one of the low cushioned seats. He pulled his hood up and leaned into the bulkhead. He looked out across the choppy water.

Russell fought off a wave of anxiety. Should something happen while they were miles from land—They could radio for a chopper. It would be okay. Evan had asked him to arrange the trip.

Ten minutes later the boat slowed and Clark signaled him. "There's a school of yellowtail off to port."

Russell handed Evan a pole already set with thirty-pound test line and a metal lead. Opening one of the built-in bait boxes, he grabbed a live squid and baited his hook. The fishy smell of the squid blended with oily smell of smoke from the idling inboard motor rumbling beneath their feet. "Throw it out and let out about fifty feet of line," he instructed. He reached for his own pole.

"How will I know if I've got anything?" Evan asked.

"If a yellowtail hits the squid it'll run the line and you'll hear it." He set up his own rig and took a seat to wait.

"You remember when you took me fishing off the pier?" Evan asked.

"Yeah, I do." Evan's face was partially blocked by the hood and he couldn't read his expression. "You had to stand on a cooler to keep your pole over the railing."

"After the divorce I used to think about that a lot, Dad."

Russell swallowed against the pain. "Me, too." The memory rose up to torment him. Evan's small face had been pink and wind-chapped, and he'd just lost one of his front teeth. He'd insisted his hair be cut in a burr that summer so he could look like the Marine recruits he'd seen on post.

"Did you know I was gay before I came out?" Evan asked. "You were the only one who didn't freak out when I broke the news."

Evan had been so withdrawn, so solitary, it had been almost a relief to know what he'd been carrying so close. "No, I didn't know. I'd worried that you were depressed, or worse, but you wouldn't talk to me. And then when you told me, I was relieved you'd finally shared what you were hiding."

Evan remained silent for a beat, then another.

Was he hiding something now? Was it something about his condition, or something else? And why the hell hadn't Gloria called?

When Evan looked up and turned to speak, Russell tensed.

Evan's pole jerked in his hand and the reel spun with a high-pitched zipping noise.

"Raise the tip of your rod, Evan. Keep it up and pull it in toward you," Russell said. He jammed his pole in the socket and stood.

Evan leaned back as he gripped the pole with both hands and the tip of the rod bent.

"You have to keep the pressure on or he'll slip the hook. That's it."

Watching him fight the fish for five minutes, then ten, the urge to help him was almost overwhelming. "You're wearing him out, Evan," he said instead.

When the struggle stretched into fifteen minutes, Evan's arms shook and his breathing grew ragged. The words 'do *you need me'* hung on the tip of Russell's tongue just begging to jump off.

The large fish surfaced and Russell grabbed the grappling hook. "One more pull and he'll be up close to the boat, Evan."

He swung the hook and it pierced the fish along the spine where the dorsal fin ran, and he lifted him on deck. "He's at least twenty pounds." The fish's gills still heaved, his yellow triangle-shaped tail whipping as he still fought for freedom.

"You've caught dinner, young fellow," Clark said from the helm on the deck above them.

"I did, didn't I, Dad?" Evan's chest heaved with every breath, and he was shaking with exhaustion, but a wide smile of pure joy curved his lips that showed every tooth.

Had he ever seen him smile like that before? Russell's eyes blurred with tears, and he bent to put the fish in the fish-box to keep it cool until they cleaned it. "You did a great job, son."

"He almost kicked my butt, but I'll get even when we eat him tonight."

Russell laughed despite the tears, and turning aside, wiped his face with his sleeve. He reached for his own pole to reel it in. The bait was gone, nibbled away while he'd focused on Evan.

"Thanks, Dad."

Russell steeled himself and turned to face him. "For what?"

"For not helping me. I know you wanted too. I need to know I can do thing for myself. I'll let you know when I can't, okay?"

The tears threatened again and he breathed through them. "Okay."

He rebated his hook and threw out his line. "What were you going to tell me before the yellowtail took your line?"

"It wasn't important." Evan smiled again. A full-fledged smile just like before.

Though he sensed that wasn't quite true, Russell let it go.

This was crazy. One minute she was nauseous as hell and the next starved. Zoe dropped butter in the skillet, and it immediately sizzled and began to melt. She poured milk into the eggs and beat them.

What was she going to do? She couldn't continue to get up an hour before Hawk to eat crackers and fight off morning sickness. He was bound to notice sooner or later. She had to tell him. Would he really be okay with being a father?

Hearing his light tread behind her, she glanced over her shoulder. His hair, still damp from his shower, moulded to his skull. His t-shirt clung to his broad chest, and his khaki shorts rode low on his hips. The sight of him never failed to make her heartbeat kick into overdrive and inspired a tangled rush of feelings she'd never known existed—until him.

He'd be good with the news. Trish was right. She'd tell him while they ate. The tension that gripped her shoulders every time she thought about keeping the secret from him eased with the decision. "I'll have omelets and toast done in a moment."

"Zoe, I need to talk to you."

"Me, too. There's something I've been meaning to discuss with you."

She glanced up from the skillet. Hawk's serious expression triggered stomach-dropping anxiety. Her hand paused in mid-action. Egg dripped from the end of the fork onto the counter.

He reached around her to turn off the skillet where the butter had begun to smoke.

Was he deploying already? He'd only been home for four months. They hadn't had enough time. Forever wouldn't be enough.

"What's wrong?" Her voice came out in a soft wheeze.

He plucked the fork from her fingers, set it aside, and offered her a smile. But there was stress behind his expression. "Easy, babe. I just need to fill you in on some things before I leave for training next week."

She dragged in a breath and leaned against the counter so he wouldn't see her legs shake. "Okay."

"Come sit down." Hawk took her arm and led her to the small kitchen table. He pulled out a chair and urged her to sit, then angled his seat to face her and sat down.

Nerves stretched taut as she took in the tight planes of his cheekbones and the deep furrow between his brows.

He cupped her hands in his and bent his head to press a kiss to each of her palms. "Yesterday when I went into the office an NCIS officer was waiting for me."

She continued to study his face. There was a tension in his features that worried her.

"They're taking another look at what went down here at the house." His gray gaze, so steady, ran over her face. "There's a federal law called the Posse Comitatus Act that prohibits SEALs from acting in the capacity of officers of the law on United States soil, Zoe. The only way we're allowed to take part is if other law enforcement organizations like the FBI make a formal request for us to act in concordance with them. Or we're activated through the chain of command and through the Department of Defense."

She nodded. Where was this going?

"The night Derrick took you and the others hostage, instead of calling the police, I called my team." Hawk began rubbing the back of her hands with his thumbs. "Because we were able to disarm Derrick without lethal force, and because NCIS has jurisdiction over crimes involving military personnel, the local police handed the investigation over to them."

"I know."

"Depending on how the events from that day are viewed, our actions can be looked at in two ways. We took an armed perpetrator down in a hostage situation. Or we disarmed a fellow team member who had become unstable and was suffering from PTSD. It's all about perception."

The full brunt of his words hit Zoe with the force of a medicine ball to the chest. He had saved her life, her brother's, and Marjorie's. But he'd risked his career and his life to do it. His whole team had risked everything for them. A quick rush of tears blurred her vision, but she blinked them back.

She tried to swallow but her mouth was dry with fear. "Are you in trouble?"

"No, not so far. NCIS is viewing the incident as disarming an unstable colleague. But there are some other things going on right now, things I'm not at liberty to tell you about. And that perception could change. If it does, I'll have no choice but to take the heat. I'm the one who called my team instead of the police. I made that decision to save lives. And I'd do it all again. But if things go south, it's a federal charge or a possible dishonorable discharge."

Zoe pressed a hand to her throat where a knot had suddenly risen to cut off her air. Fuck that! No one was going to fuck with him or his men. No one was going to tear her family apart because he'd done the right thing.

"Because my men were armed—"

"The only weapons I saw were the gun Derrick had and the Taser you used to take him down." Her face flashed hot and burned away the anxiety to leave behind a firestorm of outrage. "Brett kept Marjorie in the bedroom away from Derrick until the police arrived. She couldn't have seen anything other than that, either."

"It's all in the report I filed, Zoe. I wasn't asking you to—"

"I know you weren't. My perception was that you were coming in to help Brett disarm Derrick."

"I had my Kevlar on, Zoe."

"Of course you did. You were facing an unstable friend armed with a .357 Magnum. That's the vest your Mom bought you when you first finished SEAL training, isn't it?"

Hawk's lips quirked. "Yes, it is. We always leave our military-issue weapons and other equipment on post. The only thing I brought home from the post was my Sig. I used it for target practice."

"Doc and Bowie were just dressed in their cammies." *Dear God, they entered the house without body armor.* But Langley Marks had had his vest on. And he'd stood between Derrick and the other men.

"Derrick had more than a fair chance at killing all of us. The situation was escalating, too quickly. The police would never have made it in time. Had you and the others not acted, none of us would have survived. That's the plain and simple truth." Derrick would have killed Brett and her to get to Marjorie. "If they try and say any different, I'll be there to set the record straight."

"It's because we acted at all that NCIS even has a leg to stand on, Zo. And because we went into the situation dressed for combat."

Zoe slid out of her seat and into his lap. She ran her hands over his close-cropped hair. "Why are they doing this now?"

"Because I pissed somebody off, because I was pissed off. They were giving me the runaround, and they weren't doing their damn jobs. They didn't like having that pointed out. I'm hoping it's a warning just to stay the hell out of their business. But if it's not ... "

Could her stomach possibly get any more knotted?

He focused on her, his gaze steady while his hands moved up and down her back restlessly. "When you came back to me after our breakup, I made a promise to myself. I'd held things back from you and it caused problems between us. I'm not making that mistake again."

His words grabbed her by the throat and made her own reticence about the baby seem more a lie than an attempt to keep him safe. The words were there on the tip of her tongue begging to be spoken. But how could she drop the news on him when he was twisted up about this? He was turning to her for comfort, not something more to worry about.

She cupped his face and kissed him. "I love you, Adam Yazzie. No matter what happens, I'll never stop loving you." She kissed him again and felt the familiar heat of his response in the way his arms tightened around her, the way his lips and tongue moved against hers.

The growing intensity of his kisses, his touch as he unbuttoned her blouse, set in motion a languorous spiral of need. She wanted to spread her legs and take him inside right here on the chair. But her leg wouldn't allow it.

Hawk rose with her in his arms and dodged through the kitchen door in the direction of the bedroom. "It's going to be okay," he murmured against her lips. "We're going to be okay."

Not if you keep lying to him, her conscience whispered. *I'll tell him later, after we've held each other. After he's less upset.*

He lowered her to the bed. She shut out the nagging voice and drew him down to her.

CHAPTER 13

Brett suppressed the smile determined to bust out. The paperwork Dr. Stewart had just issued was clutched in his hand. He'd talked the man into letting him deliver the paperwork to eliminate the wait. After nearly two months of jumping through hoops, he was being returned to duty. *Finally. Yes!*

He strode down the hallway and paused outside Captain Jackson's office. He had another speaking engagement in two hours. As much as he hated it, he was trying to look at it as practice for his speech glitch. Jackson's aide motioned him to a chair.

The Captain's voice carried through the closed door. "I told you I wasn't going to be able to make it."

Brett circled the baby stroller sitting next to the aide's desk and caught a glimpse of the child, about three months old, lying lax in the stroller, sound asleep. Something about the shape of the baby's head looked strange and his eyes were unusually wide spaced. Brett frowned and glanced at the aide. What was the guy's name? Oh yeah, Crouch.

"Mrs. Jackson's in with the Captain. The baby was asleep."

There had to be some sort of emergency. It was rare for wives to come on post. Command didn't encourage it.

"This is important, James. The procedure they're talking about is dangerous, and you need to be there to hear what the surgeon says." The stress in the woman's voice seemed to elevate the pitch with each word.

"Your mother can go with you, Marsha. I have meetings all day. I have a job to do here."

"A job more important than your son?"

Silence reigned for several moments. Brett and the aide, Seaman Crouch avoided looking at each other.

Jackson's voice fell to a rumble.

A sound emanated from the stroller. Crouch's head jerked up and a look of such panic crossed his face Brett almost laughed. *Afraid of a baby?* Brett laid the paperwork aside and got to his feet. In two strides, he reached the stroller. The child had spit up and was choking, his face growing bright red with the struggle to breathe.

Brett released the belt holding the baby in place and tugged him free of the straps. He sat down, and cupping the infant's jaw, propped him on his thigh and patted his back. The choking ceased. He was rewarded by another stream of cream-colored formula. This time it had soaked his pant leg. *Shit.* But his irritation was only momentary. Definitely something wrong here. Poor little fellow. He used the bottom of the child's shirt to wipe his mouth and chin free of formula.

"Rummage in the diaper bag and find me something to clean him up with, Crouch."

The aide rushed to do as Brett asked and produced a box of diaper wipes.

"Look for a clean shirt in there. Moms always pack more clothes."

Voices rose again inside the office. Brett concentrated on the baby, though it was impossible to block out the conversation.

"You're pushing us both away because he's not perfect, and because I brought him into the world, I'm not either. No one can live up to your expectations. No one."

Whatever Jackson said in reply was spoken in a rumble.

Brett peeled the soiled shirt from the baby's body and, using the chair next to him as a changing table, cleaned him with several of the wipes. The baby's movements seemed less active than he remembered his niece Katie Beth's.

Crouch offered him a clean t-shirt from the bag. Brett slipped it over the baby's oddly shaped head and guided his arms into the sleeves. He raised the child to his shoulder and rubbed his back. The little guy's knees wedged against his chest and his head bobbed.

The door jerked open, and a woman stepped out. Brett rose to his feet.

Fragilely thin, she stood only a few inches over five feet. Her hair, a butterscotch color, was bunched at the crown of her head by a clip. She'd been crying. The skin around her eyes appeared red, as did her nose. Her gaze homed in on the baby in Brett's arms, and she rushed forward.

"Weaver, what are you doing?" Captain Jackson's voice cut across the distance, irritation in every syllable.

"The baby was choking, sir," Seaman Crouch, who'd leapt to his feet, spoke before Brett had a chance. "Ensign Weaver was lending assistance."

Mrs. Jackson captured Brett's gaze for a second before easing the baby from his grasp. "Thank you so much. Alex is having some difficulties with the formula."

Brett suppressed the urge to shake his leg and free the wet fabric from his knee. "No problem, ma'am."

"Your pants." Her distressed tone drew everyone's attention to the spot.

Brett offered her a smile to offset the quick tears shimmering in her eyes. "I've been anointed before. My sister has children. I have another pair in the car, ma'am."

"Weaver, you have five minutes to get cleaned up and in here," Jackson's irritation hadn't abated. The door slammed behind him.

Asshole. Doesn't he see his wife needs help? Brett scooped up the manila folder from the chair and laid it on the desk.

"I'm sorry, Ensign," Mrs. Jackson said. She offered him a cotton diaper.

Brett quickly wiped his pant leg off. "I can take the stroller and diaper bag out for you and get my pants, Ma'am."

"I hope you have a shirt as well," she nodded to a stain on his shoulder.

Brett's gaze followed her nod. *Shit. He'd gotten the epaulet too.*

The anxious stress he read in Mrs. Jackson's face had him saying, "Soy formula might work. My niece Katie Beth couldn't tolerate regular formula, but she did just fine on soy."

She started to tear back up again. "I'll call Alex's doctor and ask about it."

"I'll help Mrs. Jackson to the car, sir." Seaman Crouch offered.

Brett nodded. He wouldn't have enough time to change if he didn't go now. "Excuse me, ma'am." He nodded to Mrs. Jackson and jogged down the hall to the exit. He jerked his 'good humor' suit from the back seat and jogged back up the sidewalk. Crouch was pushing the stroller out the door as he raced back. He held the door for them, then ran to the men's room.

The navy blue epaulet looked a bit darker for the scrubbing he gave it, but the rest of his uniform was in working order as he paused by the desk to retrieve his paperwork.

"Ensign Weaver, sir," Crouch addressed him.

"Yes."

"Mrs. Jackson wanted me to thank you again for your help, sir."

Brett nodded.

"I appreciated you stepping up, too, sir." Crouch offered him the folder.

"No problem."

"The Captain said for you to go straight in."

Brett took a deep breath and turned the knob.

Jackson stood at the window, his hands in his pockets. "Crouch said you had some paperwork for me." He turned to face Brett.

"Yes, sir. Dr. Stewart has released me for duty, sir."

Jackson accepted the manila folder with a frown and opened it. He flipped through the paperwork, studied the documents for a few moments, and set aside the packet. "There's a problem with sending you back to your team."

Brett sucked in a breath. *Fucking knew it. Saw it coming a mile off.* The blow still hit as though he'd been sucker-punched in the nuts. He breathed through the anger, but betrayal clawed at his gut nearly choking him. "What kind of—pro- problem?" *This was not the time for this fucking speech thing to kick in.*

Jackson's eyes narrowed. "Your position on NCIS's radar for the shit about the missing boy was a catalyst. It's brought scrutiny back to the team concerning Derrick's takedown. NCIS is trying to say the men acted in the capacity of police officers. I think they're trying to put pressure on the whole team to give you and Armstrong up."

"But we didn't do anything."

"How can you be sure if you can't remember, Weaver?"

Where was the man's belief? He'd voiced it the last time he'd stood here in this office.

He studied Jackson's expression, and anger as hard and unbending as iron ate up the hurt. "I have a good reputation in the teams. I'm a SEAL, and I've conducted myself as a SEAL should in all things. My record speaks for itself. The only way my enlistment will end is if I'm killed in combat."

Jackson's gaze shifted. "You'll have to wait until this is settled before returning to the team. I'll have orders for you in a few days. Dismissed, Ensign."

Brett forced his hand up in a salute he didn't believe the fucker deserved. You could judge a man by how he treated his family. Captain Jackson had dismissed his wife and child the moment he'd slammed the door behind them. Jackson would sacrifice whomever he had to in order to bring this shit to an end.

He wasn't going to be made into a sacrificial lamb to make Jackson's life easier. *Fuck that.*

Tess hovered over the computer, reading the article she'd discovered. She'd been searching newspaper back issues all day for articles about those men and women in Congress who had been most vocal against military spending, and in particular about the high price of training SEALs. And their training was expensive. Close to a million dollars a man throughout their enlistment with the teams. That was a hell of an expense during these economic times. But how did you put a price tag on national security?

Since 9/11, the whole country was more aware of what was possible. America's vulnerability had been penetrated in the most painful way. America's complacency had been shredded. And if it took a few million for these guys to stand between America and the bad guys, so be it. They could stop things before they reached our shores. With the other military contingents, they provided a perimeter of defense. She was grateful they were there.

And she finally had something to share with Brett Weaver. But there was information she couldn't access.

Maybe her father would have some suggestions. He'd be here in twenty-four hours. The familiar feelings of excitement and dread bubbled up.

It wasn't enough that she had followed in his footsteps and become a journalist. He looked on her job as insignificant because it didn't have a wide enough reach. And she agreed. But she was working toward her place in the news community. Building her reputation. She'd recently had an epiphany, and Brett Weaver was responsible. She now had a clear plan about which direction she wanted to go.

She had no intention of sharing it with her father. He'd find some fault with it. She should have been a boy to follow in his footsteps. She couldn't change her sex to suit him. And didn't want to.

Her cell phone rang, and she glanced at the screen. Her heart leapt. She drew in a deep breath. She had to get control of her response to Brett Weaver. He was just a man. A man who trained nine months a year and who was deployed to foreign countries to fight bad guys for six months or more at a time. She pushed the accept button and raised the phone to her ear. "Hello."

"I need to see you."

Those few words spoken in that husky male tone accelerated her already fast heartbeat. "Has something more happened?"

"Yeah. I'll finish up on a public speaking gig about three. Can we meet somewhere private afterwards?" he asked.

Where could she take him? Her apartment? Did she feel comfortable taking him there?

Did she trust herself taking him there?

What was she, a teenager? He was a source to a story big enough to put her name on the journalism map. She was an adult and a professional. She could meet with a man for an interview without jumping his bones.

But most of the men she met didn't affect her in the ways Brett Weaver did. *Grow up, Tess. It's your job.*

"My apartment around three-thirty." She said in her best professional tone and gave him the address.

"I'll be there. Thanks." He disconnected.

She ran her hand over her forehead, pushing back the bangs feathering her brows. She'd have time to double-check the facts she'd learned so she could share them with him. And while at the apartment, they could start on the interview she needed to do for the paper.

The key to dealing with Brett Weaver was to keep everything professional. She'd never dated any of the men she'd interviewed. She didn't intend to break that rule with Brett Weaver.

"Can I have your autograph, Ensign Weaver?"

Of all the things he'd been asked, that was one Brett had never heard before. He'd never expected to be a keynote speaker at a political luncheon, either. The guests had asked a hundred questions at least. They'd exhausted the subject of Iraq, Afghanistan, and all portions of the war on terrorists. He'd dodged at least a thousand political hot potatoes lobbed at him. Thank you, Jesus and Master Chief O'Hara, who'd prepped him for the gig.

And now this. He stared at the teenage girl's face taking in her Cupid's bow mouth and heavy eye shadow. "I'm not a rock star or any kind of celebrity, miss."

"You're a SEAL. And that's a whole lot *more.*"

The way she said *more* flashed embarrassed heat into his cheeks. Jesus, she was just a kid. To move her along quickly, he took the small notebook the girl thrust at him and signed his name, purposely scribbling a bit.

"My name's Candy."

Of course it was. Her beaming smile of thanks made him glad he'd signed the paper, even as an uneasy tightness cuffed the back of his neck.

He shook hands, and attempted to respond appropriately to the women's greetings and their breathless words of thanks. For the most part the men in attendance hung back and offered nods. Which suited him fine. Sometimes there were assholes determined to prove to their wives or girlfriends they were just as tough as he was, and it never ended well—for them. He certainly didn't need any bad press generated by an incident. *Especially not now.*

Fifteen minutes later, he said his last good-bye and headed outside to collect his car. He handed the claim ticket he'd been issued to a young teenager there and the valet took off.

One of the young men working at the valet station approached him. "Are you Ensign Weaver?" he asked.

"Yes."

The man removed an envelope from his shirt pocket and handed it to him.

Brett recognized the name Candy, but not the address and phone number written across the envelope. The handwriting swirled with dips and curls. Brett tucked his bonnet beneath his arm and tore the end of the envelope open. A tiny scrap of fabric fell out onto the ground, and he scooped it up. He raised the stretchy scrap, a petite pair of thong panties.

The man who'd handed him the envelope grinned. "It certainly doesn't suck to be you, sir."

Heat crept into Brett's face again. Jeez, what had that kid been thinking? Shaking his head, he stuffed the paper and panties into his pocket. Wonder what her parents would think if he mailed the panties back with a thanks, but no thanks?

The valet pulled up in his car and he exchanged places with him behind the steering wheel. He set his bonnet on the seat beside him, and fastened his seat belt. The guy with the envelope was still grinning as he pulled away.

CHAPTER 14

W hat did it say about him that he was sitting in a reporter's apartment instead of turning to his teammates for answers to this problem?

Brett tracked the sway of Tess's hips and the way she placed one foot in front of the other like a model on a runway. Just watching her as she walked from the minuscule kitchen to the living room was enough to make him hard.

The apartment was smaller than his, though he knew she came from a wealthy family. While the furniture was expensive and tasteful, there wasn't much of it. The observations tweaked a momentary curiosity, until she came into the living room with two glasses of tea.

She should have been a model. She wasn't as tall as some, but she naturally had the kind of willowy figure most women had to work hard to achieve. Her movements had a grace that captured his attention. The silky camisole thing she was wearing bared her shoulders and arms. Though her skirt nearly reached her knees, her calves and ankles were an instant distraction.

"My father will be here tomorrow," she said as she set the glass on a coaster on the coffee table in front of him. "He wants to meet with you. And I have some information I thought you'd want to know." She sat down in the chair across from him, took a sip of her tea, then set the drink aside.

"What information?" Brett asked.

Tess leaned forward, her expression intent. "There are three senators determined to cut military funding. Rob Welch,

Frank Skidmore, and Eli Drummond. Welch is the ringleader, but the other two are following hot on his political heels. All three come from states with only a few military bases and a small population of enlisted personnel. Who wouldn't guess that?"

She laced her fingers together. "From what I've been able to discover, only one of them has access to military intelligence. And he has just filled a position on an arms committee."

"Rob Welch," Brett guessed. He'd heard things about the man from some of the other Special Ops guys, and learned more from articles he'd read in the last couple of months.

"This is just speculation at this point, but three suspicious situations cropping up around the same SEAL team in a matter of months is just too good an opportunity for him to pass up. If he puts pressure on the right people, the situation could prove problematic for your unit and the whole Naval Special Warfare Group. The events, if they're played just right in the press, and before Congress, could significantly dig into the group's funding as well."

His injury in Iraq had triggered all of this. There had been too many inconsistencies in the reports. He'd read them all. Doc had seen him going back into the building after the charges had been set. Why would he set charges, and then go back in. Who had hit him?

If one of the terrorists had bashed him, they'd have raised the alarm and the rest would have bugged out. That was the anomaly that led NCIS back to the six of them.

And it led NCIS to the missing Iraqi boy. It gave the person who'd attacked him motive.

Had Derrick really done something to the kid?

I wouldn't have let him.

But what if he'd been too late to stop him?

The thought had his gut roiling. Tess's voice barely pierced the panicked sound of his heartbeat filling his ears.

"If we had access to his corporate or private bank accounts, we might find a money trail, but it's doubtful. From what I've read he seems pretty cagey," she said.

"We have to find the boy, Tess." He fought hard to keep his voice even. "Once we find the boy, part of the house of cards will collapse."

"But first we'll have to make it worthwhile for the military to find him. That's where my father will come in. He has strong contacts in Iraq. He's been covering things over there since Saddam was in power. He's going to go at the story about the missing boy from the Iraqi citizens' point of view. Build up sympathy for the families and lay it on the military to see that their children are found. With the satellite capabilities we have now, we might be able to search for and find the training camps."

She was so idealistic. "We find them all the time. As soon as we knock out one, they rebuild somewhere else and take up shop again. There's no guarantee the kid hasn't been killed in a bombing raid." Unable to sit still any longer, he rose and moved to the one large window in the room.

His heart pumped like a piston. The guys with them would have reported it if something happened, even if they couldn't file the report until they reached base. They'd have said something on the radio. He had to believe that.

Brett's silence, the way he stood looking out the window yanked Tess to her feet. She ached to offer him some kind of comfort. She saw herself going to him, sliding her arms around him from behind, and pressing close against his back. But she couldn't. She had to maintain her professional distance. He was just a source. Maybe if she said it enough she'd begin to believe it.

She was getting too close to him, beginning to care. But how could she not?

"Dr. Stewart released me for duty." His voice sounded hoarse and he cleared his throat.

The words gave her a jolt. He'd just recovered from a head injury and he was going back? Though concern snagged her heart and gave it a squeeze, she forced enthusiasm into her tone and expression. "That's wonderful, Brett."

"My CO won't send me back to my team until all this is squared away."

Shit. His life had been put on hold for months because of his injury. For someone so driven, so focused, it would be hell.

"I could be in—" He paused and his jaw worked. She studied the look of concentration on his face. His lips moved though he remained silent. "Lim—limbo for months." His expression of relief was followed by frustration.

Sunlight lanced off the scar on his temple. The reason behind the hesitation in his speech suddenly struck her like a blow. An ache settled in her chest, and quick tears burned her eyes.

He'd stood up there on stage in front of two hundred women. Knowing his speech might freeze up. Knowing he'd feel humiliated if it did. The courage it must have taken.

And how hard had he worked in the past two months to get this far? Probably harder than she'd ever worked at anything in her life.

"Doc Stewart thought being back with my team might smooth things out for me. I convinced him of it. And now I'm stuck." He thrust his hands out, palms up.

"Whose idea was it for you to do the public relations thing, Brett?" she asked.

Confusion flickered across his face. "My CO's."

That asshole. Outrage tumbled through her.

The need to touch Brett, to offer him comfort, rose like a tide. She raised a hand to his cheek. The warmth of his skin seeped into her fingertips. His pale blue gaze focused on her.

"You're going to get through this, just as you have everything else." If it was humanly possible, he would. But what if he didn't?

His muscular bulk, the strength of his personality, and the focus he projected, made her more aware of his vulnerability than she'd ever been of anyone's. She rose on tiptoe to slide her arms around his neck and hold him.

His arms went around her and he stepped into the embrace, bringing their bodies close. His heart beat against her hard and fast. Too hard. Too fast. And his skin felt feverish.

She caressed the back of his neck soothing him. "We're going to find the kid. I know we will." She rested her cheek against his and breathed in the clean scent of soap and man.

The longer she held him, the more she relived those moments when they'd danced, but the memory was a sad substitute. Her breasts ached with the need to be touched. The row of bars and medals on his uniform pressed into her, stiff, unyielding. She shifted, and his arms tightened. The thrust of his erection lay like a tormenting promise against her belly. Oh God, if she raised herself on tiptoe, it would be so close.

"Brett ... " her voice came out breathy and weak. She drew back to look up at him, and his mouth was there, covering hers, his arm tightening around her even while his hand ran down over her buttocks to mold her against him. Responding to the open hunger he exhibited, her heart thundered against her ribs. Her mouth parted, offering him access, and his tongue thrust forward to find hers.

I have to stop this. I have to. The kiss went on and on. *Oh God, have I ever been kissed like this?* He cupped her breast and ran his thumb over the erect nipple that pushed against the fabric of her blouse. Her will wavered, and she leaned into his touch, encouraging him. And when his mouth left hers to follow the line of her cheek and jaw to her throat, all she could do was drag in enough air for a sigh instead of the words she needed to say.

The stiff ribbons on his shirt snagged the neckline of her blouse. Brett hastened to unbutton his shirt one handed, and then dragged it free of his pants, shaking free of it and peeling his t-shirt over his head.

Wasn't that what she'd wanted? *Yes.*

Her breathing grew choppy at all the golden-hued skin laid open to her view, her touch. And as his lips took hers again, she stroked her palms over the patch of light brown hair on his chest, then over his wide shoulders layered with muscle.

She wanted—more. She wanted him inside her, moving.

His hand trailed upward beneath her shirt and found her bare breast. He seemed to know just how to touch her, how much pressure to exert as he kneaded and caressed her.

"I want your legs around me, Tess." His voice sounded deeper, huskier.

She wanted them there too, but—Her father's accusation, *'Are you sleeping with this guy?'* rose up to slap her out of her sensual haze. If she did this, he'd know. He already thought so little of her as a journalist ... "We can't—I can't—"

Brett nibbled at the sensitive area between her shoulder and neck. She shivered and caught her breath. His heart was thundering again, but so was hers.

Tears stung her eyes. "I can't, Brett."

He froze, and for a moment continued just to cradle her breast in his hand. The warmth of his touch seeped into her flesh, and it took all her self-control not to move against it in response. His breath was hot against her shoulder, and her nerves seemed to quiver beneath that, too. She'd never been so aroused in her life.

He withdrew his touch, but continued to hold her. When he drew back, his cheeks were flushed and his pale eyes looked dark. The open expression of desire in his gaze triggered a rush of heat to her cheeks.

"I need to cool down a minute," he said. He scooped up his shirt and disappeared down the hallway to her bathroom. A few seconds later she heard water running.

Tess clenched her hands and pressed them hard against her cheeks. "Damn it." This couldn't happen again. And why the hell did she feel like crying? This was what she wanted.

She'd apologize to him. She stepped toward the hallway and her foot kicked something soft ahead of her. Was that a ponytail scrunchy? She bent and picked it up. The soft fabric spread out as she hooked her fingers in the elastic. A pair of black thongs spread damningly between her hands. What the— Shock hammered her heart. Color once again surged into her face hot on the heels of the anger that sang in her ears.

The whole time he'd been kissing her he'd had a trophy from some other woman, where? In his pocket? A sound, half screech, half growl thrust up into her throat, but she choked it back.

Apologize hell.

She was going to kill him.

CHAPTER 15

Jesus! His heart hammered, his face felt hot, and his dick pushed painfully hard against the zipper of his pants. Just touching her had almost been enough. If she'd even attempted to touch him, he'd have embarrassed himself. He'd never been this worked up over a woman.

Eleven months was too long. And then to have Tess kiss him, hold him like she was as hungry for him as he was for her. Oh, man. But why had she called a halt to things?

Brett splashed water on his face and slapped a wet washcloth to the back of his neck. He understood the professional distance she was trying to keep. It would probably be smart for him to maintain one, too. But as far as he was concerned, it was too late for that now.

He had to calm down so they could have a reasonable discussion about this, about *them.* He wiped his face with the washcloth, then set it aside. Disappointment thrummed through him as he buttoned his shirt and straightened his uniform. At least he presented an outward impression of calm and control. He dragged in several deep breaths before he opened the bathroom door and stepped out into the hall.

Something whizzed at him and hit him in the eye. It stung like hell. "What the—" He slapped one palm over his eye and snagged the object as it fell with the other hand. He stared at the thing one-eyed taking in the color and texture of the fabric. Recognition struck him. "Oh, shit."

"Damn you." Tess stomped toward him. "How dare you come in here and kiss me like—like—"

For once he wasn't the one looking for the right word. "Like I've been wandering in the desert for eleven months without a canteen and you were my first drink of water?"

Her lips moved, but no sound emerged as she mulled that over. "But I wasn't, was I? Otherwise you wouldn't be running around with a thong in your pocket." She stabbed a finger at the panties.

Was she jealous? He studied her expression. *Oh yeah.* He fought off the urge to smile. "Yes, you are, and I can explain."

She propped her hands on her hips. "Oh, I'm sure you can." Her eyes narrowed.

He withdrew the envelope from his pocket. "This is what they came in. I had a speaking engagement at Giorgio's before I came here. A valet at the restaurant handed them to me when I went out to get the car."

"You're obviously interested in the woman who left them for you. You kept them." Tess folded her arms against her waist. "Not that it's any of my business."

"No, I'm not interested in her. She's just a kid. Sixteen, seventeen at the most. I'm not a pervert. I prefer adult women." He approached her, caution in every step. Petty Officer Langley Marks said women were like landmines. You step on their feelings, and they'll go off. Lang was almost always right. "Call the restaurant. Ask to speak to the skinny kid with the diamond in his ear. He's the one who handed me the envelope."

When she didn't go to the phone, he stepped a little closer. "I didn't smell like another woman, did I?"

Her cheeks grew red as another flood of color rose to her face. She swallowed and looked away. "It isn't really any of my business who you smell like."

Brett bit his lip to keep from smiling. He eased up close enough to invade her space. He touched her bare shoulder and breathed in her scent. "Tess ... "

"We can't do this." She took a step back. "You're a source, and I'm a reporter. I'm not jeopardizing my professional reputation by getting involved with you."

"It's a little late to pull the professional distance card, honey. I already know what parts of you feel like naked."

Her brown gaze narrowed and shot him a warning. "I mean it, Brett. We're not going there. At least not together. And if the girl who gave you that thong is as young as you say, you'd be wise not to take her up on the offer."

He grasped her wrist and placed the thong and envelope in her palm. "You can do whatever you want with these. I'm holding out for a pair of yours."

Clara focused the camera on the sun worshippers slick with oil. This angle made the reclining bodies line up like sardines in a can. That was what she was shooting for. Human sardines packed in oil.

She might not ever take another award-winning photo like the one when the kids were small, but the creative spirit she'd discovered through the lens of her camera pleased her. And everywhere she looked, there was something interesting to take a picture of.

Good thing she had something to occupy her time. With Zoe back at work, Hawk gone on a three-week training op, and Brett busy with the speaking engagements his CO kept giving him, she needed something to focus on.

Sweat trickled down her side as she lined up another shot. The dank, salty smell of the ocean brushed against her. The beach umbrellas fanned out like miniature Quonset huts all across the sand. Her cell phone rang and she fished in her pocket to retrieve it. She frowned at the unfamiliar number. It was a local exchange and a private number. She pushed the accept button.

"Hello."

"Mrs. Weaver."

The voice sounded unfamiliar. "Yes," she replied tentatively.

"This is Evan Connelly."

Clara bit her bottom lip. Try as she might, she hadn't been able to dismiss their meeting. She'd told herself he was ill and had tried to forgive and forget, but the ache remained.

"Yes."

The sun beat down on the top of her head. A rivulet of sweat ran from her hairline down her cheek. The ocean breeze created a tunnel effect inside her cell phone, making it difficult to hear.

"I'm calling to apologize, Mrs. Weaver."

Clara trekked up the beach to stand in the shade of one of the lifeguard stations and leaned back against one of the supports. The camera grew heavy in her hand.

"The way I acted, the way I treated you, and my father, was rude and uncalled for."

She could agree, but it would just stir feelings she was determined to ignore. "You were tired and not feeling well, don't think any more of it." She'd just say good-bye and put it behind her.

"I appreciate your making excuses for my acting like a two-year-old." The sound of him drawing a breath filled the silence across the line. "Mrs. Weaver, I'm trying hard to build a relationship with my father. We haven't had a very good one in a long time. The way I treated you hurt and embarrassed you both. I'd really—really appreciate an opportunity to make it up to you, and to him."

"You don't have to make anything up to me. You can just tell your father you called and apologized, and I accepted it."

"That isn't enough. I really need you to help me show him you don't hold him responsible for my behavior."

Would she have felt responsible for her adult children treating a guest badly? Probably. The pain she'd read in Russell Connelly's features before she'd left the apartment came to mind. "I can call him and tell him myself, then."

"I was hoping you'd agree to join us for dinner here at the apartment," Evan said.

Did she really want to leave herself open to—?

"I promise to behave like an adult," Evan continued.

She held the cell phone against her shoulder with her ear and pulled a tissue from her pocket to wipe the back of her sweaty neck.

"Please join us tomorrow night."

Clara stuffed the tissue back into her pocket and leaned her head back against the wooden support. She closed her eyes a moment while she debated. Maybe if she accepted, she could really forget about it. Evan seemed sincere.

"What time?" she asked.

"Seven. Thank you, Mrs. Weaver."

The relief she heard in his voice made it impossible to back out. "You're welcome."

"We'll see you then. Good-bye."

She murmured a good-bye and shut the phone. She was not going to stew about this. Or about Russell Connelly.

She had her own family to think about. Like Brett and his situation. And Zoe and her new job. And Hawk being away for three weeks. And what the hell she was going to do with the rest of her life.

Clara trudged back up the beach, camera in hand, scanning her surroundings for another shot.

Zoe dragged her thoughts away from the worrisome meeting she'd had earlier and studied her patient, Marine Corporal Crowes. He'd been reluctant to put on his prosthetic leg in front of her, so she'd helped him with it.

"Doesn't that gross you out?" he asked.

She looked him in the eye and shook her head. "Not at all, Corporal."

She'd studied his records last night. He had plenty of muscle in his thigh. His knee joint was still in good working order. He was receiving counseling to help him deal with the loss. With a little work, he'd be on his feet and moving on with his life in a few months.

But often the psychological pain was just as bad as the injury. She understood that all too well. She made some notes in his file and gave him some time to study the other patients in the room as they went through their exercises. It didn't hurt for him to see he wasn't alone.

With a little urging, he gripped the parallel bars as though grasping a lifeline and dragged himself from the wheelchair. Zoe rushed to move the chair out of the way.

"Just take a few minutes to adjust to being up."

Crowes' knuckles were white with tension. Was he holding on so tightly because of pain, or was it anxiety?

"This is going to be an easy exercise, Corporal. All I want you to do is keep your spine straight and just shift your weight back and forth. Like this." She stood in front of him, and resting her hands on the bars, demonstrated. "This will help you grow used to the feel of the prosthetic and teach you how to adjust your balance."

"Yeah, right," he breathed sarcastically. The anger behind the words was part of the grieving process. The man had lost his leg. Right now he felt as though his life was never going to be the same. Zoe ignored the attitude and watched as he shifted his weight gingerly from his sound leg to the prosthetic, then back again.

"How does that feel?" she asked.

"Like there's nothing there to catch me, yet there is."

"I understand."

"Do you?" There was a challenge in his gaze and tone.

"Yes, I do."

She tugged up the leg of her pants, exposing the partially missing calf muscle of her left leg. "I have a rod, a plate, and several screws holding things together. Enough to set off airport security. There are times I have to wear a brace. Since I've been on my feet pretty much all day today, you'll probably see me in it tomorrow."

"At least your leg's still there," he said his tone husky with pain.

"Yes." And so were the scars from the skin grafts and other injuries. And the muscle pain that persisted.

She took him through several weight shift exercises, with just one hand gripping the bar and then just his fingertips. Though he did what she asked, he remained sullen.

What could she do to break through this? He needed to take his anger and use it. She bent to place two scales in front of him. "Now I'm going to monitor how much pressure you're putting on the prosthetic when you shift your weight by using these scales. We're working on balance first. Then we'll work on getting you ready for some dance moves."

"I don't dance." Crowes stepped up on the scale, his knuckles growing white as he gripped the parallel bars.

"Well, you will after I'm through with you."

"I have two left feet."

"That can be arranged," Zoe shot back before he could dwell on what he'd just said.

After a brief look of surprise, he laughed. "What's your name again?"

"Zoe Weaver."

"If we're going to be working together, I'm going to call you Zoe. You can call me Cal."

Now that she'd finally gotten him to smile, she hoped she'd be around to see him walk, too. "All right." She smiled.

"Maybe we could go out to dinner sometime," he said.

She'd just been asked out for the sixth time in one day. A personal record, since she hadn't dated for nearly two years before she met Hawk. "I appreciate the invite, Cal, but I'm involved with someone."

"Involved or *involved?*" he asked, stressing the latter word.

"*Really involved,*" she said, emphasizing both.

"Is he military?" he asked.

"Yes."

"And if he had a leg blown off?"

Her stomach roiled. Just the thought gave her heart a violent squeeze. She looked up from the needle on the scale and focused on his face. Though he had a little scruff of beard on his chin, his cheeks were smooth. He looked so young and vulnerable.

"He loves me despite my leg problems. I'd have to love him despite his."

"My girl bailed on me. She couldn't deal with this." Cal motioned to the prosthesis.

Ah, shit. The memory, like a shadow pain, rose up to give her a small pinch. "I'm sorry. I've been down that road myself, and it sucks."

He nodded.

"There's someone out there for you who won't care about your leg. Your leg isn't what defines you as a man. It's what's inside that does." She tapped her chest over her heart. "You can let what's happened make you bitter, or you can use it to come back even stronger than before."

When he remained silent, she went into the next exercise, weight shift without hands.

"Is that what you did?" he asked, his eyes focused on the bars.

"Yes. It took me over a year to learn to walk again. I had to have several surgeries." Her experience in college had stopped her progress. But she wasn't sharing that with him. "My boyfriend showed me that my leg was a very small part of the whole picture. That's how I feel about it, too."

"He sounds like a good guy. What branch is he in?"

"The Navy."

"A swabbie. I won't hold that against him."

"My dad was a jarhead like you."

"Semper Fi," He extended his fist.

With a laugh, Zoe bumped knuckles with him.

She took Cal through several more balance exercises. He was beginning to tire when the aide, a huge man at least six foot six and two hundred plus pounds, appeared and pushed the wheelchair forward. "Dr. Hanson wants to speak to you, Ms. Weaver."

"Thanks, Tank."

She spoke with Cal a few minutes about the possible swelling of his stump, since he was unused to the pressure put on it, and parted with, "You did great today. I'll see you in a couple of days." She hoped.

"Later," he said.

She wandered across the open space of the physical therapy room to the hallway. A hollow feeling invaded her stomach. She'd had to tell Dr. Hanson she was pregnant. They'd given her the job, and in a little over seven months she'd have to go on maternity leave. It wouldn't be fair to her patients.

She'd have to explain to Hawk how she got the job one day and lost it the next. But maybe the news about the baby would wipe out his disappointment. Of course it would. He'd be great with it.

Maybe they'd let her sub for the other therapists when they needed to be off. Or take on a part-time position until she found something else.

Zoe tapped on the door. At Dr. Hanson's, "Come in," she opened it.

She eyed his serious expression and tried to fight off the disappointment that lodged like a brick in her chest.

After greeting her, he got down to business. "I'd like to go over what you did with each one of your patients today, Zoe." He pointed to a seat in front of his desk.

Of course, whoever took over her job would want to know about what she'd covered today.

They went through each file. He asked about her impressions of the patients and what outcome she projected for them.

"What did you do to get Corporal Crowes to laugh?"

Had he been observing her? He must have been. "I told him I'd teach him how to dance once he mastered retaining his balance. He said he had two left feet. And I said we could arrange that."

"We couldn't really."

Zoe's cheeks heated. "No, of course not. It was just a joke."

"He wouldn't even get out of the chair for the last therapist who worked with him."

"He'd just been dumped by his girl because of his injury. He may not have felt like working with anyone at that particular time."

Dr. Hanson shut the file in front of him, shoved it aside, and leaned his elbows on his desk. "You're an excellent therapist, Zoe."

He was letting her go. She pressed her hand to her midriff where an ache had started. "Thank you, sir."

"I wish you had told me of your situation before we hired you."

Her throat tightened around the tears. And she looked down at her hand fisted in her lap. "I should have told you at the interview, but I'd just found out that morning, and the job wasn't a sure thing. That's why I told you first thing this morning. In case you decided you couldn't keep me on, you could possibly get one of the other applicants."

"I see."

She'd burned through her savings soon after Brett recovered. And because they weren't married, she didn't feel it was Hawk's responsibility to support her. She'd have to find another job somewhere. She shoved to her feet.

Hanson remained silent for a moment when he rose to his feet. "There may be some difficulties with your health insurance. The pregnancy could be considered a pre-existing condition."

"What?" She jerked her head up to look at him.

"I said there could be some difficulty with your health care coverage since you became pregnant before we hired you."

"I haven't canceled my other coverage, yet."

"I'd be certain to keep it until we sort it out."

She drew a relieved breath and fought back tears. She offered him a shaky smile. "Thank you, Dr. Hanson. I really appreciate your keeping me on."

He nodded. "I'll see you tomorrow."

Her steps were much lighter as she walked back to the storage lockers and got her purse. She'd have a job to support herself and fill her days while Hawk was gone. And just maybe she'd get used to being separated from him. Maybe, in a hundred years or so.

CHAPTER 16

Yasin al-Yussuf stood at the window of the cinderblock building the soldiers used as an office and barracks. Humvees rolled out in a wave of activity, kicking up dust and exhaust. His driver, Aban, stood next to his car waiting and watching. He fanned the particles away.

"We have not given up searching for Sanjay, Yasin. He is out there somewhere."

Yasin turned from the window to face Captain Morrow. The man was similar in age and height to him, but his hair was already graying at the temples and appeared very white against the darkness of his tan. "Have you found the record of his delivery home?" Yasin asked.

"We have the record of the radio transmission from the SEALs and their cover that he was dropped at your house and went inside."

"What kind of record is it?"

"It is a transcription of their radio message to base. The detail returned immediately to base afterwards." Morrow picked up a sheet of paper from his desk and read from it. "This is Alpha-five-zero. The package has been delivered. He is inside and secure. Out." He looked up a moment. "That transmission came in at thirteen-fifty. That's one-fifty. At exactly fourteen-fifteen, two-fifteen, the cover detail radioed their ETA of fourteen-twenty back to base. The SEALs were on a strict timeline."

Yasin already knew that. It had taken some doing, but he had gotten the information about their next mission. "How can you be sure Sanjay went into the house?"

"The radio transmission says he did." Morrow set aside the paper.

The man did not understand what he was saying.

"In order to protect themselves and your son, they would have taken a roundabout route there and back. It took them fifty minutes to deliver Sanjay and thirty for them to return to base."

"Have you spoken to the men in this cover detail?" Yasin asked.

"Four were killed the next day when their vehicle hit an IED. The others were killed in action a few days later."

Was the man telling him the truth? He read the Captain's somber expression. Morrow had never had any reason to lie to him. Yasin tried to dredge up a small particle of sympathy about the American deaths, but his own loss was too raw. He settled for a frown.

"Why has it taken four months to find this transmission?" he asked.

"We already knew the timeline of the detail, and his ap-proximate arrival. We thought our first priority was to question people in the neighborhood and physically search for your son." Morrow drew a deep breath and hiked a hip onto his gray metal desk. "We've worked hard to improve relations between your people and ours, Yasin. But we can't be sure your neighbors didn't lie to us."

"What do you mean?"

"When we questioned them the day after Sanjay disap-peared, they said our military vehicles were the only ones they saw. But when an Iraqi team went in and asked the same questions a few days later, they reported another vehicle cruising the neighborhood just hours before Sanjay disappeared."

Morrow eyed him with a frown. "I know there are several factions who disagree with your support of our being here.

That opens the investigation to many other possibilities. We are utilizing the Iraqi military and police as much as possible, hoping to uncover what happened between the time our men dropped Sanjay at your home and when he was discovered missing."

"There is just one problem with that, Captain," Yasin said, fighting to keep his tone even. "If your men brought Sanjay home, and he entered the house, why is it neither my wife nor the servants saw him?"

"I don't know, Yasin. Maybe they were in a different part of the house. When we questioned the servants, they all said they didn't see him or hear him come in. Your wife was too distraught for us to question. If it would help, do you think she would be open to us questioning her now?"

Yasin shook his head. Levla rarely spoke and only ate when he was there to urge her to. "She is not doing well."

"Can you think of any reason why Sanjay would wait for the men to leave, and then exit the house again? Does he associate with anyone in the neighborhood?"

The man truly believed Sanjay was still alive. How could a total stranger have hope when he had lost his?

Because the man still believed in his men.

The SEALs had killed Sanjay. Otherwise, it would not have taken nearly an hour to deliver him home and half that time for them to return to base.

He looked up to find Morrow waiting for his reply. "Because of the fighting, Sanjay had remained close to his home."

"Yasin. I have children of my own. I know how I would feel if something like this happened to one of them." Morrow rested a hand on his shoulder. Yasin fought not to flinch away from the man's touch. "I swear to you, I will do everything in my power to find your son."

And what if your men were responsible for killing him? The words were there inside his mouth, waiting to be spoken. But with Morrow standing over him, his expression so earnest, so sympathetic, Yasin's grief rose up to strangle them.

"I must go," he managed though his throat ached with the effort.

"Don't give up, Yasin."

I already have. His feet felt heavy as blocks of cement when he trudged down the hall and escaped the building. He flinched from the heat after the air conditioning inside of Morrow's office. Aban held the car door until he slid inside. Though the windows had remained down, the heat absorbed by the seats burned through his pants. Sweat broke out across his brow and along his sides.

Aban slid into the vehicle and started the car.

"Take me to Sanjay's friend, Gabir Abbas' home," Yasin said.

Aban nodded and pulled away from the barracks.

Clara studied her appearance one last time in the bathroom mirror. *Not too bad for an old broad, if you didn't look too closely.* Her hair didn't have any gray running through it, yet. And from a distance the fine lines around her eyes didn't look too deep. But nothing she did was going to turn the clock back twenty years. With a sigh, she swiveled away from the mirror and opened the door.

Brett's small apartment had begun to close in on her. Since Hawk was going to be gone for three weeks, he'd asked her to come stay with Zoe, so she wouldn't be alone. The added space at his house was a welcome change.

She sauntered into the guest room. The pale green walls, and the floral printed comforter that matched them, projected a welcoming serenity. She fastened her watch on her wrist and slipped on her white sandals.

The faint aroma of chicken soup reached her as she wandered down the hall to the large, bright yellow kitchen. The white cabinets gleamed with a fresh coat of paint. The pale blue countertops with their darker veins of blue added a splash of coolness to the warmth of the room. Zoe had hung wide yellow, white, and blue striped curtains on the one large window over the sink. The setting sun filtered in from the French doors that led out into the sunroom.

Zoe looked up with a smile and continued stirring something at the stove. "Is that a new outfit?"

"Yes." Clara ran her hands down over her waist and hips. "Does it look all right?"

"It looks great. That shade of blue goes just right with your hair and eyes."

Clara studied the color. Joe had loved her in blue. After twenty years she was still picking clothes she thought he'd like. How pathetic was that? She was dressing for a husband who would never see her, touch her.

"You okay, Mom?"

"Yes, I'm good." She focused on Zoe. "You were a little queasy this morning weren't you? Are you feeling all right now?"

"I'm fine. It was just a little first day at the job nerves." Zoe turned to open a cabinet door and get out a bowl.

"I don't have to go out, you know. I can stay here with you and we can fix something more substantial than chicken soup out of a can."

"I happen to like chicken soup. And you don't have to cancel your plans on my account. I've been on my own for a while now, you know." Her smile held a hint of teasing.

"I know. You could go with me. I'm sure Dr. Connelly and his son wouldn't mind an extra."

"Hawk's going to call me in a little while, and I want to be here."

She'd seen that same look of anticipation on her own face twenty years ago. And felt the excitement hearing Joe's voice could jumpstart.

Why hadn't she warned Zoe to hold back some small part of herself? If something happened to Hawk …

It was too late to say anything now. Zoe was firmly entrenched in Hawk's life and the passion they shared. Just seeing how Hawk looked at her daughter brought back memories of her relationship with Joe.

She'd told Zoe that people loved wherever their heart took them. But she hadn't warned her it could be a double-edged sword and cause as much pain as it could pleasure.

"You're going to be late if you don't leave soon," Zoe said, breaking into her thoughts.

"I won't be late," Clara said.

"I'll probably crash after Hawk calls. My first day was really busy."

Clara brushed Zoe's cheek with her lips and gave her a brief hug. "I'll check on you when I get back."

Twenty minutes later, she stood at Russell Connelly's apartment door. The anxious feeling in the pit of her stomach kicked up a notch. She drew a steadying breath and tapped at the door.

It opened after only a moment's wait, and Russell smiled at her. "Please come in, Clara."

His smile punched through the anxious feeling, but set off a riot of nerves instead. He stepped back to allow her to enter. They stood for a moment just looking at one another, an awkward silence between them. She breathed in the rich aroma of roast beef and onions and searched for something to say.

"Thank you for giving us a second chance, Clara," Russell said softly.

With his masculine features set in such serious lines, she couldn't think of anything to say but "Thank you for having me."

"Evan's been cooking." Russell drew her into the living room to the couch.

"It smells good. How is he feeling?" She set aside the small purse she carried.

"He seems a little improved."

Worry had etched lines around his mouth and across his forehead that she hadn't noticed the week before. "Good." She hoped so, for his sake and Evan's.

"You have the start of a nice tan. What have you been up to?"

"I've been taking pictures at the beach. The tan is just a side benefit. I'm not really a sun worshipper."

"So you've taken up your camera again."

"Yes. Or I'm attempting to. There are so many things to take in here. San Diego is a beautiful city."

"Have you been to old town yet, or done the walking tour of the Gaslamp Quarter?"

"No, but they're on my list."

"Once you've wandered around San Diego, you could get on the I-5 and go up the coast. It's very scenic."

"Hey." Evan's said from the kitchen doorway, breaking into their conversation.

Clara's heart contracted at the sight of his pale thin face and the fragile stoop to his shoulders. He wasn't better. In fact, he looked worse. Her voice, swallowed up by pity, came out breathy and soft. "Hello."

He shuffled forward. His gaze homed in on her face. "Thanks for coming."

It seemed completely natural to rise, take a step toward him, and offer her hand.

Evan's hand was cold as he clasped hers. "I'm sorry, Clara."

"It's forgotten," she managed around the lump in her throat. When his gaze grew glazed with tears, she put her arms around him and held him. He felt so frail. She fought to keep her own tears at bay, and when he drew back, she offered him a hard-won smile.

He wiped his shirtsleeve across his eyes. "I hope you like beef. I think I've fixed enough for a dinner party of eight or ten instead of just the three of us."

"Roast beef and beef stew are some of my favorites."

"You can take some home with you," Russell said.

"I'm going to clean up," Evan said. "I'll be right back, and we'll eat."

He disappeared down the hall. Clara turned to look up at Russell.

"He's left so I can tell you." Russell throat worked as he swallowed. "Evan has AIDs, Clara. He wanted you to know, and wanted me to reassure you that I did most of the preparation so you wouldn't worry about eating the food." His hazel gaze searched her face.

His words didn't cause the shock he was obviously expecting. Somehow, she'd known.

He cleared his throat. "We'll understand if you don't want to stay."

Did he really expect she'd leave? Were people still so uninformed and phobic?

"As my son Brett is so very fond of saying, screw that. Well, actually he'd say something stronger."

Russell's brows rose, then he laughed, his smile clearing the stress from his features and injecting charm in its place. "I think I get your drift."

CHAPTER 17

Russell offered his hand, and a jittery feeling settled in Clara's stomach. Why couldn't she look at him without feeling this way? His son had called him a player. Was that true?

"I'll get you something to drink. Wine? Beer? Something stronger?"

"Iced tea will be fine. If you have it," she said. She followed him into the kitchen.

"We have plenty."

While he filled glasses with ice, she moved to the small table covered by an aqua tablecloth. White napkins folded into swans sat in the center of each plate. The glassware gleamed, as did the silverware. Two tall candlesticks, as yet unlit, were wedged into wooden cubes. And in the center of the table was a small glass bowl with a sprig of hibiscus floating in it.

"Evan has a thing about setting the table."

Clara smiled. "It's beautiful. I wish I'd brought my camera. It could be a setup for a *House Beautiful* spread."

"He'd be pleased to hear you say that." He handed her the glass of iced tea and used his own to motion toward the table. "I'm clueless about this kind of thing."

Looking into his strong, masculine features, Clara didn't doubt it. How hard had it been for a career military man to accept his gay son? But then being a doctor might have had some part in easing his acceptance. She touched the sprig of hibiscus. "So now you've learned something new from your son."

Russell studied the hibiscus blossom for a moment, then took a sip of his iced tea, his expression contemplative. "As a child Evan was more artistic than athletic. I thought he'd be an architect."

"I might have been had my mother not insisted I go to work with Carl so often," Evan said as he entered the kitchen. He had changed his shirt and combed his dark hair. "I learned to love the intricacies of the law. There are so many ways to approach a legal problem, to defend the undefendable."

Clara's brows rose. "Are you a criminal defense attorney?"

"No, I practice family law, which at times isn't so different."

His gaze shifted to Russell. "It didn't bring in as much money as Carl's practice, but I felt I was helping families do the right thing for their children."

Russell nodded.

"But in the end, we attorneys are hired to look out for the payee's best interests. Looking back on some of my past cases, I've been wondering whether I did what was right for the kid, or the person with the wallet."

"I'm sure most lawyers are trapped in that same quandary," Clara said. "That's why you have an opponent trying to sway the judge's decision to his viewpoint."

"It sounds as though you have some experience in family court," Evan said as he pulled back a chair and motioned for Clara to have a seat.

Russell set aside his ice tea and went to the refrigerator. He returned with individual plates of salad.

"Some. I had to testify in court at an abuse case. It was ... stressful," Clara said.

"That sounds like an understatement," Evan said. He reached across the table to light the candles with a small lighter.

"You could say that. Any time you deal with family issues, emotions run high."

She removed the napkin swan and placed the cloth in her lap so Russell could set her salad plate before her. On a bed of torn Romaine lettuce and spinach leaves lay thinly sliced pears arranged like the petals of a flower. In the center were raisins and crumbled blue cheese. Evan placed a small bowl of salad dressing, obviously homemade, in the center of the table.

"Maybe you should have been a chef instead, Evan," she said as the men sat down.

"I toyed with that idea, too. I have a friend who's a chef. He's taught me a thing or two about presentation." He motioned to the salad.

When it seemed the two men were waiting for her to start, she drizzled a small amount of dressing over her salad and dug in.

Russell had to admit the food was delicious. Though he'd done most of the preparation, Evan had stood over his shoulder the whole time and given directions. Without his vigilance, the beef with roasted potatoes and vegetables would have probably turned out a burnt rock. When cooking for himself he usually ate out of the pan or carton while reading or doing paperwork. Evan would probably think that uncivilized, as would Clara.

He listened to the two of them debate the textures of poached pears and baked apples both with caramel and nuts. He'd bought pastries from a bakery down the street, so neither of the fancier options was available. He was beginning to worry whether what he'd chosen would suffice when Clara turned and smiled at him. Her cheeks looked flushed and her blue eyes reflected the color of her blouse. He was suddenly lost in just looking at her. A need to be closer physically, emotionally, overwhelmed him. She was so open to Evan. Would she be the same with him?

"What's your favorite desert, Russell?" she asked.

You could be. The thought threw him off and he reached for the first thing that came to mind. "Banana pudding."

She laughed. "You're just teasing. What's your true favorite?"

"I've had a wide range of horrible deserts over the years. And, depending on where I was at the time, I've been grateful to get them. But I'm a pie guy. I like peach pie or cobbler the best."

"À la mode or plain?" she asked.

He smiled. "I'll take the ice cream when I can get it. I have a sweet tooth. I've bought pastries for desert. I'll fix coffee."

"I'll fix the coffee, Dad." Evan pushed himself to his feet. "He's used to hospital coffee and makes it strong enough to stand without the cup."

"Once you acquire a taste for that, normal coffee isn't the same," Clara said and gave Russell a wink.

He didn't realize how closely he was watching Evan until Clara placed her hand over his. The open compassion in her expression had him looking away. He was losing his son to a disease he could do nothing to halt. He'd looked at all of Evan's medications. He'd sent out requests to other doctors with an expertise in AIDs, and they'd all said everything that could be done was being done. Helplessness spread a void inside him. It was driving him crazy.

Evan had to respond to the medication. He just had to. Especially now that they'd finally reached a truce and had a chance to build a father-son relationship.

Evan returned to the table but didn't sit down. His features looked drawn and he rested a steadying hand on the table. "Would you mind very much if I skipped desert and lay down for a bit, Clara?" he asked.

"No, of course not." She rose and Russell stood. "Dinner was delicious and the table setting was beautiful. I've enjoyed being here with you and your father."

"I'm glad." Evan's smiled. "Save me one of those apricot things, Dad."

"Will do."

They fell silent until Evan's steps receded into silence and the bedroom door closed.

Clara sat down and Russell moved to the counter. He transferred the cream and sugar to the table and collected the desert plates, forks and the pastry box.

"He was excited about you coming and wanted everything to be perfect."

She looked away, and he realized she was struggling to maintain her composure. "I shouldn't have come last time. He's ill and—"

"It wasn't about you, Clara. It was about us. Our relationship hasn't been what it should be since his mother and I divorced many years ago. My numerous deployments didn't help."

"I know how hard it is to explain to a child why his father isn't there. If a spouse is resentful—it doesn't make things any easier. There were plenty of times I was mad as hell at Joe for leaving us."

"But you never spread that to your children." She wouldn't do that.

"I was a military wife a long time. Some women aren't cut out for it."

"Gloria never was. Evan was seven when we divorced."

"And Carl is her husband and a lawyer."

"Yes."

"And she pushed Carl to replace you."

"I don't know. I don't think I've said twenty words to the man since they married. But she pushed Evan to accept him as his father."

"Obviously it didn't take completely."

He raised his brows.

"When he needed someone, he turned to you."

But why? Why now? Sure, he was ill, but there was something else going on. And why wasn't Gloria calling to check on him? And why wasn't Carl? There was more going on than Evan was sharing.

His gaze fastened on Clara's features and read concern in her expression. "I shouldn't have dumped this on you."

"How many families and patients have you comforted over the years?"

"I don't know." *Thousands.*

She tilted her head and the candlelight picked out the copper highlights in her hair. "Why not accept that you deserve to be comforted and supported, too?" She touched his forearm.

For the first time since his fiancée Valerie's death, he was tempted to reach for what she offered. He needed— everything. Evan's illness was acting as a catalyst, pointing out all the time he had wasted, all the relationships he'd missed out on. With Clara looking at him with such under- standing, it would be so easy to just go for it—go for her. But he couldn't use Evan's illness to–to put the move on her. God, they didn't even call it that any more. They called it hooking up. He didn't need to hook up. He needed more. He wanted all the things he'd hoped to have time for. *Passion, love, a real relationship.*

He forced himself to his feet at the same time Clara rose.

"I'll get the coffee," she offered.

He followed her. And before she could reach for the coffee pot, he caught her wrist and turned her to face him. "It's been a long time since—" He started over. "It's hard to think of anything but survival and the job when you're in a war zone. Just keeping everyone alive so they can go home consumes you." He had been caring for other sons while his was growing ill. He hadn't dealt with the guilt that knowledge triggered yet. "I'd been a little numb since getting back, but that day we ran into each other at the airport—" Jesus he couldn't talk either. His face felt hot. Why the hell was he so tongue-tied with her? "This isn't the greatest time for me to even—" He pressed on. "I wanted to ask you out for coffee or dinner that day."

Her frown cleared and changed to a smile. "And I wanted you to ask me out for coffee or dinner."

So he hadn't imagined that spark of interest, or the sense of awareness that seemed to bounce back and forth between them. The knot in his stomach untwisted. He smiled. "Would you still want to go out?"

"Certainly. But we don't have to go out to get to know each other. I know that Evan is a priority right now."

The tightness that banded his shoulders relaxed.

Clara placed a hand against his chest. "Take a breath, Russell."

He did, and at the same time slipped an arm around her to draw her close. Her arms went around his waist, her hands sliding up his back. Her breasts pressed into his rib cage and her head rested against his shoulder. She smelled like cinnamon. The heavy heat of arousal rushed to his groin. It had been a long time since he'd felt that. The trauma of war had leached it from him.

When Clara tilted her head back to look up at him, he lowered his mouth to hers and kissed her.

Hawk narrowed his eyes against the glare of the morning sunlight on the hard-packed sand, reached for his sunglasses, and shoved them on his face. He looked toward the east. Desert terrain dotted with scrub stretched toward the distant Chocolate Mountains. The land looked so much like parts of Iraq and Afghanistan he sometimes felt he was back there.

With every evolution he felt closer and closer to a deployment and farther and farther away from Zoe. With the distance came an almost physical ache. He'd never experienced that before. It was more than just missing the sex, though that was part of it. He missed her physical presence, missed sharing his space with her, and his thoughts.

The exercises they were conducting, night and day surveillance and reconnaissance, reinforced the impression he got that they were revisiting their last mission in Iraq. Were they gearing up for something? Or was someone fucking with them? Or it could be a coincidence? Or not.

The barracks door closed behind him and Bowie sauntered up. "You okay, L.T.?"

"Yeah."

"Jesus, it's only eight in the morning and I'm already sweating," Bowie groused, "Why can't we find a cooler climate to wage war in?"

"Do you remember that mission when we lost the IBS and we had to tread water until the boomer showed to pick us up?"

"Yeah. You'd think a goddamn nuclear sub could have gotten a little more steam up. My balls drew up so high I thought they'd gone into permanent hibernation and taken my dick with them. I swear they were lodged above my bellybutton for about a week."

"Do you really ever want to be that cold again?"

Bowie's features blanked, then he threw his arms out in an exaggerated stretch. 'Sure feels good out here, doesn't it?"

Hawk laughed. "Whenever the heat gets to me, I just remember that mission."

"I'll keep that in mind. What's up for today?"

"We'll be in a briefing most of the day. This evening we'll be doing a night maneuver. Some of the SQT troops training here will be stalking us across the desert."

Bowie's expression grew serious. "That sounds way too familiar."

For a minute they remained silent. Hawk knew he was thinking about that desperate cat-and-mouse pursuit through the streets of the Iraqi village after the building had gone up. They'd fallen back and hidden in one of the abandoned structures for a time. But Cutter's condition had grown worse by the minute, and the al-Qaeda forces had gotten closer and closer to their location, forcing them out into the desert. Waiting for the Chinook to pick them up had been one of the most dangerous times he'd had as a SEAL. The assholes had heard the helo coming and had swarmed their location.

Pinned down, they'd returned fire. He'd ordered Flash to call in an air strike to get them off their backs so the helo could pick them up. That strike had damn near been on top of them.

His men had saved Cutter's life and his. With his knee puffed up the size of a basketball, he'd been unable to walk. But by God he'd held his own in the firefight.

"I have some things to do before the briefing," Hawk said. "You know the drill. After chow, see that the rifles are fitted for Simunitions and ready to go. I'll be briefing you guys on the scenario as soon as I've got it."

"Will do."

Hawk entered the dormitory and wandered down the hall to his room. Petty Officer Langley Marks the man who had taken over as Hawk's XO after Flash's disappearance, and his roommate, came out of the room just as he reached it.

"I thought you were going to the mess hall," Lang said as they met in the passageway.

"I have to email someone."

Langley grinned, emphasizing the lantern-shaped jaw that gave his lower face a disproportionately heavy look. "You have it bad, man. You just talked to her last night—for thirty minutes. You never talk that long."

"Zoe thinks her mom is going through some kind of ... " he gestured vaguely, "thing because of her retirement and— She was just talking to me about that."

"Uh-huh. And you didn't have to reassure her you were eating like a king, sleeping like a log, and not doing anything more dangerous than shooting at targets."

"Well—"

"I know, man. I have to do that with Trish, too. I don't think she believes me anymore."

"I don't believe you either, Lang."

Langley laughed. "I'm losing my edge."

"That situation you and I discussed a couple of days ago. I thought I'd shoot off an email to Captain Morrow and see if he could shed any light on it"

Lang's smile dimmed, and he nodded. "Good idea. I'd give him a thorough briefing."

"Our being here, the timing of it, seems a bit fortuitous. Or it could be just paranoia kicking in."

"If it is, mine is doing a shimmy and a shake, too. It has been ever since NCIS showed up on base. Someone may be playing a little mind game."

"Jackson's become a real bastard. He's leaving Cutter flapping in the breeze, and he'll do the same with us. They may have waved a promotion under his nose."

"I hear that."

"We need to toe the line here, Lang. The men need to be at their best. Whoever is fucking with Cutter has an eye on us, too. This current round of exercises we're participating in is like a revisit of the mission. Someone is yanking our chain."

"I hear you. I'll go check on the men. See you in a few."

Hawk entered the room and went directly to his laptop. He shot Zoe a brief email to reassure her and tell her he loved her. In his email to Morrow, he went into a succinct briefing of the situation with Cutter and Derrick. An uneasy itch hit him between the shoulder blades as he moved the cursor to the send tab. Navy network, Navy computer, Navy brass. But Morrow was a good guy. He'd bet his trident on it. And he had to trust someone in order to get info. And if anyone was monitoring his email, they'd see a CO concerned about his men and interested in getting to the bottom of things.

He sent the email and closed the computer. And if they read anything more into the message? Fuck them.

Tess printed out the article and added it to the growing stack of research she was compiling. After having done two interviews with women, she was scheduled to sit across from a man at lunch to do the third interview about his discharge from the Navy for a "personality disorder." She was finding a growing trend that concerned her.

Those moments of anxiety Brett had gone through when they were at her apartment had played through her mind again and again. What if the Navy tried to pull a discharge on him because of his brain injury or his PTSD? There had to be a way for him to protect himself.

Thus far, with every one of the people she'd talked to, their discharges had gone through despite their attempts to fight it. And now all of them were appealing that decision, but the process moved as slowly as a sloth's digestive system. It took months for any progress.

Her hand strayed to her cell phone for the fifth time that morning. What could it hurt for her to call him and give him a word of warning? She picked up the phone, thumbed down through her address book, and hit the number.

"Hello, Tess. I was just thinking of you."

How could he have that cocky assurance in his voice and be suffering from PTSD? For a second she allowed herself to dwell on what it had felt like to hold him and offer him comfort. She had to clear her throat, and she blinked her eyes to hold the tears at bay. "I thought I'd give you a heads up about something I've been researching. I'm doing an article on how the military is using personality disorder diagnoses so they can avoid giving personnel their retirement benefits. They're forcing discharges on them, either because they've gone to their commanders with other problems, or because they have had injuries or conditions that require long-term care."

Brett remained silent for a beat then two. "I'm working with a psychiatrist now who is paid by the military, but isn't enlisted. Sort of a civilian consultant. I don't think my CO would be able to pressure him into misdiagnosing me. Also, SEALs go through psyche evals several times a year. Mine have always been clean."

But that was before his head injury.

"Some of the doctors involved have received heavy-handed suggestions through certain commanding officers to push things through. The military seem eager to shed the weight of any soldier they view as a problem. I know you work hard to be top in your field, but because of the other situation, I was concerned. Should they try and use a diagnosis of PTSD to force you out, and things escalate, your legal fees wouldn't be covered by the military."

"I'm innocent. And there isn't really anything I can do but ride it out."

How was he bearing that kind of pressure?

With more grace than I would.

"I appreciate your concern." His voice deepened. "You know what that means don't you?"

"No, what?"

"I'm growing on you."

He was more than that. He'd gotten under her skin the first time he'd looked at her with those baby blues while he massaged her legs as though he didn't realize what he was doing.

Sure, he hadn't.

"You're a source, Brett. I can't—"

"One day I'm not going to be a source anymore, and you're going to have to decide."

"Decide what?"

"Whether to stand on the sidelines and watch life go by, or be a par—" he paused while he searched for the word. "Participant."

Was that really how he saw her?

"I'm working to break through my speech issues. I'd love to be there when you break through yours, when you finally reach for what you want without holding back."

"And you think I'll reach for you?" she asked, trying to scoff, but not quite pulling it off.

"You did once. I'm hoping you'll do it again."

She felt heat rise from her throat to her cheeks. She couldn't say it was a mistake because it was what she had wanted. Dear God, how she'd wanted him. But this desire to protect him was something she'd never experienced before. "I have to go. I'll call you with firm plans to meet with Ian when he arrives."

"What are you afraid of, Tess?" he asked before she hung up.

She hit the button without answering. But she couldn't avoid the answer in her own mind. She was afraid of being a disappointment to him. *Of not being enough.*

CHAPTER 18

Yasin listened to the soft sound of his wife's breathing. Levla had cried out in her sleep during the night and had only quieted after he'd drawn her close. He studied the smooth skin of her cheeks and the graceful curve of her brows. At their wedding, she had been the most beautiful thing he'd ever seen. After eighteen years together, he still could think of no other woman who compared to her.

The first time they'd lain together, he'd been surprised and pleased by her responsiveness. But neither of them had been interested in lying with one another since Sanjay's disappearance.

He ran the backs of his fingers against her cheek. If he woke her now, could they lose themselves in each other for a time?

When his cell phone rang, Levla moved in her sleep to cover her ear with the pillow. Yasin swung his legs over the side of the bed and answered. His gaze traveled across to the hall to his daughter's room. She, too, burrowed further beneath the covers.

"I have a number for you," a strange voice said in Arabic.

"One moment." Yasin rushed from the room and down the hall to his office. He scrambled to find a pen and paper. "Yes."

The man recited an American exchange. "Use the phone that was delivered to you. Should anything happen, destroy it."

"Yes, of course."

"He will be awaiting your call."

Before Yasin could respond, the line went dead. He lowered himself into his chair. He studied the number for long moments. If he did not call Tabarek, would he go on with what he planned to do? Tabarek's hatred for the Americans was strong enough for them both. Yes, he would move forward with his plans for them. But what would Tabarek tell the men who worked for him here? Would they come here searching for him? Would they hurt his family?

Yasin bent, opened the bottom desk drawer, and retrieved the cell phone that had arrived two days ago. He keyed in the numbers, and a familiar raspy voice answered. "I am in San Diego. I have found one of the men responsible for your son's death and my brother's."

"You worked very quickly."

"There are others here who are in agreement with my cause."

Sweet Allah. He had not expected that. "That is fortunate."

"The other SEAL is in jail."

"For?"

"American women are whores. They lay with so many men, they cannot even identify the fathers of their children. They must go on television to discover it. The SEAL attempted to kill his mistress because he believed her unfaithful."

He could understand the man's desire to kill his woman for being unfaithful. But if the man were guilty of attempted murder, did that not make it almost certain he had killed Sanjay? He'd believed his hope had died, but the thought cut him like a knife.

"He is surrounded by bars that are both a prison and a protection. I have not yet found a way to get to him."

Why did he feel relieved? He wanted him dead, didn't he? "He is already being punished."

"Not enough."

"And the other man?"

"He is often on the military base. But I will be seeing him soon."

"And then it will be over," Yasin said.

"No, my friend. Then I will find the others as well. I will call when it is done. I will need more money to leave the country."

He had no more money. He had given him all he had to fly to America. How could he get more?

"I will try," Yasin said into the silence.

"You will do better than try. Otherwise, your daughter may have to be sacrificed. She is lovely. Almost as beautiful as your wife."

Rage shot blood into his face and made his ears ring. "You will not threaten my family."

"You knew there would be a price to pay."

Yes, he had. *Allah help him.* There always was.

Muzzle flashes lit the darkness to the west, illuminating the silhouettes of buildings on the distant horizon. Though the bullets were blanks, the sound seemed all too real. Hawk drew a deep breath of the cold desert air.

They'd worked their way across the hard-packed sand and taken cover. Now troops were tracking them. He'd been right. They were reliving their mission in Iraq And whatever sadistic SOB had ordered this was really pouring it on.

"I'm getting tired of this shit, L.T.," Doc said from beside him.

The binding around Hawk's knee simulating the injury he'd received while saving Brett provided a reminder he didn't need. "We can't call in an AC130 gunship to rain artillery on the guys, so we need to go to plan B."

"Which is?" Lang asked from beside Doc.

"You're going to leave me and Greenback here, and you and the men are going to work your way through the opposition while I hold down this position. Then you'll swing around behind them and take them out."

"That isn't how it went down, L.T," Doc said, his voice flat.

"Just because they're ramming déjà vu down our throats doesn't mean we can't change history."

"There are at least thirty men out there. They'll capture or kill you," Langley said.

"Not without a fight. This is the hard decision, Lang. If there's no ground cover, and no out for you to escape with an injured man, what do you do?"

"You don't leave a man behind," Lang growled.

"You do if there's a chance you can save the rest. And then you come back for him." Gunfire came closer.

The eyes of all four men settled on him.

"This could have been the real deal. It's always a possibility."

"What do you have in mind?" Lang asked.

"The men will have to ditch their packs and move light. Does anyone have any flashbangs?"

"I have a couple," Doc said.

"Me, too," Jeff Sizemore, the new guy, spoke up.

"Give me yours, Sizemore." The Seaman handed the two canisters over.

Hawk slapped a spool of trip wire into his hand. "Doc, take Sizemore with you and show him how to rig them as booby traps. I'll have to set them off manually when the troops get into range. We just want to scare the shit out of the guys, not hurt them."

Doc's grin flashed white in the darkness. "I'm on it. Come on, Jeff." The two crawled out of the trench into the darkness.

The sound of gunfire crept closer every minute.

"The enemy was firing blind that night. It was pitch black. Chief Howard may have changed that scenario. That means you need to stay close to the ground and move fast."

"They'll be bearing down on you pretty quickly. And there'll be another unit moving in from the south," Lang said. "I read your report."

He wasn't going there. It had gotten hairy. "How you doing, Greenback?" he asked.

With his head wrapped in bandages, his body secured to a makeshift stretcher, and an IV in his arm, Greenback looked very much like Cutter had that night.

"I've never felt more helpless in my life. Not sure I like it, either."

"Roger that," Hawk agreed. "Wish I'd won the coin toss instead. I could use a nap."

Greenback chuckled.

Doc and Sizemore backed out of the darkness, one behind the other, as they each fed out trip wire.

Hawk slapped Langley's shoulder. "Get moving."

Doc shoved the wire into his hand. "They're about twelve feet apart, fifteen feet out. You pull the first one, you may not need the next. We'll be on them."

Hawk punched Doc's shoulder. "Play for keeps, Doc."

"Roger that."

The men disappeared into the darkness. Hawk checked his weapon, turning it to full auto.

"Do you think you could really make the same call if you had to?" Greenback asked.

"Only if I didn't have any other choice," Hawk said. He remembered Zoe's words during the short deployment they'd been called up on. Luckily they'd never left the base, but before he left, she'd held him close and whispered in his ear, "Do whatever it takes to come home. Whatever it takes." He'd promised her he would. If this were a real mission, could he make the same decision?

He prayed to God he never had to find out.

Sporadic fire sped closer. The men playing the bad guys were taking their job seriously. He spied stealthy movement across the desert terrain at thirty feet. His NVGs revealed greenish shadows crouched and moving fast. He positioned his weapon and waited. If he fired too soon they'd pin down his position and be on him. He had to wait and give Lang a chance to work his way into position.

His heart raced and sweat ran down his back despite the cold. Just like that night.

Five guys, moving in sync, crept toward him. Fifteen feet was close. Shit.

If the flashbangs were real grenades, they'd take out at least four and injure more. Would the men fall as though injured, as they should?

Five more feet and he'd pull the pin on the flashbang. Four, three, two, one. He pulled the wire on the first grenade and turned his head aside to keep from being blinded. A loud pop sounded and all hell broke loose. Fire erupted to his right. He raised his gun and fired at the first tango that stepped through the smoke. Paint from the Simunitions round splattered the man's vest and he fell, pretending to go down.

Suddenly there were seven more there.

Hawk pulled the other wire setting off the other flashbang and turned his face away so the flare wouldn't impede his vision.

Simunition rounds hit the back of the ditch he lay in. The percussion of the grenade popped.

"Cover your face, Greenback," he yelled as he rose out of the ditch and pulled the trigger on the M4, spraying the advancing men with fire. Blinded by the flash they returned fire but the rounds went wide. Florescent yellow paint bloomed on their vests one after the other, and they fell out of sight.

"Hawk, hold your fire!" A voice came over his radio. The acrid smell of gunpowder hung in the air.

Lang came through the smoke, his distinctively shaped jaw recognizable. "We caught them in a crossfire, Hawk. They're down. The chopper is one minute out." Sure enough, Hawk could hear the distinctive sound of helicopter blades echoing across the desert. Sizemore, Turner, and Doc came at a run.

Once aboard the chopper, Hawk radioed back to the Chief Howard. Everyone had come through the simulated battle unhurt.

The new men, Sizemore and Turner, high on adrenaline, were trash talking. Doc was freeing Greenback from the bandages and IV.

"Those flashbangs were a stroke of genius. They weren't expecting them," Lang said.

"Something to think about next time." He smiled at Sizemore and Tyler's high fiving. He had once been the new guy and remembered exactly how it felt the first time you kicked ass.

"Senior Chief Thornton will want to debrief us as soon as the other men arrive back at base."

Hawk nodded. He set aside his rifle to unwrap his knee.

"You know how many guys we took out, Hawk?"

"No. I counted eight from where I stood."

"There were twenty-five. And you took out almost a third, without getting hit."

"They were blinded by the flash."

"A third. That's fucking amazing."

It was amazing no Simunition rounds had hit him. The trainees would get hell tomorrow because of that.

"If it keeps Senior Chief off our asses for a while, I'll be fine with that."

"Copy that."

And he'd kept his promise to Zoe. Even in a simulated fight, he'd made sure he'd come home to her alive and well.

Brett settled in one of the deck chairs on the small balcony, enjoying the lingering smell of outdoor-grilled steaks. He studied his mother's face and smiled. Her skin had taken on a light tan and she looked … different somehow, but he couldn't quite define what about her had changed.

Spending time with her was both stressful and relaxing. Relaxing because he was always assured of her unconditional love. And stressful because he was so tempted to come clean about what was happening in his professional life. He couldn't dump his problems on her, not yet. Not until it became a code red and he had no choice. But keeping it to himself was a form of lying, and he felt guilty every minute they spent together and he didn't come clean.

"I haven't been neglecting you, have I, Brett?"

Surprised by the question he leaned forward. "Geez, no, Mom. You've been great."

"I just worry that I haven't been spending as much time with you as I should."

Brett grinned. "I haven't been around much. In fact, I was feeling the same way about you."

Clara smiled. "Maybe we can make a date. I'm pretty booked up this week, but say next Tuesday, if you're off, I'd love to drive up the coast and take some pictures."

"I think I can arrange that."

"When do you think you'll be getting orders?" she asked.

He laced his fingers together. "I don't know. My CO's still dragging his feet."

Clara was silent for a moment. "He's still testing you, isn't he?"

"Yeah." He shrugged and fought to keep his tone light, though bitterness edged in. It didn't look like Jackson would grow a pair any time in the immediate future.

Clara reached between their chairs and grasped his hand. "As a mother, my instinct is to march on base and kick Captain Jackson's ass. But I don't guess that will help anything."

Brett laughed. "No. But I could sell tickets and make some cash."

Clara smiled. "Your speech glitch is better. I can tell. It's helped you being on post, hasn't it?"

"Yeah. The more I concentrate and use my training, the easier it comes."

"Good. This time isn't wasted, honey. You're regaining your balance more every day." She squeezed his hand and released it.

"I know."

She glanced at her watch. "I'm going to the movies with a friend." She got to her feet.

"Anybody I know?" he asked.

"Yes. Dr. Connelly. We're dating a little."

The studied casualness of the way she said it set off battle station alarms. "Define a little."

"We've been going out three or four times a week. Just eating together and doing casual things."

Four times a week wasn't dating just a little. That was leading up to seeing each other every day. And how many times a day were they calling one another?

"I told you about his son, Evan."

"Yeah."

"He isn't doing well."

The catch in her voice had the volume of those alarms escalating.

"I know how tender-hearted you are, Mom. You're not getting too involved, are you?"

She paused before speaking. "He's such a sweet boy. We've become friends."

Meaning yes. Shit.

"Russell's concerned that something has happened between Evan and his mother. She hasn't contacted him since he got here. I can't imagine not speaking to you or at least getting an email from you every week. Even when you're out of touch, you let us know you're okay in some way. And since he's so desperately ill—"

"Define desperately, Mom."

"He's dying, Brett. He has AIDs and he's dying."

Her bleak expression made it worse. *Jesus!* His mom really cared about this kid.

"I thought I'd told you."

"No, you didn't tell me." He struggled to keep his tone even. "You're being careful, aren't you? I mean—"

"I'm not being exposed to anything that could make me ill. Evan is very careful. And so is Russell."

What the hell did she mean by that? Every protective instinct was screaming. His heart thundered against his ribs, and his face burned with anger. "This guy isn't taking advantage of you, is he? Like using you as a caregiver or whatever?"

"No, Russell has hired a nurse to come in three days a week while he's at the hospital. He's cut back on his hours so he and Evan can spend time together."

"And he's making time with—for you, too?"

She folded her arms against her waist. "Breathe, Brett. You're getting worked up for nothing."

Bullshit. "I'm concerned you're setting yourself up to get hurt, Mom."

"Honey, just living can hurt. After your father died, I didn't want to live. The only thing that kept me going was my love for you and your sisters. Retiring has given me a new perspective on things. I'm fifty-five years old and I'm alone."

"No, you're not. You still have us."

"But I need more, Brett. Your sisters have more. I'm hoping you'll have more than just your job one day, too. I can't bury myself in work anymore, honey. I've done that for more than twenty years. It's time for me to explore other options now."

"So you're exploring with Connelly." God, he sounded so jealous. Of course he wasn't jealous, he was concerned for her.

"Maybe a little. We have a lot in common. And we're both single. Why shouldn't we?"

Every argument he came up with sounded selfish as hell.

Are they sleeping together? Oh jeez. Can't go there.

"I've even sold some of my photographs, Brett. Imagine that! I just uploaded them to a couple of sites and they're selling."

"That's wonderful, Mom. You haven't shown them to me." Was that accusation he heard in his voice?

"They're on your computer. I left them on there so you could see them."

What kind of pictures could she have taken that people were purchasing them? "I haven't been on the computer here, just at work." He hated when he had to make excuses when he should have been on top of all this. "I'll check them out."

Where the hell had he been while she was starting a new career and having an affair?

Not an affair. His dad had been gone a long time. And as far as he knew she'd never allowed anyone else close. Why now? And why Connelly?

He felt like hunting the guy down and beating the shit out of him.

"I need to go, honey. I don't want to be late." She wrapped her arms around him and hugged him tight.

"Be careful, Mom."

"Always."

She was such an easy mark. Her heart was right there for the pickings. If this guy hurt her, he'd ... *take him out.*

As soon as the door closed behind her, he reached for his cell phone. His hand shook as he scrolled down to Zoe's number and punched it.

"What the fuck is going on with Mom?" he demanded when she answered.

Zoe was silent for a long moment. "Hello to you, too."

"Sorry, I'm just a little—" he ground his teeth, "surprised." *This is so messed up.* "She says she's dating my doctor."

"He's not your doctor any more. And yes, they're seeing quite a bit of one another."

"Well? What the hell is going on?"

After another long pause, Zoe said the last thing he wanted to hear. "I think she's in love."

After ending the call, Brett paced the floor, restless and strangely anxious. The urge to call Tess and talk to her was strong. He shoved it away. She didn't know his mom. Hadn't gotten to know her enough to care about her. Why would she want to hear about this shit? She wouldn't. But having her here would be a distraction. If she'd come.

And why the fuck was he so driven to share things with her? He'd never been that way before.

Maybe that bump on the head in Iraq had done something to him. He rubbed his hand over his head, roughing up his hair.

She listened to him. Really listened. Her eyes would focus on his face as though he was the only person on the planet and it just ... drew him in.

He picked up the cell phone again and punched the number.

"Hey," he said as soon as she answered. "How about some ice cream?"

She laughed. Then fell silent for a moment. "I'd love some."

He scooped up his keys from the breakfast bar. "I'll pick you up in twenty minutes."

Tess rushed to change from sweats into white shorts and an off-the-shoulder gold tank top. She tossed a sweater on the bed next to her purse. If Brett put the top down it might be chilly. She went into the bathroom to freshen her make-up.

She stared at herself in the mirror. The heavy, excited thump of her heart, coupled with the shine of emotion in her eyes gave her pause.

"What am I doing?"

Afraid of the answer, she focused on applying blush, then smoothed on a light touch of lipstick, brushed her hair and secured it with a black clip.

When Brett knocked on the door twenty-five minutes later, her heart leaped. "I'm in trouble. This is trouble," she said to herself even as she rushed to let him in.

She opened the door. A slow smile curved his lips and his eyes seemed to eat her up. Every nerve in her body clamored for him to wrap his muscular frame around her.

"Come in." Those two words had never sounded so suggestive to her.

"What did you do with the thong panties and phone number I gave you?" he asked.

A dropping sensation hit her stomach. Had he lied? Was he harboring an interest in the girl? "Why do you want to know?"

"I'm just curious."

Her chin jerked up. "I threw them away." Was that a touch of defensiveness in her voice? She needed to do better than that.

Brett's brows rose. "Is that all?"

If she told him she'd pretended to be his girlfriend on the phone, he'd read too much into it. Her cheeks heated. "I called Candy and explained to her that if she wanted a boy's long term interest, she needed to play a little more hard to get next time—with a younger man. And that she should put a higher value on what she'd offered you."

He drew her close and wrapped his arms around her waist. "I appreciate you handling it for me. Thank you."

He brushed her lips with his own, stealing her breath and draining most of her wary suspicion away.

"What you did was much better than what I had in mind."

"Which was?" she asked when she could get her lungs going again.

"I was going to mail the thong to her parents with a note."

"Oooo." She frowned. "Way harsh. She has a ferocious case of hero worship. Her parents would have grounded her for months. And she'd have hated you until her dying breath."

Brett grimaced. "Uh, that doesn't sound good."

"And her father would have probably shown up on your doorstep just to make sure you never contacted his daughter again."

"Definitely not good." His eyes narrowed. "How do you know what her parents would have done?"

She directed her attention to the dark blue t-shirt stretched across his chest and bit her lip to keep from smiling.

"I was a teenage girl once myself. And I did a couple of stupid things, too."

His arms tightened. "You haven't sent panties to some other guy, have you?"

With his flat muscular stomach pressed against hers, and regions below resting intimately against her, her mouth went dry as dryer lint and she had to swallow before she could speak. "I've never been quite that aggressive."

"You can—" His features tensed as he concentrated on the word he wanted. When his expression cleared, she sighed. "You can practice on me, if you'd like," he said.

Meeting his gaze was more than she could handle, so she laughed and shook her head. "I thought we were going out for ice cream."

"And a movie?" he asked. "I have several downloaded."

He mentioned a romantic comedy just released to DVD she'd wanted to see. She glanced at her watch. She had to be up early and it was already eight. But she wanted to spend time with him.

It was just research for the article on PTSD she'd just begun to write. Wasn't it? *God, I'm such a fool to let him get to me like this. It can't go anywhere.* "All right."

"My favorite ice cream place is close by," Brett said as she collected her purse and sweater.

They went to Ben and Jerry's. Brett ordered chocolate ice cream with white and dark fudge chunks and pecans, walnuts, and almonds. She ordered chocolate with gooey marshmallow and caramel swirls and fish-shaped fudge pieces.

"I think we may both go into a sugar coma," she complained as they left the scoop shop.

He rested a hand against her waist. "You can handle it, Slim."

She smiled. "That was possibly the best ice cream I've ever had."

"My mom's homemade is pretty spectacular. She used to fix it every Fourth of July for us. If she's still here, I'll sweet talk her into fixing us some for my birthday at the end of the month."

"You don't think you'll be shipped off somewhere for some kind of training by then?"

"I don't know." His expression lost some of its animation.

"It's going to work out, Brett."

"Yeah." He opened the car door for her.

He no longer sounded positive.

What would he do if he could no longer be a SEAL? His engineering degree would be there to fall back on, but would he ever be the same man? His whole psyche seemed tied up with being a SEAL. Because it wasn't just a job. It was a calling.

Though Brett seemed to pull out of that dark moment, he had to fight for words three times as they talked on the way to his apartment. He parked the car in the lot next to the building and came around to open her door.

When he reached for her hand she asked, "What's happened that's got you so worked up?" She slide free of the car.

He closed the door and hit the locking mechanism on his key. "Nothing."

"Did I say something?"

"No."

He was shutting her down. Something he'd never done before. She studied his face as the hurt built. Maybe he'd open up when he was more relaxed.

"I heard the movie was really good."

"I did too. I thought it would be the perfect blend of action for me and chick stuff for you."

She laughed. "I happen to like a good action movie. I especially love Bruce Willis' movies. He always plays a smartass like you."

A slow grin spread across his face. "I think I have all the Die Hard series. You could spend the night and we could do a Die-Hard-a-thon."

Was that a deliberate sexual innuendo?

"I have all my hair, I'm younger, and I bet I have more stamina than he does."

Yes, it was. Her face burnt and the heat spread down her body like a conflagration. Her heartbeat tapped a staccato rhythm against her rib cage and she was having trouble getting a full breath.

They entered the building and his hand rested against the small of her back as he urged her into the elevator.

"You look flushed," he said as he brushed the backs of his fingers against her cheek.

"Don't toy with me, Brett." She caught his hand and held it.

His brows rose and his gaze homed in on her face. "I don't see you as a plaything, Tess. You're too smart for that and too wary. I'd like to know what caused that."

The dropping sensation centered in her midriff had more to do with his comment than the elevator ride. "We all have experiences that make the whole dating thing difficult."

"Share them with me, so I'll know what not to do." They stepped out of the elevator and wandered down the hall to his apartment.

She should have never said the word dating. They shouldn't be dating. He was a source. Her mouth was dry and she swallowed. "If my father can't come through for you, or doesn't, is that going to be an issue?"

Brett straightened from unlocking the door, and once again, she was captured in his intent pale blue gaze. "Are you suggesting the only reason I'm interested in you is because I want to meet your father?"

"No, I'm not saying that." But it was hard not to believe it. Hadn't it happened in the past?

He stepped back for her to precede him into the apartment. "Sounds like that's what you're saying. If you're worried about that, we can move on to the next journalist on the list and put that issue behind us. I'd prefer we do that, anyway. Mixing business with pleasure never works out."

It was too late now. "No. My father's already on his way and he's sold on the story. To give it to someone else now—" She shook her head. *God forbid. Ian would never speak to her again.*

Brett tossed his keys onto the breakfast bar that separated the kitchen from the living room. He lifted the narrow strap of her purse from her shoulder and placed her bag next to his keys. "Tess." He drew a deep breath. "I'd hoped tonight could be about us enjoying being together, not about the damn story or all the bullshit that's going on in my professional life. If it can't be, if you're not interested in spending time with me, we can call it a night right now, and I'll take you home."

Tears stung her eyes, and she bit her lip. She'd never wanted to be with anyone as much as she wanted to be with him. But the trouble he was in, his job, this thing with Ian, all added up to a recipe for emotional disaster.

She forced her gaze to his face, and her throat tightened. He looked so serious, so somber. And she couldn't say she wanted to leave when she didn't. "I'd like to stay."

He nodded. "Good."

He picked up the laptop from the bar and moved to the television. With just a few cords, he had the computer hooked up to the flat-screen like a monitor. He turned on the television. "When we're down range, we use our laptops to stay in contact with home, and for entertainment when there's time and a connection, which doesn't occur together very often. I have some of my favorite movies saved on here. I just downloaded the one we're going to watch."

He straightened from the computer. "Can I get you something to drink?"

"No, I'm good." She moved to the couch and sat down.

Brett went into the kitchen and got a bottle of water, then returning, clicked on a file and the opening symbol of one of the national film studios came on. He settled beside her, kicked off his shoes, and propped his sock-covered feet on the coffee table, but didn't try to draw her any closer.

She slipped her sandals off and propped her bare feet next to his. His feet were wider, longer, and obviously masculine. His tan legs were dusted with a sun-bleached hair, as were his forearms. She leaned her head against the back of the couch and tried to focus on the movie, but his thighs and calves stretched muscular and enticing on the edge of her vision, distracting her. Her muscles both tightened and turned to jelly when he crossed his ankles, bunching up what lay beneath his zipper. She'd felt him aroused and hard against her. She had some idea of the size of what he had to offer. Every nerve in her body sang with need. She turned on her hip, and drew her knees up on the cushion beside her.

Brett laid a hand on her thigh just above her knee, his touch warm, the texture of his palm slightly callused. Her insides turned to liquid.

His pale blue eyes held banked emotion, mirroring her own feelings. "You could give us both a break and let me hold you at least," he said, his tone husky.

She swallowed with difficulty. Brett wiggled around to wedge himself into the corner of the couch and propped his feet back up on the table. When he raised his arm in invitation, Tess slid in against his side. She found a resting spot for her head in the hollow of his shoulder, and with her arm lying across the muscular slope of his stomach she began to relax. Just being close, sharing his space and his heat eased the raw edge of her need, but that aching awareness still hummed along her nerve endings.

"How did you know?" she asked softly.

Brett's ran a hand down over her hip. "This movie is supposed to be funny as hell. We haven't laughed a single time."

He wrapped gentle fingers around her hand and held it against his chest. "I'm willing to wait while you work things out, to go slow, but you're going to have to make up your mind, Tess."

She breathed in the subtle clean scent of his cologne and him. If she said she already had, things would spiral out of control way too quickly.

Who was she kidding? They already had.

CHAPTER 19

T ess stood at the baggage claim area and scanned the crowd. She swung between excitement and dread every time her father visited. Why did she still allow Ian to do this to her? When he appeared, his battered canvas laptop case slung over his shoulder, the knot in her stomach twisted. Had she ever seen him without that case? Even during her teen years, his computer had been more a part of him than she was.

He retrieved a medium-sized black bag from the carousel, and turning, spotted her across the crowded room. As he loped toward her, she studied him. His long-legged, lanky build mirrored her own, though he outweighed her by at least sixty pounds, and at six-three, stood taller by eight inches. His red hair, tied back with a black strip, was bright ginger, as was his beard. As he drew closer, she noticed heavier threads of gray wound through his well-trimmed beard and at his temples. The crow's feet fanning out at the corners of his eyes looked deeper, but otherwise he appeared just as he had when she'd last seen him.

A year had passed, and he had only contacted her twice. Once in the middle of the night a week after her birthday. He'd sounded drunk, but insisted he'd just been out in the field with some soldiers and was exhausted. The second time he'd called to retrieve the telephone number of a friend in France and to ask her to scan the address book he'd left behind and email him a copy. She'd emailed the book out the next day. He hadn't contacted her to tell her if he'd received it or not.

"Hello, Teresa," he greeted her and gave her a brief hug. He smelled like sweat and Scotch.

She couldn't expect him to smell fresh. He had been in the air for more than twenty-four hours.

"I hope you had a good flight," she said.

"It's been a long couple of days, but I slept most of the night. I'll feel more human once I've had a decent cup of coffee and a shower."

"We can swing through Starbucks here for the coffee, then I'll drop you at the hotel. I've texted Ensign Weaver to meet us in your room for dinner at seven. I thought we might need some privacy."

"Sounds good."

After a brief stop at the closest Starbuck's, his long legs ate up the distance through the airport to the exit, leaving little time for talk. They passed artwork along the way, sculpted caricatures of a group of people standing in line waiting to check their baggage or claim it, and a model plane suspended from the high rafters. Milky midmorning sunlight glowed from behind the sloped bank of windows that decorated the front entrance of the airport.

"They're doing some construction, so I've had to park in the temporary lot. We'll need to catch one of the shuttles."

"All right."

They located the correct shuttle and boarded. Ian shoved his suitcase in one of the racks and slouched into the seat next to her.

"Where did you fly in from?" she asked.

"South Africa to Heathrow, and from there to Chicago, then from there to here."

"I appreciate you coming."

His tan gaze, much lighter than hers, swept her face. "Why have you taken an interest in this?"

"I met Brett Weaver at a luncheon. He had just been released from the hospital and returned to partial duty. He'd nearly died, and he was still talking about going back. How he'd stand between us and any threats. It wasn't hype. You could tell he meant every word." She drew a deep breath. "There's a rumor that one of his teammates tried to kill him, and that's how he ended up in a month-long coma. I wanted to know the truth."

"Of course he wouldn't tell you."

"He doesn't remember how he was injured and he won't speculate about what happened."

"These guys are used to keeping secrets, Tess. He's not likely to let anything slip. I'm surprised he's come to you."

"He's not really come to me." Though he'd agreed to an interview and to help her with the articles she was writing, he'd met with her to get to Ian. Each time she thought about it, it hurt. It was just one more instance where she didn't measure up.

Was he pursuing her just to get to Ian? Well if he was, he'd get what he wanted and disappear.

Just like Kevin. The douche bag, that asshole.

A hollow feeling invaded the pit of her stomach. She was not sleeping with Brett Weaver.

"So he thinks I can get to the truth," Ian said, breaking into her thoughts.

"I've told him you can."

Ian started to say something then veered away from it. After a pause he said, "I always thought you'd call me for help with your career, not a story."

Tess remained silent a moment. "My career path isn't the same as yours. I'm smart enough to know I'm not cut out to dodge bullets and bombs. I'd rather dodge the verbal ones here. I write about people and you write about events."

"Is that what you think I do?"

"They're events that have affected people, or will, but you rarely dig into the personal aftermath."

"And you do?" he asked, his brows raised, skepticism in his expression.

"I've been talking to my boss about a series and also a new column. It will deal with people. The traumatic experiences people go through, and how they've overcome them."

At his continued silence, heat raced to her face as defensive anger clutched her chest. "Some of the issues aren't easy. Like a woman whose son is on death row in Florida, or an internationally known artist who's lost his eyesight. Does that sound like puff to you?"

"No, it doesn't. It sounds like an excellent Sunday insert to the local paper."

Nothing she did would ever be good enough because she *refused* to compete with him. Tears burned her eyes and she was grateful when the shuttle moved forward and gave her an excuse to look away.

Why couldn't he just be a regular father and love her?

Why did she look to him for approval? Anger and pain tumbled together into a hard knot in her stomach. She grabbed onto the anger and held on.

When the shuttle finally stopped, they got off and wandered further up the row to her car. When they were in the car she asked. "Would you like to stop for a meal? Check-in time at the motel is noon."

"I'm good."

She dragged her seatbelt across her chest and snapped it shut.

"I wasn't denigrating the choices you've made for your stories, Tess."

She froze for a moment. "Sure you were." She shrugged. "I've grown used to it in the last five years, Ian." She started the car and turned to back out.

"My intent has always been to challenge you."

She paused to study his face for a moment. The tide of anger she was riding crested. "No, it hasn't." He was slapping her down, and she'd had enough.

His odd tawny eyes narrowed and his long angular face tightened "You can give me the name of the hotel and I can call a cab," he said.

"It's the Holiday Inn on the Bay. We can be there in three minutes. I'll drop you there. They have three restaurants. You can hang out in one of them and wait for your room to be ready."

She jerked the gear into reverse and put on the gas. Silence fell between them as she maneuvered the vehicle into the escaping traffic and turned south onto Harbor Drive.

"I haven't been here in a while. I'd like to go to Mission Beach. You could hang out with your old man for a while and give me an opportunity to apologize."

That was something new. He'd never said he was sorry for anything before. And he still hadn't.

But he had flown in from South Africa for this interview, an interview she had asked him to do.

"How long have you been out of the country?" she asked as she turned onto India Street toward Mission Bay.

"Two months."

Why did he want to spend months away from home in places where he could be wounded or killed? "Where were you?"

"A game reserve covering the attacks on the white rhinos. I think these ignorant bastards who poach their horns, and the even more ignorant bastards who purchase them, may finally succeed in wiping them out."

The quiet anger she heard in his voice had Tess glancing at his profile. Had he finally decided to truly care about something besides his career?

"They tranquilize them then hack out their horns with machetes. One of the cows–half of her face was gone and she was still alive."

Tess flinched away from the image.

"Seeing that massive creature disfigured and left for dead just seemed more wrong than I can find words to describe."

"What happened to her?" Tess asked.

"The vet had to put her down."

She flinched. "I'm sorry, Ian."

He shrugged. "It was just an event I wrote about."

Tess drew a deep breath as guilt tap-danced on her conscience. Had she been too hard on him or was he playing her?

What kind of daughter was she that she had to ask that?

"When is the piece you wrote going to be released to the AP?"

"Probably tomorrow since it wasn't time sensitive."

"I'll be on the lookout for it. My editor will be interested in running it." She glanced at his profile. "Did you go out with the patrols looking for the poachers?"

"Yes. Damn bastards are fast and they know the terrain. Hit and run, and they're gone long before the animal is even discovered."

Tess shook her head. "I know the situation is more complex than the killing of the animals."

"Everything boils down to money and ignorance, Tess. Everything." He ran a hand over his jaw. "What about this guy Brett Weaver?"

"I don't think he's motivated by money. But he does want to save his career."

"And do you think he's really about to be accused of murder?"

"I think he has good instincts and something has happened that's sending him warning signals. He says a good SEAL prepares for the worst and hopes it doesn't happen."

"He could be guilty and just looking for a way to cover his ass. For a small percentage of the troops, it hasn't been their finest hour."

Guilty? Her stomach muscles clenched. Brett was not a murderer. He had probably killed in defense of his country and the other men in his team, but he wasn't a cold-blooded murderer. After seeing him with his family and his friends, she'd never believe it.

"And why isn't he going up the chain of command on this thing?" Ian asked.

"I think he has, but from what little he's told me, someone is stonewalling him."

"And it only takes one link of the chain who's more interested in covering his own ass than covering his men to do that."

"Maybe he'll tell you who it is," Tess said, a wistful note in her voice.

Ian's head jerked around and his gaze went sharp and flat. "You've not gotten involved with this guy?"

There was involved and *involved.* "No, I haven't." But it didn't stop her from wishing. She just couldn't go down that road with Brett. She'd feel as abandoned as she did each time her father walked away from her. The fact that she was even imaging what a serious relationship with him would be like had her heart racing and her mouth going dry. After what had happened in her apartment and the other night in his— As soon as the series was finished she had to cut off contact with him. She had to.

Clara shifted her attention back from the pale blue early morning sky. The light was soft as though it shone through a filter. A faint smell of exhaust from the early morning rush hour still hung in the air, blending with the rose bush Russell had planted in a huge pot just outside the balcony door. That he'd done that for her gave her a special thrill.

She leaned forward on her elbows to study the chessboard. It had become their morning routine when she visited to play chess with Evan while Russell finished paperwork.

These moments with Evan were a blessing. He was witty and sharp and above all a sweet man. Their first experience together was almost forgotten in her growing fondness for him. She didn't know how to protect herself from that, wasn't sure she could if she'd wanted to. He was burrowing into her heart just as easily as Russell seemed to be doing.

She jumped Evan's pawn and moved the knight into position.

"I believe I've been hustled. You said you played, but you didn't say you were a pro," Evan said.

"Not even close, but I used to play with Brett quite a bit. He, like his father, loves war games and strategy."

"Do you have pictures of your children? I'd like to see them."

"Certainly. If you'd like to meet them, we can have a family dinner or something at Hawk's house," she offered. She hadn't wanted to push that until Evan was ready. She dragged her purse from behind one of the longue chairs and took out her billfold.

"I'd like that, when I'm a little stronger." He opened the flap where the pictures lay in their plastic sleeves and studied them.

"Zoe and—"

"Sharon," she supplied.

"They both look a great deal like you."

He flipped the picture. "That's Brett. He'd just gotten his trident."

"He's gorgeous."

She laughed at hearing her son described like that by a man. "Yes, he is."

"This is Joe, your husband?"

"Yes." She studied the picture, long faded to sepia from exposure. She'd just moved it every time she changed billfolds.

"Do you believe in soul mates?"

She smiled. "Yes, I do."

"Do you think you get a shot at more than one?"

"I hope so."

He smiled. "And these two princesses?"

"They're Katie Beth and Ali Marie. I can't believe my daughter bought into that southern tradition choosing two names for her children. It's so stereotypical. But it seems to suit both the girls. Katie Beth just turned five and Ali Marie is five months old now."

"They're your legacy. And they both favor you." He handed her back her billfold.

"For now. They could change any moment. That's the way with young children."

"I always hoped to have children," Evan said, a wistful look on his face. "Do you think it wrong for same sex couples to have children? Be honest."

Clara thought a moment. "I've seen children neglected, abused, molested, and die in accidents and of disease since I've been teaching, Evan. I don't really care if their parents are same sex, lesbian or gay, straight, married, cohabitating, divorced, bi-racial or what. If they love and take care of them, which is basically what all children need and want, I don't think it matters. The kids just need them to be there and to pay attention. The children need to be their priority, not an afterthought."

"Don't hold anything back now, Clara," he teased.

She laughed.

After a moment's silence, he returned to the chess match. He moved his knight forward.

The move posed a threat to her queen, and she moved the piece back out of striking distance.

"I wish you'd been my mother."

Her heart plunged into her stomach and she looked up to find his brown eyes focused on her face with such sadness that instant tears threatened. What had happened with his mother that could have caused him to feel that way?

"The only things my mother carries in her wallet are her charge cards. And the only attention she was willing to shower on me was when she used me like a weapon or a bargaining chip—" he stopped. He ran his fingers through his thinning hair. "I don't really want to talk about this."

A bargaining chip? How had she done that?

Clara rested her hand on Evan's forearm, and after a moment his hand covered hers and he gave it a squeeze. Her heart ached for him.

A few minutes later, when he won the match, she rose from her seat and moved to stand behind him and rest her cheek against his and give him a hug. "Shall I show you what a good loser I am by getting you a drink? I'm going to make myself a glass of iced tea."

"Do you know how to make real coco?" he asked.

"Yes, I do."

"I'd love some."

Anything that was fattening and might help him gain a little weight was fine by her. She had just stirred the coco and sugar into the milk and placed the pot on the burner when Russell came to stand next to her.

"That smells good." His gray hair was ruffed where he'd combed his fingers through it, and his glasses hung from the front of his shirt.

"Evan wanted some coco. Do you want some? I can add another helping of everything to the pot."

"No, I'll stick with tea. Though it is tempting." He slipped his arms around her waist and brushed his lips against her cheek. "But not as tempting as you."

With his tall frame pressed close against her from behind, her whole body heated with a wonderful surge of desire that left her lower limbs weak. She'd thought those feelings were long dead. But Russell Connelly seemed to trigger them without much effort at all. "That was a very good line, Captain Connelly."

"No line, just the truth," he rested his cheek against hers. "One of these days we need to spend a day together, just the two of us, Clara. As much as I appreciate your willingness to include Evan, I want some time alone with you."

She laid her hand on his forearm, felt the muscle there thick and strong, and rested back against him. She had missed the sturdiness of a man's body against hers. Missed being held and kissed. And missed other things as well.

Her mouth was suddenly dry with longing. "Whenever you're free, just give me a call."

"I hope you mean that, because I'm going to," he warned. He found the sensitive area behind her ear with his lips.

She shivered.

When he released her and moved toward the door to the balcony, she drew a deep breath of regret. He'd left her aching for more.

He paused in front of the sliding glass door. With the deep cleft in his chin and his beard-shadowed jaw, he looked heart-tuggingly masculine. His brown eyes looked dark. "What about tomorrow?"

Her face grew hot and her heart beat so hard she had to fight to draw breath. "Tomorrow would be good."

"It's a date."

Brett shoved another clip into his Sig Sauer P228 and faced the target, feet apart, knees bent, arms forward, hands in position. The stance was second nature to him. He squeezed the 4.4-pound trigger and fired in controlled bursts. Each of the thirteen plus one rounds hit the lighter circle positioned over the target's head, shredding the cardboard. He lowered the empty pistol to his side and studied the target.

"Hold fire." The command came down the line from Petty Officer Newton. Though Brett wasn't one of the BUD/S students, he reloaded his clip and held his fire.

Newton wandered down the line, checking each man's progress, and until he came to Brett. He eyed the distant black silhouette with its head in tatters. "You have a serious grudge against that target, Ensign Weaver."

Brett smiled. "Just keeping my skill level up, Petty Officer Newton."

"I know you're as good with a gun as you are a knife. We're shorthanded today. If you want to lend a hand with some instruction, we could use the help."

Finally, he could do something useful. Brett suppressed a grin. "Sure, I have some time." He secured his sidearm in his holster.

"I'll clear it with my CO," Newton said, and, reaching into his pocket, flipped open his cell phone to make the call.

Brett sauntered down the wooden railing separating the shooters from the range and checked out each man's target. The level of marksmanship the trainees exhibited ranged from excellent to mediocre. The latter performance would change in a hurry with a little more practice and a few pointers.

Newton shot him a thumbs up as he closed his phone, and Brett moved in on one of the two students he saw needed instruction. After some work on stance and sighting with the seaman, the he seemed more confident and Brett moved on to the other student.

As Newton ordered a prepare to fire, Brett slipped on the protective headgear Newton had given him. "Fire." A simultaneous explosion of sound followed, muffled to a roar by the safety gear.

When the firing stopped, he walked down to check the targets. The two men had done much better.

The short-barreled M4 rifle came next. He loved this shit. He was in his element with a rifle in his hands. Why wouldn't Jackson assign him to instructor duty?

Because the CO thought he wasn't the perfect SEAL anymore.

Mrs. Jackson's words from the other day played through his head. *No one can live up to your expectations. No one.*

Was that what this was about? Did Jackson think because he'd suffered a brain injury he was like his son, Alex?

Brett shook his head. As much sympathy as he felt for the little guy, he couldn't equate himself with the child. He'd read the evals Dr. Stewart had sent to Jackson. They were all excellent. The doctor had given him a clean bill of health and released him to full duty.

But if Jackson was fixated on the head injury, he would try to find a way to force him off the team and out of the service. And transferring to another team would be out as well. He wouldn't pass on an operator he believed wasn't at the top of his game to another team.

Jackson was isolating him from his team, and any help they might offer him. He had to find a way to protect his back.

Was he growing paranoid? Was that part of his PTSD?

He rubbed a hand down the side of his face. The high he'd experienced only moments before had taken a nosedive quicker than a FA-18 Hornet after a ground target. Shit.

Maybe he should talk to Tess about it? *Whoa*—

The woman was a reporter. They wanted each other, but the distance she kept between them ensured he reined in this insane need to share. Just because he wanted to tear her clothes off with his teeth didn't mean he could trust her with any of this shit.

And he certainly couldn't talk to her about the PTSD.

PTSD was a sneaky mother. He never knew when his heart rate and blood pressure would shoot up and he'd be thrown into a panic. He'd almost lost it when he was last with Tess, but he'd held it together. Or it could have been the way she'd distracted him when she'd changed the direction of his thoughts and feelings. *Oh, yeah.*

He couldn't mention the PTSD to his mom. She'd get worried and upset, and it wouldn't help either of them in the long run.

Maybe Zoe. She already knew about the PTSD. She always had some good advice about things, and she knew how to keep a secret. Yeah, he'd talk to Zoe. Maybe. Probably not. She was already worried about Hawk. She didn't need anything else gnawing at her.

He had to shake this shit off for a while and just enjoy doing what he was trained to do.

He sauntered down the shooting range and studied the targets. He paused just behind one of the students and waited for the firing to cease.

Brett hung his sunglasses on his shirt, approached the student, and asked his name. Accepting the rifle from Cramer, he demonstrated to the Ensign how to lean into the butt of the gun as it was fired to better absorb the impact. Though Cramer was doing that, the percussion made the barrel jump, and he wasn't bringing it back into position completely before firing again. It was throwing his aim off by a few inches. Inches that could count in a close-quarter firefight.

"Hug it in like it's a woman you're about to dance with. This lady will save your life, and you want her directed where you need it. Stiffen your muscles each time you fire so that they will pull the barrel back into place again, like a spring, before you squeeze the trigger again." Brett swiveled the rifle barrel up to return it to Cramer. The strap snagged his sunglasses and they fell to the ground.

"Thank you, sir," Cramer said.

Brett stepped away, giving Cramer room to reload while he bent to pick up the glasses. Cramer turned and the metal stock of the gun came right at Brett's face. He shoved up a hand to block it. His palm absorbed the impact, but he staggered and threw out a hand to catch himself.

For a moment the world flashed green as though he were looking through NVGs. A blurred image of someone standing over him was overwhelmed by the memory of a metal gun-stock plunging toward his face.

"Jesus. I'm sorry, Ensign Weaver," Cramer's voice jerked him back to the present.

Brett blinked to clear his vision and focused on Cramer. His hand shook as he snagged the sunglasses from the ground. Excitement jacked his heart rate up to Mach IV speed. *I fucking remembered something!*

"No harm done. You didn't hit me." he assured Cramer as he shoved his glasses back on. At Newton's prepare to fire order, Brett took two big steps back and again covered his ears with the headgear.

He closed his eyes and attempted to recall every moment of the memory. All he could see was a green blur and the stock of the AK-47 coming at him.

CHAPTER 20

Tess pulled into one of the parking lots close to Mission Beach. She and Ian followed couples, joggers, early morning sun worshippers, and tourists migrating to the sand and surf. The smell of grilled food wafted on the breeze. Tess rummaged through her purse for her sunglasses and put them on.

Desultory customers wandered in and out of the businesses. Teenagers perched on the concrete barriers that separated the boardwalk from the beach eating fast food breakfasts and listening to music.

"When you were five or six your mother and I used to bring you down here. We'd have to coat you in sunscreen to keep you from burning."

"You burn as well."

"I'm covered in freckles. My skin's like buffalo hide."

Tess shook free of the linen jacket she wore. Each time a wave rolled ashore it pushed a breeze ahead of it, cooling her skin. Though it was only ten-thirty in the morning, the sun was already heating up. The smell of suntan lotion hung in the air.

They wandered down the wide sidewalk people-watching for a few minutes.

"I could use another coffee," Ian said when they reached a small café with tables outside. Tess found a patch of shade beneath a bright blue and white-striped umbrella over one of the tables and sat down. Ian went inside the small restaurant and returned with a large Styrofoam cup.

Ian sat down. "I've been offered an editorial position at the Los Angeles Times."

Surprise held her immobile for a second, then two. She tried to imagine Ian riding a desk instead of a Range Rover across an African plain. The picture remained fuzzy and indistinct. "Are you going to take it?"

"I'm thinking about it."

He was actually considering staying in one place. Her thought processes stumbled to a halt.

Ian smiled. He did that so seldom and he laughed even less. He was always so intense. His smile reminded her he could be charming, too. "You're surprised, then."

"I'm stunned, actually."

"It's bound to happen eventually."

So it wasn't a done deal.

"While I'm here, I thought I'd drive up to LA and meet with some people and get the lay of the land."

She nodded. "What section of the paper?"

"Domestic and national news."

Of course he'd be in charge of the front page.

He removed his sunglasses and his gaze homed in on her face. "You could come with me, Tess."

"I'd be a fifth wheel at your meetings."

"No, I mean to the Times. I could make it one of my negotiation points that they take you on."

Her jaw dropped. He'd gone from criticizing her story ideas to offering her a job. The juxtaposition created a whiplash effect that left her head spinning.

He'd be her boss. *God Forbid!*

"I think you need to get a good grasp of everything the job entails before making any demands. You may decide it isn't what you want. After all, it would be completely different from what you've done in the past."

Ian's lips twisted in a wry grin. "Actually not. I wasn't born with my suitcase glued to my hand and my laptop slung over my shoulder. That came after I'd resigned my position as managing editor of a small paper in Oregon." He took a drink of his coffee.

Why hadn't she heard about this before?

"I was bored with small town news, and a friend I'd gone to school with at UCLA called. He was a journalist with the Washington Post. He was going to South America and needed a partner to travel with, for backup and to take pictures. I said yes.

"We interviewed a South American drug lord who'd been arrested. The prison was a nightmare. We were frisked the moment we walked into the building, and my camera was confiscated along with all the cash in my wallet." He grinned and excitement lit his eyes. "I was scared shitless the whole time I was in the room with the guy. You could tell the guards were more interested in protecting this guy than us. But it was a rush."

"So you became an adrenaline junkie." Was this jump of excitement and adrenaline what motivated Brett to do what he did? She hadn't realized the two men would have much in common, but—

"I got addicted to the rush you get when you break a story no one else even knows is out there."

"Like the one Brett Weaver is offering you."

"If I decide to take the Times job, this story will be my last big international scoop—if it pans out."

If he covered the disappearances and was able to pressure the military into finding the missing boy or boys, or if he somehow uncovered where they were, it would be a major coup. And what a way to go out. But he'd be in danger the whole time. And he might put himself out there even more because it would be his last big hurrah. Her heart took on a panicked rhythm and her mouth grew dry.

What have I talked him into?

Clara studied Russell's strong features in the summer sunlight and took a quick picture using the harbor as a background.

"There's more interesting scenery to photograph than me," he said with a smile.

Should she tell him about the photo essay she was creating for him and Evan? No, she'd make it a gift. "I find your face very interesting. You look like you could jump on any one of these boats and sail out to sea." Was that a flirty comment or just the truth? She was so out of practice, and when she said those kinds of things, they sounded silly instead of sexy.

"I thought about buying a boat years ago." A sad smile curved his lips.

Clara pointed her camera at a sailboat under full canvas gliding toward the harbor. "There's still time."

"I'm sixty years old, Clara."

"So, I've been thirty-five for the last twenty years."

"I can believe that." He laughed. "You have more energy than anyone I know."

"Not always. I just refuse to give into those moments when my age creeps up on me. I realized recently that I had forgotten how to enjoy myself. I've been the responsible adult for the last thirty-five years, and it's made me boring."

"I don't find you boring at all."

"That's because you've only seen the Clara who's turned over a new leaf. I've lived my life for years for my children. Now they're adults and living their own they've left me behind, just as they should." She paused to sneak up on a heron perched on the metal railing of the dock. The bird twisted its long neck to look at her as she pushed the button. He stretched his beak into the air, preening for her, and she smiled and captured the change in pose. After several more shots she lowered the camera.

Russell was smiling as she returned to where he waited. "You charmed him into posing for you."

"He's probably used to having his picture taken and just hammed it up for me."

The ocean breeze blew a strand of hair into her eyes, and Russell's fingers were there to smooth it back. "I'll have to bring you back down here at night so you can take more pictures."

"I'd like that."

He captured her hand as they walked up the sloped wooden dock to the street above. "It gets a little noisy in the Gaslamp Quarter at night. It's a little too commercial for my taste. But there are some wonderful restaurants and bars down here. I thought I'd take you to the Harbor House for lunch. The view from there is beautiful and they have wonderful food."

The ocean breeze offset the sun's burning rays as they walked up Harbor Drive to the restaurant. Terracotta-and-gray-mottled paving stones set in a walkway led up to the entrance of the restaurant. The exterior looked like weathered wood, but sat in the midst of carefully manicured and landscaped grounds. Inside, the walls glowed with the golden tint of stained wood floors and the heavy-beamed roof supports had brick accents. The waitress sat them at a window table so they could look out on the harbor while they waited for their drinks and studied the menu. The smell of charbroiled beef and shrimp followed one of the servers as he passed by, his tray laden.

The waitress returned soon with water glasses and Russell requested a double order of crab-stuffed wontons as an appetizer.

"I know I'll love them, but I hope you're hungry enough to eat more than half. I'm on a diet," Clara said when the waitress was gone.

Russell rested his elbows on the table with a frown. "Why are you on a diet? You look great."

"Thank you. I'm on a diet so I'll continue to look this way. You didn't think I stayed like this without working at it did you?"

He chuckled. "I promise not to mention desert."

"Thank you," she smiled at him. Having him all to herself was exhilarating. As much as she loved Evan, and she had fallen in love with the bright, charming young man that he was, she'd craved having time alone with Russell. "I've been thinking of taking up belly dancing."

Russell choked on the sip of water he'd taken.

"I think it will help me stay in shape. What do you think?"

"I'm sure it will. Are you going to really commit and buy a costume?"

She pushed her camera closer to the center of the table out of harm's way. She studied his features, so attractively masculine, and his charming smile. "Would you like me to?"

He laughed aloud, the sound so free of the sadness or worry he usually carried, that her heart raced.

"Yes, I'd love to see you in full costume giving it all you've got." He grasped her hand and brought it to his lips, the light caress rushing heat to her cheeks. "As long as it's just for me." His smile settled into something more intimate. "You're good for me, Clara. And good for Evan. He's ill but his attitude is lighter. Hell, my attitude is lighter when you're with me."

"I'm glad you feel that way."

"Why hasn't some other man snapped you up?"

She gave the question some thought. "Do you want the truth? It may sound like I'm man-bashing."

"I can take it."

"When I was younger, the men who were brave enough to approach me had two attitudes. I was good enough to have sex with, but God forbid I should expect them to have anything to do with my kids. Or they were looking for a replacement for their mothers, and thought becoming one of the kids was a way into the fold. Neither worked for me." And her love for Joe had stood between her and every man she'd met. How could she have let any of them touch her when the memory of what they'd had together was still there burning inside? "Once the kids were gone, and I was older, the men were either widowers or divorced and looking for a home they didn't have to pay for and a wife who would wipe their chins and do their laundry. They eyed my house and car with more lust than they did me. The only passion that stirred was a desire to kick them to the curb with a pointy, steel-toed boot."

Russell laughed for even harder then, shook his head and wiped his eyes with his napkin. "Surely they weren't all like that."

"No. There were a couple of nice guys, who wanted me for me, but Joe was a hard act to follow, and it never seemed quite right. Then about five years ago, after Zoe moved out, I had some kind of late mid-life crisis." She covered her face with her hands and shook her head. "It should have never happened, and I cringe every time I think about it."

"We've all made those kinds of mistakes at least once in our lives, Clara."

"Thank goodness, mine's only been the one."

Russell took her hand again, and though his expression sobered, a smile tilted the corners of his lips. "I don't need anyone to wipe my chin or do my laundry, and since I've never seen your house or your car, the only thing left for me to lust after is you. So, if you brought those pointy steel-toed boots from Kentucky, you can leave them in the closet."

The heated promise she read in his smile, his eyes, gave her an instant jolt, shifting her breathing into overdrive. She squeezed her thighs together when that tempting tingle of desire came to life, as it did so often when she was with him. Could she really reach for what he promised?

Russell Connelly had certainly jump-started her libido, and she loved every minute of it. But could she bear the loneliness again if it didn't work out?

Brett came to a stop at the red light and checked his watch for the third time. He was running late. Skimming a hand over his shower-damp hair, he rehashed the afternoon. He'd tagged along with the BUD/S class, doing whatever was needed. Running alongside them as they crisscrossed the base had brought back good memories of his own BUD/S class. He was tired, but he felt good. Strong. And he still had juice left.

He'd need it if Tess's dad, Ian Kelly, lived up to his reputation. He was known as a pit bull when it came to uncovering a story. If he could just point the guy in the right direction and avoid getting pressured into divulging stuff he couldn't ... This interview was going to be tricky as hell.

Was he doing the right thing?

At least he'd get to see Tess. They had spoken on the phone a couple of times since they'd watched the movie at his apartment. She'd kept it all business, holding him at a distance. He'd expected her to be pushy. Weren't reporters supposed to be pushy? Would she be more aggressive in bed?

She had her own style. Sort of subtle and smart. In a way, her low-key method made her more dangerous. Because of how she looked, feminine and non-aggressive, she lulled a guy into complacency and encouraged him to share more than he should. He could appreciate that. And even enjoyed the extra challenge she presented.

Was her dad like that? Or had she found her own way? He'd find out soon enough.

Twenty minutes later, he walked into the hotel. He glanced at his watch again. Ten minutes late. Would Tess be pissed? Women had a tendency to get upset when a guy didn't show the moment he was supposed to.

"Can I help you, sir?" A woman asked from behind a wide wooden reception desk.

"I'm supposed to meet someone at the bar."

Before the woman could offer directions, he heard his name called. He swiveled around to see Tess struggling with a large box and several bags. He strode forward and relieved her of the largest package.

She brushed at the strand of hair that had escaped her ponytail to dangle down her cheek. Her nose was pink as though she'd been out in the sun.

Because he just had to touch her, he tucked the wayward strand of hair behind her ear and immediately remembered what the skin under her blouse had felt like while he caressed her.

Tess raised her sherry-brown eyes to his face and color washed up her throat.

Was she thinking the same thing? Jesus—Every time she looked at him, really looked at him, he got hard.

"Ian likes his coffee fresh brewed and hot, and hotel room coffee leaves a lot to be desired," she said. "I've brought him a coffee maker and coffee."

"Good, we can have a decent cup after dinner."

The mouth-watering smell of Chinese food wafted up from the large plastic bag she carried.

"I can take that for you, too," Brett offered.

She shook her head. "I'm good. He's on the second floor. Come this way." She led the way to the elevators.

The doors opened and spilled out a party of five. They stepped into the elevator alone. "Do you always call your father Ian?" Brett asked.

She punched the button. The doors closed. "Yes."

The brevity of her answer, meant to dissuade him from asking another, only torqued his impatience. She was so closed off from him. "What do you call your stepfather?" he asked.

"Milton."

"You've been out in the sun today," he commented.

"Yes. We went to Mission Beach for a while before I dropped Ian off here to settle in."

"You worked today?" Why hadn't she spent the whole day with her father?

"I had a couple of interviews that I couldn't reschedule."

The elevator doors opened and they stepped out into the corridor. She turned right into a dimly lit hallway. The striped pattern of the carpet looked like it was moving beneath their feet.

"You look like you've been out in the sun today, too," she said.

"I worked as a BUD/S instructor today."

"Have you received orders?"

"No. I volunteered to fill in for someone."

She remained silent a moment. "How did it feel?"

"Great." He smiled.

"He's in room fourteen-nineteen." Tess paused in front of the door and knocked.

The door swung open and Ian Kelly braced a hand on the door facing while he raised the drink he held in greeting. "Come in." He moved aside to let them pass.

Brett's first impression was that Tess looked nothing like her father, despite her coloring. The second thing he observed was that Ian was, if not drunk, well on his way.

A half-empty bottle of Scotch sat on the end table in the sitting area of the room.

An expression of shock and uncertainty crossed Tess's features. Her cheeks grew flushed, brightening her already heightened color. Her movements jerky, she stalked to the small table in front of the sliding glass door and set her two bags next to the open laptop there.

"I'll set up the coffee pot," Brett said in the silence that followed.

The early evening light shone in from the balcony, but did nothing to lighten the tension in the room.

"I was scooped today by Sixty Minutes," Ian said his words a little slurred. "The AP has released my story, but Sixty Minutes will run a segment with the same info tonight."

Brett removed the coffeepot from the box and set it on another end table.

Tess placed a one-pound can of coffee and some filters down beside him. "Make it strong." She turned back to Ian. "It'll bring exposure to the rhino's plight, and more people will read your story tomorrow because the show will whet their appetite for more information." Though her tone was positive, she clenched her hands at her side and bit her lip.

Brett opened the coffee can, positioned a paper filter inside the machine, and using the scoop inside the can, measured out a generous amount while paying equal attention to Ian and Tess.

"Everything is about timing, Tess." Ian flopped down into a chair. The liquid in his glass sloshed over his hand. He set the container aside to sling the scotch off his fingers, then wiped them on his pants leg.

Tess flinched.

Brett went to the sink and filled the glass carafe with water.

"You know the old adage about how a picture's worth a thousand words? It's true."

"Then you need to apply for a job writing for one of the national news shows," she said, her tone edgy with impatience.

Ian tilted his head back and narrowed his eyes. "There's an idea."

Her lips tightened at his slurred words.

Brett poured water into the reservoir and pushed the on button. "Coffee's on," Brett said into the lull. *Are we having fun yet?*

Ian's gaze settled on him, his expression suspicious. "So you're the SEAL."

Ooooo-kay. Brett nodded. He was put off by this whiny, arrogant SOB. The only thing keeping him in the room was Tess.

Ian rose to his feet and sauntered over to him, a slight sway to his gait. "Did one of your team try to kill you?"

"I don't know." He'd been certain Derrick was responsible. Had that green blur behind the AK-47 been him? It had to have been.

"Have you recovered any memories since the attack?" Ian stepped closer, invading his space.

Brett focused on his face. Could that one flash even count? "No."

"Why's your CO jerking you around?"

Brett's attention shifted to Tess. He hadn't told her that. "I expect to get orders in the next week or so."

Ian's eyes narrowed and he studied him, his tawny gaze intent. "But you're not rejoining your team?"

"No. Not yet."

"Have they given you a reason?"

"They're waiting until the investigation into the boy's disappearance is finished."

"Did you kill him?"

When someone even suggested it, it was like he'd been punched in the balls. "No. I don't know what happened to him."

"Come eat something, Dad," Tess said, her voice soft.

Brett frowned at her use of Dad instead of Ian. What had it been like to dance to this self-centered asshole's tune when she was a child? It was bad enough watching her do it as an adult.

Tess studied Brett as he chewed. His silence had become conspicuous. In fact, she'd never known him to be anything but cocky and confident. This subdued Brett was unfamiliar, a new side to the man she'd begun to know.

She'd wanted to find a hole and crawl into it when Ian had opened the door. What had Brett thought?

Ian raised his coffee cup and took a sip. "Tess said your mother is here visiting."

"Yeah. She's staying with my sister right now."

"Does she know about all this?"

Brett's features tightened. "No. And I'm not telling her unless I have to."

Ian nodded. "No need to worry her until something negative happens."

With a little food in his stomach, he was showing improvement. And at least he'd given up his drink and switched to coffee. He'd smelled like scotch at nine o'clock this morning. And now—how long had he been drinking like this?

An awkward silence permeated the room broken only by the sound of chewing.

When Ian set aside his plate, Tess said, "I'll clean up in here. Why don't you two go out on the balcony and talk?"

"I'd prefer to stay in the room, Tess. Less chance of someone overhearing our conversation," Brett said. He rose from his seat, stacked his plate with hers and Ian's, and dumped them in the trash. He reached for one of the cartons and closed it. She rushed to help him. And though she tried to catch his attention, he didn't look at her.

Ian rose, retrieved something from his bag, and unfolded it. He stretched the map of Iraq out on the table.

Brett studied the map, his expression dispassionate.

"I know you can't tell me precisely where you were supposed to deliver the boy," Ian said.

"No." Brett remained silent for a long moment, a waiting stillness in the way he held himself. "There's a small market in Al Rashid. We'd stop sometimes and buy oranges. You can see the dome of the Al Rasheed Hotel from there. Have you ever stayed there?"

"Yes. When Baghdad was first invaded." Ian rubbed his hand on the side of his face.

"Really spectacular architecture. They've replaced the mosaic floor of George Bush in the lobby with one of Saddam Hussein."

"I thought perhaps that might happen," Ian said, his tone quiet.

"It may have changed again. A hotel group came in and started renovating it for some conference or other while we were still down range." He drew a deep breath. "We'd drive through the surrounding neighborhoods fourteen, fifteen blocks west of the hotel. Most of the people were friendly, especially the kids.

Ian nodded, his features tight with concentration. "The boy's name?"

Brett studied his face for a long moment, his jaw pulsing. "Sanjay al-Yussuf."

"You don't remember any of this?" Ian asked.

"No." Brett swiveled toward Tess.

He had remained still for so long that his sudden movement startled her.

"I have to go. Thanks for dinner."

He looked nothing like the Brett she'd begun to know. The shuttered, controlled look of his features was distant and frightening.

He strode to the door and was through it before she could respond. "I'll be right back, Ian."

She broke into a run as she saw him disappear into the corridor in front of the elevators. "Brett?"

He pushed the elevator button, impatience in every line of his body.

"Brett."

"I should have fucking walked away."

"Why didn't you?"

His blue eyes settled on her face, burning with anger. "Because of you. Because you still believe in him."

The elevator door opened and he got in. "He's spiraling, Tess. Desperate for a scoop, and I gave it to him. I've placed my career and my freedom in the hands of an alcoholic, a-a-," He swore beneath his breath. "Egomaniac. Fucking ridiculous."

She clutched her hand against her midriff where fear and doubt twisted. Hearing him put into words what she'd been thinking intensified the feeling.

"It will be all right," she said. "He needs this as badly as you do."

Brett studied her features. "I hope you're right. Because I'll be looking at the inside of a prison cell if you're wrong."

The words hit her like a punch.

The elevator door closed between them.

CHAPTER 21

B rett parked the rental car, a Buick, at Osprey point and exited the car. Inactivity was driving him crazy. As he approached the point, he looked out at the horizon. A grayish sheen colored the distant sky and the clouds touched with blue-gray had an angry look. A storm threatened out at sea, ensuring some good waves as long as it didn't blow further inland.

The sound of the car door shutting behind him drew his attention and he turned.

"This is beautiful, Brett," Clara said.

"Yeah, it is."

She raised the camera to her eye and started taking pictures.

Though he watched Clara as she moved around the point, the words *shouldn't have done it* beat against his brain. He couldn't think about that right now. It was over with. The only good day was today. Only yesterday sucked.

He couldn't escape the decision he'd made. He'd spilled info to Ian Kelly. He'd given him the boy's name and his location. In code, but it still counted. NCIS hadn't said he couldn't talk about it, but in Special OPS they didn't talk about anything. He'd broken the code. Hell, he'd already broken it with Tess. He'd let her in further than any other person, including his mother or sister. He'd let his dick control his brain, but never again. If he survived this thing with his career and his life intact, he'd never let anyone close enough to compromise him again.

But there had been no other choice. All the feelers he'd put out, both back in Iraq and here in the *real world,* had given him nothing. No one knew anything. Or if they did, they weren't talking. That silence bothered him more than this crap with Ian Kelly.

They were his brothers-in-arms. And he felt like he'd been abandoned in enemy territory.

Did his teammates think he'd killed the kid?

Developing a reputation with the teams was important. Living up to the reputation you'd established, even more. How long would it be before the other teams started wondering, doubting? Had they already begun to?

SEALs were pack animals. They did their best work as a team. His pack was a hundred miles away in the desert training. They'd be dirty, sweaty, and carrying forty-pound packs on their backs. God, he'd give his left nut to be there with them.

"Are you going to tell me what's bothering you?" Clara asked. "You can't just keep saying it's this delay in orders."

"I can't talk about it, Mom. It's about some things that happened down range."

"Secret or just bad?" she asked.

"Both."

"I know you took an oath to maintain secrecy. I won't ever ask you to compromise that. But if you need to talk, your secrets will always be safe with me."

Brett looked away as guilt and other emotions crashed together to form a knot in his throat that threatened to choke him. Why had he decided to trust strangers when he had her and Zoe? "I know you've always got my six, Mom," he said when he could speak.

"Always."

He had to focus on the here and now for a while instead of the what ifs or should haves. He pointed to a large rock formation in the cove, its top coated with bird droppings from the many seafowl that landed there. "That big rock is affectionately called Bird Shit Rock around here. It's Bird Rock on some maps or Reeds Rock."

"I can see why they named it that." She moved around the parking lot behind the wood and wire barriers to take several shots from different angles.

'We can walk out onto the point and all the way around so you can get some more pictures," he suggested.

The path just outside the barrier, used by tourists and locals, was well worn and far enough away from the edge to be safe. They picked their way out to the point where waves surged against the rocks. Sea spray splattered their clothes and hair. Clara laughed and used the tail of her shirt to wipe off her camera lens and took a picture of Brett as the water splashed him.

They worked their way around the cove, careful not to step on the wildflowers blooming here and there.

When they paused on the south side of the cove, Clara exclaimed, "Look at the strata on the cliffs!" She raised the camera to her eye.

Brett studied the rock formations she was fixated on. The cliff bowed out where the water had eaten away at it, leaving behind bands of color and a cluster of rocks at the bottom. "I looked at your other photos, Mom. They were amazing. The one of Greenback dancing with his baby girl cheek to cheek, I'm sure he'd like a copy of it. I know you took pictures of us kids. But I don't think it ever occurred to me that you had such a talent for it."

She grinned, her features glowing with an excitement he'd rarely seen. "I'm really enjoying experimenting. I felt a little guilty about buying the camera equipment, but I'm about a third of the way to earning the money back so I think it was a good investment."

"Why would you feel guilty for buying something you wanted?"

"I earmarked money for bills the whole time you kids were young. And even while you and Zoe were in college, though you both worked, I slipped a certain amount of money into your bank accounts because I knew you'd never ask though you needed it. I guess once you learn that behavior, it's hard to throw caution to the wind and just spend money if you simply want something rather than needing it."

"We're all grown now, Mom. You don't have to take responsibility for anyone but yourself at this point."

"It doesn't' work that way, honey. Just because you're all grown doesn't mean I don't feel responsible for you. It's a mom thing." The whole time she talked, she was pausing to take pictures.

"And dads are supposed to feel the same way?"

"Your father always did."

Had Ian ever felt responsible for Tess? *Ever?* He rubbed his forehead where a dull tension headache had begun. Was Tess's relationship with her father why she distanced herself from him?

"I'm sure you'll feel the same way when you have your own children, Brett. And it's not like I deprive myself of things. I'm just conservative. But not so conservative that I didn't invest in a telephoto lens that weighs as much as a small lap dog. I'm going to use it today to take some pictures of you surfing."

"What does any of this have to do with Captain Connelly?" Brett asked.

She lowered her camera to study his expression. "He doesn't have anything to do with my taking pictures. He has been encouraging me, though."

"You've shown him your stuff?"

"Yes, he's the one who suggested I upload them and sell them."

Brett remained silent for a moment. "You're being careful with this guy, aren't you Mom?"

She drew a deep breath and her eyes focused on the distant horizon. "You're making it more complicated than it is. Russell enjoys my company, and I enjoy his. Why does it worry you that I'm dating someone?"

"Because you've never done it before. Not really."

"I wasn't ready before. It's taken me twenty years to even look at another man since your father."

Brett's heart jogged double time. "Well, why this guy?"

"Because he looks at me like I'm still an attractive woman, not a fifty-five year old retired school teacher."

Oh, shit.

They spent twenty minutes working their way back around the cove. As they approached the car, Brett paused in surprise when Tess straightened from where she leaned against the front quarter panel. Her dark red hair shone with copper highlights as she faced them.

His gaze raked the length of her, covered from neck to ankle in a full wetsuit. The white strips decorating the front followed the curves of her body, accentuating her lithe, slender shape. Though every inch of skin was covered but her face and hands, she might as well have been naked. Desire twisted and tumbled through him and he grew hard. As usual.

He turned to face his mother. "Did you tell her where we'd be?"

Clara frowned. "She called while you were dressing. I thought you'd be pleased to have her join us."

He'd needed more time with his mom to talk to her out of this thing with Connelly. But time with Tess was—It had been hard as hell keeping his distance and not calling her. Who the fuck was he kidding? He wanted to be with her.

But the rules had to change. He couldn't keep hanging himself out there and getting nothing in return.

Brett's frown put Tess's heart into free-fall. It was a mistake to have come here. He didn't want to see her. It had been five days since the meeting at the hotel and she hadn't heard a word from him. An ache settled just under her breastbone. She clenched her hands at her sides. She had been so certain he'd wanted more from her. Wasn't that what he'd said?

"Hey," he said as he reached her.

"Your mom told me you were going surfing. I brought my gear," she said.

He grinned. "I can see that. You didn't tell me you surfed."

Was that an accusation? If it was, she probably deserved it. "I'm a better listener than a talker."

He studied her for a moment. "I noticed."

"It's a hazard of the job." She bit her lip and looked over his shoulder to Clara. "Hello, Mrs. Weaver."

"Please call me Clara."

The knot of anxiety loosened a little more at Clara's encouraging smile.

"Where are you parked?" Clara asked. "It might be easier to find parking for one car instead of two. If you don't mind leaving yours here, we can transfer your gear to my rental."

"I'm up the street. And I think that's a good idea."

"I thought we'd go further up the coast. It's a little tricky reaching the surf here," Brett said.

"I know. I've been here before."

With towels cushioning the boards, they used soft straps to secure Tess's board atop the car with Brett's.

Brett opened the passenger door, but Clara opened the back door and took a seat there, leaving the front seat free for Tess.

"We'll come back down to the point around sunset, Mom. It's amazing here. People come here just to take pictures of it," Brett said once they were in the car.

"Sounds good."

He put the car in gear and drove down the coast to the long stairs that led down to the beach.

Brett parked the car in a roadside lot and Brett popped the trunk.

"I'm going to be busy taking photos of the area," Clara said. "I thought I'd photograph you two surfing and work my way back toward the point. We can meet back here in, say … a couple of hours?"

"Then we'll dump our gear, change, and find a place to eat. What do you think, Tess?"

"That sounds good. I have a sundress and sandals in my bag."

"I'm going to wander over and take some pictures of the stairs that lead down to the beach," Clara said.

An almost painful silence stretched between them. Tess sought something to say to break it. "I wasn't certain about coming, but your mother seemed to think it was okay."

"I'm glad you came," Brett said, his tone abrupt. He propped his arms on the top of the car and leaned in.

"After the way things—the other night—I hadn't heard from you—" She wasn't entirely able to suppress the hurt in her tone.

Brett remained silent for a beat then two. "I had some things I needed to work out without being distracted." He drew a deep breath and focused on her. "I'm not completely comfortable with the way things were—are, Tess."

She swallowed. "I understand."

His gaze sharpened, the line of his jaw going taut. "I don't think you do."

"I understand you went way out on a limb with info that could come back to bite you if anyone finds out." She bit her lip. "I know you've lost confidence in Ian because of how he behaved. But if he's as desperate for a scoop as I think he is, he'll find the truth and report it."

"I hope you're right. And I hope he doesn't disappoint either of us." The flat even tone of his voice held an accusation.

"You once told me that what was happening between us was separate from what you needed from Ian."

He straightened from his leaning position on the car. "Right now, you haven't allowed anything to happen between us, Tess. I can't be the only one willing to—lower the barriers." He drew a deep breath. "I can't continue to guard every word I say for fear of seeing it in print one day either. I have to know I can trust you."

She focused on him so he'd know she was sincere. "Everything you say to me from this moment on will be off the record, Brett. I turned in the last of my articles for the series yesterday."

"I didn't think you had enough information yet."

"I called Master Chief O'Hara and got the remainder of the information I needed. You're no longer an official source."

"So?"

You're no longer a source for any kind of story." She raised her hand. "I swear it. Every word you said in that hotel room is locked away for eternity as far as I'm concerned. I never heard a thing."

Brett nodded once, and though he continued to search her face for several moments, the tension in his shoulders relaxed a little. After a moment of silence, he shed his shirt and shorts to reveal a brief swimsuit that left little to the imagination. *Oh, my.* Tess nearly swallowed her tongue at the wealth of bare skin and lean muscle. The light brown hair that dusted his chest ran down the center of his taut stomach in a line that begged to be followed. He pulled a wetsuit from a bag in the trunk. He worked the legs of the suit over his calves, the muscles in his back flexing.

Her hand shook and her heart was thundering in her ears as she ran her palm over the curve of his body between his shoulder blade and spine.

He froze for a moment, acknowledging her touch with that alert stillness she'd found so unnerving the other night. He straightened and tugged the wetsuit up over his hips.

Tess caught her breath as she glimpsed how he'd responded to her touch. Since he'd left her standing in the hallway of the hotel, a tight knot had taken up residence in the pit of her stomach. The sensation of it unraveling brought a smile to her lips.

He glanced up. "Now who's toying with whom, Tess?"

"I don't look at you as a plaything either," she said using his own words against the barrier he'd thrown up between them.

He straightened, his gaze meandering down her body as though she was an ice cream cone and he was deciding where to lick first. His hard-edged expression of raw desire barely held in check carried enough heat to fire the libidos of every woman within a hundred-yard radius. Having his unrelenting interest directed at her from point-blank range tightened her nipples and warmed intimate areas south. Her heart beat in her throat, and she felt stifled by the constricting layers of the neoprene wetsuit.

Damn. He was dangerous to her peace of mind, and her heart.

Brett wiggled into the top of his wetsuit, and, gripping the long zipper pull, tugged it up his back. Then he unhooked the pull, dropped it in the trunk, and strapped a knife to his calf.

"Is this suit anything like what you wear when you're working?" she asked, more to distract them both than because she wanted to know.

The heat banked in his expression cooled.

"No. Most of the time we're in dry suits. They're bulkier, gray, and have pockets for gear at the calves and at the top of the arms, and aren't nearly as fashionable." He started working at one of the straps holding the boards atop the car and she rushed to help with the other one.

"I took up surfing when I first came out here. It took me forever to be able to pop up on the board. I'm not a novice, but I'm not an expert either." *Why was sharing the slightest thing so hard for her?*

"How strong a swimmer are you?" he asked. "Sometimes the undercurrents can be strong here."

Was that comment double edged? "I've noticed. I think I'll be fine."

He nodded and slid her bright pink board off the top of the car and handed it to her.

"This week—I've missed talking to you, Brett."

"Good." He braced the board against the car and rested his elbow on the top. "I've missed you, too."

She studied his expression before stepping closer. "I believe in you. I have since the beginning. You're no more a murderer than I am."

His attention focused on her once again, intense, unblinking. His gaze shifted downward to her lips and settled there, yet he didn't move to kiss her.

Why wasn't he? She'd given him every reason to. His desire for her had nothing to do with Ian and everything to do with what she could give him. If she was brave enough.

"The other night, when you invited me over to watch the movie, we made a connection, didn't we?" she asked.

Some of the tension in his shoulders relaxed. "I thought so."

She'd told him it was hard for her to step out from behind the professional façade, but she hadn't delved into the depths of how truly difficult she found it. Before she could lose her nerve entirely, she rose on tiptoe and kissed him.

In an instant, his lips softened beneath hers, parting in response to the pressure. His hand cupped her hip and drew her in against him. The brushing movement she had initiated took on a clinging intensity that made her legs weak. When his tongue touched hers, she leaned into him, wanting to be closer. The kiss went on and on, growing hungry, intense, until, breathless, she had to draw back.

He was just as out of breath as she was, and spots of color highlighted his cheekbones.

"Has anyone ever told you your timing sucks, Tess?" he asked, his lips touching her temple, her forehead.

"No. Why?" She leaned back to look up at him. She'd never experienced a more perfect kiss. Hadn't it been the same for him?

"For one thing, you took your sweet time kissing me." Brett studied her, laughed, then groaned. "And another—I dare you to kiss me like that when we're not encased in body-sized condoms."

CHAPTER 22

Clara glanced over her shoulder toward the car. The hot pink of Tess's surfboard stood out, and she could see a sliver of it propped against the rental car A couple of joggers, a man and a woman, ran by. Two women walked down the path toward her, acknowledged her with a nod, and paused at the stairs to talk about the view.

Something wasn't quite right between Brett and Tess. Had they had a fight? Was that part of what was troubling him?

She drew a breath. If only he didn't hold so much inside. He'd learned to close himself off because of his job, and now it was sliding into his private life. And Tess did the same thing. How could two such self-contained people reach each other?

He was worried about her relationship with Russell Connelly. Well, she was worried about his with Tess. But he'd think she was invading his privacy if she asked questions.

Just as she'd reacted when he'd done the same.

Brett appeared on the path. He was laughing. Tess's cheeks were flushed and she was smiling. Had they settled whatever it was that had sent up the barriers between them?

Maybe this would distract him from digging into her relationship with Russell. She didn't need Brett picking at something so new and fragile. The relationship had just begun to bud. They hadn't slept together, not yet. Though she knew she wanted that to happen, she was enjoying being wooed. Their lunch date had ended with a tour of the Gaslamp Quarter and she'd taken tons of pictures. But holding hands, window-shopping, talking and flirting had meant more to her. Because she'd felt closer to Russell.

She didn't know where they were going emotionally. But she definitely didn't need an overprotective son interfering.

She took some shots of Brett carrying his eight-foot board with the trident symbol on the front. His blond hair gleamed in the early afternoon light, his jaw darkened by a shadow of beard. He looked so much like Joe, a fist clenched around her heart. He grinned at her and she took another quick shot.

When Brett and Tess were close enough, she said, "You don't mind my taking some photos of you, too, do you, Tess?"

Tess propped her board against the railing at the top of the stairs to tie her hair back with a rubber band. "No, not at all."

She was so beautiful, with her slender long-limbed frame and auburn hair, Clara couldn't resist snapping a quick picture of her right then, using the hot pink board behind her as a backdrop.

She and Brett made a striking couple, but just because their looks complimented one another didn't mean their personalities would mesh. She drew a deep breath. As protective as she felt toward her kids, she had to step back and hope they each made the right decisions about their relationships.

"I'll save a copy of the best pictures for your parents," Clara promised. "Do you still say 'hang ten dudes?'"

Tess laughed. "And 'toes on the nose'."

"Have fun," Clara called as they ascended the steps.

She clicked some pictures of the two as they picked their way across the rock-strewn beach below and headed into the surf.

Brett monitored Tess's progress as they paddled out past the break. They straddled their boards and studied the waves.

The kiss they'd shared, and the effort she'd put forth to get him to respond, made him hopeful. He'd have to keep nudging her to open up and reach for what she wanted. *But— Jesus, I want her to kiss me again. Right now.*

He had to get his mind on something else or he'd reach for her. And right now he wanted her reaching for him, instead of holding him at a distance. "Do you jog?" Brett asked, looking for other things they might have in common she hadn't mentioned.

"Not unless it's to the head of the line at Starbucks in the morning.

He laughed.

"I'm actually pretty lazy," she said. "I used to ride horseback every weekend when I was in New York. And I love this, though I don't get to come out as often as I'd like." She glanced behind her on the lookout for the perfect wave.

"This will be my first time surfing since coming home," Brett said.

"I promise not to show you up in front of your mother," Tess said falling chest-forward on the board. She paddled hard and was well in front of the break before the swell hit him, raising him up long enough to see her pop up on her board in perfect form. His board fell into the trench before the next wave of the set passed him, blocking his view of her. Then the water took him up again and he saw her wipe out.

Brett looked back to see the swell of the next set rising behind him. He stretched atop the board and dug deep to get out in front of it, and then let the excitement and joy of just riding the waves take over.

After thirty minutes passed with neither of them finding a strong ride, they settled on their boards for a breather.

"I hope your mom isn't disappointed in us," Tess said. "She's probably not getting the best shots."

"A gag reel maybe." Brett agreed with a laugh. "Mom's used to being alone and entertaining herself. Thus this adventure in photography." He nodded toward the cliffs. "She can find beauty in the darnedest things. I saw some of her pictures recently. I was amazed. I didn't know she had such a talent."

"Really?"

"She's been putting her pictures up on websites and selling them."

"Has she ever thought of working for a newspaper?" Tess asked.

Brett's brows rose. Would she like something like that? "I don't know if she'd be interested or not."

"With you and your sister both here, it would offer her even more reason to relocate."

Zoe would love it, but what would it mean to him? His mom would be closer for when he wasn't deployed, and though she'd flown out every time he came home, she'd be here waiting for him. He'd actually have a family unit here, like the other guys.

And what about Tess? Could she become part of that? A slow smile worked across his face. "I could get used to having family here. That's pretty much all you think about between missions and patrols."

Shielding his eyes from the glare of the sun, he glanced seaward. The earlier storm at sea was pushing higher waves their direction, and more surfers were paddling out past the break.

A gigantic swell rose in the distance. He leaned forward onto the board and dug deep. "We need to paddle, Tess. A big one's coming."

The wave rose beneath him just as he leapt up on his board. The board's fins caught the water, and arms extended, legs bent, he bobbled, then found his balance. The wave curled up behind him, and he hit the lip, then pivoted his board forward, working for and finding the barrel of the wave and using it to extend his ride. The displaced air pushed before the water seemed to hold him suspended on the waxed plank until the wave tumbled forward, crashing into white foam that shoved him forward a few more yards. He thrust his fists into the air in a victory sign and gave a yell.

A sudden flash on the cliffs above caught his attention. Was that light reflecting off his mother's camera lens? He hoped she'd taken plenty of pictures, because that was probably the best ride he'd ever had. A sudden shove from another wave had him bobbling. Something struck his side spinning him around and he fell headfirst into the water. He surfaced choking and spitting salt water. His hip felt strangely numb.

What the fuck?

A sudden rush of water from another wave struck his board, sending it swooping toward shore and dragging him under.

He pressed his hand against his side as he fought his way to the surface. His board drifted close and he latched onto it. The surface of the board exploded near his face, sending up wood and foam particles. "Jesus Christ!" He thrust the board away. Someone was shooting at them. He dove beneath the water, jerked the Velcro strap loose from his ankle, and set the surfboard free.

He kicked forward without surfacing, bobbed up twenty feet to the right, and looked back toward where he'd left Tess. She was paddling forward as another wave rose. "No!" The crash of the surf swallowed his yell. Another shot zipped past his head like an angry bee and hit the water. The fucker was fixated on him and hadn't targeted her or any of the other surfers—yet. He dove and came up farther down shore. What could he do? How could he protect Tess? The other surfers? No one had noticed anything.

Could he make it across the unprotected strip at the base of the cliffs and get up there? His heart beat in his ears like a bass drum. *Jesus, Mom's up there.*

Fear rocketed through him, offsetting the rush of adrenaline. Brett dove and swam hard toward shore.

Clara heard a strange noise just down the path from where she stood. She looked back toward the road that ran parallel with the beach. Was that a car door slamming? She turned her lens toward the water and looked through to find Tess, arms outstretched, riding a wave with a grace that made the whole experience seem easy. Another pop sounded. She jerked and lowered the camera.

That wasn't a slam. She'd been around gunfire all her life, and she knew the difference. She swung around trying to pinpoint where the sound had come from. Two people near the street were running down the road away from the cliffs. She shifted her focus from the water and surfers below to the path she'd traveled earlier. A man lay prone on the ground, a rifle pointed downward toward the beach. *Dear God!* Her heart thundered in her ears and tremor shook her body. She focused the camera lens on the man, dark hair, dusky skin, a black baseball cap, and pushed the camera button again and again. She swung the camera toward the water.

A surfboard bobbed and jerked as the water shoved it toward the beach.

A white surfboard with a SEAL trident on it.

Clara's heart skipped a beat and she leaned forward over the overhang as far as she dared to search for Brett through the lens. He was nowhere in sight. Just the board. Fear numbed her hands and feet and made it difficult to breathe. Her hands shook so she had trouble gripping the cell phone she jerked from the camera bag at her feet. She speed dialed 911.

A busy signal? My God, a busy signal?

Another pop sounded and Clara brought the camera to her face again, looking out to sea, looking for Tess and Brett. Tess straddled her board and was looking toward the beach. She was an easy target.

Three surfers paddled toward one of the other surfers who was signaling. Had he been shot? Dear God that man was going to kill them all.

What should she do? She hit the button on her phone again to redial the number.

A busy signal. This can't be happening.

Her breathing came in gasping breaths. "Dear God, help me," she said aloud and broke into a run toward the man with the rifle.

The ground seemed to roll beneath her feet, and she couldn't get enough air into her lungs. Her fingers gripped the camera so hard it hurt.

She was almost upon him when he turned to look over his shoulder. With a cry of panicked fear, she swung the camera down in a backhanded motion as hard as she could, hitting him on the side of the head. The telephoto lens broke away. Her fingers numb, she lost her grip on the camera and it tumbled across the hard-packed dirt. He jerked around and tried to bring the rifle into position. She staggered and fell on top of him, kneeing him in the stomach. The rifle went off. He shoved the gun into the side of her head, the steel barrel striking her just above the ear and knocking her aside.

Stunned and deafened from the shot, a high-pitched ringing dulled the crash of the waves, and made the sound of her breathing loud in her ears. She rolled onto her side and tried to rise, but her limbs were slow to work.

He staggered to his feet and pointed the barrel of the rifle at her. With his teeth clenched in a grimace and his cold, dark eyes focused on her with hatred, Clara's limbs turned to liquid. He aimed at her chest. He screamed an insult at her she couldn't understand.

"Mom!"

A shout came from the stairs and Brett half ran, half limped toward them. He held his side with one hand and the sun glinted off something in the other. The man pivoted and raised the rifle to his shoulder.

Adrenaline shot through her veins. "No." Clara lunged and, wrapping her arms around the man's legs, she heaved forward and knocked him off balance. The gun discharged into the sky. The shooter staggered and jerked away, kicking her in the jaw. She cried out. He screamed something at her and thrust the gun's stock down at her face. She rolled, and covered her head with her arm. The blow landed, brutal and numbing.

CHAPTER 23

The shooter broke into a full-out run. Brett, torn by the compulsion to give chase, slid to a stop on the dusty path, then rushed back to his mother. Blood welled between his fingers from the wound in his side. It dripped to the dry ground and onto her crop pants. He ignored it as he knelt next to her. With a violent movement, filled with frustration and anger, he thrust the knife he gripped into the ground.

Agony ratcheted through him catching at his voice. "Mom?" He drew her arms away from her head and she cried out.

"It's just me, Brett."

With a sob, she reached for him. For a moment, just holding her seemed the best thing for them both. His arms shook and his heart thundered inside him. Nausea hit next, and he sat down, dragging her close against him. He braced a hand on the ground to remain sitting. Now that the adrenaline was leaching away, his side screamed for attention. And the smell of blood was making him nauseous.

Sirens wailed in the distance and people rounded the edge of the path. Seeing them, they hesitated, then rushed forward.

"Call 911 and ask for an ambulance," he instructed one of the women.

"You're bleeding," one woman pointed out.

No shit. Brett accepted the towel she offered him and pressed it against his side.

"We found this bag full of camera equipment on the path," another woman said and sat it down close to the camera lying in the dirt.

"Someone needs to go down the stairs and check if anyone else needs medical attention," Brett suggested. *Was Tess all right? Had the fucker tried to shoot her too?* An image of her floating lifeless in the water rose up to tear at him. "Please hurry."

"I'll do it," the only man with the group answered.

"He was going to kill you all," Clara said, her voice barely a whisper. Her body shook with violent tremors. "I thought he'd shot you."

"You did good, Mom." *Jesus, she took on a killer.* His eyes burnt with tears, and he held her tighter.

Tess was suddenly there kneeling beside him, her face so pale her eyes looked almost black. "You're losing a lot of blood, Brett. You need to lie down." Her voice shook.

Clara drew back and cried out when she saw the blood streaking her arm and clothing. "Oh my God. He did shoot you." A bruise and knot were forming on her jaw and her eyes looked dull with shock. She wiggled out of his arms.

When his mother pushed against his shoulder, he was more than happy to lie down. He was feeling a little light-headed.

Tess bent to readjust the towel and put pressure on his side front and back. Brett bit back a groan of pain but sucked air through his teeth.

Tears streaked down her cheeks. "I didn't know you were hurt. I just saw you running for the stairs. Then I found your board floating in the surf and saw the hole."

"It's okay, honey. I'm breathing well, and the pain is—" He circled the word, but his mind felt dull "It's easing off." His face and tongue felt numb.

Tess's tears flowed faster. He rested his hand on her thigh and wished he could feel her skin instead of the neoprene. "It's going to be okay."

Sirens cut off abruptly. Four police officers ran in from the street, their guns drawn.

When they established the shooter had left the area, the officers started pushing people back and securing the scene. A moment later, an ambulance halted on the street and a team of paramedics ran toward them, cases in hand.

One policeman was talking to Clara while another interviewed Tess. Brett was grateful they left him out of the loop. It took every bit of his concentration to deal with the pain as they cut his wetsuit away.

One paramedic started an IV while the other applied gauze pads over his wound, then rolled a tight dressing around him that kept constant pressure on it. Something his mother was saying penetrated the place he'd taken himself to deal with the unrelenting agony. "Mom?"

"Yes." She wiggled over to be closer to him.

"What was it you just said?"

"The man was screamed something at me."

"What was it he said?"

"He said matter jinga or something like that."

"Maadar jendeh."

"Yes, that's what he said."

Brett started to sit up, but the paramedic pushed him back down. His ears rang with the effort to remain calm. "Officer. My name is Brett Weaver. I'm a Navy SEAL. I need you to clear this area as quickly as possible. And I need you to contact NCIS right now."

The uniformed cop stared at him. "Why?"

"Because the words *maadar jendeh* are Farsi, and they mean," He glanced at Clara, "I'm sorry, Mom, mother whore."

"So?"

Brett closed his eyes for a moment and swallowed back the urge to leap to his feet and grab the SOB by the throat.

"I just got back from Iraq four months ago. That man knew," he motioned toward his Mom. "that this woman is my mother. When you go down to the beach, you're going to find a hole drilled though my surfboard by a second round that missed my head by less than an inch. And one that penetrated the sand about a hundred feet from the stairs. There's probably another somewhere else down there."

"His gun went off when I fell on top of him. It shot over that way," Clara said, pointing at an angle toward the road.

Jesus. How long had she wrestled with the fucker?

"The last round, number five, the last round in the clip, was shot into the sky when Mom tried to tackle the son-of-a-bitch and saved my life. He may be looking for a house to perch on to start shooting again."

"I'm getting the stretcher and we're out of here," one of the paramedics said, and, using his radio reported, "We're doing a bag and drag. We'll be in contact as soon as we're in route." He rushed to his feet and ran toward the ambulance.

The paramedic's actions convinced the cop, and he turned aside to use his radio. Within three minutes, Brett and Clara, her arm immobilized by a gauze wrap holding it across her chest, were loaded.

Tess stood outside the ambulance with the camera bag and camera in hand. "What hospital are you taking them to?" she asked the paramedic.

"Scripps Mercy. It's the closest, and they have an excellent trauma department." He slammed the door shut and went around to get into the driver's seat. They tore away from the site with lights flashing and siren screaming.

One of the policemen helped her load her board atop the car. They'd confiscated Brett's as evidence. She set the camera bag in the front passenger seat and, spreading a towel over the leather seat, got into the driver's side. She had to adjust the seat so she could reach the gas pedal and brake. Her hands shook so much she had trouble inserting the key into the ignition. For the first time, she noticed her hands and folded them in her lap. Despite the towels and wipes the paramedics had given her, Brett's blood had stained her fingers where she'd put pressure on his wounds. He'd clutched her hand all the way to the ambulance. He'd looked so pale.

Tears streamed down her face, but she brushed them away with the back of her hand. He wasn't going to die. He was going to be fine. He was tough.

The kisses they'd shared, their moments of connection came back to haunt her. She'd been wasting time when they could have been together. What was *wrong* with her? Why was she living her life to please her father instead of herself? Why was she so set on looking for approval from a man who didn't give a shit about her? Especially when she had one who wanted her enough to slog through her *issues.*

She quashed the desire to beat her forehead against the steering wheel. She'd been a fool, but not anymore. She started the car.

Russell was already in motion as he hung up the phone. Used to dealing with emergencies, he recognized the panicked racing of his heart, but could do nothing to control it. This was Clara. Concern spurred his steps as he left his office and jogged down the hall. Nurses and corpsmen sidestepped out of his way. He reached the elevator just as the door was opening and hit the proper button. He jerked his cell phone from his pocket and called his secretary to reschedule his appointments for tomorrow.

Five minutes later he reached physical therapy. The buttercream walls of the rooms projected a positive, warm atmosphere, as did the staff. The place had a faint rubbery smell. He'd seen them work miracles with both severe injury and amputation patients.

It took only a few moments to find Zoe. She stood before a young man missing the lower half of his left leg. He was performing an exercise on his prosthetic limb.

"Zoe," Russell spoke before he reached her and she looked up, the focused concentration of her expression changing to a smile.

"Hey, Dr. Connelly."

He forced himself to take a deep breath. It wouldn't do either of them any good if this panic he was experiencing spread to her. He had to pull it together. He'd been a doctor for over thirty years. He'd dealt with situations far worse than this. No, he hadn't. This was Clara and Brett.

"Tess Kelly called me a few minutes ago. She met your mother and brother at Sunset Cliffs today."

"Yeah. Mom said she might." Zoe's features stiffened. "What's happened?"

"There's been an incident at the beach." He grasped her arms. "There was a sniper. Brett's been shot."

She flinched as though he'd struck her and blanched.

"Also your mother has injured her arm. They've taken them to Scripps Mercy."

Her throat worked as she swallowed. "Is he alive?" Her eyes, so like Clara's, looked glazed with shock and fear. Her body stiffened as though she sought to brace herself against a blow.

"Yes, they had him stabilized before they put him in the ambulance. Your mother attacked the shooter, and he hit her with the butt of his rifle."

"Dear God."

"You need to get your things so we can go to Mercy."

She turned and motioned toward the patient she'd been working with.

"I'm good. You need to go," he said.

Zoe broke into a limping run toward the door, the brace on her leg jingling.

"I'll get someone for you," Russell said to the patient.

"I'm good, Doc." He stepped from between the metal parallel beams, and though he limped some, he seemed steady on his prosthesis.

Zoe returned to the door with both her purse and a large African American man. Russell rushed forward.

He heard her say to the man. "Seaman Roby is doing balance exercises to strengthen the muscles in his thigh, and he still has twenty minutes of work to do. Don't let him wiggle out of it."

"I got this covered. You go do what you got to do."

"Thanks, Tank." She touched the man's arm.

When he and Zoe were in the car, he realized how shaky he was, and reached for her hand.

"Tess said Brett was awake and talking and your mother got into the ambulance under her own steam. They're both going to come through this fine."

Zoe features blanked as she fought back tears. "Thank you, Dr. Connelly."

This was Clara's daughter. He'd felt more of a connection to her when Brett was his patient than he did right at the moment. With Clara spending so much time with his son, why hadn't he made more of an effort?

"Russell. Please call me Russell."

The hallway was pitch black and the NVGs painted the walls, and the crates that lined them, florescent green. Keeping his steps measured, he approached the first door. He pressed his ear to the panel. Silence breathed behind the door and he shoved it open.

Crates of AK-47s and ammo lined the room. He shrugged out of his pack and unbuckled the flap to get to the DET cord inside. He strung the cord around the boxes of rifles and knelt on the floor to plug in the timer. The next moment the butt of a rifle was coming at his face. He tried to move, but the action was so unexpected he seemed frozen in place.

"You need to wake up, Mr. Weaver," a female voice said from his right.

Brett caught his breath and inhaled the medicinal burn of antiseptic lingering in the air. His mouth tasted like the bottom of a cesspit. And he was certain he'd been run over by a tank at least twice, maybe three times. Keeping his eyes closed he raised his head an inch off a pillow that crackled each time he moved. Pain shot through his side from just beneath his ribcage to the top of his thigh. He bit back an oath.

"Would you like some ice chips?" The female voice asked from beside him.

"About a gallon of water and a toothbrush ought to do it."

She laughed. "A gallon might be overdoing it, but I can get you a cup of ice and a toothbrush later."

"Thanks." He forced his eyes open and looked up into a smiling face. Her skin, the color of dark caramel, made her smile appear that much brighter, and he found himself grinning back.

"Hey. My name is Pamela Farmer. I'll be one of your nurses while you're here."

"Thanks. My mother?" he asked as his mind cleared a little and worry bounced back, sharp and deep.

"She's fine. She and your sister have been here waiting for you to come up from recovery. I'll go tell them you're in your room and they can check on you now. Your fiancé is here, too."

All right. Hmm. His thoughts were working through parachute nylon, but he'd remember something as important as a fiancé. He smiled. "Slender redhead with beautiful brown eyes and a very faint sprinkle of freckles across her nose?" he asked.

"That's her. She'll be thrilled you haven't forgotten her."

"Not a chance."

She checked his blood pressure, his IV, cranked up his bed, filled a plastic pitcher with ice, and gave him a cup of ice chips. "Think you can hold that on your own?"

Brett gave her a thumbs up, and she smiled again.

"Once we make sure you can keep water down, I'll see about getting you a real cup of water. Okay?" the nurse said.

"Okay."

He was sucking on a piece of ice when Zoe and his mom came in. When his mother hugged him, he pushed down the emotion that welled up. He held her one armed and smoothed her hair. That fucker could have killed her. He'd tried to kill them both.

"I'm good, Mom. Just groggy."

"You look like hell," Zoe said, but smiled. She turned aside to brush away tears. She stood at the foot of the bed and rested a hand on his sheet-covered calf. "Tess is outside in the hall waiting to see you. And NCIS, the local cops, homeland security and the FBI are here."

"Jesus." He fought to keep his eyes open. He felt so tired. His eyes closed, but when someone reached for the cup, he awoke again.

Clara gripped his hand. "They're looking at this like it's a terrorist attack."

"I expected as much." How could he protect his mom and Zoe if he was laid up in the hospital? The thought helped him shake free of some of the drugs. "When's Hawk due back, Zoe?"

"He's due back tomorrow."

"Good. I'd like for you and Mom to stay in a hotel until he gets home."

Zoe studied his face. "If that's what you think we should do."

"Yeah."

"Okay." Zoe moved forward to his other side and brushed his hair back, and leaning down, pressed a kiss to his forehead. "I love you." She pressed her cheek to his and her body shuddered with suppressed sobs.

"I'm okay, Zo."

"I'm not," she whispered. She straightened and brushed aside her tears. Her throat worked as she swallowed "Everyone's waiting to speak to you, and we don't want to tire you too much. You lost a lot of blood. If you get too tired, you need to say so. Tess wants to see you before the others come in."

He grasped her arm as his anxiety skyrocketed. "Promise me you'll go to a hotel," he said.

"We promise," Clara said. She kissed him. "We're fine. You concentrate on you."

He nodded. "Is your boyfriend here?" he asked.

"Russell?" Her eyebrows rose.

"Do you have more than one?"

She smacked his arm lightly. "Don't be a smartass." Her eyes narrowed. "Yes, he's here."

"I'd like to speak to him, too."

Clara frowned. "The others are getting a little impatient."

"They can wait until I've spoken to him and Tess."

"Okay."

He raised a hand to brush it over his face. "I'm sorry, Mom. I'm just—"

"I know. We're going to be fine, Brett. And you are, too."

He nodded, but he couldn't brush aside the DEFCON six alarm that kept going off inside his head. That asshole had known she was his mother. Did he know he'd been seeing Tess? Did he know Zoe was his sister?

Russell and Tess stepped into the room.

"I need you to do something for me, Dr. Connelly."

Russell stepped close to the bed. "Your physician here seems to be doing an excellent job."

"It's not that." He drew a deep breath. "Tomorrow after Hawk gets back from Camp Billy Machen, I'd like you to ask my mother to move in with you for a while."

CHAPTER 24

Tess waited for the door to close behind Russell, then approached the bed. Brett's eyes looked swollen as though he'd slept too hard. The bandages that wrapped his torso looked snow white against the golden tan of his skin. She couldn't allow herself to think about the horrible wound that had looked like a rip in his side instead of just a hole. Weren't bullet wounds supposed to look like punctures?

"You changed out of the sexy wetsuit," he commented eyeing the sundress she'd switched into after arriving at the hospital.

He offered his hand and she took it. "I thought this might be a little more appropriate for a hospital visit."

"You always look beautiful in anything you wear. Are you okay?"

"Yes, I'm fine." She brushed his hair back from his forehead. "How are you feeling?"

"A little dopey."

"No pain?"

"No. Not yet." He rested the back of her hand against the light brown patch of hair in the center of his chest.

Her hand tingled with the contact. She'd had the opportunity to touch him and hadn't taken it. She'd been a fool. She swallowed and dragged her gaze up to his face. "I know you've faced violence in the past, but I couldn't believe how calm you were."

"We're trained to keep our head under pressure. Is there someplace you can stay tonight besides your apartment?" he asked.

"You really believe this guy was after you?"

"He didn't shoot anyone else and he called my mother a whore. Until they tell me otherwise, I'm going with that. I've been seeing you on a semi-regular basis. I want you someplace safe."

Was he right and this man was after him? Or was it just paranoia from his PTSD? It wouldn't hurt to be a little cautious. "I have a friend at work I can stay with for a few days."

"Good."

She had to tell him. If the story broke and he didn't know ahead of time, he'd think she'd used him and his mother for copy. "Your mom took a picture of the man, Brett."

He paused as though to absorb that. "Jesus."

"The police confiscated her camera."

"I'll have to get her another. They'll keep it as evidence until they catch this guy."

"Getting her another might be a good idea. The press is here in droves. Even the national television news." She swallowed against the knot that rose in her throat. "And my editor has been calling every few minutes. He wants me to cover the story."

His features hardened, and he released her hand. "You can't put our names in the paper, Tess."

"The FBI has asked me to hold off on that, but I have to write the rest."

He focused on her face, but he didn't say anything.

"I don't want to do it, Brett, because I'm too close to you and to what happened, but he's insistent. I didn't want to do it without warning you."

"Consider me warned." He looked away.

He was shutting down on her, just as he had done the night her father interviewed him. "I have to do this, Brett."

"All right." He drew a deep breath and shook another ice chip from his cup into his mouth. "But I don't have to like it."

"If they gave you orders to board a plane to be shipped off to some Godforsaken country to be shot at, you'd beat everyone else to the runway," she said her throat tight. "But when I'm faced with following orders too, you're angry about it."

"My job doesn't infringe on your privacy, Tess."

She balled her fists at her sides. How could he say that? The articles she'd written had been just general information, not the in-depth interviews with him or Master Chief O'Hara she'd wanted. She'd not written a single word he hadn't shared willingly or that could be construed as intrusive to his privacy.

The door opened and four men crowded into the room.

Blinded by tears, Tess pushed through the wall of policemen and out into the hall. For hours she'd been harassed by her editor and other reporters as she waited for him to get out of surgery, then out of recovery. She'd finally turned her phone off so she could worry in peace.

Overwhelmed, she leaned against the wall outside the room. Her composure crumbled and tears streamed down her face. Several moments passed as she struggled to compose herself. Determination replaced the hurt, and she pushed away from the wall. She had a job to do whether Brett liked it or not. And better she did it herself than trust another journalist, who might decide the scoop was more important than people's lives.

Brushing away the tears, shoulders straight, she marched down the hall to the automatic doors that separated the surgical unit and the waiting room. She strode into the waiting room where Clara and Zoe sat with Russell. "I need to go," she said. "Is it okay if I take the car and drop my board off at the apartment? Then I'll deliver the car wherever you need it dropped."

"It's nearly ten o'clock at night, Tess. Take the car and we'll work out the logistics of pick-ups and things tomorrow. You'll need to go get your car at Sunset Cliffs. Maybe you can pick me up tomorrow morning early and we'll handle it." The bruise discoloring Clara's jaw looked angry and red. The one on her cheekbone showed the imprint of the barrel of the gun. With her arm in a sling, she looked battered.

"It wouldn't be a good idea for you to be behind the wheel of a car in your current condition, Clara," Russell said. "You have a slight concussion. Tomorrow you'll be sore and the bruising will be worse."

Zoe said. "I'll take care of the car. Tess and I will meet early, ride out to Sunset Cliffs together and I'll drive the car back."

Exhaustion dragged at Tess. After hours of waiting and worrying over Brett during his surgery, she just wanted to go home and have a good cry. "Thanks, Zoe."

"I have to go into the office now." She gathered her bag and slipped the strap over her shoulder. "My editor is expecting me to write the story up tonight, and they'll submit it for publication in the early edition. I promise I won't be putting in your name or Brett's. I'll just say the FBI has requested the identity of the victims be kept confidential until their families can be notified."

"Thank you," Clara said, a troubled frown marring her brow.

"I'll walk you to the car," Russell offered.

"With the way the press behaved when we got here, I think that's an excellent idea, Russell. Thank you," Zoe said, her tone laced with outrage.

"What happened?" Clara asked, frowning.

"They couldn't understand why Tess was coming up with us when they were confined downstairs."

"Because I'm one of their fraternity and I had an inside track, or they thought I did. I really don't want to write the story, Clara. I'd gladly hand this one off to someone else." Once written, it would be the death knell to a relationship that probably never had a chance anyway. An ache settled in her chest that didn't let up.

"Better you than someone else who is just out for the scoop, no matter what it might cost us," Clara said.

"I'll try to convince my editor of that. I'll call you in the morning about the car. Under the circumstances, it might be better if I stay away."

"I don't think Brett will be pleased if you don't come to see him," Clara said and began to tear up. She wrapped her arms around Tess and gave her a squeeze. "Thank you for helping."

Tess felt her own eyes glaze with tears and pulled back as soon as Clara released her. "I'll speak with you tomorrow." She exchanged cell numbers with Zoe.

A panicked breathlessness took over when she started down the hall with Russell. What if something happened to Brett while she was gone? "Brett will be okay, won't he?" Her voice shook and tears were close again.

Russell hesitated. "There are always risks because of the nature of the injury, but Brett is young, strong, and healthy. He should make a full recovery. He's in good hands here."

She tried to take comfort from his words, but the soul-deep sense of loss was crushing her heart.

Fuck-fuck-fuck. The words screamed through his head. While he'd been in surgery, she'd been conducting business as usual. He'd done the same thing when a teammate was injured. Life went on, no matter what catastrophic thing had happened. But she'd shrugged it aside so easily. And let him know exactly how important he was to her. He was just a fucking story.

An ache ripped through him with as much power as the bullet that had struck him. He ran a hand over his jaw and struggled to control his expression.

"Do you feel up to a few more questions Ensign Weaver?" The NCIS agent who spoke was one of the ones who had interviewed him in Captain Jackson's office.

Brett dragged in a breath and focused his attention on the man. "Sure, Agent Wright."

"When were you first aware that you were being fired on?" he asked.

"When a small section of my surfboard exploded inches from my face. And then again when a round hit the water just behind me.

"When did you realize you were hit?"

"When I made it out of the water onto the beach and my side was bleeding like a sonofabitch."

"How many rounds did you hear?"

"Just the one that hit my board. The surf drowned out the sound of the discharge. But I felt the velocity of a round hit the water behind me. I thought he shot another round at me while I was on the beach, but my mother said the weapon discharged toward the street when she fell on top of him. That round and the next were the only two I heard."

"There were six rounds fired."

So he'd had five in the clip and one in the chamber. An M-15 or a Barrett XM-109 maybe. The possibilities are numerous. Jesus, I should be dead.

"We recovered the twenty-five millimeter shell casings atop the cliff and the round in the sand down on the beach was found with a metal detector before the tide came in. We think he was using low velocity to suppress the sound."

"It seems to have worked."

"We haven't had time to analyze the picture of the shooter. But we've printed one off for you to look at." Wright stepped forward and handed him the photo.

Brett studied the picture.

"Would you have any idea who he might be?" Wright asked.

"No. My mother said he spoke Farsi." Brett looked up and he scanned the three men's faces. "Who have you got in Iraq investigating the incident we spoke about recently? And who would they have given my name to?"

Despite his dusky coloring, Wright's cheeks darkened and his jaw tensed. "No one, Ensign Weaver."

"No one is investigating? Or no one would have given out my name?"

"No one would have mentioned your name."

"Just what the hell are you guys talking about?" The FBI agent asked.

"Agent Wright can explain it to you," Brett said his gaze never wavering from Wright. His heart beat hard against his ribs, and his face felt hot with rage. "It's strange that you approached me a month ago and now I'm dodging bullets, Agent Wright. Not just me. My *mother. My mother! What the fuck do you think might be going on?*"

Wright looked as though his six foot six inch frame might explode at any moment. He focused on an area just past Brett's shoulder. "We don't know that the two instances are related."

Brett raised one brow. "Surely you're not that obtuse."

Wright's gaze leaped to his, and his jaw pulsed. He started to say something, but nurse Farmer stepped into the room. "Time's up, gentlemen. Ensign Weaver has just been through a trauma and had surgery."

The group started to file out.

"Agent Wright." Brett said as the man reached the door. Wright stiffened and turned, reluctance in every movement. "You know who Tess Kelly is?"

"She's a journalist for the San Diego Tribune."

"She's also Ian Kelly's daughter."

Wrights brows rose and his expression clouded.

"You know the only guy I wouldn't want on my ass besides a SEAL would be an award-winning journalist. Tess is his baby girl, and I've been seeing her."

"Don't you think that might be a bad call, considering?"

"Not if I'm innocent, which I am. If things go down badly because someone took a shortcut and didn't do their job, it won't hurt to have an international watchdog on my side."

"Meaning Kelly?"

"Yeah. And one other thing. My team has sort of adopted my sister and mother as part of their extended family, especially since my sister and my commanding officer, Lieutenant Yazzie, are so close. Since you don't believe there's any connection to my being shot and your investigation, I'd suggest you do one thing."

"What's that, Weaver?"

"Spend a little time on your knees praying nothing happens to my family while I'm in here unable to protect them, because Lieutenant Yazzie and the team are due back soon."

"I shot him," Tabarek crowed in exultation.

"He is dead?" Yasin stared out the window at the courtyard outside his home office. The yard was hard-packed dirt with patches of scruffy grass here and there. How did he feel about a man's life being over? He felt numb. It was as though the pain of Sanjay's disappearance had cauterized his emotions into emptiness.

"No. But he was taken to the hospital bleeding badly and his whore mother was taken as well."

"His mother?" Was Tabarek's jihad extending to the man's family?

"The whore attacked me while I was shooting her son." He laughed.

Sweet Allah save us. "We did not speak of attacking the families of these men, Tabarek."

"They have taken our families, why would you not want them to pay for that with their own?"

"We are talking about innocent women and children."

"No, this woman gave birth to a murderer. Besides the whore can identify me."

Yasin sank into the chair behind his desk and rested his head in his hand. "I wanted the men who killed Sanjay dead, not their families."

His tone grew rough with rage. "I want more. I want them all to suffer, as we have suffered. They are infidels. Why would you care about them?"

"I did not say I care about them. But their women and children have done no one harm."

"They harm me just by living. My own family is dead because of them." Tabarek's voice rose, growing so loud Yasin held the phone away from his ear.

Tabarek's family was dead because they had chosen to follow a different path than those peaceful Muslims who lived the Koran as it had been written.

He was being drawn deeper and deeper into a pit. How had he allowed his own beliefs to become so twisted?

"You are losing focus, Tabarek, and putting yourself and the others in danger. You have allowed your passion to rule your intellect, and it will be your undoing."

The man remained silent for a moment. "That is easy for you to say, safe in your home with your family."

"No one is safe. There is no family who has not been scarred by what has happened in our country." *The Americans have been scarred, too. If only they had not harmed my child.* Tears burned his eyes and fell in large drops to stain his pants. He wiped them away impatiently. "You must stick to the plan, Tabarek. Kill the men you went there to kill and come home."

"I cannot reach the one. He is protected by his prison walls. So someone else will have to take his place. Perhaps his commanding officer. It was he who ordered the bombing and played a part in your son's death. What was his name?"

Would this never end?

"What was his name, Yasin?"

He remembered the man reassuring him that his son would be safe with his men. Anger and pain blended together to form an unbearable ache in his chest. "Captain Jackson."

"Do you know his full name?"

"Stewart Jackson."

"I will find him and he will pay for what he has done."

The phone went dead.

CHAPTER 25

Yasin hit the off button, disconnecting the call.

"What have you done?" Levla's voice came from behind him and he started.

How much had she heard? "What do you mean, Levla?"

Her dark eyes widened with fear. Her hands clawed at her skirt. "You were talking to someone about killing. You told a man to kill someone."

She'd heard too much. He rose to his feet and faced her. "He is going to kill the men responsible for Sanjay's disappearance."

Levla staggered and pressed a hand over her mouth not quite stifling a groan. "No. Blessed Allah, no." Tears flowed down her face. "This cannot be. This cannot be."

How could she not want them punished? "They killed my son, Levla. No one has seen Sanjay since they took him from the base. He is dead by their hand."

She shook her head hard enough that her hair fell forward over her shoulders. "Nooo—No! He did not die by their hands." She fell to her knees and rocked in pain. "He died by mine."

"For the second time in your life, you've received a miracle, Ensign Weaver," Dr. Talbert said.

"I know that Doc."

Dr. Talbert leaned his six-foot frame over the railing of the bed and pointed at Brett's bandage. "The bullet had to be a low velocity round. It entered here just beneath your ribs and exited just above your hipbone. It skimmed just beneath your skin, ripped open a fissure nine inches long, and tore out the subcutaneous fat layer. Had you sustained a direct hit you would not be sitting here with me right now."

Jesus. The doc made it sound as though he'd gone out and gotten shot on purpose. "I didn't do this to myself, Doc."

Talbert's brows rose. "I'm sorry if I sounded as though I were blaming you for your injury, Ensign." He drew a deep breath. "I only meant to point out how very fortunate you are."

"*Inshallah*, as they say in Afghanistan. God's will."

The doctor nodded. "Obviously He was looking out for you. We removed particles of your wetsuit from the wound track and repaired the injury. You'll have an ugly scar, but in terms of tissue loss, the muscles were spared any major damage. You should recover pretty quickly."

"How long before I can train again?"

"Six weeks for the tissue to heal completely, maybe a couple of more just to be certain. Two months at least."

Shit. More waiting. More fighting his way back. More excuses for Captain Jackson to stall his orders. Or find a way to push him out.

"When can I get out of here?" He needed to get home. He needed to protect his mom, his sister. And that niggling worry about Tess kept tormenting him.

She'd hung around to get the scoop so she could use him as copy. He cared about someone who didn't give a shit about him. How pathetic was that? Pain like battery acid ate at him.

Dr. Talbert studied the chart for a moment. "The nurse said you'd been up and moving well."

"Yeah." It had hurt despite the pain medication, and he'd mentally cussed every step. But he'd done it.

"I can release you late tomorrow, if you're showing no signs of infection and you have someone responsible who'll stay with you."

It wouldn't be Tess. "Trust me, I have two responsible somebodies who'll stay with me. That's the one good thing about being the only male in the family."

Talbert smiled for the first time. "Good, I'll get on that paperwork tomorrow."

"You're ex-military aren't you, Doc?" Brett asked.

"Yes, I was a Naval surgeon. I just retired last year. How did you know?"

"The analysis of the wound. And the anger."

Talbert frowned. "What do you mean?"

"I got home from a seven-month tour in Iraq four months ago. And I've been angry ever since. Angry and restless. I see a psychologist twice a week. You might want to talk to someone."

Talbert remained silent for a moment. A brief smile crossed his lips though he shook his head. "I'll think about that, Ensign."

Brett extended his hand. "Thanks for patching me up."

"You're welcome." Talbert shook his hand. "I'll want to follow up in a week, just to make sure everything is healing as it should, and then again in six weeks. The nurse will be in with some paperwork for you to sign, an appointment and some instructions."

"Thanks, Doc."

As soon as Talbert left the room, Brett swung his legs over the side of the bed. He placed a bracing hand against his hip as he rose to his feet. The more he moved around, the quicker the soreness would abate, but, damn, he felt like he'd been stomped on several times.

The door swung inward behind him and he turned.

Hawk stood in the doorway. A smile broke across Brett's face.

Hawk's serious expression didn't change. "We need to talk."

Russell exited his car and headed up the walk to the house where Clara was staying. He'd called earlier to check on her, but his need to see her, just to be certain she was okay, overwhelmed his usual control. The porch stretched across the front of the house. At one end, a wicker lounge, and two chairs with a table angled before them, were arranged invitingly. The cushions on the furniture, printed with bold flowers, mirrored the hibiscus plants in the two large planters that bracketed the arrangement.

"Sir." A police officer approached him from a car on the street. "I need to see your identification."

Russell pulled his wallet from his back pocket and waited while the man looked over his license and military ID.

The door swung inward and Clara stood within its frame. "Thank you, officer. Dr. Connelly is a friend."

The police officer returned his ID, and Clara motioned for Russell to come in. She shut the door and locked it.

"I wanted to see you just to be sure you are all right," he said.

Clara's smile eased the taut knot of anxiety, and he drew his first deep breath since he'd rushed to the hospital.

Dressed in lightweight cotton pants and a summer sweater, she looked her normal self except for the brace that hugged her arm. The early morning light picked out the copper highlights in her hair and touched the fine lines at the corner of each eye and around her mouth. He didn't dwell on those, but homed in on the fragile slope of her jaw where a black bruise and a swollen area marred the oval shape of her face.

"How are you feeling?"

"I'm just a little sore."

The careful way she moved her head told him something more. Tipping her face up, Russell studied the lighter bruise along her cheekbone. Someone had hurt her. Had tried to kill her.

Every time he looked at her injuries, acknowledged them, rage shot through his system, and he wanted to punch the asshole and go on punching him until he was ... no more.

Instead, he enveloped Clara into his arms and held her. When she nestled against him, pressing her breasts into his ribs and her head against his chest, he drew a deep breath. He wanted her. He couldn't hide his response to her, nor did he want to. He'd almost lost her before they'd ever had a chance to truly know what they could have together.

Her arms tightened around him. He smiled at the color in her cheeks when she looked up at him. He bent his head and kissed her. Her lips clung to his, intensifying his need. He drew back before it got harder to stop, but his lips lingered against her cheek, her temple.

"Evan wants me to bring you over so he can see for himself that you're okay," he said.

"Maybe later." Clara drew back, but her hand lingered against the front of his knit shirt. "I've always thought when my children were grown and gone I'd have plenty of privacy to do as I pleased."

"Let me guess," he interrupted. "When you had the privacy, you didn't really need it, then when you crave it most, it's impossible to find."

Her smile held a wry twist. "Exactly."

"I've been feeling the same way." His breathing grew labored against the frantic beat of his heart.

She ran a caressing hand over his chest, and his skin heated.

"I called earlier to check on Brett. He'll be released later today." She rested her cheek against his chest, once again stirring his urge to protect and comfort. "Zoe's left to take Tess to pick up her car. She's going on to work with the rental car. And Hawk will be coming home later tonight."

Russell ran his hand down her spine to the small of her back. His pulse leaped to pounding in a matter of a nanosecond. "How's your arm feeling?"

"I took some medication earlier. It's fine."

He touched her chin, and she tilted her head back to look up at him. He searched her features one by one. "You've just been through a trauma, Clara. Are you sure?"

"What time do you have to go to the hospital?" she asked.

"Fourteen hundred." His mouth found hers again. She cupped his face, and her tongue caressed his in a slow sensuous response. He groaned.

She pulled free of his arms to take his hand and tug him down the hall into a bedroom decorated in cool shades of green.

She slipped her feet free of her sandals, and his attention fastened on the graceful shape of her ankles, her feet, and the pale pink polish on her toenails. Had he ever recognized how sexy bare feet could be? Surely not until this moment.

He toed off his own shoes and reached for his belt.

"We've had so little time alone together. I've wanted more," she said.

"I have, too."

She shimmied out of her pants and stood in just her sweater and panties.

The shapeliness of her thighs drew his attention. He slipped his arms around her. "We can take our time, Clara." He dragged the comforter down to the foot of the bed and urged her to lie down. He was aware of her watching as he shucked his, socks, pants and shirt and stretched out beside her in his boxer briefs. Her head found a place in the hollow of his shoulder and the brush of her bare thigh across his sent instant heat racing upward. He grew painfully hard. It had been too long. He drew her hand to his lips and he brushed a kiss against her fingertips. "I know we're past the need to worry about conception, but do you have protection? I'm careful at work and with Evan, but just in case ... "

"They're in the nightstand drawer." She ran a hand over his chest in a caress he felt all the way to his toes. She raised her head to look down at him and the trust he read in her face triggered a rush of tenderness for her.

"You ought to have seen the look the young girl at the pharmacy gave me when I bought them. I don't know which of us was the most embarrassed," she said, and laughed.

He chuckled. "Young people look at us and see the lines on our faces, and the gray in our hair, and nothing else." He caressed the tender curve of her cheek. Seductive and shy, generous and caring, she drew him in more thoroughly than any other woman ever had. "When did you buy them?" he asked.

"After you took me to the harbor and the Gaslamp Quarter for lunch."

He smiled. "I bought some then, too. I haven't been carrying them around with me, but I got them. Just in case."

Her smile was laced with mischief, though her cheeks grew pink with a blush. "Maybe you should start carrying them. Just in case."

He caught his breath at the depth of his response to her teasing. He kissed her, pouring into it all the intensity of his passion for her.

Clara tried to lose herself in his kiss, but the nervous tremors spread from her hands all the way down her body. For as much as she wanted him, she was terrified of disappointing him. For all the seductive teasing she'd done, she was afraid this first experience would end as disastrously as her last one.

The patient love she'd seen in his face as he looked at his son, the tenderness and humor she'd read in his eyes when he looked at her, suddenly came to mind to chase the nerves away. It was going to be okay. She loved him.

It had been so long since a man had touched her. Russell's hands running over her skin felt like something new and wonderful. She wanted to laugh with the joy of it and weep for all the barren years she'd waited. Why could she not have found him sooner?

Russell's fingers tugged the sweater upward, and she pulled it over her head. He guided the strap of her bra down her shoulder and followed it with his lips. "Your breasts are beautiful. I had to keep myself from staring at them that day at the airport."

She unhooked her bra and nearly groaned aloud when he paused to caress each one before lowering his lips to her nipple. The texture of his tongue, the warmth of his mouth as he sucked, sent ripples of pleasure arrowing down her body and her hips rose in response. Her breathing grew choppy and her hands ran over the width of his shoulders in a caress. The shape and size of him was both familiar and strange, and oh, so dear. When his lips came back to hers, she caressed the sturdy strength of his chest and felt the coarseness of the hair there against her skin. The thrust of his arousal pressed against her hip and she ran her fingertips down the length of him through the briefs. He thrust against her touch and groaned her name, his tone husky.

When he peeled her panties down, she wiggled free without hesitation. He ran his palm over her hip and down her thigh then back up, his exploration slow and thorough. As he stroked and caressed the inside of her legs, need clawed at her and she rolled her hips, encouraging his touch. At the first careful, intimate brush of his fingertips, she caught her breath. He tempted and teased her with the circling movement of his finger until her hips rocked with need. His name broke from her.

He rolled away to strip off his briefs and reached for the drawer. Seconds seemed like eons as he ripped open the condom and covered himself. When he turned back, she opened her arms and her thighs to welcome him.

The careful way he balanced atop her, the easy way he thrust so slowly inside her, gave her heart a squeeze. His eyes swept her features, his expression filled with tender passion. "I've wanted you so much, Clara." She cupped his face and drew his lips back to hers.

And after a small pause, Russell captured a rhythm, edgy with pent-up need. She welcomed the push and drag of his body moving in and out of hers. Her breathing grew ragged as the firm thrust of his erection swept that sweet spot just inside her again and again. At the swelling throb of his release, her pleasure spiked, stealing the strength from her limbs, and she clung to him as the orgasm tumbled through her.

When she opened her eyes, he was smiling down at her, his hazel eyes alight with amusement and satisfaction. "How long has it been?" he asked.

"Almost six years."

Surprise rocketed across his features. "Dear God!" He kissed her.

CHAPTER 26

Hawk wandered down the hall to the physical therapy wing. A plastic smell like the mats in a training room grew stronger the farther down the hall he progressed.

He'd wanted to see Zoe before visiting Brett, but he'd taken pity on a fellow teammate and dropped the news on him as soon as he'd hit town. Captain Morrow had a copy of the transmission between HQ and the security detail. According to the tape, they'd delivered the kid, and then bugged out back to base.

Morrow had sent NCIS a copy of both the transcript and the tape on the first stateside-bound transport. It would arrive in a few days. Knowing NCIS's reputation, the tape wouldn't completely clear Brett, but it was a start.

And now he was going to see his girl, even if it was just for a minute between patients. He lengthened his stride and excitement brought a surge in his heart rate and his temperature. He'd missed her every day and every night of the three weeks he'd been gone.

A woman passed him the hall and paused. "May I help you?" she asked.

"I'm looking for Zoe Weaver. She's a physical therapist here."

The woman's eyes ran down over his brown t-shirt and desert cammies, all the way to his boots. The come-on registered only long enough for him to frown. Not interested.

"And you are?" she asked.

Her boyfriend. Her partner. Her lover. Her man. It was growing more awkward for him each time someone asked. Zoe deserved to be a wife. He wanted to be a husband. So, why wasn't he remedying that situation?

"I'm Adam Yazzie, her boyfriend. I've been gone three weeks on a training op and just wanted to see her."

The woman's attitude changed from scoping him out to being helpful. "She's with a patient, but I'll slip into the room and tell her you're here. You can go down to the lounge and get a cup of coffee while you wait. It's just three doors down and to the right."

"Thanks." A patient with an artificial arm fitted at the elbow walked by and saluted him with his hook. Their eyes met for a moment and Hawk returned the salute. *By the grace of God.* Hawk was reminded every day how lucky he was. He wandered down the hall to a room with a kitchen, a small table and chairs, and a television mounted high on the wall in one corner. The smell of fresh coffee permeated the room He leaned against the counter uninterested. All he wanted was to see Zoe and hold her.

Five minutes passed and he was reading the same poster about the stages of grief for the tenth time when Zoe rushed in. For a split second they just looked at one another, and then they were in each other's arms. Zoe's head pressed against his chest and her arms clung tight around his waist, her breasts pushing into his ribs. He breathed in her vanilla scent. Vanilla and her. God knew what he smelled like after riding from Miramar to base in the back of a truck. Maybe he should have stopped to shower. He ran his hand down her back to her waist with one hand while he cupped her head with the other and tangled his fingers in her ponytail.

When she finally leaned back to look up at him and smiled, his mouth found hers. Her lips parted and their tongues tangled. The kiss went on and on as they tried to make up for three weeks of separation.

When he finally raised his head, her voice came wispy with emotion. "I've missed you so much."

Hawk cupped her face with both of his hands and just studied each feature. He'd never known he was capable of loving anyone as completely as he loved her. "The words 'me, too' don't even scratch the surface."

Her dark blue eyes looked even darker since the kiss. He took her lips again, this time with all the tenderness that rose inside him.

"You can't keep looking at me like that, kissing me like that. You're either going to make me cry or we're going to have to find a storage closet somewhere," she said, her laugh shaky.

"There's an idea. What time do you get off?"

A grin curved her lips. "As soon as I get home, I hope."

The erection he'd tried to control was instantly at full mast. "That's a promise, sweetheart." He kissed her again, then grew serious. "I need to know what time to be back here so I can ride home with you."

He hated watching the teasing light go out of her eyes.

"It's just a precaution, Zoe." A well-founded precaution. Did the asshole who'd shot Brett know about Zoe. Where she lived? Where she worked? Did he know where Clara was staying?

"Have you been home yet?" she asked.

"No."

"There's a policeman standing guard at the house. He'll want to see your ID. Mom's there with the alarm on."

"Good."

"So, you think the man may know where she is?" she asked, her voice rising with alarm.

Hawk kept his voice moderate. "We don't know that, Zoe. But it doesn't hurt to take precautions." He sighed inwardly. "I want to stick around and have lunch with you."

"I'd love it. But I don't get a break for an hour. And I'd feel better if you were home with Mom. If you don't mind."

"No problem."

"Do you really think this guy may be after Brett?"

"Brett believes he was targeted, and he and your mother were the only two the shooter went after."

"But why Brett?"

Shit. He hated keeping Zoe in the dark. But it wasn't his secret to tell, and even if it were, he was bound by his oath and couldn't say. "I don't know, Zoe. We were in Iraq for seven months and dealt with a lot of bad guys while we were there. This one may or may not have a tie to a mission. We don't know for sure." And now that NCIS and all the other agencies were involved, they probably wouldn't know if this guy was tied to one of their missions, until somebody was on a slab. That possibility had him and all the other guys in the team on high alert.

She glanced at the clock on the microwave and sighed. "I have to go." She pressed close against him again.

Hawk tightened his arms around her and rested his chin atop her head. "What time do you finish up here? I'll have one of the guys drop me by and I'll ride home with you."

"Five o'clock."

He kissed her again, and despite the tension their discussion had triggered, the taste and feel of her lips beneath his sparked a desire for more. He released her reluctantly. "It's going to be okay, Zoe."

She nodded. "But it sure would be nice to go more than a few months without some kind of crisis."

Amen to that.

He walked her down the hall to the PT room she was using. "I'll be back at five. Wait here for me. I don't want you walking to the car alone."

"Okay."

Aware of people in the hall around them, he bent his head and kissed her hand instead of her lips. "I'm really glad to be home, Zoe."

Her smile was something special, and her voice softened so only he could hear her reply. "I'll show you how glad I am to have you home later."

"I'm up for that, sweetheart." He gave her hand one last squeeze and strode down the hall.

She sighed as Hawk disappeared around a bend in the hall. As much as she liked her job, there was something to be said for not working. Like not having to postpone their intimate homecoming celebration. Until now, they'd only been separated a few days at a time since she'd moved into his house permanently, and each of the other homecomings had been memorable.

In fact, the last celebration had probably been when she'd conceived. And just when was she going to surprise him with that bit of news? She'd hoped he'd pop the question before she had to, but with his training rotations coming with shorter periods in between, there had been little time for them to focus on anything so serious. She'd hoped he'd want to ask her without the push of a pregnancy forcing his timing.

And time was flying biologically speaking. By her, and her doctor's, estimation she was eight weeks and sprinting toward her first trimester. The only change she'd noticed other than morning sickness was her breasts were tender and her nipples were turning a darker color. Would Hawk notice that one small thing? God, he noticed everything. She had to tell him.

Seeing Corporal Crowes waiting for her in the room, she shut her thoughts away. She had to focus on his problems right now.

"Is that your boyfriend?" Crowes asked from his seat on the four-inch thick platform they used as an exercise bed for patients with more than one amputation.

"Yes."

"He's Native American?"

"Yes, Navaho. His grandfather was a code talker in World War II."

"Cool. You said he's in the Navy, but he was dressed in desert cammies."

Zoe remained silent. Special Ops girlfriends and wives didn't spread the word about what their guys did. She'd learned that from watching Trish, not anything Hawk or Brett had said.

"How's your stump feeling?" she asked. "Not tender or sore anywhere is it?"

"It's good. I keep a close check on it like you and the doc said."

"Good. You want to stay as mobile as possible and keeping your leg healthy is a major part of that.

"He's a SEAL, isn't he?"

"I'd rather not talk about what he does." She attempted to change the subject by throwing attention onto him. "Are you growing a beard?" She studied the whiskers on his chin.

"Okay." He paused for a moment. "I understand. You're just trying to protect your guy."

The tension in Zoe's body relaxed. "Thank you." She offered him a smile.

He rubbed his hand over the unshaven spot on his chin. "I thought I might grow a goatee. No one's going to bust my chops about facial hair now. Hell, I might even get a tattoo and a motorcycle." There was an edge to his voice, a recklessness. He suddenly switched topics. "Anyone can tell. Those guys have a way of moving, a kind of aura that just sets them apart. We had a SEAL sniper that worked with our platoon. He never missed."

Zoe hated to dampen his enthusiasm, but she wasn't talking about Hawk to him. Something had happened to set Cal off. "Cal, we need to concentrate on you. As for the bike, I'd take it one step at a time," Zoe said. "There's no reason why you can't do those things, but a tattoo is a very permanent thing, and I'd give it a great deal of thought before I marked my body with something that can't be removed."

His expression darkened. "Like this." He raised his leg thrusting the prosthetic out.

If he'd hoped to shock her, he'd missed the mark. She'd seen and heard far worse. "Why don't you tell me what's happened? You're angry as hell, and I promise not to spout that stuff counselors and psychologists say about the stages of grief. You've probably already heard all of it. Did you just get up angry today, or did something happen to set you off?"

"It's my mom. She treats me like a fu-freakin' invalid. She's constantly doing things for me. Telling me to sit down and rest my leg. I don't want to rest my leg. I freakin' want to just—hell I want to go out trollin' for girls. And party with my buds."

"There's no reason why you can't do that."

"I think the guys think this—" he gestured at his leg, "will put off the girls."

"Or maybe they're afraid it will give you an unfair advantage. You're a hero, Cal. You sacrificed your leg for your country. You were prepared to sacrifice your life. Women admire warriors. And just because your girlfriend couldn't handle it, doesn't mean other women will feel the same way. You need to cut yourself some slack and stop cutting your *buds* any."

A few minutes later in the midst of an exercise Cal said, "I understand why your boyfriend snapped you up, and didn't give a shit about the scars. Out of all the bullshit, you see what's important."

Zoe blinked as sudden tears blurred her vision. She swallowed several times before her throat cleared enough for her to speak. "Thanks, Cal."

Tess stepped out of the shower and reached for the towel on the bar. The scent of her shower jell hung in the moist air. The mirror, frosted by the steam, glared at her. Thank God she couldn't see herself. She didn't need to see the dark rings beneath her eyes. The headache that pounded at her temples was bad enough.

She wrapped the towel around her body, then opened the medicine cabinet and reached for the Tylenol. The pills stuck to her palm, still damp from her shower. She scooped them off with her lips, ran water into the glass on the sink, and washed them down. The bitter taste lingered, as acidic as the hurt that ate at her every time she thought of Brett. He'd gotten what he wanted, his introduction to Ian and Ian's active interest in the story. Five days of silence following the introductions should have offered her a clue.

She should never have accepted Clara's invitation. Despite his response to the kiss, he hadn't wanted to see her.

It had happened again. She'd been used to get to her father. Tears ran down her cheeks for the hundredth time in the last twenty-four hours. She reached for the corner of the towel and it fell loose. She buried her face in the cloth and allowed her grief free rein.

Damn him! Damn him! She hit the sink counter with the heel of her hand. At least she hadn't given herself to him. The humiliation of that happening again would have been too much to bear. She swallowed back the pain and draping the towel back over the bar, ran cold water into her cupped hands to cool her face.

Was that the phone? She turned off the water. The sound of the William Tell Overture rang from down the hall. *Ian.* Grabbing her robe from the back of the bathroom door on the floor, she raced to her bedroom.

"Hello, Daddy." She shrugged into her robe and clamped the front together in a fist.

"Tess, I've found a pattern of young men being taken. I've discovered at least twenty-five between the ages of twelve and eighteen. They're not just in the area Brett mentioned. They're spread over the city of Baghdad. Once I discovered one and began talking to the fathers and other relatives, they started telling me about other boys they'd heard about. I've been following the trail ever since I got here."

"My God!" She sank down on the bed.

"The sad thing is, the Iraqi government doesn't care. And the Iraqi military are so overwhelmed here they're looking at these kids as casualties of war and writing them off. No one is looking for them, or trying to do anything about it."

The reception wandered in and out, loud, then soft, then cutting out altogether. "Ian? Ian?"

"I'm here. My SAT phone is going in and out. There's some kind of interference."

"What will you do? What do you need?" Tess asked raising her voice.

"I've written the preliminary story and sent it to the AP. I need an American military contact here in Iraq I can share information with. I think I've found a contact who knows where they've taken the boys, but I need backup, just in case."

She'd have to call Brett. Her stomach dropped at the thought. *This could mean Ian's life. She had to do it.* "I'll call Brett right away. He'll have someone there you can feed the info to. But you have to be careful, Daddy."

"I will. That's the second time you've called me Daddy. What's going on?"

Tears welled up and she blinked them away. "Nothing here. I've just been worried about you." True enough. She'd kept her phone with her constantly, except for that brief hour she'd surfed with Brett. Ian had called less than Brett had. "Please—please call me more often and let me know you're all right."

"All right. I'll call you tomorrow morning at eight, your time, for the contact information. If you get it before then you can email, but I'll still call. Internet connection can be disrupted. I'm to see Sanjay al-Yussuf's father tomorrow."

"Are you eating right and sleeping?"

"When I'm not pacing the floor waiting for interviews. I'm fine. I'm staying with an Iraqi friend who writes for Al Zaman. I have a feeling this problem is more widespread than anyone can guess. We're not talking about boys who were eager to leave their families, Tess. These are children who would have never done so, had they had the choice."

"There has to be something that can be done. I'll see Brett today. I'll have the contact for you. Ian, don't do anything until you have a backup."

"I may be driven, but I'm not stupid, Tess." Irritation crept into his voice.

Surely he wasn't drinking. Wasn't it against the Muslim faith to drink? Surely he wouldn't drink in an Iraqi household and show such disrespect. But she'd have never guessed he'd done so to excess, ever. Not before a big interview. Not before meeting Brett. She cringed from the memory.

"I know you're not stupid. But you weren't exactly yourself when you were here."

"I'm fine now, Teresa. I've found the thread that will unravel the story, and I'm waiting to pull it. I'll keep you posted. I've got to go."

"I love you, Ian."

The connection was gone and all she heard was empty air.

Russell woke and instinctively turned to check on Clara. She was curled on her side, her bare shoulder and back to him. Her skin was a delight to touch and he was tempted, but she seemed so sound asleep he didn't want to wake her. He contented himself with breathing in her scent, something with a hint of cinnamon in it.

She needed to rest after her ordeal the day before, and their lovemaking. And they hadn't just made love once, but twice and both times had been—good, really good. Who was he kidding? They'd been fantastic together. He couldn't remember the last time he'd spent the morning in bed with a woman. But he'd certainly remember every moment of their time together.

He glanced at his watch and grimaced. He had forty-five minutes to report to the hospital.

From the open doorway, he caught a glimpse of desert camouflage uniform pants and a brown t-shirt and tensed. Why hadn't they closed the door? Was this a threat?

Hawk Yazzie stepped into sight just long enough to shut the door. His soft tread in the hallway moved away.

Russell drew the covers over Clara's shoulder and eased free of the bedclothes. He reached for his discarded clothing and dressed. He paused to take in Clara's bed-rumpled hair and flushed cheeks with satisfaction and more than a little tenderness before leaving the bedroom. When he entered the kitchen, Hawk sat at the small kitchen table set before the windows, drinking a glass of iced tea. His gray eyes, sharp and watchful, studied Russell as he approached the table and sat down.

They eyed each other for a moment.

Russell leaned back in the chair. He wasn't ashamed of being with a woman he cared about. And they were adults. But Hawk's steady gaze had a predatory watchfulness that had his muscles tensing in preparation of defending himself. "I'd appreciate it if you didn't tell Clara that you saw me here. She'd be embarrassed knowing you saw us together."

"I wouldn't do or say anything to make her feel uncomfortable. She's Zoe's mother. So, she's my family." Hawk said.

So he was protective of Clara. A good thing under the circumstances. "We've been dating ever since she came out to visit. This isn't a casual thing. I came over just to check on her ... " What was he doing explaining?

"She's a special lady, and she should be treated as such."

"I agree."

"This will stay just between me and you, as long as you treat her as she deserves, Doc."

That was plain enough. "That isn't a problem. As I said, this isn't a casual fling. I care about Clara." Russell rose to his feet. "I have to report to the hospital. She's sleeping soundly and I don't want to wake her. I'd like to leave a note."

"Sure." Hawk rose, went to the cabinet closest to the phone, slid open a drawer, and removed a pad and pencil. He handed them to Russell. "When you're ready to leave, let me know. The alarm is armed, and I'll reset it when you go." Retrieving his iced tea from the table, Hawk wandered out onto the sun porch.

Russell spent some time formulating a short note and slipped into the bedroom to leave it on the pillow next to Clara. He wanted to kiss her good-bye, but didn't want to wake her.

At least he didn't have to worry about anyone getting through the policeman outside to harm her. He had no doubts at all that they'd play merry hell getting past Lieutenant Yazzie to lay a finger on her.

CHAPTER 27

B rett gripped his side and swung his legs over the edge of the hospital bed. He swore beneath his breath at the tugging sensation that gave him a quick pinch of pain along the stitches. Fucking temperature spike. He'd have been out of here if it'd happened just a few hours later.

He hiked up his pajama pants as he eased to his feet. At least his bare ass wasn't hanging out of a hospital gown. Bless Zoe for bringing him some pajamas.

A dull headache throbbed at his temples, more from grinding his teeth with every movement than the fever. He'd taken the two Tylenol the nurse had given him instead of the pain pills the doctor had recommended. He wanted his mind clear in case anything went down. The pain medication made him too drowsy.

He ran his hand over his unshaven jaw. The nurse had offered to shave him, but he'd turned her down. He might be a patient, but he'd be damned if he'd be treated like an invalid. He rose to his feet and shuffled to the sink. Jesus he was sore. His ditty kit was at home, but Nurse Farmer had left him a disposable razor and a can of shaving cream, which beat the hell out of dry shaving or not shaving at all, as they'd often had to do down range. He picked up the plastic razor and frowned at the blades. What more could a guy need or want?

A tap at the door had him shuffling around to face whoever was coming in. He couldn't twist to look over his shoulder. Tess stepped into the room. Her dark auburn hair was secured at the back of her head, leaving her face bare. She wore a white sweater trimmed with pale blue stripes that hung off one shoulder, and dark blue leggings hugged her long legs and emphasized her lithe, graceful build.

Screw the razor. She could fill the bill.

"I've come to give you an update." Her flat tone made him notice her closed expression. She looked pale, and her dark gaze moved around the room restlessly, looking at everything but him.

What was she pissed off about? He was the one who'd been under the knife while she'd been thinking about the scoop.

"I read your article. Thank you for holding back our names."

She shrugged her bare shoulder and shot him a glance. She gripped the cloth strap of her shoulder bag as though someone might wrestle it from her. "With all the different agencies breathing down my neck, you didn't really think I'd put them in, did you?"

The urge to go to her and taste that smooth creamy skin was a temptation despite his condition. He had to quit wanting her like this.

"You made Mom into a real hero. She'll be embarrassed, then secretly proud. She doesn't draw much attention to herself."

"She'll probably need to lay low for a few days, in case someone here in the hospital leaks her name." Tess shifted from one foot to the other but made no move to come any closer. "She single-handedly fought off an armed shooter with a camera and took his picture. She deserves some recognition. But the reporters out front have been overaggressive."

"You'd know, wouldn't you?"

Her eyes flashed. "Yes. They know my name, and they know I'm associated with whoever it is who was shot, so they've given me hell every time I've come into the hospital."

He frowned as anger raced through his system. Assholes. If he were able— But he wouldn't be for a while. *Damn it.* "What did you come to tell me?"

"Ian has discovered a pattern of missing boys all over Baghdad. He has a lead on who's responsible and where they may be taking them, but he needs a military contact who can help should he get into trouble."

"Holy shit," Brett breathed. The son of a bitch had really done it. "Has he found the kid?"

"No, not yet. But he's documented a pattern of disappearances and must have interviewed some people in the government and the Iraqi military. He says they've written these boys off as casualties of war. He's written a piece and sent it to the AP. And he needs backup before he follows the thread he's discovered to who may have taken them and where."

"I have someone in mind, but I'd like to talk to Hawk and see if he concurs."

"Ian will be going to see Sanjay's parents tomorrow. He said he'd call me for the name tomorrow morning."

"Can I borrow your phone to make the call now?" he asked.

She fished inside her bag and came up with her cell. She hesitated before she crossed the distance between them and extended it to him. Up close, the dark circles beneath her eyes stood out like bruises. She looked tired. He accepted the phone and caught her wrist when she would have stepped away.

"Tess—"

"Save it. You got what you wanted. Ian got what he wanted. And I learned a valuable lesson."

"And what was that?"

"Don't ever-*ever* allow another man close who wants to meet my father for any reason. At least this time I was smart enough not to sleep with you." She jerked away, moved to the window to look out, and folded her arms.

Brett's heart skipped a beat. If there were a sniper on any of the structures close by—"Get away from the window, Tess."

Her features tensed at the sharpness of his tone, and she jerked her chin up. Stepping away from the window with a slow sway of her hips, she shot him a narrow-eyed look over her shoulder.

Once she was safe from the immediate threat, his mind leapt back to what she'd just said. *This time? This time?* Jealousy clamped down on his lungs and for several moments, he couldn't breathe. Some other guy had sex with her to get an introduction to her father? Jesus, he'd kill the fucker.

He pushed his hand against his side and strode to her with as natural a gait as he could manage. "What do you mean this time?"

"Fuck you, Brett Weaver. It's none of your damn business."

Whoa—He'd never heard her swear before. Her eyes had grown dark, her lips tightened, and tears started to give her eyes a glaze.

"If he slept with you just to meet your father, he was a fucking fool, Tess. Your father's an asshole."

She made a choking sound, and then laughed. And laughed. And once she started, she couldn't stop. He didn't know whether he should laugh with her or just wait until the storm passed. When she finally stopped and drew a deep breath, she had tears in her eyes. She wiped away the moisture with the back of her hand. 'That asshole may just save your bacon, if he doesn't get killed first."

Was worry over her father what had brought that drawn look to her features? *What am I missing here?*

"Why did you hang around until I came out of surgery?"

"You'd just been shot. Did you really expect that I'd just go home and wait for word?"

"It wasn't for the story?"

"What story, Brett? I've written all I can about what happened. Sure, they may release your name and your mother's, but now the story will revolve around the attempts to capture the shooter. You've had your fifteen minutes of fame."

Wow—Talk about a reality check. He flinched as another thought hit him. Hard. He'd misjudged her motives for staying at the hospital. And given her hell. He'd allowed his anger to cloud his judgment. Shit, he'd really screwed up.

He ran a hand over his jaw. "I behaved like an asshole night before last."

"You've been behaving like an asshole for the last week. In fact, you and my father should compare notes." The pain in her expression had guilt slapping him upside the head. Had he done such a bad job before of showing her how he felt, telling her how he felt? Going five days without calling, then jumping down her throat over the story hadn't exactly shown her anything but how big a prick he could be. How could he fix this?

He raked his fingers over his close-cropped hair. "I didn't call because I was too busy beating myself up for giving your father the info."

"So you took it out on me by not calling."

"Yeah, I did. But I didn't not call because I didn't want to see you." Exhaustion suddenly weighted his limbs and he eased back onto the edge of the bed. He turned the phone over and over in his hands. Could he trust her? The hurt he'd read in her features only moments before gave him a sharp jab.

"I have this anger thing." He swallowed. "I've been angry ever since I woke up from the coma. And when I get angry, I want to punch something. I've seen what that kind of anger can do to the people around you." *Jesus, I will not become Derrick Armstrong.*

"And you were angry with my father for not living up to your expectations, and angry with me for looping you into a situation where you spilled what you felt were secrets."

"We don't talk about what we do, Tess. Never."

She sat down next to him. "You'd never raise your hand to a woman, Brett. As protective as you are of your mother and sister ... " She shook her head. "No way. But you can't keep shutting down and holding all that rage inside. It isn't healthy."

"What would you suggest?" he asked.

She remained silent for a moment. "Would it really be that scary to let it out?"

"With my CO, it could get me court-martialed."

"But if you'd come to me a week ago and we'd had this discussion, you'd have probably gotten laid." She stood up and shrugged her shoulders again. "Your loss."

Brett tossed her phone on the bed and, catching her hand, scrambled to his feet as quickly as his injury would allow. "I'm sorry, Tess."

She studied his face, her gaze narrowed, probing. "Are you sorry because you screwed up, or because you didn't get to have sex?"

If he smiled, she'd punch him. Well, as long as she didn't hit him where he'd been shot, he'd be okay. "Actually both." He drew as deep a breath as his side would let him and grew serious. He tipped her face up so he could look into her eyes so she'd know he spoke the truth. "But mostly because I hurt you and made you think I was as big an asshole as your father, and the other guy who hurt you. I'm not that guy, Tess."

Tears ran down her cheeks and she turned her face away. "It sure felt like you were."

At the sight of her dark eyes wet with tears, a knot formed in his stomach. He peeled the bag from her shoulder, dropped it to the floor, then drew her against him. "I'll promise not to close myself off from you when I'm angry, if you'll do the same."

When she went completely still, he tensed. Had he said too much?

Tess listened to the steady beat of his heart beneath her ear. That strong rhythm soothed her. Heat seemed to radiate off him. She drew back with a frown and laid the back of her hand against his forehead. "You're running a fever." Her stomach tightened as concern hit her. She'd been harping at him, and he'd been running a fever. But he'd deserved to be harped at for treating her just as her father did.

"They're going to hook me back up to an IV and start giving me fluids and antibiotics again."

She bit her lip. "Don't you think you need to lie down and rest?"

"You could lie with me." He cupped her hips and tugged her with him as he sat down.

Standing between his legs, her own temperature spiked at the thought. "That won't really encourage you to rest."

He raised one brow and grinned.

When he smiled like that, she saw the reckless, sexy side to him that had drawn her from the moment she'd first seen him. "You really need to relax and let your side mend, Brett."

"I was going to shave. Would you like to help?"

Desire shot through her at the idea of touching him so intimately, quickening her heartbeat and making her breathing choppy. She cupped his cheek and ran a thumb over the rough stubble darkening his chin. "Yes."

The look in his eyes intensified that tempting, empty ache. Emotion rose high in her throat and took her breath. *She loved him.* The realization weakened her knees. She dragged air into her lungs. *But could he love her?* She swallowed. "Are you sure you trust me?"

"You know things about me even my mother and sister don't. What do you think?"

He was talking about the PTSD and the anger issues. *Issues that could end his career should they come to the attention of the wrong person. If he could trust her with his secrets, surely he could love her. S*he cupped his jaw and bent to press her lips to his. "Your secrets are safe with me."

"Tess." He tried to pull her down into his lap, but she resisted.

"Let's make you more comfortable with a shave."

His blue gaze latched onto her with such intensity that an aching heat settled between her thighs and she grew breathless. She took his hand as it rested on her hip and tugged him to his feet, then drew a chair close to the sink and urged him sit.

She reached for the shaving cream and sprayed the foam into her hand. She hesitated, uncertain.

Brett's grin was both challenge and temptation.

Her fingers followed the strong structure of his jaw and chin, spreading the foam over his beard. She ran warm water into the sink and picked up the plastic razor. "I was very angry with you when I first got here. Are you sure you're okay with me standing over you with a razor my hand?"

He studied her expression. "You're not going to hurt me."

Pressing the razor's blade against his skin gave her a sense of both control and anxiety. She wouldn't nick his handsome face for the world. She loved his face. Concentrating on each area, she studied every angle and slope as she scraped away the dark brown whiskers. His jaw was decidedly masculine. His chin had a faint hint of a cleft. And his lips surrounded by the foam were a prime example of how male lips should be structured. She knew from firsthand experience how they could be firm yet soft when they trailed over her skin.

"You keep looking at me like that, Tess, we're going the give the nurse a shock."

Heat climbed into her cheeks. "I'm just concentrating on what I'm doing. I don't want to nick you."

He raised one brow. "Uh-huh."

She tilted his chin up and scraped the blade along the stretched skin beneath. When she'd rinsed the blade for the last time and set it aside, she wet a hand towel and wiped the last of the foam from his face.

Brett was on his feet before she realized he was going to rise. His body brushed all the way along the length of hers, his arousal blatant as he tugged her close. He worked a hand beneath her sweater to cup her breast, at the same time lowering his lips to her bare shoulder. She caught back a groan as his teeth scraped, with careful pressure, the tender skin between her neck and shoulder. She shivered and pushed against his erection. The gentle pinch and tug of his fingers as they played with her nipple drove her need to a fever pitch. She wanted to spread her legs and take him in *now.*

She dropped the towel to cup the back of his head and thread her fingers through his hair. His mouth turned to hers and his tongue delved into her mouth as though hungry for contact. She sucked on it and he groaned, the vibration of the sound triggering a whimper of her own.

The William Tell Overture played from the bed, and she broke from the kiss. "Oh my God, I forgot about Ian."

CHAPTER 28

Yasin sat on the edge of the bed opposite Levla and pressed the heels of his hands against his aching eyes. He had been furious with her after listening to the whole story. Why had she not told him the truth about Sanjay? For his insolence toward his mother, he'd have punished him. For striking her, he would have certainly done so. But to lie and say she hadn't seen him after the SEALs had delivered him to the house, *Dear Allah.*

She blamed herself for allowing him to leave the house. Blamed herself for his disappearance. She'd grown thin and withdrawn in the last five months. The guilt continued to eat at her. She left the house with two of the servants every day searching for their son. *While I continued to work just as I did before Sanjay's disappearance. Why have I not been searching with her?*

Because I had already decided what had happened. He had believed his son dead. And now he was afraid to believe he might still be alive.

And where was Sanjay? Had he run away that day, afraid of being punished for his disrespect? Or had he been taken, as Levla believed?

Would she have ever told him had the American reporter not come to their home and asked to speak with him about Sanjay? And what would he say to the man when he arrived in a few minutes?

Levla sat up on the edge of the bed, her back to him. "Will you allow me to speak to the American reporter?" she asked.

"I will be there with you. So, yes, you may speak to him, if you wish."

After a pause she asked, "What will you do about the man you spoke with in America?"

How could he stop Tabarek's jihad against the SEALs without exposing his own involvement?

He couldn't. He had condemned innocent men to death. But they were not innocent of killing Tabarek's brother. They *had* blown up the building he was in. But his brother had also been a member of the Taliban and had probably created bombs to kill the Americans.

"There is nothing I can do, Levla."

He had become judge and executioner to men who had done his son no harm. He would have to learn to live with that. Unless Tabarek was captured and unable to finish what he had started. If Tabarek confessed and named his conspirators, he, Yasin, would pay for his part in the whole plot. As much as Tabarek hated the Americans, perhaps he would remain silent. And Allah would forgive him for directing his anger and grief at men who had not wronged him.

But who had taken Sanjay?

The American reporter had told one of the servants he had stories of other missing boys taken off the streets. And what did this American reporter hope to do about it?

"He called you a traitor to your people. He said he was ashamed to call you father. And I struck him. He would have hit me in the face had I not turned aside." Her voice sounded hoarse with pain.

He had heard this the night before. His pain crouched like a cancer, eating at his insides. Were these things spoken out of anger because he had not accompanied Sanjay home? What had happened that had made Sanjay see what he was trying to accomplish as something shameful? The businesses he was directing were growing, and their profits were helping his people rebuild. Why couldn't Sanjay see that?

"It is my fault that he is gone," Levla said.

When she had first told him of their argument, he had been angry with her. Now he'd thought things through and realized there would have been nothing she could have done to stop Sanjay from leaving.

"It is Sanjay's fault for being disrespectful to us both. It is his fault for allowing his anger to control him. And for leaving our home when he knows how dangerous the streets are when traveled alone. How many times have we cautioned him?"

And why had he not moved his family to a safer area? Because there were no safe areas.

"I am afraid to believe he is alive and cannot or will not come home to us, Yasin."

The anguish he heard in her voice ratcheted up his own despair. "We will listen to what the reporter has to say and decide what is to be done." He rose to his feet and moved around the bed to where she sat. He knelt to take her hands in his and bent his head to touch his lips to her palms. "I have worked with many of the American base commanders, Levla. I will persuade Captain Morrow to help find Sanjay. He has already been attempting to do so."

The hope he read in her face brought an ache to his chest. Hope was as cruel as death. What would it do to her, if they could not find their son?

"Baba, there are two men here to see you," Amira, their daughter, said from the open doorway. "Hakim says one is the same man who came here looking for you yesterday."

"Thank you, Amira." He rose to his feet and offered Levla his hand.

Her fingers were cold and she was trembling.

He rested his hand against her waist as they left the bedroom and walked down the hall to the formal living room where they received visitors. The only time he used this room was to entertain guests. The less formal living area for the family was next door. He eyed the stiff, formal furnishings without interest.

The tall man who rose to his feet looked imposing because of his height and the intensity of his expression. His bright red hair and beard looked so *American.* Another man, an Iraqi, stood beside him.

"I am Yasin al-Yussuf. This is my wife Levla."

Both men shook his hand and tipped their heads to Levla.

The red-haired man said, "My name is Ian Kelly and this is Ahmed Hannah, a reporter for Al Zaman."

"Please sit down." Yasin motioned to the two large chairs and guided Levla to the long couch positioned against the interior wall of the room away from the windows. How long would it be before they no longer had to live in fear of a bomb blast or stray bullet? "What do you wish to ask?"

"We have been all over the city and have learned about many missing boys, just like your son, Mr. al-Yussuf," Ian said.

Yasin had heard the rumors, but had not believed Sanjay was one of the boys. "Yes?"

"Ahmed and I want to bring enough attention to this issue that the American military will become involved and help find the boys. They have the technology and the resources. I've already been to the Iraqi police and spoken with several members of the government." His features creased in a frown. "I'm afraid this may not be one of their top priorities. They are overwhelmed."

"But the American military may be more helpful?" Yasin asked. Was that hope he heard in his own voice? Was he actually allowing it to grow in his heart as well?

"It would be in their best interest to help because they are trying to build a cooperative relationship with your people and your country. It would also be good international public relations. No one, no matter what their nationality, likes it when children are abducted and hurt."

"That's how we are trying to approach the story," Ahmed Hannah said.

"Where do you think they are taking the boys?" Yasin asked.

Ahmed spoke. "There have been reports from witnesses that men have forced the boys into pickup trucks at gunpoint.

But who these men are isn't clear. Perhaps Taliban. Perhaps al-Qaeda. We do not want to speculate about who they are or where they may be. But we all know where the training camps have been destroyed in the past."

"When your son disappeared, did anyone see him on the street? Has anyone come forward with any information?" Ian asked.

Yasin looked to Levla. At the anguish in her face, he shook his head. "No one has come forward."

"Do you have a picture of your son we might have? It will help in our hunt for him, and the military's."

"Levla?" Yasin gestured to her, and she quickly rose to her feet and left the room.

"Do you believe your son may have been abducted like the others? Or is there a possibility he may have left home for some other reason?" Ian asked.

Would it make a difference if he told them of the fight Sanjay and Levla had had? Would they think he might have run away? "Sanjay had no reason to leave our home."

The two reporters looked at each other. "What direction would he have gone if he had arrived home, then left again?" Ian asked.

"I thought perhaps west," Yasin offered. "That would have been toward his friend's house."

"What is his friend's name?"

"Gabir Abbas. But I have already spoken to him, and he did not see Sanjay."

"So Sanjay may have been taken somewhere between here and the Abbas' house," Ian said.

"If you would be so kind, we would appreciate it if you could call the Abbas household and ask if we might talk to Gabir when we leave here. It will smooth the way," Ahmed said.

"Certainly." Yasin nodded. Levla returned with a five by seven photograph of Sanjay. Her eyes grew wet with tears as she handed it to him and he patted the sofa cushion for her to sit down again. He'd hired a photographer the year before to take pictures of his wife and children. Living on the edge of a war zone had given him the idea that he wanted some kind of representation of them, should the unthinkable happen. He paused to study the color photo. Sanjay was short of stature and thin, but the image captured the intensity of his personality. His brown eyes, so much like Levla's, looked alight with concentration. Yasin extended the picture to Ian. "I have had some contact with the base commanding officer here."

"Captain Morrow?"

"Yes. He is already aware of Sanjay's disappearance."

"We intend to see him tomorrow and give him the information we've compiled. We need to know if your son has any birthmarks, moles, distinctive features, that kind of thing that could help identify him."

"He has a small overlap of his front teeth that is not evident in the picture, since he is not smiling, but no marks."

After he had given them information about Sanjay's height and weight, and answered a few more questions, the two rose to leave. "I will call the Abbas' house and encourage them to meet with you." He handed each of the men a business card with his contact information on it and closed the door behind them. His muscles shook from the release of tension that followed their departure. Would they be able to find Sanjay? *Please, Allah.*

Would they investigate him? Would they find some evidence of his contact with Tabarek? Surely not. No one knew they had met, and the phone he used to speak to Tabarek was anonymous and untraceable. Wasn't it? He was safe, for now. *But was Sanjay?*

Russell knocked on Brett's apartment door and glanced up and down the hall. The idea that Clara had actually come here alone to clean the apartment in preparation for Brett's coming home was mind-boggling. What had she been thinking?

He heard steps approaching the door and a pause. At least she was checking through the peephole.

The door opened and a young man, vaguely familiar, stood in the doorway. Russell's gaze moved past him to Clara standing just behind him. The tension in his back and shoulders relaxed somewhat.

The bruise along her jaw had turned green and was only faintly visible. The brace they'd given her was absent.

"Good to see you, Captain Connelly," the man said and offered his hand.

Recognition struck Russell. He'd met him at the hospital during Brett's stint as his patient. "Ensign Rivera, isn't it?"

"Bowie."

He shook the hand Bowie offered. "I appreciate you keeping Clara company."

"No problem, sir." Bowie smiled flashing dimples and white teeth. His swarthy skin appeared darker than the last time Russell had seen him. He remembered he was a member of Hawk's team.

"How was the desert?" Russell asked as Bowie stepped back to allow him to enter the apartment.

"Hot as hel-Hades." He glanced in Clara's direction. "Sorry, Mrs. Weaver."

"For what?" She shot him a smile. "What can I do for you, Russell?"

"I thought you might have come over here alone, and I was concerned."

"Bowie came over to keep an eye on things while I cleaned up and packed Brett a suitcase. I've tried to talk Brett into staying at Hawk's house, but he insists he's going to a hotel. Hawk's security system is state of the art, and he's even put in cameras around the exterior of the house."

"You know why they're staying away from each other, Clara."

"I know, but I don't have to like it. He's hurt, and he's so vulnerable right now."

"He's still a SEAL, Clara. And hurt or not, he knows how to handle himself. You know that."

She compressed her lips. "I have to finish this." She turned and went into the bedroom.

Were they getting ready to have their first fight? Russell glanced at Bowie.

"She's already heard the same thing from me, Doc. She's got her momma bear vibe going."

"So I see."

"I can hear every word you two are saying," Clara said from the bedroom.

Bowie grinned.

"I'll just talk with her." Russell pointed at the bedroom.

Bowie lowered his voice. "Good luck."

Russell strode to the bedroom. "Can I help with anything?"

Clara shook her head. "He said casual and about a week's worth of clothing. I'll put in a couple pair of dress slacks, just in case."

"Brett is just as worried about you as you are about him, Clara. Why do you think he suggested you call Bowie to come over?"

"How do you know he did?"

"Because I know how independent you are. And I know how protective he is."

She bit her lip.

"Evan needs to go back to San Francisco to see his doctor. He wants you to go with us," Russell said.

"I can't go, Russell. I can't leave Brett."

"This would be the day after tomorrow. Brett's out of the hospital and back on the mend. I've examined him myself."

"I can't leave him, Russell. If something happened, I'd feel like I'd abandoned him when he needed me."

Russell sat on the bed and took her hand. "I'm not asking you to choose between our children, Clara. Brett wants you to go with us. He asked me to get you out of town for a few days until this guy is caught. I want you to go with us."

"He really asked you to take me out of town?" Her tone fell somewhere between hurt and exasperation.

"You can identify the shooter, Clara. You got a close look at him. Brett's afraid for you. I'm afraid for you, too."

Her gaze shifted away. "I need to talk to Brett first."

"Okay." Russell rested his cheek against her palm then turned his lips against it. "I know Brett needs you. He'll always need you. He's your child. But I need you, too."

Worry drew her brows together. "Is Evan all right?"

No he wasn't. He was losing ground every day. And it was killing him, knowing there was nothing he could do. "Evan is doing as well as can be expected. But I wasn't talking about that."

Her voice dropped to a whisper. "I've been afraid to come over."

"I know. But if you go out of town with us, you'll be out of harm's way, and that will be one less concern for Brett to deal with. It will leave him free to concentrate on himself. And you'll be safe because no one will know you're with us."

"But Zoe will be here alone."

"Hawk's got that covered. They're going to stay with friends a few days."

"It seems the three of you have it all worked out."

Was that a note of pique in her voice? "If you all go in different directions, they'll have a harder time figuring out where you might be. It's just for a few days."

He could see she recognized the logic of it. "I'll take you home in my car just to be certain you're safe."

"Hawk dropped me off and will be back to pick me up."

"I want to spend some time with you, Clara."

Color flooded her face and then she smiled, her expression seductive, yet shy. A tight knot clogged his throat. She was so much what he needed and wanted. If anything happened to her—He couldn't go through that again. He had to keep her safe. She had to go to San Francisco with them.

CHAPTER 29

Hawk stood before Captain Jackson's desk as he pulled a folder toward him. He'd seen the man be a total asshole under pressure, but he'd never seen him sweat. And he was sweating now. His expression remained so controlled that his features looked wooden.

The muffled sound of someone walking down the hall at a quick clip traveled through the door then receded. The smell of the industrial wax used on the floor lingered. Hawk remained at parade rest rather than take the hard-backed seat Jackson had pointed to. If this were bad news, he'd take it standing.

"There's someone high up the food chain who's been pulling reports about every mission your team participated in while in Iraq. Those you led in particular," Jackson said, finally breaking the silence.

"What do you think they're looking for?"

"Any instance that you or your team may have screwed up."

The words *fuck you* hung on the tip of Hawk's tongue. "We didn't screw up."

Jackson raised a brow.

Hawk's temper fired and he mentally counted to ten. "If you really want to start pointing fingers, we can do that. I have copies of every report I made in Iraq and the ones I've filed since. That includes my conversations with you about Derrick Armstrong before and after his meltdown. I've followed protocol in every situation. Nothing we've done can be considered a fuckup."

"You'd better hope you're right, Lieutenant."

Hawk took several deep breaths and forced the angry tension from his muscles. It was counterproductive to punch your commanding officer. "It might be helpful if we knew who gained access to our files."

"I don't know who specifically, but they're using the reach of the Senate Arms Committee to gain access."

Rob Welch. Who were the other two Tess had mentioned? Brett had spoken to him weeks ago about Tess's suspicions that they were using the negative situations that had happened to their team to put pressure on the committee to cut funding.

"You don't seem surprised."

"No, I'm not. Brett said there are three members of the committee who have a record of unsupportive behavior toward the teams. Three who don't have significant populations of military personnel in their state."

"How would he know that?"

"His girlfriend, Tess, is a reporter for the San Diego Tribune."

"He's dating a reporter?"

"Yes, he is." Should he tell Jackson about Ian and the story he was pursuing in Iraq? No. It would point Jackson toward Brett and open him up to questions he wouldn't want to answer.

Jackson's lips compressed. "You could approach her and see what else she's found out."

"I can do that."

"I believe this same entity may be responsible for the investigation into your last mission in Iraq, as well as the Iraqi boy's disappearance. And I'm certain they're putting pressure on the Justice Department to bring charges against you and the other men for subduing Ensign Armstrong."

Jackson readjusted a stack of files on his desk. "There has been some discussion about your team doing an early deployment." His focus shifted to Hawk's face. "It would make things more difficult for the Justice Department to prosecute a team of heroes serving their country down range, rather than cycling through training rotations."

Did that mean an indictment was inevitable? The thought punched the breath from Hawk's lungs, and a wave of nausea hit him. Zoe. What about Zoe? Oh, Jesus. Three weeks had seemed like an eternity. A six-month deployment would be forever. But if he was convicted and sent to the federal pen—

"Admiral Cane is aware that you just got back from a tough seven-month deployment." Jackson continued.

It was his fault they were even scrutinized. Why hadn't he tried to take Derrick down himself? Because he'd been focused on saving all three hostages, Brett, Zoe, and Marjorie, Derrick's girlfriend. The chances that one or more might have been hurt or killed had been too high. "You could transfer me to another team and deploy just me. The rest of the team could remain home."

Jackson studied him for a long moment. "You'd be willing to take responsibility for everything that went down at the house?"

"We saved three lives, sir. I truly believe we had no other choice." A knot the size of a baseball lodged in his throat, and his breathing grew constricted as a band of emotion tightened around his chest. "They're my men. They came because I asked it of them."

Jackson's eyes fell to the stack of papers again, and he remained silent for a long moment. He cleared his throat. "There were five SEALs in your home when you took Ensign Armstrong down. And though it's admirable—damn admirable—for you to take sole responsibility, there would be no guarantee the others would be cleared, despite your sacrifice. If it happens, it'll be all or none, Hawk."

Hawk nodded. "The whole platoon, sir?"

"Yes."

"When?"

"Two weeks possibly."

It's too damn soon. Jesus. I'm going to pay for this in every way.

Tess paced the floor and glared at the cell phone. Ian was late calling her. Every time this happened, her anxiety level spiked. A knot spiraled in her stomach and pushed against the confines of her rib cage. Though she was grateful for the place to stay, Eva's living room, as small as it was, seemed to grow tinier as her focus narrowed on the phone. She dragged in a breath and continued to pace from the leather couch that took up most of the room to the breakfast bar that separated the living room from the miniscule kitchen.

When the William Tell Overture began to play thirty minutes later, every muscle in her body relaxed at once and she hiked herself up on one of the bar stools, her legs shaky. "Hello."

"We've discovered something else," Ian said from the other end of the line, the connection made sporadic by static. "There's someone else following our investigation. I think it might be the Naval Criminal Investigative Service." The connection cleared and his voice sounded more natural. "We went to see Captain Morrow yesterday, and he wasn't surprised by what we've uncovered. He was receptive to the info and he's going to follow up. He's also pretty much promised to keep me apprised of any developments."

"That's great Dad."

"We spoke to Sanjay's parents. They're hiding something, Tess. I can smell it. I think they know something they're not sharing. I had my doubts about Brett's innocence when I first started, but not anymore. This kid was snatched off the street. I know it. I just can't find anyone to collaborate it. We're going to question one of Sanjay's friends today."

"It sounds as though you're making good progress."

"So far. How's Brett?" Ian asked.

"He was released from the hospital this morning and has settled into a hotel. One of his team members is picking me up and taking me to the hotel to see him." She eyed the suitcase she'd packed. Her heart raced just thinking about it, and a jittery feeling of nervous excitement tap-danced along her nerve endings.

"If someone leaked info, Tess, it wasn't us. His name has never come up in our questioning of the people here."

"I know that, Ian."

"If terrorists are after him, that means someone here fed some very bad people his name and location. It might be better if you stayed away from him."

Tess drew in a deep breath. "I can't do that."

He remained silent for a moment, then swore under his breath.

Tess rested her head in her hand. Tears blurred her eyes. "I never expected to fall in love with someone who trots the globe like you do. I swore it would never happen. I tried to keep my distance. Tried to think of him as just a source. But I couldn't."

"He'd better love you. And he'd better not let anything happen to you. I'll be on his ass for the rest of his days."

The tears that had threatened streamed down her cheeks. That was the closest he'd ever come to saying I love you. "I'll be fine, Dad. Brett won't allow anything to happen to me. That's why he's sending his friend to pick me up. You need to be careful, too."

"I will. I'll call again tomorrow."

"I love you." There she'd said it.

He remained silent for a beat then two. "It's hard for me, Tess."

"I know." They were so alike in that way.

His tone grew husky. "I know I've been a disappointment to you."

"Not always."

He loosed one bark of amusement. "Thank you for that. You've never been a disappointment to me."

The connection broke. Tess shook her head, but a smile blossomed.

Brett shook his head. "So headquarters is going to allow politics to dictate when they deploy us—you." In all the time he'd known Hawk Yazzie, he'd never seen him this agitated.

"Yeah, they don't really have a choice. Remember when you said you felt like you had a target painted between your shoulder blades? Well, I've got that itch between mine right now. Jackson as good as said they were close to indicting us for taking Derrick down."

"If I ever see Derrick Armstrong again I'm going to beat the crap out of him." Brett shook his head as rage forced heat into his face. The hard thump of his heartbeat filled his ears.

"I'll help." Hawk said. "I need a favor."

"Anything," Brett said without pause.

"Do you think Tess could do some more research on Welch and his crew?"

"Sure."

"We need to find out why Welch has a hard-on for us, Cutter. Jackson said someone was putting pressure on from on high and it was coming from the Senate Arms Committee."

"Okay. Tess is great at research. You've read her articles. And I've told you about everything she ferreted out about Welch and his buddies. Doc's bringing her over in a few minutes."

The seriousness of Hawk's expression ratcheted up his own tension. His stomach muscles tensed. The pain reminded him to relax, but it was easier said than done.

Hawk's hands clenched and unclenched at his sides. "I know I don't have to ask this, but I need you to look after Zoe for me."

"Done. No one's going to fuck with her on my watch."

Hawk tipped his head. "There's a chance that even getting sent to the sandbox won't keep the indictment from coming down." He swallowed and the struggle to maintain his composure was evident in his labored breathing. "I want to pop the question, Cutter. I want to be with her for the rest of my life. But if I go to prison—I can't ask her to wait for me. I can't ask her to marry a felon. That will follow me for the rest of my life, and she deserves better than that."

Why was all this happening? "First, these bullshit charges are going to go away, Hawk. And second, it's already too late. Zoe would have never let you lay a hand on her if it wasn't the real deal for her. She won't give up. She doesn't know how, any more than you do."

"I can't ask her until I'm sure I have a future to share with her, Cutter."

Brett understood that. But Zoe wouldn't. She wouldn't give a damn about anything but Hawk. She'd done hard before and she'd just look it as another obstacle to overcome. "I'll look after her." But she'd still be heartbroken and he'd be useless to help with that. *Fuck.*

Hawk nodded "I know you wish you were going with us."

Brett forced a grin. "Why would you think I'd want to eat MREs and sand for six months, not to mention dodging bullets, and going days without sleep?"

Hawk smiled for the first time. "You're right. You'd be crazy to want to do that."

I'd give my right nut to be going with them. His gaze locked with Hawk's. "There's worse things than crazy."

Hawk nodded. "I have to go. We need that intel ASAP. Once you find some connections, maybe I can find some on my end. Right now all I have are the missions we covered on our last deployment."

"I have my laptop here. Since I can't do anything else, I'll help Tess."

Hawk slapped his back.

Brett suppressed a flinch. Damn he was sore. "I'll call you as soon as we find something."

Hawk nodded. "Do you have backup? Your personality might not be strong enough to keep the bad guys away."

"You're off your game. That insult was subpar for you. I have a nine mil in the dresser drawer."

"You have a permit to carry?"

"Yeah."

"Well, start carrying it. It's not going to do you any good out of reach."

Brett nodded and moved from the sitting room section of the room to the bedroom, the areas divided by a thin decorative panel that ran from floor to ceiling. He opened the dresser drawer and retrieved the Sig Sauer. He checked that it was loaded.

Hawk's gray gaze sharpened as soon as he returned. "That isn't your service weapon?"

"No, L.T. It's a registered backup." Brett checked through the peephole before opening the door. He looked down the hall in both directions. Nothing. "Go home and wait for Zoe. You need to be with her, Hawk. And I wouldn't tell her tonight. Let the dust settle. This deployment may not happen." *He hoped.* Because his sister was going to be devastated, though she'd try to act the good little military girlfriend. She'd be supportive and true. But while he'd been recovering from the head injury, he'd seen her wander the house and grieve when they'd gone wheels up before. Hawk loved the job, loved being a SEAL as much as he did. But it was always going to be an issue for Zoe. And the way Hawk was so twisted up about it, it was going to be hard for him, too.

He grabbed Hawk's arm when he started to leave. "Tess and I will find something. There has to be some reason why they keep coming back to our team."

"I'll work on my end until Zoe gets home. And call if I find anything." Hawk strode down the hall to the elevator, a man on a mission.

Fifteen minutes had passed when a tap came on the door. Brett picked up the pistol and headed for the door, his gate slightly stiff. He suppressed the urge to put his hand over his side. He had to quit doing that. Tess would be afraid to touch him and he sure as shit didn't want that. His heart revved like a Humvee with a stuck gas pedal. And his breathing was uneven. If he had anything to do with it, they were going to make love *tonight.*

With everything going down, he needed to feel connected to her, physically, emotionally. The way she'd held him and comforted him in her apartment kept springing to mind. He'd never needed that before. He'd always been the one to offer support, comfort, whatever was needed. To know he needed it, and that she would offer ...

But what do I have to offer her? One thing came to mind but his thoughts veered away. He wasn't ready for that yet. With all the trust issues they'd had up until now—And they hadn't even slept together yet.

After looking through the peephole, he opened the door to Tess and Doc. Doc motioned Tess into the room, then set a suitcase down just inside the door.

Tess wore a silk shell and a wraparound skirt that flowed around her long legs. Her auburn hair hung just past her shoulders, dark against her pale skin.

Aware of Tess's innate reserve, Brett controlled the urge to kiss her senseless, despite Doc's presence, and brushed her cheek with his lips instead. His hand wandered down her back to bring her in close enough that she could feel how glad he was to see her. Her cheeks flushed pink and her soft "hey" had him grinning like a fool, he was sure. The constant interruption of medical personnel and family at the hospital had held him in check. He didn't think he'd have so much control when they were alone.

When he released her and turned his attention to Doc, the guy had a knowing grin plastered on his face and there was suppressed laughter in his Irish green eyes. "I can't stick around. I have things to do at the base. We weren't followed, I made sure of that."

"Good. Thanks, Doc."

"I rented a car. I thought they might look for mine," Tess said and actually put her arm around him and pressed close to his side.

Brett looped an arm around her and gave her a squeeze "Good idea."

"Hawk fill you in?" Doc asked.

Brett tipped his head. This fucking terrorist bullshit sucked for them all. Especially now with deployment hanging over their heads. He was reasonably sure his family was covered. But what about Langley Marks' wife, Trish, and the kids? And what about Greenback's wife, Selena, and the new baby? "Is everybody okay?"

"Greenback's wife and baby are spending some time with her family. And Lang's taken Trish and the kids on a before-school-starts R and R close by. The rest of us are on alert."

"Good." He drew a deep breath of relief.

Doc pointed a finger at him. "Get fit so you can get back to the team."

"Bank on it, Doc." They bumped knuckles.

"Thank you for bringing me over," Tess said.

"No problem, Legs."

She shook her head at Doc, though a small smile peeked out.

"Call if you need anything." Doc said in parting and left.

Brett secured the door behind him and pivoted to face Tess. The words "let's get naked," perched on the tip of his tongue, but he swallowed them. He'd once promised himself that he'd romance Tess, and thus far he'd really sucked at it.

"Would you like to order something to eat?" he asked.

"No thanks. Maybe later. How's your side?"

"Better. Itching, so it must be healing." He leaned back against the door.

"What did Doc mean when he asked if Hawk had filled you in?"

"There's some political stuff going down, and they're being deployed."

"But they just got home what—five months ago?"

"Yeah."

She studied his expression. "Can you share it with me?"

"Yeah, but I was hoping to spend time with you first."

When she smiled, he knew he'd finally gotten something right. He pushed away from the door and linking his fingers with hers, guided her to the couch.

Her expression grew grave as he placed the Sig on the oak end table.

"It's just a precaution."

"I've never been around guns, Brett."

"There's nothing to be afraid of." He picked up the weapon, released the magazine, and ejected the round in the chamber, double-checked, then offered her the empty pistol, butt first. "It's a part of who I am, Tess."

Her hand wrapped around the gun's grip, and she held it in her lap. "It's heavier than I thought it would be."

"I can take you to a public range and let you shoot it."

She bit her lip and ran her fingers over the barrel of the weapon.

He slid his arm around her and guided her into holding the pistol in a firing grip.

She smelled like citrus and spice, her hair lay against his cheek, the texture a little coarse compared to the silky smoothness of her skin. The contrast mirrored the qualities in her personality. She had complete confidence when she had the recorder in her hands or a pad and pen. She was intelligent, focused, and patient when doing an interview. She'd wooed him into dropping his guard and giving her what she needed. And then there was her uncertainty when it came to the sharing herself with him. Had she always been that way? Or had it happened after the asshole she'd told him about had betrayed her?

"Maybe you'd better take this," she said. The Sig looked weighty and foreign in her hand, and she held it awkwardly, her fingers wrapped around the trigger guard and ejection port.

He took the weapon by the grip, and then caught his breath as her hand dropped to his thigh and ran up the inside of his leg toward his groin.

Had he thought her shy? Her smile was laced with amusement.

"Have you ever seen that movie where the guy calls his rifle a gun and his drill instructor makes him repeat over and over this is my rifle, this is my gun?"

"It's called *Full Metal Jacket*," he managed, though he couldn't draw a full breath with her fingers resting high inside his thigh.

"I've handled your weapon, now I'd like to touch your gun."

CHAPTER 30

Just the thought of her touching him sent blood rushing to his cock so quickly he thought he'd explode. When Tess leaned forward and kissed him the last remnants of surprise dissolved into full-fledged, raging need. He tossed the pistol on the cushion next to him to free his hand and reached for her. The hot hungry way her lips and tongue tangled with his drove his desire higher. His erection pushed against his zipper, painful and hard.

"I was trying not to pounce on you the moment you walked in the door," he said when the kiss broke. She turned and straddled his lap and his hands ran down over her slender hips. He grabbed one of the round bolster pillows from the end of the couch and shoved it behind him to support his lower back.

"Me, too." Her cheeks were flushed and her lips berry red from the pressure of the kiss. "I tried to talk Doc out of coming up with me." Her fingers rolled up the bottom of his t-shirt and when she dragged it upward, Brett wiggled free eager to be skin-to-skin with her.

When he followed suit with her silk tank top, she shimmied free, then pressed her bare breasts against him. His breath seized, then released. Oh God, her skin was as soft as the silk she'd been wearing and her breasts were high and perfect, a lush handful that peaked against his palm. "You're the most beautiful thing I've ever touched, Tess," he said his tone husky. She was, with her long, lithe body and pale skin.

Her sherry brown eyes turned dark and sultry as her hand grazed the bandage over his side. "Are you sure you're okay to—"

He kissed her, cutting off the question. *Screw the pain.* He'd die if he didn't have her, right now. His hands ran up her thighs beneath the wraparound skirt and encountered, instead of lacy underwear, only luscious, warm, bare skin. He groaned aloud.

She sat next to Doc in the car without any panties on. Jesus. The need to claim her, to mark her as his, raged through him, raw and basic. He slid a hand between their bodies and found the intimate heart of her with his fingers and caressed her, tempted her. She was so warm and wet.

Tess caught her breath and soft color rose to her cheeks. Her voice turned breathy and weak as she said his name. The way she responded to his touch sent a wave of heat through him. The urge to free himself and thrust up inside her was almost overwhelming. Instead, he palmed the rounded curve of her buttocks and wiggled down, aligning their bodies so when she pressed down she'd ride against the bulge beneath his pants. *Jesus, his damn side hurt, but this felt too good to stop.* He drew her lips back to his again and tried to slow things down by guiding the movement of her hips. *Can't take that for very long without something major happening.* His fingers found his zipper. *And where the hell did I put that condom?*

Tess rose up on her knees to give Brett room to shove his pants down. He jerked his wallet free from a pocket and produced a condom. "I've been carrying this around, in hope, since we first met." He tore open the packet.

Tess plucked it from the wrapper. The hard length of his erection brushed against her intimately beneath her skirt and the desire just to sink down on top of him was almost uncontrollable. Had she ever wanted a man like this before? *Never.*

"Let me put the safety on," she said, her voice a husky whisper.

Brett groaned again. "You're killing me, baby. I'll never touch my weapon again without thinking of you," he said, his lips finding her throat, her collarbone. The moist heat sent arrows of sensation downward to her breasts.

As she rolled the condom down over his erect penis she caught her breath, he was so warm and thick. She slid back and guided him inside her. Brett's head fell back against the couch cushions and a sound, half groan, half sigh, escaped him. She bit her lip to keep from echoing it. For a few breath-taking moments she contented herself with just rotating her hips and pushing down, taking him as far inside as she could.

She brushed a hand over the blond hair at his temple and the scar there. She brushed her lips over his brow, his cheek, until she found his lips again. He ran his palms up over her bare back and, when she drew back, looked up at her, his blue eyes alight with desire. She braced her hand atop the couch and began to move—slow, careful, mindful of his injury. But when his hips rose to meet her, her heart stuttered as pleasure spiraled through her. The compulsion for release took over, and she captured a slow, steady rhythm, guided by the pressure of Brett's hands and the upward thrust of his hips. His breathing grew as ragged as hers. Her muscles tensed as, with every movement, the elusive moment of release crept closer and closer. Brett murmured her name as he swelled, filling her to the point of pain, and an orgasm hit her so fierce prickles rolled outward from her core to her fingers and toes. The answering pulse of Brett's release brought on another wave, this time gentler, yet enough to make her hum with pleasure.

She rested her forehead against the back of the couch. With Brett's breath hot against her neck, she tried to catch her own. Minutes passed before she started to ease away, but his arms tightened around her. "I know your legs are probably killing you, but don't move yet," he said.

Her heart turned over, and, smiling, she straightened enough to look into his face.

He brushed the weight of her hair over her shoulder and his hand trailed down the slope of her back from her shoulder to her waist, then around to cup her breast.

As he played with her distended nipple, nerve endings fired, running from the peak of her breasts downward to where their bodies were still connected. She drew in a shaky breath.

"I could spend hours just touching you," he said, huskily.

"I've felt the same way about you," she said, and when the heat of a blush rushed into her face, she looked away.

He cupped her cheek and ran a thumb over her cheekbone, then, thrusting his fingers through her hair and cradling her head, he drew her lips to his. He kissed her with a long, slow thoroughness that left her weak and aching.

"Just thinking about you sitting next to Doc in the car without your panties on ... Promise you'll only do that with me from now on."

It had taken her hours to build up the nerve to ditch them, and all the way to the hotel she'd felt self-conscious and uncomfortable. But his reaction when he'd discovered them missing had been worth it. "Doc didn't know."

"Promise."

That possessive, protective look on his face stole her breath and thrilled her.

"I promise."

He kissed her again. When she moved to rise, he steadied her.

Her legs ached from being in one position too long. Brett's movements were a little stiff as well as he slid off the couch and hiked up his pants. He disappeared into the bathroom.

Tess retrieved her tank top from the floor and slid into it. She stretched luxuriously. Every muscle in her body felt loose, and there was a wonderful languorousness in her lower limbs.

She plucked the discarded pistol from between the couch cushions and gripped it. She held it in her hands as Brett had directed her and pointed it at one of the watercolor seascapes hung in a grouping on the wall.

"You need to widen your stance a little," Brett said as he came out of the bathroom. She frowned in concern at the careful way he moved.

"Like this?" She increased the distance between her feet.

He wrapped his arms around her waist and pressed close to her from behind. "Yeah."

How could she want him again so quickly? "Where's the safety?" she asked.

"It's a military-grade Sig 226, so it doesn't have one." He nuzzled her neck.

She shivered and glanced over her shoulder at him. "Neither do you."

He laughed. "A well-trained SEAL is always prepared."

She smiled and turned to cuddle against him. She held the gun down at her side. "You can prove it after you've rested a while. And in the meantime you can tell me about this political issue you and your team are worried about.

"I'd rather take you to bed for about a week instead."

"When you're completely healed, I'll hold you to that."

His grin was something special. "Okay. But what I'm about to tell you has to stay off the record."

She tensed. Would he ever learn to trust her?

"After we find who's responsible, you can do what you want with the story. But you can't use Hawk or me as corroboration. We have to stay below the radar on stuff like this."

Understanding eased the momentary hurt. "Okay."

He drew her over to the bed to sit down. "About four months ago Derrick Armstrong had a meltdown. Because my team disarmed him instead of calling the police, someone's looking for a way to prosecute them for acting in the capacity of police officers. If they're able to do that, four of my teammates could go to federal prison. One of them is Hawk."

Shock tumbled through Tess, taking her breath. "They can't do that."

"Yeah they can, unless we can figure out who's putting pressure on the Justice Department to bring charges, and figure out how the hell someone in Iraq got my name."

"Those two instances may not be related," Tess said. "But my dad called this morning, and he thinks NCIS agents are following up his interviews. He reassured me your name hasn't been shared with anyone through him. But someone must have said something, because he made a point of reassuring me."

"I think both things may be connected, Tess. And if we can find the person responsible for one ... "

"Think in terms of what would motivate someone to leak your name," she said.

"Money, power, revenge, being an evil asshole. In Iraq, all of those could apply. People there are poor, and though their religion encourages them not to get hung up on possessions, they have to eat."

"But who there would have access to your background information and information about your missions there?"

"No one outside of the Special Ops community."

"Who here would have access?"

"The same, but anyone on the SAC could if they knew who to approach. And someone on the committee is accessing information."

"All right. Then we concentrate on the person we think might be involved, and ask ourselves what does he, or they, have to gain by going after you and the others?"

"They already have money and power so that only leaves being an evil asshole or revenge. I'm not ready to rule evil out, but why revenge? What could we have done in Iraq that would inspire someone to leak my name there, or go after the others here?"

"We have to look for a reason. And maybe somewhere along the way we'll find out if our suspicions are correct. Even if they're not, it might still lead us in the right direction."

"There are five guys from the same team, me included, who are counting on what we can find."

"Then I suppose we'd better get started."

"First I need you to do something for me." He slid his hand into hers and smiled in a way that her heart leapt to double time.

"What is it?"

"I need you to put on some underwear. Otherwise I won't be able to think of anything but how you feel without them."

Clara looked over her shoulder between the car sets to check on Evan. Even in sleep, his fingers gripped the pillow. His legs were bent and his bare feet braced against the opposite door. Despite his six-foot height, he looked small and so very young. How was it possible for anyone to be so thin and still be mobile? His elbows looked sharp enough to pierce his skin.

Russell folded his fingers around her hand where it lay on the seat between them. "How's he doing?"

"He's still sleeping. We should have flown. It would have been so much easier on him."

"Evan wanted you to have the opportunity to photograph some of the coastal areas. He loves being with you."

Tears tightened her throat. She focused her attention on the winding road ahead until she could trust her composure. "I love being with him, too." Russell squeezed her hand.

"Where are we, Dad?" Evan asked from behind them.

"We're almost to Santa Barbara. I thought we'd stop there for the night and get something to eat."

"The harbor there is small, but beautiful. You should take some pictures, Clara."

"Maybe I will."

Thirty minutes later Russell pulled beneath the portico of a hotel near the harbor. The structure, constructed in a Spanish villa design, had clay tiling on the roof and arched doorways. The terracotta rooflines thrust out in tiers. Clara caught a glimpse of the ocean at the end of a high stucco wall connected to the hotel that shot nearly to the beach highway.

The sounds of splashing water traveled from the pool behind it and reached her through the open car window while they waited for Russell to check them in.

"Simon and I stayed here about a month before he left me," Evan said. "They have excellent food in the dining room and a walking bridge that extends above the street and leads directly to the beach. We had a wonderful time. We got full body massages and facials."

Clara's throat nearly closed at the sadness she read in his face. *Dear God, this is so hard.*

'Your father wouldn't have chosen this hotel if he'd known, Evan. We can go somewhere else."

"No. These are good memories, Clara. It doesn't hurt me to think about them."

But she could tell it did.

"Simon gave me the virus. He was unfaithful." He paused. "I never was. I never wanted to be with anyone but him. You know how that is." It was a statement, not a question.

She answered anyway. "Yes, I do."

"It wasn't until I got sick the first time and was diagnosed that I realized he had infected me. He admitted to having strayed. We broke up, but he stuck by me until I was well again. When I started getting really sick, he couldn't take it. I don't know if it's cowardice or guilt, but he hasn't spoken to me since."

"I'm sorry, Evan."

"Should something happen to me, you'll stick around for Dad, won't you?"

She looked away while she struggled to maintain her composure. "You don't have to ask me. You know I will."

"I was being selfish. I didn't want to share him with you. That's why I behaved like an idiot before. I'd just never had his undivided attention before."

She swallowed against the knot in her throat. *And he was running out of time to experience that.*

"It wasn't entirely his fault. My mother wanted him out of her life and mine."

Clara reached between the seats to take his hand. "Sometimes when you're unhappy it's easy to make bad decisions."

He smiled and squeezed her hand. "Your being very generous to a woman you don't even know."

"None of us is perfect, Evan. We all make mistakes. I've made some doozies."

"Probably none as bad as her. I can say that, because every decision she made affected me."

"Is that why she hasn't called?" Clara asked.

"Yes."

"Would you like me to call her?"

"No." He tilted his head back against the seat. The late afternoon sun struck his features, shadowing his hollowed eyes and the sunken areas beneath his cheekbones.

A rush of fear and anguish struck Clara that was so deep she had to fight against the wail of grief that pushed up her throat. When the time came, how would Russell bear losing him? How would she?

Her voice shook despite her effort to control it. "I didn't just fall in love with your father, Evan. I feel in love with his son, too."

CHAPTER 31

Zoe stretched, then rolled onto her side. The pillow smelled like Hawk. And she nestled her head more deeply into it. He had been so tender, so needy last night when they'd made love. She'd almost cried as he'd held her afterwards.

His arm slipped around her and he pressed close from behind. She smiled. Even in sleep he sought her out. And she could tell he was asleep, otherwise he'd be caressing her, ready to come inside her and get as close as he could. They'd been together almost six months. And in that time she knew his moods, his food preferences, his favorite sexual positions, his private fears and dreams. Just as he did hers. They'd held nothing back from each other. Except the secret military stuff he did.

Her hand ran down to her abdomen and she cradled the small roundness there. She had to tell him. She had to tell him today. *She was telling him today.* The decision took a weight from her and she rolled toward him to find him awake.

She smiled. "Hey."

He studied her face one feature at a time and traced the curve of her cheekbone, with the back of his fingers. "I love you."

Every time he said those words, her heart seemed to rise up to catch them. "I love you, too."

He kissed her. Morning breath, scratchy beard and all. She didn't care. All that mattered was this connection between them. Her arms went around him to hold him close.

The brush of his body against hers was all it took to make her crave more. It was the perfect time to tell him about the baby.

When the kiss broke, she drew back to look into his face. "Hey, there's something I need to tell you."

The distinctive ring of his cell phone sounded from the nightstand. "Hold that thought, sweetheart."

He rolled, scooped the phone up and looked at the number before pressing the accept key. "Yazzie."

The way he said the word, all business, Zoe knew it was the base. Just when she'd finally built up her nerve—With a sigh, she slipped from the bed to go to the bathroom while he dealt with the issue and glanced over her shoulder at him. The tension in his body, his expression, gave her pause. She shivered as her skin grew chilled, and grabbing her robe, slid into it.

"Yes, sir." His hand fell to the bed still gripping the phone. His attention shifted to her.

"We're being deployed."

Her body tensed and her heart reared up into her throat, beating so hard she could barely breathe. "When?"

"Eleven hundred."

She glanced at the clock then froze. *Three hours, dear God, three hours.* She gripped the bathroom doorframe.

Hawk jerked the bedclothes aside and strode to her. His arms came around her hard, tight, every muscle in his naked body taut.

I will not cry, I will not cry. Though every muscle in her body tightened in the attempt to suppress them, the tears still came and flowed down her face like a dam had burst inside her. Hawk kept holding her.

"I'm sorry. I'm trying not to," she managed after several minutes.

"I know, sweetheart. If I wasn't supposed to be such a badass, I'd be bawling like a baby."

His attempt at humor only made the tears flow that much faster. "I love you." *Forever.*

"Always, Zoe. Always," His voice cracked.

His steady strength allowed her to compose herself. She wiped her face with the sleeve of her robe. One-handed, Hawk reached for the tissue box on her nightstand and offered it to her while his other continued to hold her.

She blew her nose, wiped her face one more time, then drew a deep breath. "What do you need me to do?" she asked.

Though his features remained composed, pain flickered behind his eyes. "Nothing. I just need to tell you some things. Then I'll have to go." His throat worked as he swallowed. "HQ thinks that if we're deployed it will keep the indictment we've been threatened with from going down. It's a political thing."

So this was all about politics. They were tearing apart families because of politics. "Who's doing this?"

"Cutter and Tess are looking into it. And HQ is trying to trace who's pulling the strings, too." His hand cupped her cheek and rested his forehead against hers. "It's only six months, Zoe. And if it makes this legal shit go away—it'll clear me, Lang, and the others."

She nodded. *Damn whoever was doing this! Damn them to hell!* The guys had saved her life, Brett's and Marjorie's. Why wasn't that enough? "You knew this was going to happen?"

"Yesterday Captain Jackson said two weeks, Zoe. I thought I'd have time to ease you into it."

She nodded.

"My pay goes directly into the account, so the bills will be taken care of. I have a list of repair people next to the phone, should anything happen here at the house. And there's a list of other team members you can call on if anything else come up. They'll protect you. Don't hesitate to call any of them if you notice anything that makes you anxious. Keep your guard up, baby." His arms tightened around her again and he drew her in against him. "I'm glad Cutter will be here with you. It makes it easier for me, knowing you have him close by. Keep the doors and windows locked and the alarm on the whole time you're here. Promise me."

She nodded. "I'll be okay." Her arms tightened around him. "You'd better get ready. I'll fix you something to eat."

"Zoe—After all this shit is behind us—"

The hoarse note in his voice gripped her by the throat. It was too much. Things were happening too quickly. Though grief had settled like stone in her chest, she forced herself to look up at him and maintain her composure. She cupped his face. "I'll be right here waiting for you to come home."

He nodded. "I have to get going. The guys on the list. They'll be taking turns making sure you get to the hospital safe." He smiled though the effort was forced. "If any of them tries to put the move on you, tell them I'll kick their ass when I get back."

"I'll do it for you." She kissed him, then pulled away. "Get in the shower; I'll fix you some egg sandwiches and a goody bag to take with you."

She turned away because she had to. She had to take care of him in the only way she could, until she couldn't anymore.

Brett looked down at his bandaged side, then to the creased khakis he'd fallen asleep in while on the computer. Tess must have closed it down and set it on the nightstand, because he didn't remember doing so. He stretched and caught his breath. Bad move. God, he was sorer today than yesterday.

He studied Tess as she slept. Early morning sun lanced across the bed from a crack in the heavy green drapes drawn across the balcony doors. It fell across the inside of her bare thigh giving it a pearl-like sheen. He longed to trace that small section of skin with his finger then move higher up beneath the sheet, but she slept so soundly he didn't want to wake her.

He'd been pushing her, in one way or the other, trying to get her to reach for what she wanted ever since they'd met. And now she finally had, and he felt guilty for manipulating her. She deserved better than he could give her.

His career was hanging by a thread. Even if they cleared him of these suspicions, there was no guarantee he'd ever get back to active duty. Though his speech thing was getting better, when he was tired or upset it reared its ugly head and had him struggling. He had to accept the possibility he might never get back to top shape. And he wouldn't put someone else's life in danger because he couldn't call in a location for an air strike or give orders under fire.

But he hadn't been given the opportunity to find out how he'd do out in the field. If they'd just give him a chance. If he couldn't cut it, he'd walk away. It would kill him, but he'd do it.

And what about Tess? If he stayed with the teams, she'd be stuck with a guy who bugged out at a moment's notice, just like her father. He'd be gone long stretches of time. Six months, sometimes longer. Could she handle that? Would she want to handle that? Why would she want to handle it? And why was he thinking long term here? His stomach muscles contracted and he sucked in his breath, more from the rising panic that flip-flopped inside him than the painful tug at his stitches.

Oh, shit! He lay there waiting for the feeling to subside. This was not just about getting laid. He'd had those kinds of relationships in the past and been left feeling empty and dissatisfied. His attention strayed to Tess again to find her awake and watching him. *Oh, man. This was way beyond that.*

"What is it?" she asked, her voice soft and breathy, as though she hadn't quite found it after sleep.

Jesus, he loved that. His half-staff erection started while studying her bare thigh grew to full-fledged woody in a heartbeat. He couldn't say the words, not yet, he had to be back to full speed, for her, for himself. "I'm sorry I crashed on you last night."

"You just got out of the hospital, Brett. The trauma of being shot, the surgery, the drugs. You didn't really think you'd walk out in top form after three days, did you?"

"A guy can hope."

She smiled. "Your mom called last night after you fell asleep with the computer in your lap."

"She okay?"

"She was fine. She was just checking on you. They'd stopped in Santa Barbara to spend the night."

"And Captain Connelly's son?"

"She didn't say."

He nodded. She probably wouldn't have shared that info with him either. After years of keeping students' issues private, she didn't gossip.

Now that Tess was awake, Brett brushed his fingertips over the soft patch of skin the sun had christened. He leaned forward and kissed her.

"I haven't brushed my teeth yet, Brett."

"Neither have I." He slid downward and, lying on his good side, touched his lips to that tantalizing strip of skin resting in the sun.

Tess caught her breath. When he tugged the sheet aside, he found the white cotton bikini panties she'd slipped on at his request, coupled with the t-shirt he'd worn and tossed aside. He grinned. Telling thing when a woman wore your clothes.

He nuzzled her pubis and breathed through the cotton.

She made a soft sound of surprise, and, raising up on an elbow, ran her fingers through his hair. "Brett?" The uncertainty in her tone gave him pause.

"Hasn't anyone ever tasted you, Tess?"

She swallowed and two spots of color bloomed on her cheeks. "No."

Virgin territory. His pulse jumped to racing speed. His breathing grew labored. He could claim her in a way no one else ever had. He was so aroused by her inexperience it was almost painful. He lowered his lips to the area just above the waistband of her bikinis. "Will you let me, Tess?"

"Oh, God." She fell back on the bed and covered her face with her hands.

He stifled a chuckle and raised the t-shirt up over her breasts to home in on them. Her coral-tinted nipples puckered before he'd even touched them. He played with one while his mouth covered the other and he sucked. Her hands dropped away from her face to caress the back of his neck and shoulders.

He ran tempting fingers along the inside of her thighs and brushed his touch over the crotch of her panties while he shifted to the other nipple. When the fabric began to grow wet and her hips moved in response, he slid downward to press moist hot kisses down her belly and circle her navel with his tongue.

Tess's ragged breathing became evident, and the soft sound of it made him ache. God, he'd never dreamed he could be this crazy about a woman. Her every response sent a new wave of heat straight to his cock. But his side and hip were so sore, and the activity of the day before might have made things worse, though he didn't regret a moment of it.

He hooked his fingers in the cotton fabric at her hips and tugged her panties down. Tess lifted her hips, then raised her legs to help him take them off. His lips and tongue followed the ridge of her hipbones, then the dip just above her pubic bone. The hair, a lighter red there, brushed his chin as her hips rolled. The faint scent of her arousal teased him.

He parted her nether lips with a questing finger and found the sensitive nub there, tempting it with the gentle rub of a fingertip while he nibbled the inside of her thigh. Her legs trembled and she spoke his name in a pleading, husky tone, the same voice that had started this whole thing.

Raising her hips, he laved his tongue over the intimate heart of her, tasting her salty sweet heat. She writhed beneath his strokes and gripped the bedclothes. He settled on the opening of her body and again and again tempted her with a thrust and flutter movement. Her muscles tightened around the invasion. Her hips began to work against his mouth with more and more intensity. He kissed her and thrust his tongue as deep as he could go. She cried out, her hips jerked and he felt the orgasm roll up her body in the contracting tension of her muscles.

Tess opened her eyes. Brett's head rested on her stomach and his hands were still splayed beneath her hips. *Oh my God, what had she just done?* What had he done? Should she be embarrassed—or grateful? Or both?

His cell phone rang from the bedside table, and he raised his head. Tess reached for it and extended it to him. He rested his head against her again. "Weaver." He went still for a moment then eased further down to the bottom of the bed and rose to go into the bathroom, moving more carefully than the day before. After several minutes, the commode flushed, water ran and splashed, then he opened the bathroom door.

He carried a hand towel and wiped his face and hands dry. His features were set in grim lines, and his blue eyes gleamed with anger. "Hawk's been deployed. He'll be wheels-up in an hour."

Tess dragged the sheet up over her nudity and swung her legs over the side of the bed. "Just like that?"

"Yeah. It happens that way sometimes." He sat down on the edge of the bed next to her, his movements slow.

"Zoe?"

"She didn't want to talk." Pain flickered across his features. "God damn it, there's not a damn thing I can do for either of them." He clenched his fist.

"Yes, there is." Tess said.

His attention fastened on her and embarrassed heat climbed into her face. Every moment of what they'd just done all came rushing back. She jerked her thoughts back to the moment at hand. "Can you access information on a Corporal Michael Theodore Masters, USMC?"

"Yeah, why?"

Because he was killed in action on December 21, 2010 and he was Senator Rob Welch's stepson. The two of them were extremely close—real father and son close. Would there have been any possibility that you met him while in Iraq?"

Brett stared across the room, his expression intent. "The name doesn't mean a thing. He shook his head. "We worked with a number of Marine Corp divisions. There's no guarantee we didn't have contact. If I saw a picture of him, I might remember his face."

"I can access the picture I found of him last night." She slipped out of bed, and hyper-aware of her nudity beneath the t-shirt, tugged the garment down, and retrieved her laptop from the coffee table in the sitting room. She sat down beside him and flipped open the top so the desktop came up. She clicked on a folder, then scrolled down to a specific file. She opened it. The picture was of a Marine in his dress uniform.

Brett stared at the picture for several minutes. He shook his head. "He'd have been in cammies and probably thinner. The stress, lack of sleep, and the food throws your system off, and you always lose weight."

"We need particulars on how he was killed, the specific mission or patrol he was on, any information you can get. You know what I'm saying. If I were going to go after a specific team, there'd have to be a very personal reason for it. There may be a connection between you and him or your team."

"I agree. I'm on it. I need to make a few phone calls."

"I'll clean up while you do that." She shut the laptop and set it on the floor.

He slipped his arm around her to hold her in place beside him. "Did you like what I did, Tess?" he asked, his lips brushing her shoulder, his hand inching beneath the t-shirt to trace the curve of her hip and waist.

Could your whole body blush? Hers certainly felt like it. She couldn't meet his gaze. "Very much." She fled to the bathroom.

Russell eyed Evan through the review mirror. There was something off with him.

Evan wouldn't let him examine him. He'd drawn a well-defined line between what he expected his Dad to know as a parent and what he'd share with him in his role as a physician. He had agreed to allow a colleague to examine him before they'd left San Diego, just to be sure he was strong enough for the trip. Dr. Hal Minor was an expert in autoimmune diseases. He'd assured them both that everything that could be done was being done as to medications.

But what had Evan asked Hal to hold back? His gut told him there was something.

What was he missing?

Was there more color in Evan's cheeks than usual? Was he running a fever?

Clara placed a hand on his arm and gave it a gentle squeeze. His gaze swung to her. She got a bottle of vitamin water out of the cooler, and turning in her seat, offered it to Evan. "You look like you could use a drink," she said.

He smiled. "A dry martini, shaken, not stirred, with an olive please."

"I'm sorry, Mr. Bond, but the bar seems to be out of gin and vermouth at the moment. If you still want one later, I know how to fix it."

"I'll hold you to that when we get to my apartment." He opened the bottle and took a drink.

Russell set aside his worry. There was nothing he could do. One day at a time. He had to take it one day at a time. But it was torture. He shook his head when Clara offered him water and reached for her hand instead. Just touching her made him feel better.

"You're going to ignore propriety and stay at the apartment with us guys aren't you, Clara?" Evan asked.

Clara's cheeks grew a little pink.

"I want you to stay. You and Dad are an item, so I don't understand what the big deal is."

Russell smiled when she bit her lip and looked away. At their ages, it was ridiculous for them to have to sneak around like they were doing something wrong when they wanted to be together. He kissed the back of her hand.

"We both need you, Clara. Neither of us will sully your reputation by saying anything," Evan said.

She laughed and looked over her shoulder at him. "All right. You're making me sound like a Victorian miss. And I'm not."

Evan leaned back with a smile. Russell met his gaze in the rearview mirror. Evan winked.

Russell smiled and shook his head. Evan had Clara wrapped around his little finger. She'd grown so attached to him. Had he not pursued their relationship, he could have spared her this pain. But Evan was right, they both needed her. She came across as soft and feminine but a core of steel shone through now and then. He hoped that would stand her in good stead when the time came. Maybe them both. Because there were times he wanted to howl from the pain. To watch his son struggle so tore the heart right out of him.

The Oakland Bay Bridge came into view. "We should stop so you can take pictures, Clara," Evan said.

"I'll have plenty of time later, once we've rested and had a meal," she said. "I'm a little tired after the drive and need a nap."

Russell gave her hand another squeeze. There were a hundred kindnesses she'd shown his boy every day. And she did it in a way that didn't draw attention to Evan's illness. He'd loved her for that. And a thousand other things.

The apartment building, all limestone-finished concrete and steel, stood on Market Street surrounded by similar buildings. A dark green canvas awning jutted out from the main entrance, shielding the occupants from the elements as they entered or exited. The parking structure at the back spiraled upward, a catacomb for expensive vehicles nearly half the height of the building.

Russell watched surreptitiously as Evan unfolded his fragile frame from the back seat and leaned against the car for support. In the seven weeks he'd been in San Diego he'd grown weaker. How long would it be before he'd be forced to enter the hospital? Not long.

Russell had spent all of his adult life inside of hospitals or temporary structures converted to them. He didn't want the antiseptic emptiness of a hospital room to be where his boy spent his last days. He'd keep him here surrounded by his own belongings. If he could.

The entrance foyer of the apartment was a narrow hall. The double doors of a wide closet took up the wall on the right.

"This is my book closet." Evan said resting a hand against the doors as he passed it. I'm a terrible book hoarder."

The passageway opened into a wide living room that was all light and gleaming wood surfaces. Bright red drapes hung open, revealing a distant view of San Francisco bay. A soft, butter-colored leather sofa sat against one wall, walnut end tables on either side. A lounge the same color as the couch thrust diagonally beneath the window, a small occasional table to one side. A book lay face down on the table's surface as though Evan had just risen from reading. A chair and ottoman, brightly striped in red, green, blue, and yellow finished out the ensemble. A dramatic abstract painting hung over the couch, reflecting the warm colors of the room.

An area rug as bright a red as the curtains stretched toward a galley-like kitchen with stainless steel appliances. A small walnut table and chairs, just large enough for two, sat opposite just down the wall from the couch.

"The bedrooms are through here," Evan said, his steps deliberate as he led the way down a short open passageway. "This is the guest room. You'll have your own bathroom." He opened the door.

"Oh, my, look at the headboard, Russell," Clara said as she wheeled her suitcase into the room. He set his own case just inside the door, and the implication of that small action was so right, so freeing, he smiled.

He studied the chrome piece she'd commented on, more a work of art than a headboard as it looped across the dark teal wall in wave-like swirls. "That's amazing."

"An artist friend made it as a wall hanging, but I thought it worked better as a headboard," Evan said.

"It's gorgeous, Evan. The whole apartment is."

"Thanks. I spent a long time choosing each piece."

"This is my room." He ran a hand along the wall as he walked toward it. The stark contrast of blues and grays was a surprise after the bright colors of the rest of the apartment. A small balcony opened off the bedroom. The sliding glass doors allowed the light from a cloudless blue sky the color of the walls into the room. Russell wheeled Evan's suitcase in and parked it next to a large chest of drawers.

"That nap Clara mentioned sounds good about now, Dad. I'm going to lie down for a while. You two make yourself at home." Evan sat down on the side of the bed, the action fraught with exhaustion. His hand shook as he pushed his fine brown hair back.

Russell controlled the urge to touch a hand to Evan's forehead. He wanted more and more often to take him into his arms and hold him. Could he make up for just a fraction of the hugs they had missed over the years? "We may lie down for a while, too. I'm a little tired myself."

"A friend picked up some groceries, so the fridge should be well stocked with dairy and vegetables if you're hungry."

"We're fine. We'll order dinner in a while."

"Sounds good."

Russell rested a hand along Clara's hip as they moved toward the door.

"Clara. Could you stay for a moment? There's something I want to give you," Evan said as they reached the door.

Clara studied Evan's drawn features with concern. He needed to rest. She exchanged a glance with Russell, then moved back to the bed. "It can wait until you've had your nap."

"No, I want to give them to you now." He opened the nightstand drawer and withdrew two large manila envelopes. "These are the arrangements I've made should something happen to me."

He handed her one of the envelopes. "I made them before I left for San Diego. Everything's taken care of."

Clara looked away from him, her composure hanging by a thread.

"This time with Dad has been all I hoped for when I arranged the trip, Clara. I'm glad I didn't wait too long."

"He's been very grateful you came, that you had time to work through things."

Evan nodded. "Me too." He focused on the other envelope, this one padded and sealed. "I've been debating about who I could entrust this to, and if you don't think you can handle it, just tell me, and I'll try to think of someone else."

She drew out a chair from the large desk near the foot of the bed. "You can lie down while we talk." She waited until he'd stretched out atop the comforter before she sat down beside the bed. "What is it?"

Evan rested a hand on the heavy package. "This is a taped deposition about a child molestation case. After—I'm gone I want you to hand it over to the district attorney here in San Francisco."

Oh my God. Why would he choose her to do this?

"It's an old case and the statute of limitations has run out, but it might start an investigation. You see, I thought there was only one victim, but there's a real possibility there may have been more."

"Why me, Evan? Why would you want me to be the one and not your father?"

He remained silent for at least a minute. He opened his palm in a seeking gesture and she rested her hand in his. "Because I don't want my Dad to know. The case is mine, Clara. I was the victim twenty years ago. And Carl Hanson, my stepfather, molested me when I was nine."

CHAPTER 32

"I've pulled some strings. You have an interview with Welch at nine a.m. day after tomorrow. You need to get on a plane and get prepared. You prove this, Tess, and you'll be stepping into the political news arena with the big dogs," Ian said.

For once, the SAT phone connection was clear. Tess moved farther away from the bathroom door so the sound of the shower running didn't interfere with hearing him. "If I don't fall flat on my face first."

"No guts, no glory. You'll have to get your mind right to face Welch. He's been pushing some radical ideas about foreign policy to his constituents. It's a sort of tough love policy aimed at the Middle East. You could call Kevin Hale and talk to him. He's made himself quite a name at the Washington Post for staying on top of situations like these. But don't even hint at what you're going for. He'll steal it, or screw it up for you, depending on where his loyalties lie."

Kevin Hale had no loyalties. He'd screw his own mother to get a story, or anything else he wanted. Tess fought against the wave of pain that assaulted her. "I'm surprised to hear you talk like that about him. You were quick enough to write him the letter of recommendation for the Post job."

"I wrote him the letter to get him the fuck away from you. He's a self-centered prick, and I wanted him away from my daughter."

Stunned, it took her a beat, then two, to shut her open mouth and gather her thoughts. "Why didn't you tell me?"

"At the time, you wouldn't have listened to anything I said, and I figured you already hated me, so I didn't have anything to lose."

"I've never hated you, Ian. And I never held you responsible for anything associated with Kevin Hale. In fact, had you told me later why you wrote the letter, I'd have thanked you."

"Had I known I'd finally done something right with you, I would have. It's a bitch that I had to go nearly eight thousand miles away to finally find you."

Tears blurred her vision and her throat tightened. "I'm sorry, Daddy."

After a moment's pause Ian said, "You saw my article from the AP, didn't you? It was picked up by all the majors."

'Yes, I read it. It was excellent work and there's already television coverage here mentioning it. You'll be inundated by people wanting to interview you."

"Good thing I'm hiding out and they don't know where to find me."

Tess's heart skipped a beat. "Are you safe?"

"Yeah, I'm good. As soon as this is over, I'm coming back to California to take the LA job. I understand why you don't want to come work for me."

"I never said that."

"You didn't have to, Tess. I know how I've pushed and prodded you, trying to force you down my path instead of accepting that I needed to let you choose your own. This isn't what I'd want for you. I've finally realized that."

Dear God! He was in danger. Real danger. "Can you reach out to the military for cover, Ian?" Her heart hammered against her chest and her limbs grew weak. She swallowed against the dryness of her mouth. She glanced at the bathroom door. Could Brett do anything to help him?

"Not yet. I don't need it yet."

"Are you sure? No story is worth risking your life."

"Nothing's ever certain, Tess. But I think I'm good. I have to go."

"Please call the base. Tell them where you are. *Please.*"

"The folks I'm meeting in a few hours won't show if they even get a whiff that the military are involved. This is it. The big break in the story. I'm going to find out where the boys are. I want it. You want it. And your boyfriend needs it."

"There's enough reasonable doubt about what happened to the boy to clear Brett of any wrongdoing, Ian. That coupled with his military record, he'll be okay."

"But what about the kids? What about their families? They deserve to have their children back, don't they?"

Tears started rolling down her face. "Yes, of course. But I don't want anything to happen to you." *Not now that we're finally able to talk, and share things like a real father and daughter.* "I need you to come home in one piece, Ian. It was my idea for you to do this. If something happens to you—"

"Hush, Tess. I went into this with my eyes wide open. It was my decision to follow the story. That's what I've always done. And I needed it. It's made me realize that I have to move on to other things. I can guide the next generation into covering stories like this. It will be just as challenging."

He didn't sound quite convinced. But the fact that he was even thinking about quitting his globetrotting was a miracle.

"I'll be fine. I'll be coming home soon."

"Please call the base, Ian," Tess said.

"I'll think about it. I'll call this same time tomorrow."

Why wouldn't he listen? Because he had story fever and was following a lead. And it was her fault. "Please be careful."

"Will do. Bye, Tess."

The connection broke. The bathroom door opened. Tess focused on Brett as he came out of the bathroom, a towel wrapped around his lean hips and a plastic bag taped over the gauze pad covering his stitches.

"Ian's in trouble. What can you do?"

Brett shut off his phone and reached for a pair of khaki shorts from his suitcase. "He's on it. Captain Morrow will have the info in just a few minutes and he'll call Ian. But he can't force him to accept protection, Tess."

"I know."

She was trembling visibly, so Brett thrust his legs into the shorts, dragged them up, and zipped them. Sitting down next to her, he drew her close. "It's going to be okay."

She pressed against his bare side and clung to him. "He's finally talking about giving up his nomadic ways and settling somewhere close by, possibly LA. How many times have you heard of people having just a week to go—?"

Too many times.

"God, forget I said that."

"It's okay. You don't have to pussyfoot around me about anything, honey. I know you're afraid for your Dad. But he's been around the block a few times, and he's street smart. Otherwise he wouldn't have lasted at his game as long as he has."

"Yes, you're right."

"You're just as tenacious as your Dad, you just have a different style. But I'm glad you don't have any interest in covering international news. The idea of you being in places like Kabul or Kunar province damn near stops my heart."

"But you've been in those places?"

"Yeah, but I had my team with me, and we were covering each other's backs. It's a different world there, Tess." He had to say something to get her mind off of Ian. "It's a world of extremes. In some places the earth's packed hard as concrete, in others it's sandy and dry, yet they keep trying to cultivate crops. The poverty in some areas is numbing, but they have a pride in family and culture that we could learn from. You'll see these dry dusty fields with just a few scattered sheep trying to find enough food to stay alive, and in their midst will be beautiful, dark-eyed children watching over them or just playing." He drew a deep breath. "The summers are so hot you think you've been dropped into hell and the winters are brutal. But they keep on surviving."

"You sound as though you found something to admire, despite the violence there."

"Yeah. I did." He smiled. "But there aren't compromises, Tess. The way they've lived for thousands of years, the violence they've lived with, has hardened them. When every moment is a struggle to survive, you learn to stand your ground and hold it. Until that's understood, and respected ... " He shook his head. He wasn't going there.

"Maybe you understand it because you've had to stand your ground and face violence, too."

"Maybe."

"I need to go on line and book our flight," she said.

"We'll go by the airport and book it with cash. No credit cards. And we'll book it for today. We need to change hotels, and we might as well be in Washington as here."

He'd already called to check on his mom and Zoe. Everything was quiet on those fronts. He'd call them later and tell them where he was, after the fact. Otherwise he'd have to listen to them worry over him traveling injured.

Tess gripped his hand. "I've noticed something since the shooting."

"What's that?"

"Your speech. Instead of getting worse, you've not had *any* incidents of stuttering. At least not while you've been with me."

Brett thought about it. "When I'm taking action, training, or doing things for my job, I don't have any problem. My training takes over and I'm good to go. Maybe feeling as though we're under siege has jump-started that mindset." He hesitated. "Or there could be another possibility."

"What's that?" she asked.

"It's because of you." He was hanging out on a limb again instead of waiting for her. When would he learn? But he wanted her to acknowledge how she felt in some way.

"Me?" Her perfectly shaped brows rose. "What do I have to do with it?"

"You're protective of me, I'm protective of you. That only happens with couples who truly care about each other. Just having that kind of takes off some of the pressure."

She slipped an arm around his waist careful of his bandage and leaned her head against his shoulder. "I've heard that relationships that begin under duress rarely last."

Shit. No help there. "I guess we need to stick it out until the situation isn't so intense, just to test the theory."

She edged back to look up at him. "You left out something?"

"What's that?"

"Jealousy."

"What about it?"

"How jealous are you going to be when I call my ex?" she asked.

Brett's brows rose and his jaw tightened. "Why would you call your ex?"

"He's a reporter for the Washington Post. He can give me some insight into Senator Welch before I do the interview."

"As long as I'm in the room during said interview, I'll be fine." No he wouldn't. He'd be thinking of the guy putting his hands on Tess, doing other things, and would want to rip him to pieces.

"You don't look fine."

"I can handle myself."

"He's an asshole. I was well rid of him."

"He's *the* asshole, isn't he?" Blood rushed to his face and rage stormed through his system. He felt like his head might explode.

"Relax, Brett. He's not important anymore." She turned his face toward her to meet his gaze. "He's no more important to me than the young girl who gave you her panties was to you. Even less."

That wouldn't keep him from wanting to rip the guy's head off. He drew a deep breath to try and calm himself. "So, you were really jealous about the panties, huh?"

Tess slipped out of his arms, stood up, and reaching beneath the sundress she wore, wiggled free of the scrap of lace he'd watched her put on this morning with such deliberation he'd nearly chewed a hole in his pillow. A white lace thong dangled from her finger right in front of him. "You said you were waiting for a pair of mine. These are yours." She narrowed her eyes. "They'd better be the only pair you own from now on."

Clara shut the bedroom door softly, leaving Russell asleep, and moved down the hallway. She eased the door open and stood just inside the room. Morning light shone through the fine curtains, following the contours of Evan's thin shape beneath the comforter. She'd gotten up in the night and checked on him several times, just as she used to do when her own children were young.

Seeing his eyes open, she approached the bed.

He cleared his throat and his hand rolled off the side of the bed to hang limp, his shoulder at an awkward angle. Her breath caught and she crossed the space to switch on the nightstand light. Her heart leapt into her throat as she bent to grasp his hand and place it back on the bed. His skin felt cold and his fingers curled but didn't move.

"Dad." That one word came out with an effort, slightly slurred.

No, not yet. The words were a scream inside her head. "I'll get him."

She broke into a run and tripped halfway down the hall, falling against the wall and burning her arm. Her fingers were clumsy and the knob didn't want to turn. "Russell." His name came out a sob as she flung the door open.

He turned in the bed, his gray hair askew from sleep, but his eyes were instantly alert.

"It's Evan. He needs you."

He jerked the comforter aside and leapt from the bed. Clara grabbed her purse hanging from the closet door and jammed her hand into it in search of her cell phone. Her hands shook as she dialed 911.

The call made, she crept back down the hall to look in. "The ambulance is coming." She clung to the wad of Kleenex she'd found in her purse and wiped at the tears determined to stream down her cheeks. She forced herself to step back into the room and face what was happening to Evan. He was facing it, and so could she. Drawing a deep breath, she sidled around the bed and sat down.

"His right side is paralyzed. It's affecting his speech," Russell said, his voice hoarse. His features looked wooden with control.

Another wail of pain built inside her. She smothered it and reached for Evan's left hand. She held it tight in her own. "You'll need to get dressed. You'll want to ride with him in the ambulance. I'll follow you in the car."

He nodded and rose. He set Evan's hand along his side and when he bent to brush a kiss against his son's forehead, Clara had to look away for fear of losing her composure. "I'll be right back," he murmured.

Evan turned his head and focused on her. "Afraid."

"I'm right here, Evan. I love you."

"For him."

Dear God. "I won't leave him. He'll be okay."

Evan fingers squeezed her hand, and then relaxed, and his eyes closed.

CHAPTER 33

"They have run away, Yasin. The SEAL I shot has gone into hiding. The Captain has disappeared into the desert at one of their training camps. We are watching his whore wife and son. He will return and we will be ready."

"Who is we, Tabarek?" Yasin bent forward in his chair and rested his forehead atop his desk. He had not slept in many hours. He paced the house, the yard, the street, eaten alive by guilt and worry. "You do not need to know, Yasin. You need to send the money."

He had no more money. They had drained him. Nausea cramped his stomach and he dragged a trashcan close. "The SEALs did not kill my son, Tabarek. Someone took him."

"How do you know this?" Tabarek's tone grew sharp, intense.

"An American newspaper reporter has been investigating missing boys. There are at least thirty who are missing, possibly more. They have been taken off the street. The military believes they have been taken to a training camp by al-Qaeda."

"If this is true, your son is to be revered, Yasin. He has become a warrior against the Americans."

Sanjay would be considered a terrorist by the Americans and his own people. Would his captors convince him to become a martyr to their cause? Would he be forced to give his life as a suicide bomber? Tears ran down his cheeks.

"The Americans did not kill your son. But they killed my brother, my cousins. They must pay for that. We are watching Brett Weaver's sister. Since her lover has gone, there have been many men at the house, driving her to the hospital where she works. I am sure her SEAL lover knows nothing about how she consorts with these men. She is a whore like all American women."

Stop! Yasin smothered the urge to scream into the phone. He rubbed at the ache above his eyes. Since Levla's confession, they had not been able to touch each other without crying. Losing their son had irrevocably changed their relationship.

"Have you discovered the names of the other men who killed my brother?"

He would no longer help this man. The lie came easy. "I have tried, Tabarek. But the base commander guards his men's names well. Weaver and Armstrong are the only two the American investigators mentioned."

"Who were these men? Will the Americans be able to identify you as the source?"

What if they could? By giving Tabarek the men's names, he had become as much a terrorist as Tabarek. Allah would punish him for this. He was already being punished with this never-ending ache inside his chest. "I do not know. But I was not the only one they spoke to."

"You must keep trying to discover the names. We will kill as many as we can. Our lives will not be lost in vain."

Yasin flinched. A man who had made a conscious decision to give up his life was more dangerous than a rabid animal. "And what if this jihad is not Allah's will, Tabarek?"

"It is. Do not doubt it." He paused. "Send the money, or we will come for your daughter."

Always the same threat. He lived in fear every moment he was away from the house. How could he free himself of this?

He could go to the base commander and tell him everything. But they would arrest him, leaving Levla and Amira unprotected. They were all he had left. He would not allow them to be hurt. But he had no more money.

He reached inside the bottom drawer of his desk and withdrew the gun he had purchased on the street. It was an American pistol. One like the military used, probably stolen from a dead soldier's body. He had not asked when he had paid for it. He loaded the weapon and placed it carefully in the top drawer. He stared at the cell phone that lay in the center of his desk and scooping it up, rose to his feet. "No more." He left his office and went downstairs into the kitchen.

Amira, his daughter looked up from the table where she read. "Are you well, Baba?"

"I am well, daughter." He moved to a large cabinet in the corner and withdrew a hammer from one of the drawers. He sensed her movement behind him, but moved on through the back door to the concrete patio behind the house. He knelt on the ground, and placed the phone on the edge of the concrete slab. He swung the hammer with all the pain and anguish he held inside him. With every swing the hard knot eased a little more, and was replaced with resolve. He pounded every component of the phone into tiny pieces, then scooped them up in his hands. Leaving the hammer, he moved outside the courtyard wall through an iron gate and flung the pieces onto the hard-packed earth.

Amira stood waiting just inside the kitchen door. "Why did you do that, Baba? Will you not now need a new phone?"

"I have a new one already. I did not wish anyone to find and use the old one."

She nodded. He paused to cup her face in his hands and look down into her dark eyes. Levla had been as lovely at this age and just a little older when they'd been promised to one another. But had she ever been so trusting, so loving as Amira? "You are my world, Amira. You and your mother are everything to me."

A smile spread across her delicate features, her thin arms looped around his waist and she hugged him. 'Sanjay will come home soon, won't he, Baba?"

"He will come home soon," he said. But it no longer mattered if his son came home. A man who had decided to give up his life for a cause was a dangerous being. He would wait for Tabarek's men to come. And he would protect the family he had left. But they would not take his daughter.

Tess drew a deep breath, attempting to settle the uncontrolled, nervous flutters beneath her ribs. She had to calm down. At this point, if they called her into Senator Welch's office, she doubted she would even be able to speak. She ran through the information Brett had gotten during his trip to the base the day before. Why had no one discovered it before?

She scanned the room for a distraction, and noticed the warm gold color of the walls, the foot-wide crown molding that decorated the ceiling, the expensive artwork that hung behind the secretary's desk, and the heavy maroon area rug that covered the floors.

History had been made within the Russell Senate Office Building since 1909. And it was an impressive place, with its rotunda and highly polished marble floors.

She focused on the woman behind the large maple desk in the anteroom. She had introduced herself as Madeline Schaffer, the Senator's secretary. She looked to be in her early forties. Her hairstyle was short and hugged her head like a cap. Her clothing, a skirt and blouse, appeared all business. Her movements confident and quick, she opened envelopes and sorted the correspondence into neat stacks. "How long have you been with the Senator?" Tess asked.

"Nearly ten years. I worked in his law office before he ran for the Senate."

"It's a shame about his stepson," Tess said. She truly felt sympathy for any family who had made such a sacrifice.

"Yes, it is. Michael was mischievous and smart. Always laughing and pulling pranks. We were all stunned when he joined the Marines."

Tess read grief in the woman's face and said, "I'm sorry for your loss."

The woman nodded. "Thank you." When the phone buzzed, she reached for it. "The Senator will see you now." She rose and came around her desk. Tess, on shaky legs, followed her back out into the main hall. The cream-colored walls glowed with care beneath the lights. The sound of their shoes on the marble echoed along the way. Tess curbed the urge to place each foot as lightly as possible.

Ms. Schafer paused outside the second door on the right and tapped lightly. At the sound of a male voice from within, she opened the door and stood back. "Good luck," she murmured softly.

Tess's face felt stiff as she smiled in response. She was trying to ambush the woman's boss and she was wishing her luck. Her thoughts jumped to Brett waiting for her at their hotel. If Senator Welch was responsible for releasing his name to terrorists, directly or indirectly, the world deserved to know. If he wasn't, no harm would be done.

Tess stepped past the woman into the office and the door closed behind her.

'Hello, Miss Kelly." Senator Welch strode toward her, his hand extended. His grip felt warm around her nerve-chilled hand.

Welch stood about six feet. When elected to the Senate for the first time, his hair had been prematurely gray. Since then, it had turned completely white, the color a striking contrast to the healthy tan of his skin. For a man of fifty he appeared in good physical shape. She'd read somewhere he played tennis and golf every chance he got.

"I would have known you were your father's daughter just from looking at you. But you're a darn sight prettier than he is." He smiled.

Tess forced a smile to her face. "Thank you, Senator."

"Please come in and have a seat." He pointed to the dark leather couch against one wall. The room, decorated in gold and blue, had a decidedly masculine tone to it. Welch took a seat in a chair diagonal to her. "Would you like anything to drink?"

"No thank you, sir. So, you've met my father?"

"Yes, possibly four, maybe five years ago, during my re-election campaign. He's a sharp man and doesn't beat around the bush."

"No, he doesn't."

"I read the story he's covering in Iraq." His features settled into solemn lines. "Darn shame about the missing boys over there. I hope they're able to find them, or at least give their families closure."

"I hope so too, Senator."

He scooted back in his chair and crossed his legs. "What sort of story are you doing that you wanted to interview me, Ms. Kelly?"

"I have a large readership of military families in my area, Senator. And I know that you and some of the other senators have been working on a package to help those families whose husbands and fathers will be discharged once they're home. My thoughts are to write a piece that might assuage some of their concerns.

"I think we can do that to a certain degree, but not completely. The problem is a complex issue and may take years to address satisfactorily."

She drew a deep breath. "Understood. Might I use my recorder, or would you prefer I use pen and paper, sir? I prefer using both, so there's no question of my misquoting you."

"Both will be fine."

She eased into the interview, asking some background information. She asked how he felt about being on so many committees and how he had time to do so. Welch projected the charm and wit of a practiced politician.

Tess looked down at the notes she'd taken and the questions she'd written down.

"There are one hundred thousand military personnel in San Diego alone. What kind of financial package are you working on for those who are discharged?"

"We've spent billions paying military salaries. Once they are discharged, some of that money can be redirected to create civilian jobs and training programs for those coming out."

"And what about those who have been injured during their service? Do you have programs in mind for them?"

"We've spent millions caring for them. Some of that burden may have to be shared with the individual states they settle in. We've been at war for twenty years, and our debt is astronomical. We have serious economic issues. It's time to find a way to solve them. Everyone is going to have to make sacrifices."

"What kind of incentives are you going to offer the individual states to make it worth their while to take on this extra burden, sir?

"That will all be part of the financial package we're working on."

She waited for him to finish, and when he continued to look at her, she moved on. "Don't we have to make sure the country is secure before any of this can take place?"

"Certainly. But there are other methods we can use more thoroughly to ensure that what happened on 9/11 never happens again."

"Are you talking about covert technologies?"

"Yes, as well as more strenuous use of diplomatic channels. We can use harsher economic sanctions against those countries that harbor terrorists."

"President Clinton tried that in Iraq to control Saddam Hussein. The SEALs had to go in and board vessels to confiscate the oil cargo ships were smuggling for the sanctions to have any affect. If you cut funding for the SEALs and other special operations, who do you plan to have take on those types of missions?"

"It has always been my belief that we need to revisit our policy on foreign aid. If we cut aid and combine that with sanctions, it will put pressure on countries to turn over terrorists in exchange for payments. Eventually they'll police themselves."

"Are you talking about Afghanistan?"

"Among others."

It was like wading through sludge trying to pin him down. When she asked another couple of questions and got similar answers, she nearly sighed aloud in frustration. She changed tactics and moved on to the harder questions.

"There has been speculation that you, Senator Skidmore, and Senator Drummond, have a history of voting for cuts specifically directed at the Naval Special Warfare Group. Is there some reason for that?"

His eyes narrowed and his jaw hardened. "Special Operations soldiers are costly to train, and their equipment is more expensive. It is our belief that they've had carte blanche far too long. We don't need to fund their toys any longer."

"They are experts at using those stealth technologies you mentioned earlier. And they're already trained and possess the expensive *toys* they'll need to complete covert missions. Isn't cutting their funding counterproductive?"

He didn't bother to answer but rose to his feet instead. "I'm afraid that's all the time I have for now, Miss Kelly. I hope you got what you needed. I have another appointment in ten minutes."

"Of course. Thank you, Senator."

He herded her toward the door with a hand that brushed her arm but never quite grasped it.

"I meant to offer my condolences on the death of your stepson. I'm truly sorry."

"Thank you."

"I'm sure the SEALs who tried to rescue him did all they could, sir."

His jaw tightened and his expression grew angry. "It wasn't enough." His eyes suddenly widened as he realized what she'd said.

"The way my son died is not common knowledge, Miss Kelly."

"No, it isn't. And I don't really know any of the details. But there are Marine Corps personnel who know about it and are sympathetic. Is there some reason why you don't want what happened to him to be common knowledge? He died a hero."

"He died needlessly because some—CO in an office somewhere didn't want to risk his Special Ops team."

"But they went in, didn't they?"

"They went in too late."

"How many others did they save?"

"Fourteen men, but three died needlessly. Had they gone in an hour earlier, they would have all survived."

Tess swallowed. God, she hated to push him anymore. "How do you know that?"

"I've read the official report. I know what happened," he said, his tone sharp.

Sympathy for his pain nearly prevented her from saying more.

"If I felt so very strongly, sir, and had the resources to do so, I believe I'd send in someone to look into the way things were done and who was responsible."

Welch's features turned to stone. "The incident has already been reviewed, Ms. Kelly."

"Is it very hard to maintain your objectivity when dealing with Special Ops funding because of your experience, Senator?"

The anger drained from his features and he became distant and cold. "Of course not. It's part of the job. I have another appointment now, Miss Kelly."

It was a good thing he wasn't the only man on the committee. "I appreciate your help with my article, Senator." Tess extended her hand. He was slow in taking it.

"I'll be looking for it, Miss Kelly." His tone was a warning.

"I won't misquote you. I promise. Thank you for seeing me." She nodded, and sauntered out of the room. But all the way down the long hall, she was aware of his gaze burning into her back.

Brett stared out the window toward the Washington Monument. He narrowed his eyes against the piercing blue of the sky.

How would he tell her? She'd be on a high from the interview. God, he'd have to crush that. His stomach churned as though filled with gravel. Jesus. If anything happened—

He turned as he heard an electronic key being used in the lock. Tess was smiling as she came in, her cheeks flushed.

"I'm so relieved. He was very receptive to all my questions, but the last one. He ignored it. I don't think he caught on to what I was doing until then. He was mad as hell when I left. But he did send someone to investigate the mission, Brett, and he holds some CO he wouldn't name responsible for not sending in your team in time. He is manipulating things in the background. He said the mission was investigated. But I couldn't figure out a way to ask about the investigation into the boys. Ian said another team of military investigators was following them. Do you think he put them on it?"

"I don't know, honey." He smiled at her excitement, though nausea threatened. He enfolded her in his arms and held her tight. "You left your cell phone here."

"Yeah. I didn't want it ringing while I was doing the interview."

"A man called while you were gone. His name was Ahmed Hannah."

"Yes, he's Ian's friend. He's a writer for Al Zaman."

Brett swallowed, though the action did nothing to relieve the dryness of his throat. She had done everything in her power to help him, help his team, and he could do nothing to cushion the blow. "He was calling about Ian, Tess. He was kidnapped off the street last night."

CHAPTER 34

Hawk followed Captain Frank Morrow's progress from the open door to the front of the room where a small table supported a projector. The thirty-two SEALs, members of Hawk's platoon and one other, rose to attention.

"At ease," Captain Morrow said as he reached for the remote. He motioned for his aide to adjust the focus on the projector. When the image was crystal clear, he forwarded the first slide. "I know some of you have only been on the ground for thirty-six hours, but in light of all the shit that's gone down, I thought you'd all want to be a part of this mission."

"Hooyah," The room full of SEALs bellowed.

"Twelve hours ago, Ian Kelly was kidnapped by an extremist group associated with al-Qaeda. For several weeks, Kelly has been investigating the disappearance of young men and boys in the area. With Kelly's help and the use of satellite technology and local intel, we've discovered the location of the boys and believe that Kelly has been transported to that location as well.

Morrow hit several slides showing a clustered group of ramshackle buildings. "The location is just outside the village of Zalem, which lies close to the border of Iran. If we don't move quickly, the group may slip over the border into Iran, taking Kelly with them. We all know what will happen after that."

He muted the view on the projector. "We have an opportunity, gentlemen, to return at least thirty young men, possibly more, to their families here in Baghdad. This mission has the possibility to earn us some major goodwill from the Iraqi people and cooperation in the future."

Morrow's attention swung to Hawk for a moment. They'd had a long briefing about the political situations driving the deployment, the indictment, as well as Brett's situation, including the fact that he was dating Kelly's daughter. Though they couldn't allow personal relationships or feelings to direct the missions they chose to undertake, other considerations carried enough weight to drive this one forward.

"Ian Kelly came to this country to investigate a situation that we, and the Iraqi forces, had overlooked. He was the main source of information about where these boys are being held. The assholes who have him don't know that he had an opportunity to pass that info on to us some hours before he was abducted. This gives us the opportunity to make things right. He did our job for us. He deserves to go home in one piece."

Morrow hit the mute button again, uncovering the next slide. "This is a detailed analysis of the complex. We've already got people designing a simulation of the main building where the boys are being held so you can do practice runs. We'll be sending out drones to do surveillance before the raid to make sure no major changes have taken place. Now let's look at the firepower they have at their disposal."

For the next two hours, Morrow covered every aspect of the mission. Every scrap of information they'd been able to collect was gone over, as well as numerous pictures of the complex and the terrorists' movements in the last twenty-four hours.

When he finally killed the projector, he concluded, "You'll have twelve hours to prepare, gentlemen, then get some rest. You'll need it. Dismissed."

Hawk rose to his feet and bowed his back to relieve the cramped stiffness from sitting too long. Morrow approached him. "In my office. We have some things to discuss that have a bearing on the situation in San Diego."

Hawk turned and instructed Lang to gather the team in their barracks and fell in behind the Captain as they made their way down a narrow hall to the Captain's office. The small square room barely had room for a green metal desk and an office chair. "Have a seat, Hawk." Morrow motioned to a sturdy metal folding chair with little padding.

"The team sent in to investigate Weaver and Armstrong's protection detail were special investigators, sent at Senator Welch's request. He also sent in a team to go over every aspect of his stepson's death, including your team's part in the rescue."

Hawk shifted back in his chair. "I'm not surprised." He controlled the urge to run a tired hand over his face. Jet lag, and, though he didn't want to admit it, emotional issues had drained him over the last thirty-six hours. And now they had twelve hours before they stepped into a rescue and recovery mission.

"I know you and your team are still finding your feet after this sudden deployment. But I don't have to tell you how important your platoon's part in this rescue will be. It will be harder for someone to sling mud on a team who've just rescued kidnapped kids than one being investigated for overstepping their boundaries at home."

"We're all well aware of that, sir. That's why we're here to begin with."

"Good. I'm documenting Welch's movements in all these matters. And a copy will be sent to the Secretary of the Navy, as well as all the other interested parties at WARCOM. It will be up to them to pass these concerns onto the Senate Arms Committee. The possibility that these investigators might have identified some of our operators to the people they spoke with opens the possibility of the Senator taking some heat. I'd like to open a full-fledged investigation, but we may never be able to prove that's what happened. The suspicion may be enough to make him back off."

"Thank you, sir."

"As for the particular boy you've been looking for. We did recover some information from Kelly's room on each of the boys. We've made copies of all the stats and pictures. You should be able to identify all of the kids. The one that will hold a special importance in completely clearing Weaver and Armstrong will be included. I hope he's there. I'll be sending that information out to you in about an hour."

"Thank you, Captain."

Morrow rose and Hawk followed suit.

"I know you don't want to be here. Hell, none of us do. But I'm glad you and your team will be involved in this, Hawk," Morrow offered his hand.

Hawk shook it. "We'll do our best."

Taking his leave of the Captain, Hawk stepped out of the building and breathed in the dry desert air. The sun beat down, hot and relentless. Sweat pooled in his armpits and ran down his sides before he'd made it halfway across the compound.

It would be about two a.m. at home and Zoe would be sound asleep. She'd be soft and warm, and if he were there, he'd be spooning her while they slept.

He brushed his hand over his forehead and wiped the sweat onto the leg of his cammies. He had to get his head in the game. He had to put Zoe out of his mind. His men needed him focused. She needed him focused. He'd promised her he'd do whatever it took to come home. And he intended to live up to that promise. Being prepared was part of that.

He reached the two-story cinderblock dormitory where his men were being housed, and, giving a nod to the men on guard outside, entered. The meeting room they'd agreed on was on the first floor and he walked down the long hallway to what was supposed to be a rec room, but only contained a television and gaming system. He shoved open the door.

"Rock a bye baby. On the tree top," fifteen men's voices blended in an off-key rendition of the lullaby while they swung their folded arms like they held babies. He stood in the doorway transfixed. His gaze jerked to Langley Marks's face as he grinned at him and grasping his hand, pumped it up and down as though he were drawing water.

"Congratulations, Hawk. Trish told me just before we left."

"Trish told you?"

"Yeah, she said Zoe'd been trying to tell you for weeks, but then we had the three weeks at Billy Machen and then everything went to hell for Brett."

There's something I need to tell you. Those words looped through his head. *And then the phone had rung and he was out the door. Oh Jesus!*

"Zoe's pregnant." He said the words out loud. Shock spiraled through him, his heart started racing and his breathing grew labored. *Jesus, he'd left her there at the house unprotected, and she was carrying their child.*

"Yeah, man. You're going to be a dad."

Outside of Evan's hospital room, Russell braced an arm against the wall and leaned in close to Clara so their conversation would not be overheard. The faint scent of her shampoo registered dully beneath the smell of antiseptic and some industrial cleaner.

"Evan's too weak to survive surgery or chemo," he said, repeating what the oncologist had told him. "Dr. Reynolds shared Evan's scans and lab work with me. I looked over his complete chart. Reynolds is right."

Clara ran her fingers through her hair, brushing it back from her face. A single tear ran down her cheek and she wiped it off. Worry and exhaustion had deepened the lines around her mouth and eyes. In the forty-eight hours that had passed since Evan had been admitted, they'd left his side only minutes at a time.

"Did he know about the cancer before he came to see you?" she asked.

"Yes."

She nodded and leaned back against the wall. Her throat worked as she swallowed. "I'm so sorry, Russell."

"He's probably been doubling up on his meds. He's been sleeping more the last week or so."

"What can they do for him?" she asked.

Pain swallowed his voice and he shook his head. Her arms went around his waist and she held him, sharing his grief, offering him strength.

When he could speak he said, "They'll keep him comfortable. He's developing pneumonia despite the antibiotics and steroids they're giving him. It won't be long,"

A familiar figure strode toward them, her strides short and choppy, as though every step were an impatient stomp. *Ah hell. I don't need this. But Evan might.*

"Russell," she spoke as she reached him and flicked a glance down Clara's back as though she didn't exist. Dressed in a dark navy suit and white blouse, she looked as though she'd just come from a luncheon. Her blond hair was arranged within an inch of its life, her makeup perfect, and it appeared as though she might have had some plastic surgery to remove the fine lines around her eyes since the last time he'd seen her. With her high-arched brows and symmetrical features, she was an attractive woman, but for the discontent in her expression.

Had she been that unhappy when they were married? Or had it continued to build throughout the years?

"Hello, Gloria."

Clara turned in his arms to face their visitor.

"We've been out of town on a month-long cruise and I just played your message on the answering machine. How is he?" Gloria asked, continuing to ignore Clara.

Angered by her rudeness, his face grew hot and his tone clipped. "He's—not good. He's very weak and he's heavily medicated."

"I'd like to see him."

"You should prepare yourself. He's very gaunt, and one side of his body is paralyzed," Clara said, her tone careful.

"And you would be?" Gloria asked.

"This is Clara," Russell said. "My girlfriend."

Gloria raised a brow at the word "girl." "Thank you for staying with Evan, but now that I'm here, you can go home."

Clara tilted her head and a glint came into her eye. "No thank you. I promised Evan that I wouldn't leave him, or his father, and I intend to honor my promise."

Russell squeezed her hip gently. *Good.* Gloria had finally met someone who wouldn't take her crap any more than he would.

Gloria's lips tightened. "You both look as though you could use a break. Why don't you wander down to the cafeteria and get a cup of coffee or a meal? I'll call your cell should anything happen, Russell."

"Thanks, but we've both eaten. We'll wander down the hall and be back in a few minutes," Russell said. After Gloria entered the room, he guided Clara away from the door.

"She's always gotten her way by acting the lady of the manor where everyone is supposed to do her bidding," he said. He struggled to keep the bitterness from his tone, but didn't quite manage.

"That's not what we call it from where I'm from," Clara said, two angry spots of color riding high on her cheeks. Her expression changed to a frown of anxiety. "Do you think it's a good idea to leave her alone with Evan? She hasn't spoken to him in weeks."

"Has Evan told you what happened between them?" he asked.

Clara hesitated long enough that he stopped and turned to face her.

"Has he asked you not to tell me, Clara?"

She nodded. Her gaze wandered back down the hall to the room again. Her anxiety triggered his concern.

Gloria's behavior was more heavy-handed than usual. The way she'd arrived, like a woman on a mission, and her lack of concern when he and Clara had told her of Evan's condition triggered an edgy feeling of alarm, kicking his heart into a sickening beat.

The elevator door opened and two orderlies pushed a bed and patient out of it and down the hall. They followed behind it back toward the room, their progress slow.

Russell eased the door open a crack and waited. If he was wrong, he didn't want to curtail their reconciliation.

"It's a lie, Evan. You have to say it's a lie."

"No." That one word answer sounded so labored, fear twisted inside Russell.

"He didn't do it. I would have known. Carl was a good father to you."

"No."

"He would have never hurt you."

"He did."

Clara's hand tightened around his. Russell pulled away and shoved open the door hard enough that it hit the wall stop mounted behind it. Gloria jerked and straightened.

"What are you doing, Gloria?" Russell asked as he advanced toward her.

Evan gripped the sheet and his one good leg moved as though he'd escape the bed if he could. His breathing came so labored and fast, his oxygen mask fogged from the effort.

"We were just talking."

Her guilty flush set fire to the rage Russell attempted to control. He grabbed her arm and half dragged, half marched her from the room. Once outside, he shoved her against the wall and held her there, the need to strike her perfect, surgery-enhanced face so sharp and fresh he trembled.

"Is there a problem, Dr. Connelly?" one of the nurses asked, while another brushed by to enter the room.

"Yes there is. This woman is harassing my son, and I need you to call security."

Gloria's face blanched white beneath her makeup and beads of sweat. "You can't do that, Russell."

"Yes, I can. And my next call will be to the police. Our only child is dying, Gloria. And his last memory of his mother will be of you standing over him like some kind of fucking harpy. If I read the conversation you just had right, you can tell Carl Hanson that he'll be seeing me, *soon.* My son needs me right now."

He thrust his face closer and she flinched, bumping her head against the wall.

"I couldn't protect him when he was young. You made certain of that. And I should have tried harder. I should have filed for custody. But I didn't, and I'll have to live with that." His fury surged, threatening to eat his control. "You have more to answer for, and you will. Did you keep him from me because you were afraid of what he might tell me? Was the money so important to you that you turned a blind eye?"

"It isn't true."

"Yes, it is. Our child just gave you deathbed testimony. And all you could do is be the fucking bitch you are. The bitch you've always been."

Two uniformed security officers exited the elevator and trotted down the hall.

"Is there a problem, sir?" One of the men asked.

With an effort, Russell released Gloria's arm, the desire to snap it strong.

"No problem. I was just leaving," Her voice trembled, and she jerked the sleeve of her suit jacket down where his hand had bunched it.

"Don't come back, Gloria," Russell said.

"My purse," she said.

"I'll get it." Anything to be rid of her. Anything to get her as far away from him and Evan as possible before he lost it and hurt her. For the first time in his life, he wanted to raise his hands against a woman. He wanted to beat her into nothingness.

Clara looked up from her seat next to Evan's bed, her expression anxious. Evan had curled onto his side, his breathing, though still labored, had evened out. His eyes were closed.

The nurse stepped back from the IV stand, a hypodermic in her hand. She dropped the used syringe in the medical disposal box next to the bed. "I've given him his pain medication just a few minutes early. He's asleep now."

Russell grabbed the expensive leather clutch Gloria had left on the chair, and, going to the door, thrust it out to one of the security guards and shut the door.

He went to the bed and brushed his hand over Evan's head, smoothing his fine brown hair back from his forehead. He was a grown man, but in that moment Russell saw the fragile child he had been. Every moment he hadn't been there for his son compounded, ripping through him like shrapnel. A wail of pain and rage clawed upward, begging for release. He collapsed in the chair beside the bed, dropped his head to the edge of the mattress and wept.

The plane hit a small patch of turbulence and bounced. The seat belt sign flashed on and the pilot spoke over the intercom to warn them of rough air ahead.

"They probably traced him through his SAT phone," Tess said. "I should never have insisted he call me every night. I led them right to him, Brett." Her insides felt raw with worry, as though a virus had settled somewhere between her stomach and her heart and was gnawing away at both. Her plateau of anxiety never eased.

She started shaking again and wrapped an arm around Brett's. She'd never been a clinging vine, but having him there to hold on to was the only thing keeping her from falling apart.

"You don't know that, Tess. You can't continue to beat yourself up and second guess what you did or didn't do." The concern in his expression was both a comfort and a reason to cry again. "Beat me up instead. It was my fault he was there. If you have to blame someone, blame me."

She turned her face against his shoulder and breathed in the scent of hotel shampoo and soap and him. "I can't. Ian said he was where he wanted to be. That he'd be fine. I'm so fucking mad at him."

"No you're not." Brett tugged his arm free and looped it around her to hold her. "You're afraid. But he's a tough SOB, and he'll be okay. They may just try to ransom him."

"If they were going to do that, they already would have."

"Not necessarily. You have to give the powers that be time to work on this, Tess."

She tilted her head back to look up at him. "Do you think they are? Do you think they even care?"

"I think they're on top of it and you'll get some news in the next couple of days."

A couple of days! That was a lifetime. "What would you be doing if it were your father?" She turned her face against his chest. "I'm sorry, Brett."

"It's okay, honey. I'd be doing the same things you're doing right now. My hands would be just as tied as yours are. I'd be holding on to the people who cared about me and praying."

She drew back to look up into his face. Did he know something? Had they told him something when he'd called the base and talked to—whomever he had talked to? And why couldn't he tell her, if they had?

Because he didn't want her to get her hopes up—just in case.

The plane landed and they exited the terminal. Tess turned her phone on as they walked through, but there were no messages or missed calls.

Brett paused just outside debarkation to answer his phone, which rang as soon as he turned it on. "Yes, sir." He listened for a moment a frown working its way across his face. "I'll swing by on my way home, sir." He hung up and studied his missed call log.

"What is it?" Tess asked.

"Jackson's been trying to get in touch with me for the last four hours. Yet when he called just now all he said was that he needed me to come by his house so we could talk about the change in my orders."

"Maybe he has plans later in the week and he's trying to clear his desk."

Brett shook his head. "We don't talk about anything work-related outside the base, Tess. If he wants to talk about something off-post, it's got to be something he wants to say off the record."

"So, what do you think it might be?"

"He's been pressuring me for months. I think he wants me to resign my commission and take a medical discharge."

Tess studied his features. "You're not going to do it."

"No. I had doubts when my speech thing was at its worst, but not anymore. I think I've broken through whatever block was causing it. As soon as I'm back a hundred percent from this last injury, I'm requesting a transfer out of Jackson's command. And I'll take it up the chain as far as I have to."

On the one hand, hearing him say it triggered a wave of disappointment, but she couldn't wish for him to be any less than what he was. If she loved him, she had to accept his job, just as she loved Ian, despite his.

"That might mean a transfer to the East Coast," she said.

"And how would you feel about that?" he asked, his attention focused on her in such a way her stomach dropped.

"I'm from the East Coast, Brett."

"So you wouldn't be completely opposed to moving back?"

She searched his face. Was he asking her to go with him?

When she remained silent, he said. "It isn't the time to talk about it with all this other stuff going on. But it won't hurt to think about it."

Oh, my God, he was.

"I just had to hear your voice, Zoe. Just to know you're okay," Clara said.

There was a tone in her voice that tightened Zoe's stomach with dread, and she pressed a hand against her midriff. "What's going on there, Mom?"

"Evan's in the hospital. He hasn't much longer. He's such a sweet young man. I've learned to love him. It's a hard thing to watch. To feel."

"I'm sorry, Mom. Is there anything I can do?"

"Just take care of yourself. I can't leave him and Russell, Zoe. I promised Evan I wouldn't leave his father while he's going through this."

"How is Russell?"

"Not good. Losing your father was hard. But losing a child—I couldn't bear it. I don't know how Russell is going to. I don't think he'll ever be the same."

"I understand." Zoe pressed her fingertips against her lips to still their tearful trembling. Had she said too much? "Brett and I are fine, Mom. Just do what you need to do there. We're being careful, and everything has been quiet since you've been gone."

"I don't like the idea of you being there at the house by yourself."

"Hawk has the house set up like Fort Knox, Mom. The alarm is always on. And I check the video recorder every night to make sure no one's been around. The sensors are motion-activated and record anything that moves. If the alarm goes off, a security company responds immediately. The man who runs it is a retired SEAL. Hawk has weapons all over the house, and he's taught me to use them."

She didn't mention that a couple of his buddies came by morning and night. One to take her to the hospital, and the other to deliver her home and make sure she got in okay.

"Could you use one without hesitation, Zoe?"

She might have hesitated before the incident with Derrick Armstrong. But not now. She'd seen what people were capable of. And she had someone besides herself to think of now, her baby. "Yes, I could. And I would. No one is going to hurt me, Mom. I'm going to make sure of it."

"Is Brett okay? I tried to call earlier and all I got was voicemail."

"He's in the air on his way back from Washington with Tess." Zoe debated whether or not to tell her what was going on. She was under so much stress already, but she'd be upset about being kept in the dark. "Tess's father was kidnapped. They believe he's being held hostage by the same militant group who kidnapped the boys."

"Oh my God. Tess must be crazy with worry."

"Brett said she was taking it hard. But he's giving her all the support he can. They'll be back on the ground in an hour."

"Tell him to text me when he lands, so I'll know he's okay."

"I will."

"Keep me posted. I need to know you're both all right."

"Call us and keep us posted on things there. And know that I'm thinking of you and Russell. I wish there had been time for me to meet Evan."

"I do, too," Clara's voice broke. "I love you, Zoe."

"I love you too, Mom."

Zoe hung the phone up and sat for a moment, trying to shake the feelings of grief her mother had projected. Clara loved too easily. But who was she to judge? Though a man in uniform had been the last on her list as a possible mate, she'd fallen for Hawk almost as soon as they'd met.

And now he was seven thousand miles away and eleven hours ahead of her, but it hadn't changed the intensity of her feelings for him. He'd emailed her to let her know he was okay. And they'd instant messaged. Hearing his voice would have been better, but she'd take what she could get. Just knowing he was alive and unhurt made it easier to function.

But how was she supposed to tell him about the baby when he was in constant danger? She couldn't.

She rose to put the finishing touches on her makeup and tugged her hair up into a ponytail. Her cell phone rang and she limped back into the kitchen to pick it up. "I'm here," Petty Officer Norm Hamilton said.

"On my way out." She gathered her things, looked through the peephole in the front door, and disarmed the alarm. She re-armed it and pulled the door closed, checking the lock. "You're the only woman I know who is really ready when she says she'll be," Norm said from his position on the porch. "If Hawk weren't such a good guy, I'd be tempted." He grinned.

His homely face was almost handsome when he smiled, but Zoe shook her head. "I hate to be blunt, Norm, but you don't stand a chance."

He gripped his chest and staggered. "Damn, you could have sugar-coated it, darlin'." His west Texas drawl reminded her of Bowie's.

Immediately her thoughts went to Hawk, and she forced a smile despite the wave of longing that hit her. "I shoot from the hip, Norm."

The moment she started toward the steps he became all professional SEAL. His gaze sharp, he scanned the street for any movement. He placed himself just a little ahead of her, positioning his body to take a blow or a bullet, should either materialize. He opened the car door for her and she wasted no time getting in. "I'm sorry you have to keep doing this. I know you'd rather be doing something else," she said, when he was behind the wheel.

"If Hawk and Brett say I need to be here, I'm here, Zoe. They know their stuff. If something's making them itchy, there's a legitimate reason. Besides, they've both saved my bacon numerous times."

"I really appreciate you doing this." Her hand moved to cradle the small roundness of her abdomen.

"It won't be for long." He glanced at her, his expression reassuring. "They'll catch the SOB who shot Brett and it will be over."

"I hope so."

He swung past the parking structure and pulled up to the front door. The large round disk over it read Naval Medical Center San Diego around the edge. Every time she saw it she thought of how many times she'd passed by going to see Brett. She slid out of the vehicle in the midst of a group.

"I'll see you tomorrow. If you need me, you know the number. If I can't come, I'll send out the Navy."

Zoe laughed and threw up a hand as she strode toward the entrance. A dark-haired man with a prosthetic arm held the door for her, and she nodded her thanks as she went into the building. He fell into step just behind her as she wandered through the labyrinth of halls to the physical therapy wing.

The man stayed to her right and five or so feet behind her all the way to the clinic. With every step she fought the urge to look over her shoulder at him. She didn't know every patient, and the fact that she didn't recognize this one didn't necessarily mean anything. But she increased her pace, though the strain on her bad leg had the damaged muscles in her calf aching. Her heart was thudding in her throat. The few people they passed in the wide halls didn't seem to take notice of either of them.

He continued to keep pace with her. When she saw the entrance to the clinic, she drew a calming breath. She opened the door and ducked in. The man caught the wooden panel before it swung shut behind her. She passed through the waiting room, and, jerking open the door leading to the therapy rooms, swung through and yanked it shut behind her. The door to the office proper where the clerical staff worked was propped open, and she paused to look through the window as he approached it. He signed his name to the list just as any patient would, then picking up a magazine from a rack, and sat down in one of the gray-blue padded chairs.

He was just a patient. She leaned against the wall. Her heart beat in her ears, her leg throbbed, and she was trembling. *He was just a patient.* Had he been anything else he could have caught up to her at any time. She waited for the worst of the fear to pass before she straightened and limped down the hall to the employee locker room.

Tomorrow she was going to ask Norm to walk her into the office.

CHAPTER 35

Hawk rested his head against the metal bulkhead behind him and tried to block out the voice in his head that kept harping at him every few minutes. Why hadn't she told him? There had been opportunities. She'd told Trish, but she hadn't told him. But then how many times had she said *'I need to talk to you'?* Now that he was thinking about it, he remembered several. And there'd always been an interruption. A problem to deal with. The morning he'd talked to her about the legal issues stood out—Jesus, he'd dropped that fucking bomb on her, and she'd brushed everything else aside to offer him support and tell him how much she loved him.

And now he'd walked out the door and left her—*Jesus!* But even if he'd known, he'd have still have had to go. She knew that. She understood that. A lump the size of a softball lodged in his throat, he swallowed against it.

As soon as this mission was behind them, he'd call. Though use of the SAT phone was limited, he'd get it and he'd talk to her about … *their baby.* The words created such a jumble of emotions into his chest it was hard to breathe. Joy, excitement, possessiveness for their baby and for Zoe, and love. But a hint of anger tinted those feelings, too. *She should have told him.*

He had to set this aside and get his head in the game.

The men were quiet, the tension inside the compartment thick. His gaze scanned the faces of the three new members of his team, Sizemore, Tyler, and Logan. Sizemore had transferred in at the last moment to fill Brett's position, but he was no stranger to action and had been in the teams for nearly two years. During their practice drills he'd fallen into the rhythm of the team seamlessly. He was an excellent sniper. Tyler and Logan, though new, had been working with the rest of the team for three months now. They'd seen action, but not like they'd see tonight. He'd paired them with Bowe and Doc just in case. They'd do fine, as long as they followed their training.

The helo caught a downdraft and dipped; Hawk grabbed his seat and braced his feet. Lang, sitting beside him, did the same. It was his fault Doc and Bowie were mentoring two new guys who'd been with their team too short a time. It was his fault Langley Marks was sitting here beside him, away from his family. It was his fault the four of them were taking heat because of Derrick Armstrong. He should have never called any of them. They were on this fucking helo because of him. He'd apologized to them all, but that wasn't going to make up for them being away from their families. Or that they were back here again in this desert, eating sand and risking their lives.

"Let it go, Hawk," Lang said, close to his ear.

Hawk's gaze shifted to Lang's face.

Lang's expression was solemn, his lantern jaw taut with emotion. "Every man on this helo is here because we're SEALs. This is what we do. We all knew Armstrong was on the edge. But the only one who reached out to him and tried to help him was you. You did everything right. And it still went to shit. And that isn't your fault, or mine, or anyone's but his. You're not the one who put us on this chopper. Command did that to make a bullshit political situation go away. Every man on this team knows that and understands. You can't take the weight of every goddamn thing that happens onto your shoulders. And you can't control everyone's actions any more than you could control Derrick Armstrong. So, *let it go.*"

Digesting, analyzing what Lang had said, Hawk remained silent. Lang was right. There was nothing he could do to change the situation, so he had to just ride it out. "Thanks, Lang."

"You're welcome." He folded his arms over his chest, tilted his head back, and closed his eyes. "Wake me when we get there."

Hawk let out a short bark of laughter and shook his head. Lang smiled but didn't open his eyes.

"Ten minutes out." The landing controller's voice came over the intercom. Hawk checked his watch. An hour's hump to the complex, then they'd get to work. If everything went according to plan, he'd be back at base soon enough to call Zoe around the time she got ready for bed.

Five minutes out, Hawk signaled for them to prepare for touchdown and poked Lang in the ribs. "COMs on," he ordered.

"Intel says all's quiet," the landing controller said.

A few minutes later, the CH-47 pitched backward, then shuddered as it went into a hover. The ramp lowered even before the big machine touched down. Hawk double-timed it off the chopper into the desert with Lang on his heels and the other fourteen SEALs close behind.

The helo's blades kicked up a dust storm as it bugged out to drop the other sixteen SEALs at another location and to take cover five miles farther north.

Using hand signals, he ordered his men to fall in. The shamal wind that had been stronger during the day had eased. It feathered across his face, chilling the sweat that ran down his cheek. It was a double-edged sword. The wind could cover their approach to the complex, yet if it were too strong and kicked up a dust storm, it would impede the choppers from moving in to transport the hostages and them from the area.

As they approached the small village of Zalem, Hawk turned to the west, farther into the desert and away from the sleeping town. They had half an hour to take position for the raid. The terrain was steep hills and desert with little vegetation. The mountains in the west were sharp purple summits etched against the night sky.

The sand dragged at Hawk's boots as they climbed the next hillside and paused to look down on the block-like buildings below. He signaled for the men to spread out and take cover. He knelt beside Jeff Sizemore as he set up the M-11 sniper rifle and the night vision scope. The weapon was capable of taking out a target at fifteen hundred yards, and Sizemore didn't miss.

Hawk raised his night vision binoculars and studied the area around the buildings. "Six standing post," Hawk said. The images of the men as they paced the area looked like green shadows. He studied the size of the images but couldn't tell if they were men or boys. "We'll need to take out the two on the roof of the east building." The direction from which they were approaching. "And take the chance they aren't the kids. Condor two will take out the others."

"Roger that," Sizemore said.

"First light. Wait for my signal." Hawk said.

"Aye, sir."

Waiting for dawn was a risk, but without light the possibility of killing some of the boys by accident was too great.

Hawk signaled for two men to dig in. One would spot for Sizemore while the other guarded their position. He checked his watch, then motioned the others to move.

He motioned to Jack Logan, his communications specialist, to follow and the two of them worked their way downhill to a small trench. Logan set up the radio, checked the system, then they settled in to wait.

The sound of Evan's breathing had changed in the last hour. Each inhale had grown further apart and shallower. Clara caught herself drawing a breath every time he did. It was all happening too fast. But he had nothing to fight the pneumonia with. His body was just too weak.

Even if he could beat back the infection, the cancerous lesion in his brain had already paralyzed his right side and was eating away at him. At the moment he wasn't in pain. If he were, she didn't think she could bear it.

Russell sat forward in his chair, his gaze focused on some distant spot beyond the room. He clenched and unclenched his hands, the movement laced with frustration and pain. Since he'd broken down earlier, he hadn't spoken.

What could she do for him? How could she help him? She rose to her feet and moved around the bed to where he sat. She knelt at his feet and took his clenched fists in her hands. "I love you. I love your son. Tell me what I can do to help."

Russell shook his head. He drew her up to sit on his thigh. He rested his head against her breast and she stroked his hair, the back of his neck. "I love you," he said. "You're the strongest woman I know. You give your heart so freely, so fearlessly."

Hearing the words brought her a profound sense of relief. "You're wrong. I was terrified when we first met."

He tilted his head back to look up at her. "Why?"

"Because I hadn't even attempted to allow another man into my life since my Joe died. And then there you were at the airport, and I felt that special spark between us I hadn't felt in twenty years. And I was scared to death."

"But you still let me into your life, and you took Evan in, too."

"I couldn't have done it if you hadn't been you and Evan hadn't been Evan."

He turned his face against her breasts again. And she held him tight.

"I failed him, Clara." His voice cracked.

"Had you known, you'd have taken action. But you didn't. It's in the past. Evan didn't hold you responsible. And you're here now when he needs you more than he ever has before.

And he knows you love him, Russell. That's the most important thing."

He nodded. And some of the tension drained from his shoulders. "I wish there was something I could do to make it up to him."

The file Evan had given her came to mind. She'd had her doubts about being the one to hand it over to the District Attorney. She'd promised to do it to save Russell as much pain as she could. But perhaps Russell was the one who needed to deliver it. "You know that old saying about what goes around, comes around?"

"Yes."

"Well, sometimes it's true."

Zoe paused in the hall outside the therapy room and glanced at her watch. One more patient and she'd take her lunch break. Removing the phone from her pocket, she checked for messages from Clara and, seeing none, texted Brett, reminding him to contact Mom when his plane landed. She slid the phone into her pocket and leaned against the door facing while she waited for Cal Crowes.

A double amputee lay on one of the padded exercise beds doing flutter kicks with his stumps to exercise his thigh muscles. Another gripped the parallel bars while practicing balance exercises. The sight of these young men fighting their way back from such terrible injuries triggered a wave of empathy. They were maimed, but they weren't quitters. Though she'd helped other people work their way back from serious injuries, the work she was doing here was more fulfilling than anything she'd ever done.

Cal Crowes came around the corner and walked toward her. She studied how he shifted his weight and placed each step. Had she not been watching closely, she would have never known he had a prosthesis, but for the metal rod leading into the flex foot. He'd been practicing. A smile leapt to her lips. "You're doing great."

A man turned the corner behind him. His dark gaze focused on her as he approached. The same man had entered the clinic earlier this morning. Had he been sitting in the waiting room all this time? Why hadn't he been seen?

The man stopped fifteen feet behind Cal. His prosthetic arm with its metal fingers lay folded across his chest. "Zoe Weaver?" he asked. He raised his uninjured hand.

"Yes." What was in his hand?

Cal turned to glance over his shoulder. He caught his breath. "Bomb!" With a lunge, he shoved Zoe through the open doorway, his large body forcing her sideways into the room and down. Her damaged leg folded and Zoe struck the tile floor hip first. Cal's body landing atop hers forced the air from her lungs at the same time the blast shook the cinderblock walls, the floor. Debris shot from the hallway, hit the door, and ricocheted into the room. Ceiling tiles fell and one of the four-foot long plastic covers for the lights crashed to the floor along with the metal strips that held it in place. Concrete dust billowed through the air like smoke.

A fire alarm went off, piercing Zoe's blast-dulled hearing as she fought to get air into her lungs. Cal rolled off of her, his unshaven face pale. He pivoted onto his good foot, balanced on his hands, and bracing his shoe-covered prosthesis on the floor, he straightened.

His mouth moved as he yelled something at her. The screaming alarm made hearing him impossible. He bent and offered her a hand.

Zoe's first full breath was filled with grit and she coughed. *They had to get out.* She sat up. *The baby. Was the baby all right?* Her hand went to her abdomen. No pain, just a bruised feeling along her left hip where she'd struck the floor. Grasping Cal's hand, she braced a palm on the floor to push upward while he tugged. Two feet from her splayed fingers lay a human tooth.

Nausea rolled through her, and she closed her eyes. The screaming alarm was joined by a ringing deep in her ears. She opened her eyes and the world narrowed to a pinhole of light. Her stomach felt hollow, her legs weak. She bent at the waist and fought to keep from heaving.

"Look at me, Zoe," Cal's voice coming close to her ear penetrated the other distracting sounds as he grabbed her arm and put his other around her waist. "We have to get out of here."

She nodded. *The other therapists and patients?* She scanned the room. One therapist was helping the double amputee put on his prosthetics. The other was guiding his patient toward the door.

Tank, the large corpsman assigned to the therapy clinic, skidded to a stop just outside the door. "Is everyone okay?" he yelled, his words nearly impossible to hear. He motioned for everyone to hurry and shoved into the room to help.

Zoe focused on putting one foot in front of the other. Out in the hall sparks flew as a live electrical wire swung from the damaged ceiling and hit the wall. Rubbery-smelling smoke drifted through the air, but no fire was evident. The cinderblock walls were blackened and pocked from the blast. Daylight from the therapy room beamed through one area of the wall, but the structural damage seemed limited to the direct spot where the man had stood.

If Cal hadn't shoved her, they'd both be dead.

Another cramp of nausea hit Zoe. They turned away and hurried down the hall to the emergency exit. She kept walking, following the other evacuating employees through the hallways.

Once outside in the employee parking lot, they moved away from the building and joined a large group standing along the strip of grass that surrounded the lot, the metal fence surrounding the property preventing them from going further.

"You okay?" Cal asked.

She nodded, though she'd begun to shiver with reaction. She wrapped her arms against her waist. She needed to go to the emergency room. She needed someone to check her out and make sure the baby was okay. Would she have pain right away if she were going to miscarry?

"That fucker knew your name, Zoe. He was after you."

She nodded. The urge to cry was strong.

"Why was he after you?"

This man had saved her life. She owed him everything. "Someone leaked my brother's name to terrorists in Iraq. He was shot about a week ago while surfing, but not killed. The man tried to kill my mother as well."

"They've declared a jihad against your whole family."

"I'm so sorry for everything. You've been through enough already. The FBI and all the other agencies didn't think any of this would happen. They kind of shrugged it off."

Her shivers increased. And where was Brett? Was he okay? Her mother had been okay earlier, but was she safe now? She reached for her phone and hit the dial button to call Brett. His phone went to voicemail, and she waited for the beep so she could leave a message. "Call me right away Brett. Something's happened at the hospital. You may be in danger."

She hung up. And thought about what to do next. Someone had to find Brett and warn him. She pushed the next number. Norm answered immediately.

"Something's happened. I need the Navy."

CHAPTER 36

B rett pulled into the horseshoe-shaped driveway before the brick, one-story ranch style home. A privacy fence, hooked to one end of the house, looped around the side yard and disappeared around back. The yard was immaculate, the flowerbeds across the front well-tended, the sidewalks edged. On the porch, a weeping fig with its braided trunk and waxy leaves sat in a pot near the front door. "You can stay in the car if you like, Tess," he said. He removed the Sig from his shoulder holster and shoved it under the seat.

"No, I'm going in with you. If he's going to threaten to end your career, I'm going to be there to back you up."

Even with her mouth compressed, and her features set in an aggressive scowl, she was beautiful. He smiled, leaned over, and kissed her. "This may be just what he says it is. But save all that righteous outrage, just in case."

With her expression softened by the kiss, she nodded, and reached for the door handle.

Brett exited the vehicle and waited at the end of the sidewalk for Tess to join him. He pushed the keypad and locked the car, then offered her his hand. When she took it, he wove his fingers through hers.

"You're moving a little easier," she commented.

"It must be all the TLC I'm getting."

Soft color lit her cheeks.

He grinned. "Being with you is something special."

She leaned her cheek against his shoulder.

Brett let her go ahead of him up the two steps to the porch. He pushed the doorbell and the door opened immediately.

"Ensign Weaver." Marsha Jackson's smile looked brittle. Her blond hair hung limp around her face and her makeup was smeared beneath her eyes as though she'd been crying.

Were they fighting again?

"James has been calling you." Her fingers trembled as they crept beneath her jaw as though she meant to cup her throat, then dropped to a place just over her heart.

Brett frowned. Was that just a nervous gesture? "We've been out of town, ma'am. I called as soon as I got back."

"No, harm done. But he's eager to see you." She cupped her throat again, and then her fingers brushed down her blouse to settle over her heart, the first two folded under so that only the last three showed.

No gesture. She was signaling hostage. Brett met the woman's gaze and read the desperation in the stiffness of her features. He nodded slowly. She shifted her eyes toward the door.

"Please come in." She motioned with those same three fingers and stepped back.

Brett's arm tightened around Tess's hip when she started to step forward. *No way was she walking into this.*

"Tess is just dropping me off. I need her to pick something up for me while we're on this side of town." He thrust his hand into his pocket and retrieved the rental car's keys. Taking her hand, he put them in her palm and closed her fingers around them. He delved into her brown gaze, hoping she'd catch on. "Honey I forgot to write that address down for you. Do you have a scrap of paper?"

She frowned at him, confusion in her expression, but she stuck her hand into her bag and produced a small notebook and a pen.

Brett wrote a quick note, jammed the pen between the pages to hold the place, and handed it back to her. "If the guy says it isn't ready, tell him I need it ASAP and wait for it. Okay? The place is just around the corner from here."

The confusion dissolved, replaced by fear. "Okay." Though she'd never met the woman she said, "It's nice to see you, Mrs. Jackson."

"You too, Tess. See you in a bit."

Brett paused to watch her walk to the car. When she'd gotten behind the wheel, he turned back to Marsha Jackson. Her gaze had settled on him, and she gripped her skirt in her fists.

As Tess pulled away behind him, Brett said, "How's your little boy, Mrs. Jackson? Is he doing better with the formula?" He stepped over the threshold one pace, then two and lunged against the edge of the door with his shoulder shoving it back as hard as he could. The wooden panel hit something solid, initiating a startled yelp. The door thrust forward, the man behind it shoving back. Every muscle in Brett's side screamed as he heaved against it again, mashing the tango back against the wall. The wood at the end of the door exploded near his head, though the report from the fired gun was muffled to a soft hiss. The shooter had a silenced weapon. Brett hit the door again and another round went off into the ceiling.

The tango couldn't aim the weapon behind the door, but Brett couldn't disarm him, either. Brett swiveled around the edge of the door and jerked it forward, releasing him. His face bloody, his nose broken, the man jerked the weapon down to fire.

Brett punched him in the throat. The gun went off, the round hitting the flat screen TV across the room. Brett gripped the silencer on the barrel of the weapon, and thrust it upward and back. The pop as the man's finger broke blended with his coughing and wheezing as he clawed at his neck trying to breathe through his crushed trachea. He tumbled to the ground, the gun still looped around his finger. He lost consciousness and grew still.

Brett jerked the weapon free of the man's mangled hand. The French door shattered and Brett turned toward the new threat as the slugs hit the wall behind him. A man stood outside on the patio, taking aim once more.

"Down." Brett jerked Marsha Jackson onto the floor, raised the pistol, and fired twice in quick succession, striking the man once in the head, once in the throat. He fell face forward against the frame and slid down. "How many more of them are there?" Brett asked.

"Just one. He has James and Alex out by the pool. They beat James after he talked to you. He's—I don't know if he's still alive."

Jesus. "How long have they been here?"

She began to cry. "Two days. They've been waiting for you to come back." She began to rock.

What had they done to her in those two days? Terrorized her, certainly. Rage built inside him. Thank God he'd sent Tess away to get help.

A man stepped in front of the sliding glass doors with Alex Jackson in his arms. He pressed his Beretta up against the baby's chin with steady pressure, forcing Alex's head back until he began to cry.

Marsha Jackson's squealed and staggered to her feet, fear for her child etched in every line of her face. "Please don't hurt him, he's just a baby." Tears streamed unchecked down her cheeks.

This is how they'd controlled her for two days. A cold, hard rage formed in the pit of Brett's stomach.

"Come join us by the pool, Ensign Weaver. And leave the gun behind."

The man's English was good and held the same inflection as the Iraqis he'd worked alongside during his deployment. His dark brown hair was cut short. Acne scars roughened his skin, and his dark eyes glittered like obsidian. It was the man his mother had photographed. The same one who'd shot him.

Brett laid the gun down on the floor. With his first step, he felt the pull and tug of his torn stitches. He'd probably ripped them all out. *Fuck it.* He strode to the French door, his steps crushing the shattered glass into the carpet. He turned the knob, pushed it open. He stepped over the body outside and followed the man as he backed toward the limp figure secured to a lawn chair next to the pool. Marsha Jackson followed behind him, her ragged sobs dogging his steps.

Tess pulled the car around the corner from the house and parked. Her hands shook as she opened the note Brett had written. *Hostage situation dial 911, 3 men.* He'd said, "If the guy says it isn't ready, tell him I need it ASAP and you'll wait for it. Okay? The place is just around the corner from here." Call 911 and wait for the police around the corner.

Her hands trembled as she jerked her cell phone out of her purse and punched in the number. The pop-pop report of a gun reached her just as the operator answered and she jerked. *Brett.* Tears ran down her face. "Shots have been fired at four-thirty-three Locust Street. Three men are holding Captain James Jackson and his wife and baby hostage. My boyfriend Ensign Brett Weaver is in the house too. Please hurry."

"Ma'am, where are you calling from?"

The dispassionate voice drove her anxiety higher. "Outside the house. Hurry—*please* hurry!"

They weren't coming fast enough. What was happening to Brett? What was happening to the Jackson's and their baby? Tess unclipped her seat belt and shoved the car door open.

"Ma'am, units have been dispatched to your location. Stay on the phone."

Tess reached beneath the seat and withdrew Brett's pistol. Did it have to be cocked to fire? She knew it was loaded. Just holding the weapon in her hand made her tremble. "I have to go." She pushed the button to disconnect the call. When the phone began to ring, she dropped it onto the driver's seat and shut the door.

She had to know what was happening. *She had to do something.* They could all be dying while she waited. She held the weapon pointed down against her thigh, as she'd seen Brett do, and cut across the unfenced yards back toward the house. *Please God, don't let anything happen to him.* Tears streaked her cheeks and she brushed them away with a swipe of her shoulder. The privacy fence surrounding the pool blocked her way. She jogged around to the front of the house.

The front door hung open and one of the hinges was partially pulled loose. The thought of entering the house numbed her limbs and leached the strength from them. Her legs refused to move. The gun suddenly weighed two tons.

Tess clinched her teeth to still their chatter. Her breathing grew choppy and quick. *She had to do this.* She breathed through the worst of the fear, then straightened her shoulders. Wary of approaching the door head-on, she crawled onto the porch, and, reaching the opening, braced her back against the wall beside it for support, and shoved upward until she was standing. The house was quiet, too quiet. Her thigh muscles jerked as she swiveled, and thrusting the pistol out in front of her, she stepped over the threshold.

A large man lay face down just inside. A startled yelp escaped her. The flat screen TV across the room had a hole in the center of it. A gentle breeze drifted in from the open French door, while the shattered glass scattered across the carpet reflected the late morning light. Tess circled around the mess and went to the door that wasn't broken.

"What the fuck do you want?"

Brett's voice carried to her from outside and she breathed a quick sigh of relief. How could she help him?

While he waited for an answer, Brett assessed Captain Jackson's condition and looked for signs of life. The man's face was distorted by the beating he'd taken. His nose was flattened and both eyes were swollen shut. Red and purple bruises had already formed where blood had pooled beneath the skin. Brett couldn't tell if he was still breathing, but his body slumped loose-limbed in the chair, his arms secured to the metal chair arms by duct tape. If he wasn't already dead, he soon would be.

"I want you to die and all your family with you. You Americans have killed my family, one by one." The baby's head flopped back, and he nearly tumbled backwards out of the man's arms. He jerked the baby forward against his chest. "Perhaps I should kill this creature and end his suffering." He ran the barrel of his pistol along the baby's cheek. Marsha Jackson shrieked as though she'd been sliced with a knife.

Brett's stomach clenched with rage. *The sadistic bastard.* "And you know it was me that did this, how?" he asked, in an attempt to distract the man while he scanned the area for anything he could use as a weapon. The concrete that surrounded the kidney-shaped pool was as pristine and free of debris as the grass out front. A glass table and chairs positioned in one of the rounded curves had its umbrella up and offered the only spot of shade. A gas grill was shoved against the side of the house, the implements dangling from beneath the cover too far away to offer any hope.

"Were you not among the men who blew up a building in Fallujah last April?"

Jesus. That fucking mission kept coming back to haunt him again and again. "I was in a coma for a month after my deployment, and I've lost all memory of my last two weeks in Iraq."

The guy extended his arm and aimed the gun at him. "Your Captain told me it was you and this Derrick Armstrong."

"No he didn't," Marsha Jackson said behind him.

The man raised one dark brow and with a careless motion dropped the baby into the pool.

"No." Marsha screamed and broke from behind Brett at a run. The man swung the gun toward her, tracking her movement. Brett lunged forward in an attempt to cover the distance between them, even as he knew he'd never make it. Like Lazarus rising from the dead, Captain Jackson heaved his chair backwards into the man, striking him thigh-high. The gunman staggered beneath the weight, the gun going up and discharging into the air. Jackson landed on his back and hit the concrete with a meaty thunk.

Brett heard the splash of water as Marsha dove into the pool. Brett launched himself over Jackson to reach the gunman. He hit the man chest-high and his momentum carried them into the water. The tango swung the gun against the side of his head right over the scar. Brett's ears rang and the strength drained from his limbs. Blackness threatened, and he fought it. Just as he'd fought it that night. A memory of Derrick Armstrong standing over him with a rifle broke through the blackness. Brett lost his grip on the man's arm. The terrorist kicked away toward the side of the pool.

He had to fight. They'd all die if he didn't. Brett kicked upward, breaking the surface and gasping for air. The terrorist grabbed the side of the pool and started to heave himself up. Brett gripped the back of his shirt and jerked him back into the water. He looped an arm around the tango's neck and, using his weight, dragged the man under. The terrorist thrashed and tried to head butt him. Brett wrapped his legs around the man from behind and allowed them both to sink. The gun dropped from the tango's hand. He clawed at Brett's arm, his movements desperate. Brett tightened his grip around his neck and held on.

Tess ran to the side of the pool as Marsha Jackson surfaced with the baby. She set Brett's Sig down on the concrete and reached for the child. His eyes looked glazed, and he wasn't breathing. Tess laid him on his back on the concrete, clapped her hands loudly and thumped his shoulder then pressed her ear to his chest. Nothing. She began CPR. His small chest seemed so fragile, she prayed she wasn't doing more harm than good. She counted off the 30 compressions, then placing her mouth over his mouth and nose, and gave him two short breaths.

Marsha dragged herself from the water and sat staring at her, her slack expression dull with shock.

Siren's sounded in the distance, growing louder by the moment. Tess fought back the urge to scream when Brett still didn't surface. *Please come up. Please.*

"Go get help, Mrs. Jackson. Go out front and wait for the police. Tell them we need help." She bent to put her mouth over the baby's again. After half a breath, the baby choked and spit up water. Tess rolled him on his side and patted him on the back. His sharp cry was a beautiful sound. *Thank God.* Tess staggered to her feet holding the baby against her shoulder.

"Brett." She tried to shout, but the sound was choked off by fear. "Please—"

A figure rushed upward and breached the surface with a gasp. Brett's dark blond hair clung to his head like a cap and he gasped for air, one breath, then two. His movements slow, he swam to the side of the pool, dragged himself up on the concrete, and fell back on the hard surface. His chest heaved while he caught his breath. Blood stained the bottom of his t-shirt and Tess knelt next to him and raised the cloth. The gaping wound where his stitches had torn loose had instant nausea crawling up her throat.

Scooping up the pistol from the side of the pool, he stared at the weapon then at her. "Jesus, Tess. I can't believe you came in here."

"I thought you were drowning, and the baby wasn't breathing, so I couldn't come in after you." Though she fought to keep the tears from coming, they coursed down her cheeks. Brett dragged her close, wetting her clothing. She didn't care. All that mattered was that he was there, alive, holding her. He continued to hold her and the baby while they both cried, and the sirens screamed right outside the fence.

CHAPTER 37

Silence, oppressive and heavy, hung over the room. After hours of struggling to breathe, Evan had quieted. Russell continued to hold his hand though his chest no longer moved. The nurse came in with a doctor in tow to check his respiration and heartbeat.

"He's gone, Dr. Connelly," she said softly.

"I know."

The two words spoken with such finality nearly broke Clara's heart. She rose from her chair and, motioning for the nurse, went out into the corridor with her. She handed the woman a piece of paper with the funeral home information on it, then leaned back against the wall. The doctor exited the room. He nodded to her and wandered down the hall. She remained where she was, offering Russell some time alone with his son. Exhaustion dragged at her limbs, and when Russell came to the door, it was a struggle to straighten from her position.

"Do they have what they need?" Russell asked.

"Yes."

"Let's go to the apartment," he said. She retrieved her purse and he took her hand in his.

Leaving the hospital, they stepped into a different world. The late afternoon sun had knocked the chill out of the breeze, but there was a strangeness to the sound of their shoes on the concrete, the movement of the traffic, the clearness of the sky. How could all this still be here when Evan wasn't?

"What have you got in that thing?" Russell asked, motioning to her bag. "It weighs a ton."

"Just some things Evan gave me to hold on to."

The weight of the shoulder bag seemed to increase with every step, and when they reached the car Clara was glad to toss it in the back seat. She tilted her head back against the seat and studied Russell's hands on the wheel. They were strong hands, large hands, healing hands. Those hands had healed thousands of other people's sons and daughters, including her own. Those hands had held his son's for hours, had soothed him when he was at his worst. And now they gripped the wheel to take them back to the apartment where they'd both rest and try to put the pieces of their hearts back together.

As though he were aware of her thoughts, Russell laid his hand on her leg and she placed hers over it.

When all this was settled, and they had some time to adjust to being just the two of them, would she still feel like this? Would he still feel the same for her? She hoped he would, because she couldn't imagine her life without him anymore.

At the apartment building, they stepped off the elevator and walked down the hall to Evan's apartment. Russell paused before putting the key in the lock.

"If you want, we can stay at a hotel for the night, and then come back in the morning," she said.

He shook his head. "I want to sit in his reading chair and touch the book he was reading before he came to see me."

Emotion rose to the back of her throat, but she swallowed it down. She nodded.

He unlocked the door and shoved it open, then stepped back to allow her to enter ahead of him. Clara froze as she eyed the room. The closet door stood open and books covered the floor of the narrow entrance hall and spilled into the living room. From where she stood, she could see the couch cushions lay askew.

Russell followed her gaze. "Son of a bitch!" He stepped past her, and skirting the books, strode down the hall. After a moment's pause in the living room, he continued into the bedrooms.

Clara placed her feet with care so as not to step on the books and stood surveying the kitchen. Every cabinet door and drawer stood open. This was not a burglary. It was a search. A slow burning anger began to build inside her. *That bitch.*

Russell returned to the living room, his features were taut with rage. "This was Gloria, wasn't it?" He ran his fingers through his hair grabbing the sides of his head with his hands as though it might explode. "I can't believe I ever had a single thought or feeling for that—" He dropped his hands. "What the fuck was she looking for?"

Clara pulled the padded envelope partially out of her bag. "For this. It's proof against her husband. It's Evan's proof. And tomorrow morning, we'll deal with it—you'll deal with it, when you take it to the proper authorities. And they'll arrest her husband and make her life hell. Which, in my opinion, is exactly what she deserves." *The bitch.* She drew a deep breath and tried to beat back the righteous anger. She shoved the envelope back in and set her bag on the rumpled couch.

He drew a deep breath. "I could call the police and press charges against her for this, but she probably has a key and would say she had just as much right to be in the apartment as I do."

"Yes." She bent to pick up a copy of *Bonfire of the Vanities* from the floor and smiled as she read something underlined and commented on in the margin. She extended the book to him and he turned it to read what was written and smiled.

Clara picked up another, *To Kill a Mockingbird*, and found similar highlighting and comments on the text and smiled. She started picking up the mess.

Russell took the Thomas Wolfe book with him to the couch, straightened the cushion, and sat down. He thumbed through the pages, pausing to read an occasional note Evan had penned about what he'd read. The closeness he still felt with his son while reading his words eased his anger and his grief. He glanced up to find Clara still sorting through books and stacking them.

"Clara."

She turned and straightened. Exhaustion deepened the lines around her eyes and mouth. Her clothes were wrinkled, her hair mussed, her makeup non-existent, exposing the scattered freckles across her forehead, but she had never looked more beautiful to him than she did at this moment. And he'd never loved anyone more. He motioned for her to join him. "Leave the mess. We'll pick it up in a while."

She set the books on the nearest stack and wandered over to where he sat. She flopped down beside him. He slid an arm around her and drew her close against his side. He laid the book face down on the table next to him.

"When we get back to San Diego, I want you to move in with me," he said.

She drew back to look up at him, surprise in her expression.

"I know, with everything that's happened since we met, you'll need some time to be certain about how you feel. But I want us to be together while you make up your mind."

"Does that mean you've already made up your mind how you feel about me?"

Had he never said the words? He tipped her face up to him and kissed her with all the tenderness he could offer. For standing by him and his son, for being Evan's champion she deserved all the love he had to give her. "I love you, Clara. I want you with me, and when you're ready, I want you to marry me, if you'll have me."

A smile curved her lips, and he kissed her again. When he raised his head, she nestled close. "I love you, Russell and neither one of us is getting any younger, but I'd like some time for you to convince me to marry you, when we're both up to it."

He smiled. The love she gave him cushioned his heart a little against the pain. "When we're both up to it, I'll give it my best shot."

Hawk sighted down the barrel of his M-4 rifle and kept a steady pace down the dimly lit corridor. Speed and surprise had been on their side when rushing the compound. They'd taken out seven terrorists and captured one. None of his men had been injured. But that could change. Anyone left in the building would be waiting and preparing. They knew they were coming. And there was no guarantee that some of the locked doors they faced might not be booby-trapped.

He paused outside the door and waited for Greenback to take position with the breaching tool. The metal tube had a flat head mounted at one end and handles on the top. Greenback swung it, sprung the lock and the door thrust inward. He hustled out of the way while Hawk, Bowie, and Kelsey Tyler rushed in, each yelling *down* in Arabic. The three boys locked inside the room looked about thirteen. They obeyed immediately and lay on the floor while they were searched and secured with plasticuffs.

The rooms were little more than prison cells with mats on the floor for sleep and a bucket in the corner for human waste. The smell of urine, sweat, and human misery were strong.

Hawk handed off the three to another team for transport and moved on to the next door.

Ian Kelly had been a no-show thus far. Hawk shoved aside his concern. If he was here, they'd find him. If they'd taken him somewhere else, they'd keep looking. Five breaches further down the corridor, he paused outside another door. Greenback rushed up to take position. "Stay sharp," Hawk cautioned. The repetition of what they were doing was mentally dulling. Though they'd met with little resistance, there was always a possibility it could take a drastic turn.

Greenback swung the breeching tool. The door bounced open. Hawk saw a man secured to a chair, a blindfold covering his eyes and a gag pulled taut across his mouth. Bright red hair hung around his head to his shoulders. It had to be Kelly. Hawk stepped forward. A small figure bobbed up from behind Kelly and pointed a pistol at his head. Hawk froze.

Sanjay al-Yussuf held the pistol as though he knew what to do with it. There was no tremor in his hand, and his eyes never broke contact with Hawk's face.

"You do not want to do that," Hawk said in Arabic.

"Yes, I do, American," Sanjay said in English.

"We are here to rescue you, Sanjay. Your father and mother are waiting for you to come home."

"My father is a traitor and my mother a whining cow. They have welcomed you with open arms into our country. You have no business here."

"We are leaving soon," Hawk said. "We only wish for your army to be strong enough to protect you and your countrymen from terrorists. The same terrorists who took you."

"They did not take me, American. I waited for them to come." Sanjay flicked Ian's ear with the barrel of the pistol.

Ian flinched and made a sound from beneath the gag.

Lord, he didn't want to kill this kid. But if he started to squeeze that trigger, he'd have to put him down.

Bowie shifted a fraction behind him, changing the angle he would shoot from should Hawk need backup.

"You have to release Mr. Kelly."

"No."

"Why not, Sanjay? Do you really want to live the rest of your life in a place like this for killing a man? Is there not more waiting for you at home with your parents?"

"Ever since my father has been helping your military, providing services for your men, I have no life. The other boys remind me daily of what he does. I am tired of listening, tired of being spit on."

"And do you believe that taking a man's life will change any of that? Will it make you feel better?"

Sanjay remained silent, but his eyes narrowed.

"The man you are holding hostage searched for you, Sanjay. He led us here hoping to return you to your mother and father. They are grieving because you were taken from them. Your father has been to the base numerous times waiting for word of your rescue. They love you. You are their son." Hawk shifted his gun closer and looked down the barrel to the boy's face. "But if you harm Mr. Kelly, I have no choice but to shoot you, Sanjay. And I will shoot you."

The boy studied his face.

Sweat ran down Hawk's back between his shoulder blades, but he didn't move from his stance. If the kid so much as twitched, he'd get a shot off and put the boy down.

Sanjay's attention shifted to the gun and Ian Kelly's head.

Hawk's finger tightened on the trigger.

Anger flickered across Sanjay's face. He stepped back from Ian and dropped the pistol on the floor.

"Walk toward me Sanjay, and lie face down on the ground."

"Are you afraid of a defenseless boy, American?" he asked as he walked forward arms thrust out in defiance.

"You were holding a loaded weapon to Mr. Kelly's head just a moment ago. That makes you neither a boy, nor defenseless. It makes you a terrorist," Hawk replied. "Lie down on the ground."

"No." Sanjay raised his chin. "I will not bow to the likes of you."

The urge to step in and knock the kid on his ass was strong, but Hawk curbed it. He sighted the kid, "You make a move, and I will put a bullet in your brain, Sanjay. Bowie, take him."

Bowie slipped past him, jerked the teenager's hands behind his back, and secured them. Hawk didn't say anything when Bowie searched Sanjay for weapons and didn't handle him with the kid gloves he had the others.

Bowie marched the boy out of the cell. Hawk lowered his weapon and moved to Ian Kelly's side. He slung his rifle and removed the blindfold and the gag. Kelly had a bruise that covered his cheekbone, but otherwise he appeared in good shape.

"That little fucker is a sadistic prick, and I wish he'd given you reason to kill him," Kelly said.

Hawk untied his hands and grimaced as Kelly drew them around to rest in his lap.

Kelly shuddered in pain. "They broke my fingers one at a time, and the whole time that little asshole was in the room, grinning."

Hawk couldn't say he was surprised. The kid was trouble. "You'll get to testify to that when we get back to base, Mr. Kelly." Hawk hit his COM button. "We need a medic in here."

"You'll be hearing from that little fucker again sometime down the road," Ian said. "And if it's all the same to you, I'd like to walk out of here before I'm seen by anyone. I need to see the sky above me, and breathe air that isn't tainted by filth."

"We'll wait until we're ready to transport you out. Though we're patrolling the perimeter, there might be bad guys hanging around. I don't want to have to explain to your daughter why I didn't get you back in one piece."

Kelly looked up and his eyes narrowed. "You know my daughter?"

"Brett Weaver's my girlfriend's brother."

Ian smiled and shook his head. "Small world isn't it?"

"Yeah."

An hour later, Hawk sat next to Ian on the CH-47 as it lifted off. The excited chatter of the rescued boys was like a tenor drone that melded with the sound of the propellers. Though their hands remained secured, the helicopter ride was too big a novelty for them to sit in silence. Three SEALs stood guard, their feet braced against the movement of the helo, their rifles resting in the bend of their arms.

"I didn't realize until they picked me up off the street that I'd lost my edge," Ian said. He leaned his head back against the metal bulkhead behind him. The shot of morphine Doc had given him had eased his pain and made him sound a little drunk. "I've always been able to focus on the story; I never let my guard down. But my mind was on Tess, and they slipped up on me. Caring about the people back home, thinking about them, worrying about them, is a distraction you can't afford when you're here." Ian opened his eyes and looked at him. "Know what I mean?"

"Yeah, I know what you mean." *She didn't tell me.* Because Zoe understood that, had heard him say it. That's why she hadn't told him. She'd rather take it all on her shoulders than be a distraction. *Do whatever it takes to come home* were her last words every time they emailed. It was the promise he'd made. And putting her and home out of his mind was what it took.

The anger and hurt he'd been nursing dissolved. She loved him enough to hold back the things she knew would worry him, the things that would distract him. She loved him a hell of a lot.

But could she hold out from telling him the whole time he was deployed?

Special Agents Wright and Scott came into the hospital room. Thus far, it had been a who's who of law enforcement parading through.

"Go away. I'm not talking to you without an attorney," Brett said.

"Why would you need an attorney, Ensign?" Scott asked.

Brett narrowed his eyes and studied the two agents. They both looked like hell. Scott needed a haircut and some sleep from the size of the bags under his eyes. And Wright looked like a big, hulking thundercloud about to rain on someone's parade.

Well it wasn't his job to make their life any easier. They certainly hadn't made his all gumdrops and lollipops.

"Give Senator Welch my regards, and tell him to go fuck himself."

Where was Tess with that drink? His mouth felt as dry as the Iraqi desert. The damn medication they'd given him was kicking up his stomach. And these two assholes weren't helping with that.

"What does Senator Welch have to do with the terrorists you took out?" Agent Wright asked.

Brett raised a brow. "I know his son got killed in Iraq and he blames my team. I know he's had every move my team made in Iraq examined under a microscope. I know he's putting pressure on someone to make what happened at the house with Derrick Armstrong seem like something it wasn't to get some payback. Find out who he sent to Iraq to investigate the allegations of murder against me, and you'll probably find out who leaked my name and to whom. I'm not giving him another shot at me."

"You haven't been watching the news, have you?" Wright asked.

"No. I've been busy getting shot at."

The door opened and Tess stopped to eye the two agents, her expression suspicious. Her clothing had been wet and spotted with blood, and the green scrubs they'd given her to wear were too big. She tugged at one pant leg as she strode into the room. She handed Brett a soft drink and a straw. "Don't say anything," she said.

Brett laughed.

Agent Scott scowled then continued. "You and Armstrong have been cleared of the murder allegations. A Captain Frank Morrow has sent photo identification to us of the boy. He and thirty-two others were rescued from a training camp. Al-Qaeda forces kidnapped them off the street, just as you told us, and attempted to train them as terrorists. Seven of the eight al-Qaeda operatives died during the raid on the complex."

"Yes!" Thank God. The relief was unbelievable. He might actually get his life back.

"Your father was being held there at the complex, Miss Kelly. He's being treated for his injuries. We weren't told specifically what they were, but none of them was life threatening."

Brett laughed at Tess's soft squeak of joy. But her smile was something special. And when the tears started, he tugged at her shirt until she bent down for him to give her a hug.

"He's okay, Brett," she repeated, her eyes tear-glazed with joy and relief. She kissed him.

"I knew he would be. He's as tough as you are."

She laughed. That did more for him than all the pain pills in the hospital.

"We know what happened at the house," Wright said bringing them back to the reason for their visit. "Look, Ensign Weaver." He rubbed a hand over his forehead. "We got off on the wrong foot. We were told to investigate a situation and we did. And you have to admit, the boy not being seen at the house after you dropped him off looked pretty suspicious."

"Had anything happened to the kid on our watch, Agent Wright, we would have reported it. The guys covering us would have reported it. We aren't murderers. We're peace-keepers. We're there to protect the innocent and take down the bad guys."

"Noted," Scott said, and shot his partner a look. He pulled a notebook from his inside jacket pocket and flipped it open.

"Mrs. Jackson is being treated for shock, but she's been able to tell us a few things," Scott said. "We'd like for you to confirm them for us."

"How are Captain Jackson and the baby?" Brett asked. He popped the top on the soft drink, stuck in the straw and took a long pull.

"He'll have to have some reconstructive surgeries to his cheekbone and nose. He's suffering from a concussion and they've checked him for internal bleeding. He took a hell of a beating. It's going to take him some time to come back, but he'll make it. The baby is being monitored for pneumonia, but they think he'll be okay. He has a rare birth defect and will always have some issues."

Brett squeezed Tess's hand. She'd saved a life. His girl had saved a child. And come back into a house invaded with terrorists to save him. And they'd all survived to tell about it. It didn't get much better than that.

"We've shared more information with you than we should, Ensign. We'd like some quid pro quo. We need you to confirm what happened inside the house," Scott pushed.

They *had* been downright talkative. And they'd brought some really good news to Tess and to him. "I'm listening."

"We know that Captain Jackson called you repeatedly while you were in flight from Washington, D.C."

"Yeah. When I turned on my phone, there were several calls from him and voice mails. When I called him back, he said he needed to speak with me about my change of orders and asked me to come by the house."

"They were holding a gun to Mrs. Jackson's head at the time of that call," Scott offered.

"Jesus." If even a fraction of what he'd guessed about the situation was true—

"When you arrived at the house, Mrs. Jackson answered the door. What made you aware there was a situation?" Agent Scott asked.

"She used a hand signal. I thought at first that it was just a nervous gesture. She looked upset, as though she'd been crying. But when she repeated the signal, I knew there was a hostage situation going down."

"Miss Kelly was with you at the door."

"Yeah. I sent her on a bogus errand to get her the hell out of there."

"We've found the rental car you were driving with the note, your phone and possessions, Miss Kelly. We know you dialed 911, talked to the operator, then hung up."

"Yes. I heard shots. I had to go back to the house. I had to know what was happening to Brett. He'd gone into the house unarmed."

"We know you took out the first terrorist at the door, Ensign. Broke his nose, crushed his trachea, and dislocated his index finger."

"You left out the part where he tried to shoot me in the head and got the door, then tried to shoot me again and killed the TV."

"You took out the second terrorist at the French doors with the gun you took from the first one."

"After he got off two rounds through the door and nearly hit Mrs. Jackson and me."

"Then you put down the gun and walked outside to face the other man."

"He had a gun to the baby's head."

"You could have left then, Ensign, escaped."

Anger surged through Brett, and the soft drink can popped when his grip tightened around it. "Fuck you. I wasn't walking off and leaving three defenseless people alone with an armed asshole."

Scott and Wright exchanged a glance.

"You didn't have a weapon?"

"No."

"Where did the Sig come from?"

"I brought it with me from the car. Brett had left it there when he went into the house," Tess said.

"It isn't very polite to enter your commanding officer's house armed," Brett said with a shrug. He ran his hand down her arm. "We really have to hit the target range, babe. If you're going to go around rescuing me, you've got to learn to shoot."

"I'm hoping this is the last time I ever have to do anything like that, Brett. I was terrified." Color leached from her face just talking about it.

Brett tugged her down next to him on the bed and put an arm around her.

"He dropped the baby in the pool," Edwards persisted.

"Yeah. And Mrs. Jackson jumped into the water to save him. The fucker tracked her with his gun all the way. I was too far away to reach him in time. I knew he'd shoot her. If the Captain hadn't shoved his chair back and knocked the tango off balance, he'd have killed her." Brett drew a deep breath and ran a hand over his head. "I thought Jackson was dead. He looked pretty messed up. I'm glad he's going to make it." Despite their differences, he wouldn't have wished any of this on him.

"We found the gun at the bottom of the pool."

"After I knocked the asshole into the water, he hit me in the head with it and I nearly blacked out." He pointed to the knot at his temple already beginning to bruise. He almost made it back out of the pool to go after all of us again, and I dragged him back in, and I held onto him until … " He chose his words carefully, "he was no longer a threat."

Edwards shut his notebook and returned it to his pocket. "The forensic evidence will substantiate everything you've told, and Mrs. Jackson has made a corroborating statement. There will be no charges brought against you on this matter or any other, Ensign Weaver. You have my word."

"Thanks."

"You'll need to come down to the office and sign a formal report."

"Okay."

"The FBI has found the apartment the terrorists were living in and they've confiscated several computers, phones, and other evidence. From what I've heard through them, they think the rest of the men are on the run, looking for a way out of the country. So for now I think you and your family are pretty safe. It may take some time, but between the different agencies on this case, they'll be apprehended."

"Good. Thanks for letting us know."

The two Agents approached the bed, and first one, then the other, offered his hand and Brett shook them. "I'm glad things worked out for you, Ensign," Agent Wright said.

"Thanks." Glad didn't say the half of it for him. "Who was the guy?" Brett asked as they reached the door. "He was the same dude who shot me at the beach."

Wright turned to look over his shoulder. "His name was Tabarek Moussa. His brother was killed in the building you destroyed in Iraq during your last mission."

"Well, how did he get my name?"

"We don't know yet, but we will." Wright promised.

After the two left the room, Brett set aside the soft drink on the hospital table and scooted over to make room for Tess. "Come lie with me."

"The nurse will have a fit if she comes in and I'm in bed with you," Tess protested, though she slid beneath the covers and pressed against his side. It was a tight fit, but that made it even better.

"Darlin' if there was a lock on that door over there, we'd be doing more than just lying here together."

"You're in no shape for any added exercise. The doctor said you might have a concussion." She nestled in closer.

"Your coming back to the house today was a dangerous thing to do, Tess," Brett said.

"I know."

He turned on his side so they could lie face to face and he could see her expression. "I don't think you'd have done that for just anyone. So, I suppose that means you like me pretty well."

Her brown gaze scanned his face and she touched his cheek, her fingers gentle.

"You think you'll ever be able to tell me straight up how you feel?"

Her throat worked as she swallowed. "I love you, Brett. I think I fell in love with you when you danced with me at the barbecue."

Thank you, Jesus!

Hearing her say it was the sweetest moment of his life. Brett moved in and kissed her. And for a moment they were lost in the response of lips and tongues and heated bodies. The need to be closer ran through him like a torrent. But damn the room had been like a revolving door for doctors, nurses, and cops. He drew back to rest his forehead against hers. "If we were somewhere private—"

"I know." She laughed.

"I had my eye on you from the moment you walked down the aisle between the tables during my speech at the Del. Your dress flipped up and I thought, if I could get a closer look at those legs, all that discomfort I was feeling would be worth it."

"And you did."

"Yeah, and I loved every moment of it. And I love you, Tess."

"I can feel it," she said, placing her hand over his heart.

Brett grinned. "You better believe it."

Zoe curled on her side in the hospital bed and studied the ultrasound picture. This was her baby, their baby. She traced the shape of the baby's head with her finger, so much bigger than the rest. But she could see the line of its tiny body, its little bottom and its hands and feet.

She wanted Hawk to be here with her so much her chest ached with it. But he couldn't. She'd save this picture for him to see later.

The door opened and Brett stuck his head in. "Hey, Sis. You all right?" he asked. Zoe smiled as he sauntered into the room, dressed in a hospital gown and pajama pants. Bet he loved that. He drew Tess into the room and approached the bed.

"I'm fine. They just wanted to keep me overnight for observation and I think the FBI felt better about me being here than at home alone," she said.

"Same here." He nodded.

"How's your side?" Zoe asked.

"Stapled this time. It looks pretty wicked. I think they put in about ten."

"Agent Wright and Scott just left a few minutes ago. They seemed to have had an attitude adjustment concerning you. They didn't say exactly what it was you did. Maybe you can share it later. And they told me about your dad, Tess. Wonderful news."

"Yes it is." Tess fairly glowed with happiness. Zoe's eyed her brother for a moment.

"I called Mom and told her we were both okay, just in case she watched the news tonight."

"I did, too."

Brett clasped her hand. "It's over, Zoe."

She squeezed his fingers. "I'm so relieved. I just want our lives to go back to being as normal as possible." But what would normal be until Hawk came home. She couldn't share the news about the baby with him, not right now. But she could share it with her brother. "Look at what I have," she said.

He took the piece of paper from her and turned it several ways, studying it. The moment he realized what it was, his lips parted and he jerked in her direction. "You're—"

"Yes, I am."

"Does Hawk know?" he demanded.

"No, he doesn't. And he's not going to until he's right here where I can tell him in person."

"You can't keep this from him, Zoe. You have to tell him. Right away. I mean—" An expression of outrage crossed his face. "He knocked you up, and he's damn well going to marry you, or I'm going to kick his ass."

Tess laughed, and though she tried not to, Zoe joined her.

"It's not funny," he said, a scowl working its way across his features.

"Hawk and I will get married when we want to," Zoe said. "Not when you decide we have to. Now, quit playing the outraged brother and listen." She pushed a button on her phone and played the recording for him. The waha-waha sound she'd recorded on her phone wasn't loud, but the heartbeat, fast and strong, was easy to pick out.

Brett lowered himself to the side of her bed. "Oh, man."

The surprise and wonder on his face brought a smile to Zoe's lips, but tears blurred her vision, too. Hawk was going to miss all of this.

Brett put his arm around her and gave her a gentle squeeze.

"I'm going to save pictures and sounds of every moment for him, until he comes home."

The phone rang. She blinked hard to clear her vision and frowned as she looked at the screen. She hit the button to answer the call.

'Hello, sweetheart. How you doing?" He sounded like he was inside a tunnel, but it was Hawk.

Bittersweet tears slid down Zoe's cheeks. She brushed them away with the corner of the sheet. "I was just wishing I could hear your voice."

Tess tugged Brett up from his seat and pulled him toward the door.

"I meant what I said, Zo. I'll kick his—" Brett said, but the door closed behind him cutting him off.

"Who was that?" Hawk asked.

"It was Brett. He and Tess just left."

"I love you, Zoe. I miss you so much."

"I love you, Adam Hawk Yazzie," she answered.

He filled her in on some of the things he'd been doing. How the team was. And entertained her with some of the humorous things that went on in the block dormitory where they slept. If they slept. She could tell he tried to put a positive spin on everything so she wouldn't worry.

When it came her turn to share she said, "The FBI says they've tracked the terrorists, and they're on the run and possibly trying to leave the country. So, we're safe now."

"Good, I'm relieved. I didn't want to leave you unprotected."

"Norm has been looking out for me."

"He hasn't been putting the move on you, has he?"

"Every morning. But there's nothing for you to worry about. He doesn't stand a chance."

"That's my girl."

Though her throat was filled with emotion, Zoe answered, "Always."

EPILOGUE

Five and a half months later.

The C-17's engines vibrated beneath his feet, the sound dulled by his earplugs. They'd been packed into the aircraft like sardines for hours, but the discomfort meant nothing to him. They were almost home. Hawk's throat worked as he swallowed. He clenched his hands to still their nervous tremor. Jesus, how long had it been since he'd felt that? His heart was pumping a mile a minute and his palms were sweating. It had been a long six months, but it was behind them. And he was going to see his girl.

Hawk gestured to Greenback as he wandered by. Greenback pulled out one of his earplugs and Hawk did the same. "Who won the pot?" Hawk asked.

"Lang, but I think he had an inside edge because Zoe talks to Trish all the time, and Lang talks to Trish. We all think he needs to forfeit the pot and hand it over to the rest of us."

Hawk laughed. It hadn't taken the men long to figure out he hadn't known about the baby. He suspected Lang might have been the one to spread the word. He also probably set up the pot hinging on when Zoe would break down and tell him. Every man in the platoon had picked a date when they thought she might cave. Some had picked several to hedge their bets. Greenback had been the man chosen to keep the pot.

Lang had been adamant from the first that Zoe wouldn't cave. That she'd settled in for the long haul. If Trish's info had given him an edge, he deserved it.

"You'll get some of it back the next meal we share at Lang's house, so think of it as a team food allowance."

"Point taken, L.T.," Greenback said with a grin, stuffed his earplug back in place and moved on to his seat.

Hawk replaced his earplug and pulled the latest picture of Zoe from his pocket. Zoe had sworn Trish to secrecy after they'd deployed. Trish had emailed Lang not to tell Hawk about the baby, but too late. The secret already out, she'd emailed Lang pictures to pass on to him as Zoe's pregnancy had advanced.

The rounded bump beneath Zoe's blouse looked as though she'd smuggled a basketball under her shirt, and she was wearing her brace. Possibly the added weight had thrown her balance off. She looked beautiful as ever. She'd tucked her hair up into a bun baring the tender slope of her neck and showing the spot just beneath her ear he loved to kiss so he could feel her shiver.

He shoved the picture back into his pocket and looked up. Damn, he wanted this plane on the ground. Impatience revved through him like the stuck throttle on a Humvee.

"May I have your attention, please," the flight controller announced over the COM. We have started our descent for landing at Marine Corps Air Station, Miramar, and San Diego, California."

Every man roared his approval.

The controller waited until the sound dissipated. "The temperature is 70.4 degrees and the weather is clear. All electronic devices must be turned off at this time. Please remain seated until all engines have come to a complete stop. Deplaning instructions will be given as soon as we are on the tarmac."

Ten minutes had never seemed so long.

The plane cruised in, the landing a little heavy, but smoother than some he'd had. The engines came to a stop.

And when the announcement went up that no formation dismissal would be done, the men sounded off another roar of approval.

Hawk secured the seat against the bulkhead and grabbed the small duffle he'd carried on board. His heart pumped a mile a minute with every step. It seemed to take forever for the men ahead of him to file off the transport. When he hit the doorway, he spotted Brett behind the barrier and scanned the crowd for Zoe. He thought he spotted the top her head, but there were too many people between them. He jogged down the ramp and strode toward the group, using Brett as a navigation point. He dodged around several people. Trish and Lang were in a welcome home-clinch that promised more to follow. He skirted them.

And there she was. His feet were suddenly glued to the asphalt as he got his first good look at her. She was *round*. Ready to pop any day, if the scuttlebutt Trish had fed him was true. And she looked *beautiful*. She limped toward him, her expression a little anxious. He smiled, strode forward, and took her in his arms.

"I didn't want to worry you," she said her voice shaking and on the edge of tears.

"I love you, Zoe." He kissed her with all the pent-up love and longing he'd stored up for six long months. When he drew back, he studied the bump resting against his stomach. "God, Zo. What a homecoming gift."

She laughed. "I love you so much."

He palmed her belly, fascinated by the shape and feel of her beneath his hand. "Are you, both of you, okay?"

"We're wonderful, now that you're home."

She held his fingers against her and he felt something move beneath his touch. *His baby, their baby.* He wasn't waiting another moment. Hawk reached into his jacket pocket for the rings. "I'm a little late from the look of things, but I have something for you." He popped open the box. He let her get a good look at them. "They say forever in Arabic, Zoe. I took a chance and bought wedding bands to match hoping you'd make an honest man of me? Will you marry me?"

Her eyes were tear-glazed, and he thought she might cry, but she laughed instead.

"Yes. Oh yes."

Emotion clogged his throat as he slipped the ring on her finger. She was the woman he was supposed to be with for the rest of his life. He loved her, more than anything else in the world. They needed each other. "What do you think?"

Everything he was feeling was reflected in her eyes. And she sounded breathless when she said, "Hooyah."

Hawk laughed and drew her against him to kiss her again. She felt so good. Smelled like heaven, and he couldn't get close enough to her.

Brett strode forward to join them. He figured he'd given them enough privacy. He was too far away to hear what Hawk said as he popped open the ring box, but he understood fine when Hawk tugged one free and slid it onto Zoe's finger. Lang and Trish grinned from ear to ear as they watched. His throat tightened with emotion as he glimpsed Zoe's happy expression. She deserved this.

"Welcome back, future brother-in-law," Brett said as he reached them. He punched Hawk in the arm. "You've been saved by a ring. I was going to kick your ass if you didn't do right by my sister."

"Brett!" Zoe admonished.

Hawk narrowed his eyes, then smiled. "I may be late, but I'm not a fool." He laughed and hugged Brett. They pounded each other on the back.

"Good to have you home, Hawk," Brett said when they drew apart. And meant it. He'd missed him and the other guys like hell.

Hawk reached for Zoe again and held her against his side. "Thanks, Bro. How's the training coming?"

Brett grinned. "I've finished advanced sniper training and been assigned to the third Platoon, Team Seven. So, you'll still be seeing my ugly face. I just won't be rubbing elbows with you."

"I'm glad, Brett. You deserve it." Hawk extended his hand and they bumped knuckles.

"Mom and Russell are at your house preparing a welcome-home feast for you and the other guys. As soon as you collect your gear, we'll hit the road."

"I've got my duffle." He raised the bag. "Everything else I need is right here," Hawk said, giving Zoe a squeeze. "The rest will be delivered to the base."

Brett handed Zoe the car keys. "You two wander to the car. I'll go say hello to the usual suspects and put out an invite. I think Mom reached everyone but Doc, Tyler, and Logan. I'll hunt them up and get them moving in that direction, if they want to join us."

He grabbed Langley around the neck and slapped his back. "I'd kiss your ugly face, but your wife's already done it. Glad you're home, man." Next to Hawk, he felt closest to Lang. For the first time Brett acknowledged how relieved he was that they were home safe.

Trish laughed and Brett bent and kissed her cheek, to cover the emotion he knew was plastered on his face. "Go get the kids and come to Hawk's for some food."

A few minutes later, he wandered back to the car to find Hawk and Zoe standing next to his cherry-red Mustang. Hawk had a look on his face Brett had never seen before. As soon as he saw Brett appear, he signaled double time it, the hand gesture abrupt, filled with— panic. Hawk never panicked. Hawk was a rock. Brett broke into a run. "What's wrong?"

"My water just broke," Zoe announced.

Brett's eyed the wet spot around her feet, her wet crop-pants and his heart surged. The panic on Hawk's face was suddenly a living breathing entity inside him. "Oh, shit."

"Take a breath, guys. I'm okay." Zoe said. She fought the urge to bite her lip as a contraction hit. The pain seemed to start in her back and circle around her belly, the muscles tightening like a vise. It felt like a giant Charley horse encompassed her whole torso.

Hawk looked pale beneath his tan as he jerked the passenger car door open. "Come on, baby, get in the car."

Zoe eyed Brett's cream-colored leather interior. "I'll ruin the seat."

"Fuck the seat, Zoe. Get in the car," Brett said, his tone abrupt.

She started to laugh, then caught her breath as another contraction hit. Where was that transition thing that was supposed to happen? She'd had a backache all day and a few twinges she'd thought were Braxton Hicks contractions, but nothing major. This was—*bad.*

"Give me your jacket, Hawk," she said.

He bailed out of the garment like it was on fire. She spread it over the seat and lowered herself onto it. He knelt to help her swivel her legs into the car and she cupped his face. His pale gray eyes were filled with concern. She shoved her own fear away and forced a smile to her lips. This was not the homecoming she'd hoped for him. He should have had some time to get used to the idea of having a baby before it actually happened.

"The baby and I are fine. It takes hours for babies to be born. We'll go to the hospital and this homecoming gift will be in your arms in a little while."

He nodded and helped her lift her legs into the car. Zoe gripped the seat as another contraction hit. How close were they coming? She couldn't tell.

Hawk slammed the door, rushed around the car, tossed the keys to Brett and, shoving the bucket seat forward, dove into the back seat. Brett got behind the wheel, jammed the key into ignition, and cranked the engine.

His tires squealed as he backed out of the parking space and Zoe reached for the seat belt. He pulled out of the lot into a total gridlock. Cars sat bumper to bumper in front of them. "Shit!"

Zoe mentally seconded the expletive as another contraction hit. She started to shake. When she could breathe again, she said, "Guys, I think we need to dial 911."

Brett handed the phone across the back of the seat to Hawk, turned his flashers on, and pulled off the asphalt onto the grass. Hawk spoke to the 911 operator while Brett laid on the horn and passed the line of cars until they reached an eight-foot tall section of fence and could go no further.

Her throat dry with fear, Zoe turned to look at Hawk. He reached between the seats and offered his hand. She gripped it. Her lifeline.

Brett hung out the window and motioned for the guy next to him to roll down the window. "We have a medical emergency. We have to get through."

The man motioned him ahead of him, but once again they were gridlocked in the row of cars that stretched on to the front gate.

Hawk put the 911 operator on hold and dialed another number. "Doc, we're stuck in traffic. Zoe's water broke, and she's hurting bad. We need you, man."

Oh no. That wasn't happening. Doc was not going to deliver her baby. Doc wasn't seeing her up close and personal like that. He wasn't seeing any part of her. Pain raced around her, cutting off her breath. Her face felt numb and she realized she was hyperventilating. What if all this was hurting the baby? Fear raced through her. Zoe reached for the door.

"What the hell are you doing, Zoe?" Brett asked as she climbed out of the car.

"I'm getting in the back with Hawk. I need to lie down." She pushed the seat forward, and climbed into the back seat.

"I need you to hold me," She said. She lay across Hawk's lap on her side.

He stroked her hair back from her face, his forearm beneath her head supporting her. "It's going to be okay, Zoe. I've got you."

Zoe nodded. She *was* going to be okay. *Her baby was going to be okay.* Nothing could happen to either of them as long as Hawk was holding her.

Doc's sweat-misted face appeared through the open door, he was breathing hard. "The guys are coming. We're going to clear this traffic so you can get through."

"Thank, God," Brett spoke for them all.

He slammed the car door and disappeared. Zoe gripped Hawk's hand as another contraction tore through her. "It's happening too fast," she said more to herself than him.

"They're getting people to pull over, Zoe. And the ambulance is coming," Hawk soothed, his arms around her. But he was trembling as badly as she was.

In a few minutes, the car pulled forward. The sound of an ambulance approaching reached them, the siren closing in and becoming a scream.

Brett bailed out of the car like he'd been shot out of a cannon and pulled the seat forward. Hawk eased Zoe into a seated position and exited the vehicle. When he reached in to offer her a hand, his expression was grave with worry. As soon as she'd stepped on the asphalt, he scooped her up in his arms. Every bounce jarred her and she bit her lip and buried her face against his t-shirt to keep from crying out as another pain struck.

He lowered her to a gurney. It seemed to take too long for them to secure the straps around her.

Zoe lost her grip on Hawk's hand as they pushed her into the ambulance.

"I'm coming, baby." He climbed in.

Zoe looked up into his face. Her body no longer felt as though it was hers. It was all contracting muscles and pain. And a driving force beyond her control. "I have to push."

Hawk's face reflected panic, the young female paramedic's calmness. "No." they said in unison.

Clara sprinkled paprika over the bowl of potato salad she'd fixed to give it a little color, then slid the baked beans out of the oven. Now, if Brett would just arrive with Hawk and Zoe, everything would be perfect.

She turned to look out the window at Russell as he stood at the grill flipping burgers. He seemed to have that under control. What was it about men and the grill? Since they no longer had to hunt, maybe the urge to burn something replaced that.

She smiled at the thought and wandered into the dining room. She stared at the perfectly set table. The glassware gleamed as did the silverware and each paper napkin had been folded into a swan and left to swim across each plate. Tears burned her eyes as memories of Evan played through her mind. The ache was still there and would be for a very long time.

The sunroom door eased shut and Russell placed long-handled tongs he was using on a plate as he wandered through.

"When did you set the table?" she asked.

"While you were at the store."

"It's lovely. But we'll probably have twice as many people, and they'll end up eating in the living room and sun room, too," she commented.

"Well, it'll be nice until they get here," Russell said, with a smile.

Clara turned to wrap her arms around his waist and press close. "I wish he'd been mine, Russell."

"I do, too." He laid his cheek against her hair. "Gloria and Carl have gotten exactly what they deserved. He's filed bankruptcy and his lawyers have dropped him. He'll eventually go to jail. She'll probably divorce him before that happens and try and save whatever she can."

She didn't want to say she was glad for Gloria's misfortune, but she felt justice had been served. The woman's social standing and money had been stripped from her.

"You did a beautiful job on the table." Clara touched one of the paper swans. "I was thinking maybe June would be a good time for a wedding. Nothing really elaborate, just the family, a few friends, and us."

Russell tipped her face up to him, and kissed her. His hazel eyes searched her face. "You wanted to wait until Hawk was home, and he will be in just a few minutes. I want a date, Clara, not just a month. Because we're going to have a honeymoon and that takes a little planning."

The thought of a honeymoon brought a flush to her cheeks. Almost fifty-six years old and the thought of having married sex with him gave her a hot flash.

The phone rang. "How about the third Monday in June. It's cheaper to fly during the week, if we fly somewhere." She pulled away. With people coming, it might be someone checking to see if Zoe and Hawk had arrived.

"I'm holding you to that," Russell said.

Clara answered the phone, and Brett's voice came over the line. "Mom, Zoe and Hawk have gone to the hospital."

Yasin closed and locked the front door behind him. He had searched a section of Baghdad north of their home. Every boy they passed on the streets he thought was Sanjay. After nearly four months of searching, he had yet to find him.

Had they done something to him during the month they'd held him for questioning? Had they threatened him? Why had he left them again?

The house lay quiet around him. Levla spent much time in Amira's room keeping vigil over the only child they had left. With Tabarek dead in America, and after so many months, he was confident his threats were forgotten, but Levla still watched over their daughter.

He went into the kitchen and found a plate wrapped in a towel. The evening meal had long since passed, but Levla always left him a plate for when he returned. He sat down at the dining room table and began to eat the roasted lamb wrapped in flat bread, but the food had no taste and he pushed the plate away.

When a knock came at the front door, he rose to look out one of the windows. Two men stood beneath the awning. They each held a large flashlight and wore the desert cammies of the American military. Yasin cracked the door and looked out.

"Yasin al-Yussuf?" One of the men asked.

"Yes."

"We would like to speak to you about your son."

Yasin's heart leapt with hope. "Have you found him?"

"No, sir. We were unaware he was missing again."

"He left about a week after the Iraqi army released him." This time he had taken his possessions. Some of his clothing and the MP3 player he had gotten him from one of the soldiers.

"I'm sorry, sir." The man sounded sincere in his sympathy. "May we come in and speak with you?"

Yasin studied them. "I would like to see your identification."

"Certainly, sir." The two men handed him their military identification. He looked over the laminated cards. The dark haired one was Rice and the other Austen. Both were Naval investigators.

Yasin returned their cards, and, opening the door, motioned them in. He led the way to the formal living room where he and Levla had talked of Sanjay's disappearance with the American journalist.

He motioned for them to have a seat.

"We are here to ask you some questions about Sanjay's disappearance before. During that time, did you have contact with him at all?" Agent Rice spoke, while Austen sat studying his home and him. What did the man see, but a man? A man broken by loss. His son was gone. His wife, obsessed by the fear of losing their remaining child, had turned away from him. Amira, his daughter was the only one who still spoke to him, still showed him affection.

"No. We had not spoken to him until he was returned to Baghdad by the Navy SEALs who rescued him."

"Mr. al-Yussuf, do you have a cell phone?"

"Yes."

"May I see it, sir?"

"Certainly."

Yasin rose to remove the phone from his belt and hand it to him.

"This is the only one you have, sir?"

"Yes."

"Might I write down the number, sir?"

"Certainly." Rice removed a small notebook from his pocket and wrote the number down. Then handed it back to him.

"We have discovered that calls made from America came to a phone close to your location. We've been able to trace it to a cell tower nearby. Do you know a man named Tabarek Moussa?"

Yasin had been waiting months for someone to come to him with questions. "No. I do not know that name."

Rice mentioned three other names that truly were unknown to him.

"No, I do not know those men."

"We know you have done business with the American military units and that is not a popular thing to do in this area."

"But it brings money to those who need it."

"Are you aware of anyone who would have had a reason to direct al-Qaeda to your son in order to hurt you?"

Was that what had happened? Had his son been targeted in order to punish him? His throat hurt. Why had he not thought of that? "I know of no one."

After a few more minutes, the men rose to leave and Yasin showed them to the door.

"Thank you for allowing us into your home, sir." Rice said. "Have a good evening."

Yasin closed the door and locked it once more. The Americans did not suspect him. With the phone destroyed, there was no connection between him and Tabarek. He turned from the door. Amira stood in the hallway. Her dark eyes held a question.

"You did not tell them of the phone you hit with the hammer," she said.

"That was long ago, Amira."

She continued to stare at him for a long moment. "You spoke to one of those men on the phone. I heard you. You said his name."

Yasin's heart plunged.

"It is your fault Sanjay is gone, Baba." The conviction in her face, in her voice, pierced him like a knife.

"No."

"Yes, it is." As he read the sadness in her face, so much a mirror of her mother's, he stepped toward her to explain his mistake, to beg her not to look at him with such disillusionment. She was all he had left.

Amira turned and walked away from him.

The silence of the house settled around him.

Hawk and the doctor stood outside the labor room door. "This isn't normal, is it?" Hawk asked. "I read about labor and delivery while I was in Iraq, but nothing I looked at said anything about this."

Dr. Lester, a woman of about fifty, seemed friendly and competent. "It's called a precipitous labor and it's a complication we didn't expect for Zoe, since this is her first child. It's a frightening and intense situation for a first time mother," she explained.

Well it hadn't been too great for him, either. He was sweating, and though they'd made it to the hospital and were surrounded by medical help, his heart kept up a pace just short of a gallop. His legs shook as though he'd run a five-mile race.

"The nurse will bring you a paper gown in a moment. You'll have to hurry and put it on if you want to stay with Zoe while she delivers."

"I'm staying," Hawk said. His insides twisted with fear at the idea, but he was sticking it out. Seeing her in such pain— Jesus. He hadn't been prepared for that. He'd thought he was going to lose her. And it wasn't over yet.

"We're taking her to a delivery room instead of allowing her to stay here in the labor room and deliver."

He nodded. Did that mean they were worried about complications? *Oh God, don't let anything happen to her.* He should be thinking of the baby, too, but he couldn't. Not yet. Zoe had to be okay.

Hawk forced himself back into the room. They'd made him leave while they prepped her. The lights overhead glared and stung his eyes.

"I have to push. You have to let me push," Zoe begged from behind the curtain.

Jesus. He couldn't take this. It was torture hearing her hurt like this.

The nurse thrust a paper gown, at him. "Get a move on, Papa. This baby wants to come *now.*"

Hawk shook the garment out and put it on the best he could. He shucked his boots and put the booties on over his socks.

Another nurse jerked the curtain back and started pushing the bed out of the room. Hawk fell in beside Zoe and covered her hand with his as she gripped the bars.

Her cry of pain as she fought the contraction kicked his fear up a notch. God, he'd rather be facing down armed terrorists than see her like this.

They shoved through a door into a room all white walls, steel tables, and large lights. When the nurses asked Zoe to slide over on the table, he went around the delivery table and lifted her onto it.

"Hold me Hawk. Please hold me," she begged.

"I've got you, sweetheart." He raised her, wrapped his arms around her above her belly, and held her back against his chest as they pulled out the stirrups, positioned her feet, and covered her with a sheet. He had never been more aware of Zoe's vulnerability. The scars on her legs stood out stark white. He wanted to cover her, protect her from the other people in the room.

The doctor finally appeared, gowned and gloved. She scooted the stool close to the end of the table.

"I'm going to do an episiotomy, Zoe. This is a big baby, and we don't want you to tear." The nurse handed the doctor a syringe.

Nausea struck Hawk. His baby was going to tear her. It was his fault they were here. His fault she was hurting. They were never going to have sex again without a condom. He'd see to it.

"You're fully dilated and can push with the next contraction, Zoe," the doctor said.

Every muscle in Zoe's body seemed to tighten as she pushed. Each time she bore down, he caught himself holding his breath along with her. He'd never felt so useless in his life, so he changed tactics, adding his encouragement to the nurses'. And with every push, he prayed for it to be over. Twenty minutes later, he understood what the word labor truly meant.

"The head's out. I see dark hair, just like papa's." The doctor smiled up at Hawk.

He couldn't return the gesture. If it had taken her this long to deliver the baby's head—What if she couldn't do the rest? Damn, this had to end.

"Really big push, Zoe." Dr. Lester encouraged.

"I'm so tired," Zoe said. He could feel her panting for breath, could see her red cheeks and the sweat-darkened hair clinging to her face.

"We're almost there, Zoe," Hawk said, against her ear. "One more big one and you'll be done. Just one more and it'll be over."

She caught her breath, and Hawk laid his hand on her belly, putting steady pressure against the muscles, giving her something to push against. He felt the baby leave her body the moment it happened. Tears of relief burned his eyes and he blinked.

Thank you, Jesus.

"It's a boy." Dr. Lester said. She suctioned the baby's nose and mouth and he let out a high-pitched squeal of protest. She lifted the baby, wrapped in a disposable chub, onto Zoe's stomach. Hawk slipped from behind her to allow her to lie down. He placed a protective hand against the wrapper, holding the baby in place. His son. His hands were fisted and waved in the air. His tiny, features swollen from the ordeal, crumpled, and he began to cry as though someone had pinched him. Every finger and toe was exactly where it was supposed to be.

"Would you like to cut the cord, Lieutenant?" the doctor asked.

"Uh—" He shook his head. "No."

The nurse whisked the baby away as soon as the cord was cut.

Hawk focused on Zoe. Her cheeks were still flushed, her eyes swollen, and her hair lay in a tangled mess about her shoulders, but she'd never looked more beautiful to him.

"Is he okay?" she asked.

"He's fine, he's perfect." He bent to kiss her forehead, her cheek, then her lips. "I'm sorry you had to go through this, Zoe. I'm sorry I wasn't here with you."

"You're here now. And I couldn't have done it without you. I knew as long as you were holding me, we'd be okay."

Humbled by such trust, Hawk's eyes blurred with tears. He pressed his face against her breast and felt her fingers run through his hair.

"We have to clean you up a little, Zoe," Dr. Lester said.

Hawk straightened and found a nurse standing beside him with the bundled baby. "Here, papa. You can hold your son while Dr. Lester finishes," she said. Hawk automatically closed his arms around the tiny package she thrust into his arms.

With the crisis over, he was finally able to focus on this new little creature. His son. The baby yawned, exposing a tiny tongue and gums. And a smile curved Hawk's lips. Oh, man. He was beautiful.

Zoe studied Hawk's face as he looked down at the baby. She'd never seen anything quite so perfect as the sight of him holding their son. As protective and loving as he was to her, he already had everything he needed to be as good at fatherhood as he was at being a SEAL.

She flinched as she felt the pull and release of the afterbirth. When Dr. Lester started putting in the stitches, she was able to relax.

The doctor looked up and nodded toward Hawk. He was doing a rock and sway movement while he held the baby, "The bigger and badder they are, the harder they fall," she whispered.

Zoe smiled. Amen to that.

Brett paced the floor in the waiting room, just outside the OB area. "You'd think somebody would come tell us something," he complained.

"They will as soon as there's something to tell," Tess said. "Come sit down. You're making the rest of the guys nervous."

Brett tried to curb his impatience and sat next to her. He scanned the room, full of military camouflage uniforms. Everyone invited to the house had postponed the party and come to the hospital to wait for news. Bowie and Doc sat slumped half-asleep across the room. Now and then Doc would rouse and look inquiringly across the room at him and

Tess. Logan and Tyler, though they didn't know Zoe very well, were there to support Hawk. Lang and Trish were sitting with his mom and Russell. Greenback and his wife Selena were cuddled up in the corner, enjoying each other. They were a family. His family. And that included the woman sitting next to him.

Doc wandered over and sat down next to Tess. His eyes were swollen from jet lag and rust-colored whiskers stubbled his jaw. "There's something I wanted to say to you, Legs," he said. "I guess this is as good a place to say it as any."

"Me?" Tess pointed to her chest with her fingers, surprise in her expression.

"Yeah, you."

"The cover you and your dad gave us after we rescued those kids made the legal crap go away. You saved our butts. And it was a bonus when you put Senator Welch and his followers under a microscope and made them back off. We owe you, and your dad, Legs. You need anything—all you have to do is say the word."

Tess cheeks were bright red with embarrassment, but there was a gleam in her eyes, and her smile was something special. "Thanks, Doc. I'm glad I could help."

Doc rose to his feet. "I need some caffeine before I fall asleep. Can I get you guys anything?"

Brett shook his head.

"No, but thanks for asking," Tess said.

Doc sauntered down the hall.

Brett turned to study Tess's face. "Doc's right. Hawk's in there with my sister without any kind of legal bullshit hanging over his head because of you and your dad, Tess. I'm sitting here, instead of facing a court-marshal or prison, or both, because of you and your dad. This is my family and you gave them cover. You gave me cover."

"I did it because it was the right thing to do, Brett, and I believed in you. I did from the start." She smiled. "And it hasn't hurt my career any either." She ran her hand down his thigh. "But mostly I did it because I love you."

Brett cupped her face and brushed her lips with a kiss, soft and tender. "Have you ever thought about having kids?"

"Eventually, one day." She looped her arm through his and rested her head against his shoulder. Her red hair fanned out, gleaming with copper highlights against his sleeve.

"We could do it, Tess."

"Do what?" she asked.

"Make beautiful babies together. But we'd have to get married first."

Her eyes widened, and she studied his expression.

"I love you. And I want to have a family with you. You can let me know when you're used to the idea."

"The idea of getting married, or of having babies?" she asked.

Always the stickler for details. That was another thing he loved and appreciated about her. "The marriage thing has to come first."

She studied him, speculation in her gaze. "I never knew you were so old-fashioned, Brett."

"It isn't old-fashioned for a man to want to lay claim to the woman he loves, honey. That's just man stuff."

Tess laughed and shook her head.

Hawk shoved through the door. He wore a paper gown over his cammies and paper booties covered his stocking feet. He looked as though he'd just taken a beach single-handed, but he was smiling.

Brett hustled to his feet taking Tess with him. Everyone in the room followed suit.

"Zoe's fine and so is the baby. It's a boy," Hawk announced. "Eight pounds, six ounces."

A happy cry went up and everyone converged on Hawk offering congratulations.

Smothered with relief for his sister, Brett barely caught Tess's words. "What?" he asked.

"I said, I love you, and I think I could be convinced about the marriage thing," Tess said, then smiled.

Brett scanned her face and a slow smile built across his features as excitement leapt inside him. *Yes!* He molded her against him, bent his head, and kissed her with more than a little heat, until she hummed beneath the pressure. He drew back to look into her flushed face. "I'll get right on that."

OTHER BOOKS BY TERESA REASOR

BREAKING FREE (Book 1 of the SEAL TEAM
Heartbreakers)

BREAKING THROUGH (Book 2 of the SEAL
TEAM Heartbreakers)

BREAKING AWAY (Book 3 of the SEAL TEAM
Heartbreakers)

TIMELESS

HIGHLAND MOONLIGHT

CAPTIVE HEARTS

Short stories

AN AUTOMATED DEATH: A STEAMPUNK
SHORT STORY

TO CAPTURE A HIGHLANDERS HEART: The
Beginning

Novellas

TO CAPTURE A HIGHLANDER'S HEART: THE
COURTSHIP

COMING SOON!

TO CAPTURE A HIGHLANDER'S HEART: THE
WEDDING NIGHT

Children's Books

WILLY C. SPARKS THE DRAGON WHO LOST
HIS FIRE

HAIKU CLUE (COMING SOON)

CONNECT WITH TERESA ON SUBSTANCE B

Substance B is a new platform for independent authors to directly connect with their readers. Please visit Teresa's Substance B page (substance-b.com/TeresaReasor.html) where you can:

- Sign up for Teresa's newsletter
- Send a message to Teresa
- See all platforms where Teresa's books are sold
- Request autographed eBooks from Teresa

Visit Substance B today to learn more about your favorite independent authors.

31105270R00246

Made in the USA
Lexington, KY
01 April 2014

For the LORD is good; His mercy is everlasting;
and His truth endureth to all generations.
~ Psalm 100:5

The Lord taketh pleasure in them that
fear Him, in those that hope in His mercy.
~ Psalm 147:11

_____

For the LORD God is a sun and shield: the LORD
will give grace and glory: no good thing
will He withhold from them that walk uprightly.

~ Psalm 84:11

And we know that all things work together for good to them that
love God, to them who are the called according to His purpose.

~ Romans 8:28

Oh that men would praise the LORD for His goodness, and for
His wonderful works to the children of men! For He satisfieth
the longing soul, and filleth the hungry soul with goodness.

~ Psalm 107:8-9

_____

And of His fulness have all we received, and grace for grace.

~ John 1:16

_____

Being confident of this very thing, that He which hath begun
a good work in you will perform it until the day of Jesus Christ.

~ Philippians 1:6

_____

_____

_____

_____

_____

_____

_____

_____

_____

_____

_____

_____

_____

_____

_____

_____

_____

_____

_____

_____

_____

_____

The Lord is good to all: and His tender
mercies are over all His works.
~ *Psalm 145:9*

_____

Blessed is every one that feareth the LORD; that walketh
in His ways. For thou shalt eat the labour of thine hands:
happy shalt thou be, and it shall be well with thee.

~ *Psalm 128:1-2*

For the eyes of the Lord are over the righteous,
and His ears are open unto their prayers.

~ 1 Peter 3:12

_____

_____

_____

_____

_____

_____

_____

_____

_____

_____

_____

_____

_____

_____

_____

_____

_____

_____

_____

_____

_____

_____

"Blessed are the pure in heart: for they shall see God."
~ Matthew 5:8

The name of the LORD is a strong tower:
the righteous runneth into it, and is safe.

~ Proverbs 18:10

Arise, shine; for thy light is come, and
the glory of the LORD is risen upon thee.

~ Isaiah 60:1

The path of the just is as the shining light,
that shineth more and more unto the perfect day.

~ Proverbs 4:18

Rejoice evermore. Pray without ceasing.
In every thing give thanks: for this is the
will of God in Christ Jesus concerning you.

~ 1 Thessalonians 5:16-18

_____

_____

_____

_____

_____

_____

_____

_____

_____

_____

_____

_____

_____

_____

_____

_____

_____

_____

_____

_____

_____

_____

Trust in the LORD with all thine heart; and lean
not unto thine own understanding. In all thy ways
acknowledge Him, and He shall direct thy paths.

~ Proverbs 3:5-6

The LORD shall preserve thee from all evil: He shall preserve thy soul. The LORD shall preserve thy going out and thy coming in from this time forth, and even for evermore.

~ Psalm 121:7-8

Cast thy burden upon the Lord, and He shall sustain
thee: He shall never suffer the righteous to be moved.

~ Psalm 55:22

_____

Cause me to hear Thy lovingkindness in the morning;
for in Thee do I trust: cause me to know the way
wherein I should walk; for I lift up my soul unto Thee.

~ Psalm 143:8

God be merciful unto us, and bless us;
and cause His face to shine upon us.

~ Psalm 67:1

_____

Now the God of hope fill you with all joy and peace in believing,
that ye may abound in hope, through the power of the Holy Ghost.

~ Romans 15:13

The blessing of the LORD, it maketh rich,
and He addeth no sorrow with it.

~ Proverbs 10:22

_____

Mercy unto you, and peace, and love, be multiplied.

~ Jude 2

Thou wilt shew me the path of life: in Thy presence is fulness
of joy; at Thy right hand there are pleasures for evermore.

~ Psalm 16:11

Blessed be the God and Father of our Lord Jesus Christ, who hath
blessed us with all spiritual blessings in heavenly places in Christ.

~ Ephesians 1:3

The Lord hath prepared His throne in the heavens;
and His kingdom ruleth over all.

~ *Psalm 103:19*

And therefore will the LORD wait, that He may
be gracious unto you, and therefore will He
be exalted, that He may have mercy upon you.

~ Isaiah 30:18

There are many devices in a man's heart;
nevertheless the counsel of the LORD, that shall stand.

~ Proverbs 19:21

But my God shall supply all your need
according to His riches in glory by Christ Jesus.
~ *Philippians 4:19*

Behold, the eye of the Lord is upon them that
fear Him, upon them that hope in His mercy.

~ Psalm 33:18

Eye hath not seen, nor ear heard, neither have
entered into the heart of man, the things
which God hath prepared for them that love Him.

~ 1 Corinthians 2:9

"If thou canst believe, all things are possible to him that believeth."
~ Mark 9:23

The LORD taketh pleasure in them that
fear Him, in those that hope in His mercy.

~ Psalm 147:11

For the LORD is good; His mercy is everlasting;
and His truth endureth to all generations.

~ Psalm 100:5

_____

For the Lord God is a sun and shield: the Lord
will give grace and glory: no good thing
will He withhold from them that walk uprightly.

~ Psalm 84:11

And we know that all things work together for good to them that
love God, to them who are the called according to His purpose.

~ *Romans 8:28*

_____

Oh that men would praise the Lᴏʀᴅ for His goodness, and for His wonderful works to the children of men! For He satisfieth the longing soul, and filleth the hungry soul with goodness.

~ Psalm 107:8-9

And of His fulness have all we received, and grace for grace.

~ John 1:16

_____

Being confident of this very thing, that He which hath begun
a good work in you will perform it until the day of Jesus Christ.
~ Philippians 1:6

The Lord is good to all: and His tender
mercies are over all His works.

~ Psalm 145:9

Blessed is every one that feareth the LORD; that walketh
in His ways. For thou shalt eat the labour of thine hands:
happy shalt thou be, and it shall be well with thee.

~ Psalm 128:1-2

For the eyes of the Lord are over the righteous,
and His ears are open unto their prayers.

~ 1 Peter 3:12

_____

"Blessed are the pure in heart: for they shall see God."
~ Matthew 5:8

The name of the LORD is a strong tower:
the righteous runneth into it, and is safe.
~ Proverbs 18:10

Arise, shine; for thy light is come, and
the glory of the LORD is risen upon thee.

~ Isaiah 60:1

The path of the just is as the shining light,
that shineth more and more unto the perfect day.
~ *Proverbs 4:18*

_____

Rejoice evermore. Pray without ceasing.
In every thing give thanks: for this is the
will of God in Christ Jesus concerning you.

~ 1 Thessalonians 5:16-18

Trust in the LORD with all thine heart; and lean
not unto thine own understanding. In all thy ways
acknowledge Him, and He shall direct thy paths.

~ Proverbs 3:5-6

_____

The Lord shall preserve thee from all evil: He shall
preserve thy soul. The Lord shall preserve thy going out and
thy coming in from this time forth, and even for evermore.

~ Psalm 121:7-8

Cast thy burden upon the LORD, and He shall sustain
thee: He shall never suffer the righteous to be moved.

~ *Psalm 55:22*

Cause me to hear Thy lovingkindness in the morning;
for in Thee do I trust: cause me to know the way
wherein I should walk; for I lift up my soul unto Thee.

~ Psalm 143:8

God be merciful unto us, and bless us;
and cause His face to shine upon us.

~ Psalm 67:1

_____

Now the God of hope fill you with all joy and peace in believing,
that ye may abound in hope, through the power of the Holy Ghost.

~ Romans 15:13

The blessing of the LORD, it maketh rich,
and He addeth no sorrow with it.

~ Proverbs 10:22

Mercy unto you, and peace, and love, be multiplied.

~ Jude 2

Thou wilt shew me the path of life: in Thy presence is fulness
of joy; at Thy right hand there are pleasures for evermore.

~ Psalm 16:11

_____

Blessed be the God and Father of our Lord Jesus Christ, who hath
blessed us with all spiritual blessings in heavenly places in Christ.

~ Ephesians 1:3

The Lord hath prepared His throne in the heavens;
and His kingdom ruleth over all.

~ *Psalm 103:19*

_____

And therefore will the LORD wait, that He may
be gracious unto you, and therefore will He
be exalted, that He may have mercy upon you.

~ *Isaiah 30:18*

There are many devices in a man's heart;
nevertheless the counsel of the LORD, that shall stand.

~ Proverbs 19:21

_____

But my God shall supply all your need
according to His riches in glory by Christ Jesus.

~ Philippians 4:19

Behold, the eye of the LORD is upon them that
fear Him, upon them that hope in His mercy.

~ Psalm 33:18

_____

Eye hath not seen, nor ear heard, neither have
entered into the heart of man, the things
which God hath prepared for them that love Him.

~ 1 Corinthians 2:9

"If thou canst believe, all things are possible to him that believeth."
~ Mark 9:23

The Lord taketh pleasure in them that
fear Him, in those that hope in His mercy.

~ Psalm 147:11

For the LORD is good; His mercy is everlasting;
and His truth endureth to all generations.

~ Psalm 100:5

_____

For the LORD God is a sun and shield: the LORD
will give grace and glory: no good thing
will He withhold from them that walk uprightly.

~ Psalm 84:11

And we know that all things work together for good to them that
love God, to them who are the called according to His purpose.

~ Romans 8:28

_____

Oh that men would praise the LORD for His goodness, and for His wonderful works to the children of men! For He satisfieth the longing soul, and filleth the hungry soul with goodness.

~ Psalm 107:8-9

And of His fulness have all we received, and grace for grace.
~ *John 1:16*

_____

Being confident of this very thing, that He which hath begun
a good work in you will perform it until the day of Jesus Christ.

~ Philippians 1:6

The Lord is good to all: and His tender
mercies are over all His works.

~ Psalm 145:9

_____

Blessed is every one that feareth the LORD; that walketh
in His ways. For thou shalt eat the labour of thine hands:
happy shalt thou be, and it shall be well with thee.

~ *Psalm 128:1-2*

For the eyes of the Lord are over the righteous,
and His ears are open unto their prayers.

~ *1 Peter 3:12*

"Blessed are the pure in heart: for they shall see God."
~ Matthew 5:8

The name of the LORD is a strong tower:
the righteous runneth into it, and is safe.
~ *Proverbs 18:10*

_____

Arise, shine; for thy light is come, and
the glory of the LORD is risen upon thee.

~ Isaiah 60:1

The path of the just is as the shining light,
that shineth more and more unto the perfect day.
~ Proverbs 4:18

_____

Rejoice evermore. Pray without ceasing.
In every thing give thanks: for this is the
will of God in Christ Jesus concerning you.

~ 1 Thessalonians 5:16-18

Trust in the LORD with all thine heart; and lean
not unto thine own understanding. In all thy ways
acknowledge Him, and He shall direct thy paths.

~ Proverbs 3:5-6

The Lord shall preserve thee from all evil: He shall
preserve thy soul. The Lord shall preserve thy going out and
thy coming in from this time forth, and even for evermore.

~ Psalm 121:7-8

Cast thy burden upon the LORD, and He shall sustain
thee: He shall never suffer the righteous to be moved.

~ Psalm 55:22

_____

Cause me to hear Thy lovingkindness in the morning;
for in Thee do I trust: cause me to know the way
wherein I should walk; for I lift up my soul unto Thee.

~ Psalm 143:8

_____

_____

_____

_____

_____

_____

_____

_____

_____

_____

_____

_____

_____

_____

_____

_____

_____

_____

_____

_____

_____

_____

_____

God be merciful unto us, and bless us;
and cause His face to shine upon us.
~ Psalm 67:1

_____

Now the God of hope fill you with all joy and peace in believing,
that ye may abound in hope, through the power of the Holy Ghost.

~ Romans 15:13

The blessing of the LORD, it maketh rich,
and He addeth no sorrow with it.

~ Proverbs 10:22

Mercy unto you, and peace, and love, be multiplied.

~ Jude 2

Thou wilt shew me the path of life: in Thy presence is fulness
of joy; at Thy right hand there are pleasures for evermore.

~ Psalm 16:11

Blessed be the God and Father of our Lord Jesus Christ, who hath
blessed us with all spiritual blessings in heavenly places in Christ.

~ Ephesians 1:3

The LORD hath prepared His throne in the heavens;
and His kingdom ruleth over all.

~ Psalm 103:19

_____

And therefore will the LORD wait, that He may
be gracious unto you, and therefore will He
be exalted, that He may have mercy upon you.

~ Isaiah 30:18

There are many devices in a man's heart;
nevertheless the counsel of the LORD, that shall stand.

~ Proverbs 19:21

But my God shall supply all your need
according to His riches in glory by Christ Jesus.
~ Philippians 4:19

Behold, the eye of the Lord is upon them that
fear Him, upon them that hope in His mercy.

~ Psalm 33:18

_____

Eye hath not seen, nor ear heard, neither have
entered into the heart of man, the things
which God hath prepared for them that love Him.

~ 1 Corinthians 2:9

"If thou canst believe, all things are possible to him that believeth."

~ Mark 9:23

The LORD taketh pleasure in them that
fear Him, in those that hope in His mercy.

~ Psalm 147:11

For the LORD is good; His mercy is everlasting;
and His truth endureth to all generations.

~ Psalm 100:5

_____

For the Lord God is a sun and shield: the Lord
will give grace and glory: no good thing
will He withhold from them that walk uprightly.
~ Psalm 84:11

And we know that all things work together for good to them that love God, to them who are the called according to His purpose.

~ Romans 8:28

Oh that men would praise the L ORD for His goodness, and for
His wonderful works to the children of men! For He satisfieth
the longing soul, and filleth the hungry soul with goodness.

~ Psalm 107:8-9

And of His fulness have all we received, and grace for grace.

~ John 1:16

_____

Being confident of this very thing, that He which hath begun
a good work in you will perform it until the day of Jesus Christ.

~ *Philippians 1:6*

The LORD is good to all: and His tender
mercies are over all His works.

~ *Psalm 145:9*

_____

Blessed is every one that feareth the Lord; that walketh
in His ways. For thou shalt eat the labour of thine hands:
happy shalt thou be, and it shall be well with thee.

~ Psalm 128:1-2

For the eyes of the Lord are over the righteous,
and His ears are open unto their prayers.

~ 1 Peter 3:12

_____

"Blessed are the pure in heart: for they shall see God."
~ Matthew 5:8

The name of the LORD is a strong tower:
the righteous runneth into it, and is safe.

~ Proverbs 18:10

Arise, shine; for thy light is come, and
the glory of the LORD is risen upon thee.

~ Isaiah 60:1

The path of the just is as the shining light,
that shineth more and more unto the perfect day.

~ Proverbs 4:18

Rejoice evermore. Pray without ceasing.
In every thing give thanks: for this is the
will of God in Christ Jesus concerning you.

~ 1 Thessalonians 5:16-18

Trust in the L ORD with all thine heart; and lean
not unto thine own understanding. In all thy ways
acknowledge Him, and He shall direct thy paths.

~ Proverbs 3:5-6

_____

The LORD shall preserve thee from all evil: He shall
preserve thy soul. The LORD shall preserve thy going out and
thy coming in from this time forth, and even for evermore.

~ Psalm 121:7-8

Cast thy burden upon the LORD, and He shall sustain
thee: He shall never suffer the righteous to be moved.

~ Psalm 55:22

Cause me to hear Thy lovingkindness in the morning;
for in Thee do I trust: cause me to know the way
wherein I should walk; for I lift up my soul unto Thee.

~ Psalm 143:8

God be merciful unto us, and bless us;
and cause His face to shine upon us.

~ Psalm 67:1

Now the God of hope fill you with all joy and peace in believing,
that ye may abound in hope, through the power of the Holy Ghost.

~ Romans 15:13

The blessing of the Lord, it maketh rich,
and He addeth no sorrow with it.

~ Proverbs 10:22

Mercy unto you, and peace, and love, be multiplied.

~ Jude 2

Thou wilt shew me the path of life: in Thy presence is fulness
of joy; at Thy right hand there are pleasures for evermore.

~ Psalm 16:11

_____

Blessed be the God and Father of our Lord Jesus Christ, who hath
blessed us with all spiritual blessings in heavenly places in Christ.

~ Ephesians 1:3

The Lord hath prepared His throne in the heavens;
and His kingdom ruleth over all.

~ Psalm 103:19

_____

And therefore will the Lord wait, that He may
be gracious unto you, and therefore will He
be exalted, that He may have mercy upon you.

~ Isaiah 30:18

There are many devices in a man's heart;
nevertheless the counsel of the LORD, that shall stand.

~ Proverbs 19:21

But my God shall supply all your need
according to His riches in glory by Christ Jesus.
~ Philippians 4:19

Behold, the eye of the LORD is upon them that
fear Him, upon them that hope in His mercy.

~ Psalm 33:18

_____

Eye hath not seen, nor ear heard, neither have
entered into the heart of man, the things
which God hath prepared for them that love Him.

~ 1 Corinthians 2:9

"If thou canst believe, all things are possible to him that believeth."

~ Mark 9:23

The LORD taketh pleasure in them that
fear Him, in those that hope in His mercy.

~ Psalm 147:11

For the Lᴏʀᴅ is good; His mercy is everlasting;
and His truth endureth to all generations.

~ Psalm 100:5

_____

For the LORD God is a sun and shield: the LORD
will give grace and glory: no good thing
will He withhold from them that walk uprightly.

~ Psalm 84:11

And we know that all things work together for good to them that
love God, to them who are the called according to His purpose.

~ Romans 8:28

_____

Oh that men would praise the LORD for His goodness, and for
His wonderful works to the children of men! For He satisfieth
the longing soul, and filleth the hungry soul with goodness.

~ Psalm 107:8-9

And of His fulness have all we received, and grace for grace.

~ John 1:16

Being confident of this very thing, that He which hath begun
a good work in you will perform it until the day of Jesus Christ.

~ Philippians 1:6

The LORD is good to all: and His tender
mercies are over all His works.

~ Psalm 145:9

_____

Blessed is every one that feareth the LORD; that walketh
in His ways. For thou shalt eat the labour of thine hands:
happy shalt thou be, and it shall be well with thee.

~ *Psalm 128:1-2*

For the eyes of the Lord are over the righteous,
and His ears are open unto their prayers.

~ 1 Peter 3:12

_____

"Blessed are the pure in heart: for they shall see God."
~ *Matthew 5:8*

The name of the LORD is a strong tower:
the righteous runneth into it, and is safe.

~ Proverbs 18:10

Arise, shine; for thy light is come, and
the glory of the LORD is risen upon thee.

~ Isaiah 60:1

The path of the just is as the shining light,
that shineth more and more unto the perfect day.

~ Proverbs 4:18

Rejoice evermore. Pray without ceasing.
In every thing give thanks: for this is the
will of God in Christ Jesus concerning you.

~ 1 Thessalonians 5:16-18

Trust in the LORD with all thine heart; and lean
not unto thine own understanding. In all thy ways
acknowledge Him, and He shall direct thy paths.

~ Proverbs 3:5-6

The LORD shall preserve thee from all evil: He shall preserve thy soul. The LORD shall preserve thy going out and thy coming in from this time forth, and even for evermore.

~ Psalm 121:7-8

Cast thy burden upon the LORD, and He shall sustain
thee: He shall never suffer the righteous to be moved.

~ *Psalm 55:22*

_____

_____
_____
_____
_____
_____
_____
_____
_____
_____
_____
_____
_____
_____
_____
_____
_____
_____
_____
_____
_____
_____
_____
_____

Cause me to hear Thy lovingkindness in the morning;
for in Thee do I trust: cause me to know the way
wherein I should walk; for I lift up my soul unto Thee.

~ Psalm 143:8

God be merciful unto us, and bless us;
and cause His face to shine upon us.

~ Psalm 67:1

Now the God of hope fill you with all joy and peace in believing,
that ye may abound in hope, through the power of the Holy Ghost.

~ Romans 15:13

The blessing of the LORD, it maketh rich,
and He addeth no sorrow with it.

~ Proverbs 10:22

_____

Mercy unto you, and peace, and love, be multiplied.

~ Jude 2

Thou wilt shew me the path of life: in Thy presence is fulness
of joy; at Thy right hand there are pleasures for evermore.

~ Psalm 16:11

_____

Blessed be the God and Father of our Lord Jesus Christ, who hath
blessed us with all spiritual blessings in heavenly places in Christ.

~ *Ephesians 1:3*

The LORD hath prepared His throne in the heavens;
and His kingdom ruleth over all.

~ Psalm 103:19

_____

And therefore will the LORD wait, that He may
be gracious unto you, and therefore will He
be exalted, that He may have mercy upon you.

~ Isaiah 30:18

There are many devices in a man's heart;
nevertheless the counsel of the LORD, that shall stand.

~ Proverbs 19:21

_____

But my God shall supply all your need
according to His riches in glory by Christ Jesus.
~ Philippians 4:19

Behold, the eye of the LORD is upon them that
fear Him, upon them that hope in His mercy.

~ Psalm 33:18

_____

Eye hath not seen, nor ear heard, neither have
entered into the heart of man, the things
which God hath prepared for them that love Him.

~ 1 Corinthians 2:9

"If thou canst believe, all things are possible to him that believeth."

~ Mark 9:23

The Lord taketh pleasure in them that
fear Him, in those that hope in His mercy.

~ Psalm 147:11

For the LORD is good; His mercy is everlasting;
and His truth endureth to all generations.

~ Psalm 100:5

For the Lord God is a sun and shield: the Lord
will give grace and glory: no good thing
will He withhold from them that walk uprightly.

~ Psalm 84:11

And we know that all things work together for good to them that
love God, to them who are the called according to His purpose.

~ Romans 8:28

_____

Oh that men would praise the L<small>ORD</small> for His goodness, and for
His wonderful works to the children of men! For He satisfieth
the longing soul, and filleth the hungry soul with goodness.

~ Psalm 107:8-9

And of His fulness have all we received, and grace for grace.

~ John 1:16

_____

Being confident of this very thing, that He which hath begun
a good work in you will perform it until the day of Jesus Christ.

~ Philippians 1:6

The LORD is good to all: and His tender
mercies are over all His works.

~ *Psalm 145:9*

_____

Blessed is every one that feareth the Lord; that walketh
in His ways. For thou shalt eat the labour of thine hands:
happy shalt thou be, and it shall be well with thee.

~ *Psalm 128:1-2*

For the eyes of the Lord are over the righteous,
and His ears are open unto their prayers.

~ 1 Peter 3:12

_____

"Blessed are the pure in heart: for they shall see God."
~ Matthew 5:8

The name of the LORD is a strong tower:
the righteous runneth into it, and is safe.
~ Proverbs 18:10

Arise, shine; for thy light is come, and
the glory of the Lord is risen upon thee.

~ Isaiah 60:1

The path of the just is as the shining light,
that shineth more and more unto the perfect day.

~ Proverbs 4:18

Rejoice evermore. Pray without ceasing.
In every thing give thanks: for this is the
will of God in Christ Jesus concerning you.

~ *1 Thessalonians 5:16-18*

Trust in the Lord with all thine heart; and lean
not unto thine own understanding. In all thy ways
acknowledge Him, and He shall direct thy paths.

~ Proverbs 3:5-6

_____

The LORD shall preserve thee from all evil: He shall
preserve thy soul. The LORD shall preserve thy going out and
thy coming in from this time forth, and even for evermore.

~ Psalm 121:7-8

Cast thy burden upon the LORD, and He shall sustain
thee: He shall never suffer the righteous to be moved.

~ Psalm 55:22

Cause me to hear Thy lovingkindness in the morning;
for in Thee do I trust: cause me to know the way
wherein I should walk; for I lift up my soul unto Thee.

~ Psalm 143:8

God be merciful unto us, and bless us;
and cause His face to shine upon us.
~ Psalm 67:1

_____

Now the God of hope fill you with all joy and peace in believing,
that ye may abound in hope, through the power of the Holy Ghost.

~ Romans 15:13

The blessing of the LORD, it maketh rich,
and He addeth no sorrow with it.

~ Proverbs 10:22

_____

Mercy unto you, and peace, and love, be multiplied.

~ Jude 2

Thou wilt shew me the path of life: in Thy presence is fulness
of joy; at Thy right hand there are pleasures for evermore.

~ Psalm 16:11

Blessed be the God and Father of our Lord Jesus Christ, who hath
blessed us with all spiritual blessings in heavenly places in Christ.

~ Ephesians 1:3

The LORD hath prepared His throne in the heavens;
and His kingdom ruleth over all.

~ Psalm 103:19

_____

And therefore will the LORD wait, that He may
be gracious unto you, and therefore will He
be exalted, that He may have mercy upon you.

~ Isaiah 30:18

There are many devices in a man's heart;
nevertheless the counsel of the LORD, that shall stand.

~ Proverbs 19:21

But my God shall supply all your need
according to His riches in glory by Christ Jesus.
~ Philippians 4:19

Behold, the eye of the LORD is upon them that
fear Him, upon them that hope in His mercy.

~ Psalm 33:18

_____

Eye hath not seen, nor ear heard, neither have
entered into the heart of man, the things
which God hath prepared for them that love Him.

~ 1 Corinthians 2:9

_____

_____

_____

_____

_____

_____

_____

_____

_____

_____

_____

_____

_____

_____

_____

_____

_____

_____

_____

_____

_____

_____

_____

_____

_____

_____

"If thou canst believe, all things are possible to him that believeth."
~ Mark 9:23

The Lord taketh pleasure in them that
fear Him, in those that hope in His mercy.

~ Psalm 147:11

For the LORD is good; His mercy is everlasting;
and His truth endureth to all generations.

~ Psalm 100:5

For the LORD God is a sun and shield: the LORD
will give grace and glory: no good thing
will He withhold from them that walk uprightly.

~ Psalm 84:11

And we know that all things work together for good to them that
love God, to them who are the called according to His purpose.

~ Romans 8:28

_____

Oh that men would praise the LORD for His goodness, and for
His wonderful works to the children of men! For He satisfieth
the longing soul, and filleth the hungry soul with goodness.

~ Psalm 107:8-9

And of His fulness have all we received, and grace for grace.

~ John 1:16

_____

Being confident of this very thing, that He which hath begun
a good work in you will perform it until the day of Jesus Christ.

~ Philippians 1:6

The LORD is good to all: and His tender
mercies are over all His works.

~ Psalm 145:9

Blessed is every one that feareth the LORD; that walketh
in His ways. For thou shalt eat the labour of thine hands:
happy shalt thou be, and it shall be well with thee.

~ Psalm 128:1-2

For the eyes of the Lord are over the righteous,
and His ears are open unto their prayers.

~ 1 Peter 3:12

"Blessed are the pure in heart: for they shall see God."
~ Matthew 5:8

The name of the LORD is a strong tower:
the righteous runneth into it, and is safe.

~ Proverbs 18:10

Arise, shine; for thy light is come, and
the glory of the LORD is risen upon thee.

~ Isaiah 60:1

The path of the just is as the shining light,
that shineth more and more unto the perfect day.

~ Proverbs 4:18

_____

Rejoice evermore. Pray without ceasing.
In every thing give thanks: for this is the
will of God in Christ Jesus concerning you.
~ 1 Thessalonians 5:16-18

Trust in the LORD with all thine heart; and lean
not unto thine own understanding. In all thy ways
acknowledge Him, and He shall direct thy paths.

~ Proverbs 3:5-6

_____

The LORD shall preserve thee from all evil: He shall
preserve thy soul. The LORD shall preserve thy going out and
thy coming in from this time forth, and even for evermore.

~ Psalm 121:7-8

_____

_____

_____

_____

_____

_____

_____

_____

_____

_____

_____

_____

_____

_____

_____

_____

_____

_____

_____

_____

_____

_____

_____

_____

Cast thy burden upon the LORD, and He shall sustain
thee: He shall never suffer the righteous to be moved.

~ *Psalm 55:22*

Cause me to hear Thy lovingkindness in the morning;
for in Thee do I trust: cause me to know the way
wherein I should walk; for I lift up my soul unto Thee.

~ Psalm 143:8

God be merciful unto us, and bless us;
and cause His face to shine upon us.
~ Psalm 67:1

_____

Now the God of hope fill you with all joy and peace in believing,
that ye may abound in hope, through the power of the Holy Ghost.

~ *Romans 15:13*

The blessing of the LORD, it maketh rich,
and He addeth no sorrow with it.

~ Proverbs 10:22

_____

Mercy unto you, and peace, and love, be multiplied.

~ Jude 2

Thou wilt shew me the path of life: in Thy presence is fulness
of joy; at Thy right hand there are pleasures for evermore.

~ Psalm 16:11

_____

Blessed be the God and Father of our Lord Jesus Christ, who hath
blessed us with all spiritual blessings in heavenly places in Christ.

~ *Ephesians 1:3*

The LORD hath prepared His throne in the heavens;
and His kingdom ruleth over all.

~ Psalm 103:19

_____

And therefore will the LORD wait, that He may
be gracious unto you, and therefore will He
be exalted, that He may have mercy upon you.

~ Isaiah 30:18

There are many devices in a man's heart;
nevertheless the counsel of the LORD, that shall stand.

~ Proverbs 19:21

But my God shall supply all your need
according to His riches in glory by Christ Jesus.
~ Philippians 4:19

Behold, the eye of the LORD is upon them that
fear Him, upon them that hope in His mercy.

~ Psalm 33:18

_____

Eye hath not seen, nor ear heard, neither have
entered into the heart of man, the things
which God hath prepared for them that love Him.

~ 1 Corinthians 2:9

_____

_____

_____

_____

_____

_____

_____

_____

_____

_____

_____

_____

_____

_____

_____

_____

_____

_____

_____

_____

_____

_____

_____

_____

_____

"If thou canst believe, all things are possible to him that believeth."

~ Mark 9:23

The LORD taketh pleasure in them that
fear Him, in those that hope in His mercy.

~ Psalm 147:11

For the LORD is good; His mercy is everlasting;
and His truth endureth to all generations.

~ Psalm 100:5

For the LORD God is a sun and shield: the LORD
will give grace and glory: no good thing
will He withhold from them that walk uprightly.

~ Psalm 84:11

And we know that all things work together for good to them that
love God, to them who are the called according to His purpose.

~ Romans 8:28

_____

Oh that men would praise the Lᴏʀᴅ for His goodness, and for His wonderful works to the children of men! For He satisfieth the longing soul, and filleth the hungry soul with goodness.

~ Psalm 107:8-9

And of His fulness have all we received, and grace for grace.

~ John 1:16

_____

Being confident of this very thing, that He which hath begun
a good work in you will perform it until the day of Jesus Christ.

~ Philippians 1:6

The LORD is good to all: and His tender
mercies are over all His works.

~ Psalm 145:9

_____

Blessed is every one that feareth the LORD; that walketh
in His ways. For thou shalt eat the labour of thine hands:
happy shalt thou be, and it shall be well with thee.

~ *Psalm 128:1-2*

For the eyes of the Lord are over the righteous,
and His ears are open unto their prayers.
~ 1 Peter 3:12

_____

"Blessed are the pure in heart: for they shall see God."
~ *Matthew 5:8*

The name of the LORD is a strong tower:
the righteous runneth into it, and is safe.
~ *Proverbs 18:10*

Arise, shine; for thy light is come, and
the glory of the LORD is risen upon thee.

~ *Isaiah 60:1*

The path of the just is as the shining light,
that shineth more and more unto the perfect day.

~ Proverbs 4:18